"Wilder has been writing S̶ gained the attention merited Perhaps this masterfully executed new novel will remedy this. . . . Rich interactions between fully fleshed characters as well as quirky but compelling style."

—*Booklist*

"I'm still glad I introduced myself to this fine writer."

—*Asimov's Science Fiction*

"Wilder handles the complications caused by the castaways' power struggle and their eventual contact with the natives with skill and insight. . . . Shapes up into a thoroughly believable and wholly absorbing venture."

—*Kirkus Reviews*

"There's a high level of poetry in the language, which still remains crisp and light. There's a great sense of place, and a great sense of the poetry of the Unknown."

—*The New York Review of Science Fiction*

"This study of microcosmic society nicely integrates space and nautical themes. Recommended."

—*Library Journal*

SIGNS
OF
LIFE

CHERRY WILDER

A TOM DOHERTY ASSOCIATES BOOK
NEW YORK

SIGNS OF LIFE

Cover art by Nicholas Jainschigg

Edited by David G. Hartwell

A Tor Book
Published by Tom Doherty Associates, Inc.
175 Fifth Avenue
New York, NY 10010

Tor Books on the World Wide Web:
http://www.tor.com

Tor® is a registered trademark of Tom Doherty Associates, Inc.

ISBN: 0-812-55396-9
Library of Congress Card Catalog Number: 96-41

First edition: May 1996
First mass market edition: January 1998

Printed in the United States of America

0 9 8 7 6 5 4 3 2 1

Remembering Wanda, Will, Dave and Horst,
Easter 1989.
On the road to Rouen . . .

1

Twelve hours before the alert First Lieutenant Anat Asher, media and education officer on the Argosy Transporter *Serendip Dana*, felt the need to take a look at her environment. Perhaps it was a whiff of fresh oxygen on Sanity Row, topside, where the high brass did dwell. It was the little sideways lurch of the humdrum workgrid on her bunkside monitor. It was a word half-heard on the smooth nowhere reaches of the ringroad. She processed other data of this kind and had a dream.

She saw the Lord God Jehovah, an entity that her unconscious often used as a discussion partner and bearer of bad news. He stood in the main recreation area kitted up in a silversuit and said *"Exodus!"* Then he said, going away into a cloudy wilderness, full of wailing and gnashing of teeth, "Did you switch off the cooking gas?" In her dream, young Anat cried out that this was pretty crass even for Him; He was just trying to frighten her. By God, she would do it, she would join World Space, and she would have sex with whom she damn pleased. Then she was awake in her cozy quarters and she was fifty years old and she had done all that she said she would. She believed she understood the dream's message.

Lieutenant Asher rose up in the emptiest hours of ship time, took the tube down, and paced out the whole of the Rec area. She walked down the sloping radial arm, known as the Hill, which was used as a training run. Behind the blue doors on the Hill were "special quarters" used by nonservice travelers who were not VIPs: nurses for Arkady, media teams, Alpha students on their great adventure. The KONO media team was purest gold: fresh, smooth, adaptable with a range from shayrag to gagaku, supremely efficient in all the technical aspects of media production. No complaints there, but Anat had asked, like everyone else, why in mother heaven the *Serendip Dana* was carrying such a large media team. Twelve, count 'em, twelve souls. On a transporter?

The answer was Kamalin, the Kamalin movement. It wasn't a church, and to call it a cult was vaguely insulting. Kamalin was as omnipresent as yoga, as difficult to define as Zen. "An attempt to synthesize certain world philosophies," as one popular databank put it. The Kamalin Life Enhancement Movement had been founded by Marni Devi, a Vietnamese-American woman living in California in the twenty-first century. Why had Kamalin flourished when other cults had not? Because its members did not push, they spoke or sang in soft voices, stored up no worldly treasure: free classes, exercise groups. They cured headaches, relieved stress. Personal publicity, ego hype of any kind was discouraged: Kamalin leaders and senior teachers were not widely known. Yet they existed, and one of them was traveling to the planet Arkady with a media team. Kamalin was popular with the World Space Service. In space the enemies were violence and boredom; Kamalin relieved both conditions.

Anat Asher knew the breakdown on religious affiliations in the crew of the *Serendip Dana*. Twenty Christians (six practicing, fourteen nominal), four practicing Moslems, one Sikh, thirty-two persons who had no religion, including six raised in the Jewish faith, and thirty-four who "went with Kamalin." These were hard-core, or as hard-core as Kamalin ever got. An even larger portion from all denominations took part occasionally in Kamalin dancing or exercises.

Anat thought of the konos asleep or awake behind the blue doors and thought it would be a loozy damned shame if they got caught this way and died. Myrrha, the coordinator, had special powers; would she know about the threat to her family of konos?

At the foot of the Hill was the Rec area: the radial arm slotted into a section of the circumference ring of the ship, lying between two sets of bulkheads. To her right was the production area with the moving stage platform, overhead lighting gallery, all part of the trivid installation. Left was the relax round, also known as the Pits, with recliners and old red norofoam contour lounges near the rows of commissary outlets. It was the dead watch, but there were always loungers in the Pits. Directly in front of her across the star-patterned floor space was the open door of a watchpost and the door to Special Service Quarters.

Time was when Lieutenant Asher had traveled with assigned companies of Pioneers, Medics, the crews of disabled ships. She could have wished them back again. The members of the Silver Cross Air Space Maintenance Unit were the bane of a peaceful stretch to Port Garrett, Arkady.

The core of the World Space Service were the specialist crews of the space vessels with their own morale, their own neuroses. Around the core there were a cluster of satellite organizations: medical and nursing units, the Systems Establishment Resource, the Greenholme centers where Auxiliary Personnel were developed and trained; education and counseling teams. . . .

Only the Silver Cross Air Space Maintenance Corps, with training camps in the USNA, Australia, and at Armstrong Base, clung to its paramilitary trappings. Its generals took care to point up the complicated relationship between World Space and the Armed Services of former times. The military tradition died hard. The world still had its dress regiments in military academies, as life guards to president or dictator. Trimmest of all were the techs and mechs of the Silver Cross, who went into space, making life hard for themselves and for the crews and colonists they encountered.

How they shone, the Silvos, how they shaped up, hung together, reacted to the crew with arrogance and aggression. The interface was so bad that *this* door was seldom used: the Silvos came and went through Maintenance and Supply. When the time came what would their rating be? Would some of those shiners break because they could not bend?

She crossed the dimly lit starry floor, lifting up her eyes to the gallery above the watchpost. There was a small hydroponics garden, known as the Rain Forest; an observation window of thickest plex let in the blackness of space.

Inside the watchpost a security sergeant, Fallon, was imbibing coffee and playing back the latest talent quest program, "Seeing Stars."

"Catch this cheel . . ." he said.

A young black man in fantasy body paint was whistling and making bird noises to the accompaniment of Kyle, the kono on synthesizer. They listened to the mockingbird. The lieutenant gave Fallon an early cut and took over the post. When she was alone she idly checked the console, then took a key plaque from her belt and activated two locks. A section of paneling slid back, and there it was, a sleeping beauty, all its systems waiting for the prince to come through the hedge of thorns. The emergency comcen for Emergency Capsule Five, for Capem Fiver, the unwieldy hammer-shaped section of the *Serendip Dana* in which she was presently contained. Lieutenant Asher did not activate the systems. She leaned so close that she saw her own face reflected in the small dark screens.

She closed up the panels and looked furtively out of the watchpost in the direction of the Pits. Yes, there was a mensh she could use. She called with her blip and saw Ray Green receive the call. He was sitting nose to nose with another oxper, George King, blowing rainbow bubbles with CG6 cleaning solution. The bubbles were large and durable, and the game was to enclose your partner's head in a rainbow helmet. The konos had started the game; their expert Zena could enclose a human form inside two iridescent layers of CG film.

"Sorry to pop your bubble!"

She grinned at Ray Green as he strode into the post. She wondered how he saw her, if he saw that she was worried. She could not help but see him as a shade impassive. He was of uniform height with all the auxiliary personnel, one meter eighty-nine, strongly built with clean-cut features, blue eyes and brown hair. Green was an android, a particularly dour example of the artifact. Human beings, even those who did not work regularly with "oxper," could recognize androids at once: the timbre of the voice, a precision of movement that verged on jerkiness, the close texture of the skin, with a lack of hair on the lower face ... these things were unmistakeable. The age of an auxiliary was more difficult to determine: some looked middle-aged, others were "new batch" types, who looked boyish. Anat thought Ray Green looked a little older, more mature than the other oxper.

"I want you to take a Walk, Ray," she said.

"Lieutenant!"

"I want you to take a Walk with full harness and backup," she said. "I want you to inspect the fabric of the Rec area, namely Capem Fiver. I want you to pay particular attention to the heat shield installations and to the housings of the drogues. If there is visible damage to any drogue, it must be exchanged."

"I'll take one them little floater-skips, Lieutenant," said Green, "with couple extra drogues."

"This is a secret mission," said Anat Asher, "as between you and me. Anyone rumbles you . . . say it is a routine Walk to unfoul the ports. I don't want you to communicate this to any mensh or system on this ship. Understood?"

"Understood, Lieutenant."

"I know I can trust you, Ray!"

They smiled at each other, showing their teeth.

"Just the way I'm made, Lieutenant!" he said.

Oxper were very good at keeping secrets.

When old Ray of Sunshine had gone, Anat ran a check on the assigned complement of Capem Fiver. She found this getting to her and took a mild trank, a pink. It was two hours before her shift began; after that she had to be on top. She went over to the Pits and dialed a good breakfast. She checked the familiar menu for all the food and drink outlets and upped all the Replenish calls to Urgent. A friend came by and it was Rose Chan, Security. They bad-mouthed the daily round for a while, and Anat said:

"You still on Vippwatch? Taking care of the little eye doctor?"

"Sure," said Chan.

"Don't change!" said Anat. "Stick with that capem."

Chan extended her long legs on the old red couch and blinked at her friend.

"Some sharp-head asking the same . . ." she murmured.

"Who?"

"Gregg."

"Don't transfer!" said Anat. "That loozy Gregg . . ."

"Wasn't asking for himself," grinned Chan. "For his lover. Specialist Marna Rossi. Innocent cheel."

So time crawled by; this was the difficult period of the prealert when the emergency was known but not acknowledged. Insecurity was taking hold by 1200 hours. The order went through for everyone to take a pink. Matters of life and death were taken up throughout the ship. Outside in the silence of the moving dark, Ray Green patiently checked the fabric of Capem Fiver, cleared the heat shields, lubricated the lids of the drogues, swept away a few inexplicable little crusty space-turds, like gray sheep droppings. In the course of his perambulations he scared the living daylights out of Second Lieutenant Wemyss, P.H., who was tending his plants in the Rain Forest, high on the hammerhead of the Rec.

Green moved on when he was done and checked Capem Four; he replaced one of the drogues. Before he ended his Walk, his sharp senses had registered an extraordinary degree of yaw in the great ship. The stars were like white holes in the fabric of the dark; their pattern had changed. The *Serendip Dana* had altered course for the fourth time.

Anat Asher met and touched hands with friends, glassy-eyed they passed, spoke, called over the heads of others. She stood with her lover, Ren Beattie, on her last visit to the comcen, up forward. The Old Man, Batten, A.R.K., captain of the *Serendip*

Dana, began to broadcast, and they heard him where they stood; they did not go into Reception Round and watch him speak. He praised the "skilled and brave officers who have met this grave emergency," gave the names, Astrogator Trenchard, Lieutenant-Commander McGrath. Fit to be remembered. Maybe he was passing the buck. Anat recalled that Batten himself was of pioneer stock: his family had been in the Space Service for generations. She hardly grasped the schema when it was given: *"second planet of a G-class star . . . optimal human environment potential."*

After the speech there was a thin scatter of applause, music cut in: Ananda. Then they went inside to pay their respects; the air in the spacious gray-paneled room was hot and foul. In a corner there gaped Emergency Capsule Six, Capem Sexer. Complement of seven or eight. No auxiliary personnel. A weird point of honor. All the brass were there, walking about stiff-legged, some suited up, the fear of death on their necks.

She did not know which of the seniors had drawn command duties in Fiver. Ren had a command himself: Capem One, Bulk One, with the cargo and livestock. *"Second planet of a G-class star, entry corridor over the northern landmass."* Anat Asher went into a kind of fugue, moving like a zombie, came to herself as they went down in the tube. She kissed Ren good-bye; they parted in the crowded corridors.

The sound system blared out, was muted quickly, a woman's voice was putting out the first call to Emergency Stations. *First alert for the first time.* The voice was her own: Eva McGrath had revamped the vocal couple of journeys back, used Anat for the female vocal and Lieutenant Savage from Maintenance, since retired, for the male. He barked, she soothed. *Serendip Dana*, the undying mother, first female head of the World Security Council, might not have approved.

Now she came to Fiver; the hurdles had been raised so that no one could run down the hill. Lieutenant Asher gathered her wits about her and went to brief the konos. She knocked on a blue door, and it was answered by Tiria, the female lead dancer from the Duo. She had wondered on earlier visits if the Special Quarters would ever be the same again: the konos had altered their environment. It looked different with their silks hung on the

walls; it smelled of almond and sandalwood. She suspected a little forbidden cooking, secret brews of black Indian tea in the
long ship hours. The place was lived in, but it had none of the
bleak workaday disorder of service quarters.

There was always a little thread of music, someone plucking,
strumming, playing back. There were always a few konos warm-
ing up, hanging by their toes from the bunks or leaping to the
ceiling, catching each other around the hips or under the arms.
On this ship-time afternoon the music had stopped and the exercise. They were all damped right down. Anat went quickly to
the central bay where Myrrha, the coordinator, lived. She had a
small VIP suite topside in the after module, but it was mainly
used as a prop room.

"Thank you for cooperating!" said Anat.

"You're welcome!" said Myrrha Devi.

They smiled at each other. The konos had given an under-
taking to use the same prescribed medication as the crew during
any emergency. Now Anat was seeing them on pinks for the first
time. They acted as they always did, like a family, even if the
schwung had gone out of them. Anat's feelings towards large families were ambivalent.

She scrutinized Myrrha as closely as she dared. She was concerned about the coordinator's health. She had no way of knowing Myrrha's true age, and there was no medical service aboard
ship that she would accept. Myrrha looked very much as usual:
middle-sized, well-covered but not fat, with beautiful high cheek-
bones and glistening dark eyes. Her hair was coiled around her
head; she wore blue on her eyelids, red on her lips. She was sick,
uncomfortable, possibly in pain, thought Anat.

"Now," said Myrrha, "tell us what to do."

Anat took a long breath, gave it from the manual. She put
Azamo, Tiria's partner, into his silversuit, demonstrated its systems. They had had a number of drills, this was not a drill. She
explained again about the bulkhead, top of the Hill, the firedoors at the entrance to the Rec area. She thought of the Rec
doing a burn, the Hill miraculously preserved in an alien landscape, the konos all alone in a new world.

Myrrha gave some sign to the troupe, and they went away to

get kitted up. When they were alone the coordinator said, almost shyly:

"I have learned to spend a good part of my time in meditation."

She reached out and touched Anat's hand.

"I have seen . . . I can often see . . ."

"Yes?"

It was no time to deny the powers of a religious leader.

"I believe with all my heart," said Myrrha Devi, "that we will land in this section of the ship. You will bring us down safely."

Anat clasped her hand; she could not speak. A sound had penetrated from the Rec.

"Marching band music!" cried the fair boy, Halprin, looking into their bay. "The Silvos are doing a number!"

Down in the Rec area Chief Master Sergeant Winkler, G.H.D., could not keep his mind off his cruel fate. He was the oldest mensh aboard the *Serendip Dana*, six months from his pension, his pink slate shack on the shores of Port Garrett, his two dear old girls, Em and Philla. He had the stage area dismantled now; the sight of the airlock in the forward bulkhead made him queasy. The next step was to secure the after bulkhead, other end of the Silver Cross quarters. He put it off in the hope his lieutenant would show.

Early birds had been drifting into the Rec even before first call. They hovered around the Pits, most kitted up, helmets in the shoulder position along with the Q-packs of emergency rations and personal possessions. Wink could have laughed thinking of the unpalatable tack in those Q-packs. They were all going to die a fiery death, and everyone was clutching wafers in hopes of a glorious resurrection.

The morale was holding. Mood cerise . . . everyone on pinks. A bunch coming from the hospital. Pearly White, the dentist, *he* was their top medic, shee-it! Yeah, and there was the big gal, Frost, and the cook-sergeant. Wemyss, the plagged plant-lover, was up in his forest. Capem Fiver was some kinda rubber-ward, a tank of hat-fish. A young black man came up to the sergeant and unexpectedly gave him a salute. Ensign, just out of cadet school. Wink felt his stomach roll over. He was being spared nothing; he was part of a system that sent kids to be killed.

"Ensign Loney, H.A.L. I'm assigned to Fiver, Sergeant."

Sure enough, he was. Wink reeled off instructions. Cut back on food and especially liquids. Do not connect your waste system until instructed. Extra chemo-cans in the toilet block yonder. No contact lenses, earrings, nose ornaments, skin stickers, hair grips, removable dental bridges or medication strips inside the helmet.

"Take your pink?" he inquired.

"Sure," said Loney. "Sergeant, what will we really do first? I mean, I read the manual. . . ."

Gene Winkler saw that the young man was absolutely unafraid. He could not conceive of dying. He believed in this new world, this set of coordinates that the magicians upstairs had conjured out of the void. Wink looked down the shiny corridors of his own life and saw his grandmother, the Systems Administration expert, who could not believe in the planet Arkady. Yet it was real: his house by the strange sea, his garden, his two alien flowers.

"First thing," said Wink, "is get out in the air, Hal, my boy. When the bolts blow on the bulkheads it's through the locks *fast* and *safe*. No broken limbs, y'hear. The locks may not be operative, you understand . . . if the air is good, we'll simply open 'em up. Now before you go, you assume shock, you take a red, through the applicator inside the helm. Outside you form up, headcount, fifty meters or so from the capsule till she cools. I'll give you a duty, something to concentrate your mind. Take one of the foam guns from the door of the storage locker other side the Pits, bring that bastard out when you go. I give the word you play it all along this end wall here with the watchpost and our own comcen."

"Got ya!" said Loney. "I see it we come down in some kinda desert."

"I see it as some kind of tree growths," said Wink. "Maybe like those cycadics, grow on Arkady."

"Want to bet, Sarge?"

"Credits have fallen, Loney. Who'll be needing money?"

"You'll think of something."

Wink laughed, and they slapped hands.

At that moment the door of Special Quarters opened, a Silvo

appeared, the head mugger himself. Captain Boyle, T.R.R., had
not yet donned his silversuit; he was still scalpel sharp in his neon
blues with the silver cross. The sergeant gave him a salute; the
captain gave him one back that was one hundred percent better.
Boyle was a handsome man, clean-cut as the androids but looking a shade less human.

"Sergeant," he articulated, "the Silver Cross Unit preparing
for descent."

"Yessir!"

"We'll take that floor space for a turn of drill before we get out
of our blues."

"*Now,* sir?"

"Morale booster!" said Boyle.

He handed the sergeant a music cube.

"Tell your people what they're gonna see, Winkler!"

Wink went ahead obediently.

"Now then, here's a real treat," he announced. "The Silver
Cross Space Air Maintenance Unit will do a short drill before
they get kitted up. Yeah, thank you, Frost. If you could all help
clear the floor there."

The medley of marches was played by a Silver Cross band, all
live blowers and bangers, not one synthesized note. The drill-
master was a Lieutenant Fogg, T.I.K., with the foghorn voice.
Winkler knew his nickname: "Thick" Fogg. All the Silvos had
these nicknames within the unit, received, so the legend ran, at
a painful hazing ceremony called The Switch. Anyhow, they
drilled perfectly, the sergeant conceded. What they did went far
beyond marching drill or even gymnastics; it was a faggidy art
form. The glowing blue figures made stars, climbed up into pyra-
mids, wove intricate patterns on the starry floor of the Rec. The
officers worked with the other ranks: the captain went forward
and took part in certain figures, then he gave the commands
while Fogg took his turn. One of the mechanics turned an ankle,
let down his side of the double pyramid momentarily, but the
glitch was quickly covered up.

There were more marchers than spectators. All thirty-six Silvos were on the floor. Sergeant Winkler knew what this meant:
three maintenance companies still had to leave their crack troop

and go to their assigned emergency capsules. This was a farewell performance, an act of togetherness. After twenty-five minutes, the blue-and-silver mannequins whirled and clicked to a halt; their faces shone, they controlled their breathing. There was loud applause from the bodies in the Pits.

In the main entry from the Hill crowded the konos, some in silversuits, some in their harlequin coveralls. They applauded very gently like the sound of one hand clapping, then they were gone, back into quarters.

Lieutenant Asher came briskly around the Silvos and gave Captain Boyle her best salute.

"A magnificent display!" she said. "Convey our thanks to the Silver Cross, Captain!"

Boyle inclined his head a fraction.

"Dismiss!" he said softly.

Thick Fogg marched the troop back into quarters.

"Captain Boyle," said Anat Asher, "I will come through Special Service at the second call, secure the after bulkhead and check the emergency placement with your duty officers."

Boyle loomed over the lieutenant, teetering a little in his half-smooth dress boots. His face was flushed; a fine scar at his hairline twitched. Winkler was seized with fear for the lieutenant. Boyle would punch her out, chop her windpipe, something. . . . He spoke up:

"Your music, Captain Boyle, sir!"

Boyle put out a gloved hand, and Wink dropped the cube into it. The captain threw another salute and went back into quarters. Anat Asher, who had not moved, turned to the sergeant. They both spoke at once.

"Was he . . .?"

"I thought . . ."

"Holy hell, Lieutenant," continued Winkler. "He's plagged."

"Gets to us all."

Anat Asher opened the emergency comcen.

"Time to heat up the kitchen."

Inside Special Quarters Captain Ronin Boyle felt the shock-wave of his presence run down the shining rows. The final inspection. Shadow Adams, his personal aide, fell in behind along with Lieutenant Atom Klein. The air in quarters was thick and tainted. Boyle ran his eye over half the troop, then cried out in a loud voice:

"Last time in your blues. Don't disgrace them. The following placement has been generated randomly by old Shadow here. Company Cherokee assigned to the service block, Capem Two; Company Fox to Bulk one; Company Etzel right next door here to Capem Four."

There was a quiver of reaction, nothing more. Boyle strode on and found Specialist Mechanic Johannsen, P.P.N., nick-named Hunk, who had turned his ankle during the drill. He administered a mild chastisement: a slap in the face with his open hand.

"Something to remember me by," said Captain Boyle, smiling sadly.

Hunk was in Etzel Company. He reeled obediently at the slap, then resumed his parade ground stance. The captain nodded to the lieutenant, who shouted:

"Kit up! Silversuits at the double!"

The Silvos usually did not care for their silversuits: they had no fit; they were sloppy like the shitsack regulars for whom they were made. Now the baggy suits left room for contraband: drugs, food, homely devices for lighting and cooking. Above all the parts of certain sporting weapons, heavily prohibited by World Space, and concealed throughout the voyage. The continual bad interface with the regular officers and noncoms discouraged spot-checks and searches. And the Silvos knew Captain Boyle was on their side: old Ronin liked to hunt. The Silver Cross had planned to go out shooting on Arkady; now they had a new world for their hunting parties.

The heat in quarters was oppressive. They went at it by numbers; the sight of their blues folded in the headlockers moved some to tears. The members of Cherokee, Etzel, and Fox companies automatically stowed their blues inside their silversuits or tried to fold the tunics into their Q-packs, against regulations. Shadow assisted the captain. Lieutenant Klein sluiced water over her body before fastening herself in. She made supertempo, bounced out to give the next order.

"Helm and Q-pack ready. Abacus, Barnard, and Detroit companies remove the recliners from the bunks ready for transfer!"

There were faint murmurings. She was asked to "have a heart!" Lieutenant Petrova, G.R., strapping a man's wrist, said: "Captain?"

"Easy time!" said Boyle. "Easy time! Big Doc's orders."

There was a thick wave of sound; the Silvos groaned, talked, laughed loudly for a few seconds, then dropped the noise level. Only Shadow knew when the second call would come; he prompted the captain, who gave warning. Mary Klein ordered the three outgoing companies to fall in. They went through the door on to the ringroad at the double, repeating in unison:

"Silver Cross! Stand fast!"

Captain Boyle felt a great surge of loss and anger as he saw them go. World Space Service was killing his troop. He had honed them to perfection, and they were being snatched away, sent to help out the regulars on this ship-that-failed. He was forced into decisions no man could bear. Of course Shadow had not generated any random selection. Cherokee, Etzel, and Fox were chosen by Ronin Boyle alone, with reference to the areas they had to service and how well he could do without those guys.

The time for a soothing female voice was past. A man's voice was barking out the second emergency calls. Lieutenant Asher and a security oxper, Victor Burns, moved quickly past the remaining ranks of the Silvos to the after bulkhead. Abacus, Barnard, and Detroit companies were still distinguishable from the crew by the way they stood at attention. A sergeant from Capem Four, name of Dyall, came running with two oxper to complete the ceremony from his side.

". . . *down there!*" cried Dyall.

Anat Asher could not recall what she cried out. Good-bye? Adios? Go with love? On the second try the massive bulkheads wheezed into place. No way between anymore. The young Silver Cross lieutenant, Klein, M.L., a thin, dark woman like Anat herself, stood by, frozen-faced, rude, even now in the face of death, and brayed orders to Detroit Company without meeting the eye of her regular sister. The Silvos lowered and secured the air lock before the bulkhead. A way out into a new world.

The eighteen remaining members of the Silver Cross marched into the Rec area carrying their recliners and fixed them with the vacuum cups to the positions marked on the starry floor. The furniture of the Pits had been rearranged. A phalanx of recliners clustered together for the descent: man, woman, human, android, officers, other ranks, crew, Silvos, they would lie cheek-by-jowl, searing out and down on a last trajectory.

Second call for the third time. Look who was here. A man whose random number had come up: Lieutenant-Commander Gregg, R.K.G. Instead of living or dying with his fellow brass in Sexer, now he was ranking officer in Fiver.

Popular for a security chief; not much changed since he starred in that recruiting trivid. Anat Asher did not value him as an officer. He had brought along his girl, Rossi, M.A.; first he had tried to get her into Capem Tree, allegedly one of the safest berths, now they planned to see it through together. Anat watched Gregg and Boyle exchange salutes; she pierced the veil of the future and thought: Gregg and I have no pull over the assigned mensh outside this ship. *Down there* . . .

She led Ensign Rossi to one of the last places on a double couch alongside Doc White. He was in the act of removing his contact lenses; one blue eye was large and lustrous, the other small and tearful. He was a loose-limbed, bland, inconsequential young man. She *had* wondered if he might be slightly insane, a little fish who had fallen through the net of psychological testing.

"Hello, hello!" he said, squinting at Rossi, who was pale and beautiful. "Anything I can do, Lieutenant?"

He pronounced it *lefftenant*.

"Yes, Doc," she said. "Put on your spotter."

It was a device worn on the wrist to send and receive location calls. She moved away after settling Rossi and looked everyone in the eye. Time for inspiration, words of comfort, but all she could manage were a few practical suggestions. The *Serendip Dana* gave a perceptible yaw and the suggestion of a pitch. A sound far too light for a scream was squeezed from the reclining mass.

In Capem Four, a second lieutenant ranked high for stability began to shout and rave. He was tranked out by the medics and strapped into his recliner.

Inside the smallest capem, contained in a corner of the VIP suite, Chan, T.N.R., found herself alone with the civilian passenger, Dr. Valente, nervous but brave, clambering into his silversuit. She knew the capsule would hold as many as seven persons. Wasn't Fiver full to the brim? Could Anat Asher deliver her coupla mensh? She put in a call, received no reply. The after module, which housed the VIP suites, the officers' quarters, and one of the life support systems, juddered crazily. Second call for the third time resounded as if the walls were screaming. A tall figure came through the suite and entered the capsule beside them.

"Assigned, Capem Tree!"

It would have to do. Chan wasn't going out there no more.

In Capem Two, a woman from the planet Arkady, one of four Alphas on the ship, began to sing softly inside her helmet. It was an old hymn tune, Scottish or Welsh, which had taken hold on her new world. Other voices took up the refrain on the open channel. Lieutenant-Commander Pike told the singers to save their breath. Once lost, insisted the singers, now they were found. Once blind, now they could see.

Two Rottweilers, a German shepherd, and an Australian blue, all tranquilized and equipped with respirators, lay peacefully beside their loved ones in Bulk One. Captain Beattie was strung up, eager, making changes at the last minute. He considered sending one of the oxper to assist in cargo, sent a man instead, his pal Ryder, E.D.D.

Peter Wemyss clambered down from the Rain Forest, the map pocket of his silversuit filled with cuttings. The last place near the watchpost was waiting for him; he put on his helmet correctly first time. Sergeant Winkler made a comment to Lieutenant Asher on the open channel. Twenty persons in Capem Fiver were able to laugh.

In the forward module, the systems busily worked out their doom. Inside Capem Sexer, Astrogator Trenchard, following, gave a grunt of triumph. Faintly, through their helmets and the thick walls of the emergency capsule, the officers heard the sirens begin to shriek.

Myrrha Devi, weary of traveling in space, weary of being a mother, weary of selfless hope and acute physical discomfort, let her spirit go free. She swung far out in the void, voiceless, alone, then in cloud. She created the new world, its oceans and seas, mountains, rivers, vast tracts of jungle and forest, deserts of sand and deserts of stone. There was an alteration in her soaring spirit flight, and she was confronted by an image. A woman stood alone upon a stone balcony high up in the cold air, just before sunrise. She was wrapped in a white cloak of quilted cotton, she had a clear brow, deep-set brown eyes; ragged locks of dark hair streaked with gray flowed down over her cloak. She grasped a tube of polished wood with metal bands, held it to her right eye.

The vision passed. Far, far below, through a rift in the clouds, Myrrha saw a little group of men and women, oddly dressed, clustered upon a bleak hilltop staring upward. She sighed and laughed in her flight. *"Ah . . . they are here to welcome us!"* Then she was alone again, lost, tumbled about in the void, the threads of her concentration tangled. "Oh, give me that world again!" she cried in spirit. "Give it me for my children. . . ."

The *Serendip Dana* seared through thick cloud followed by a diffuse wave of sound. The ship divided into burning fragments. The six emergency capsules were flung outwards and plunged toward the surface of an unknown planet.

2

F
ar to the west in the Red Ocean, within sight of Gline's Cape, where the last of the great seafarers of Rhomary had died, the brig *Dancer* lay out to sea. In the southeast another vessel hovered in the morning mist; the trader *Seahawk*, named for Gline's own ship, was leaving her kelpground. Cap Varo kept the boy, Paddy Rork, on watch in the crow's nest. A fresh breeze came up, clearing the mist; it held Cap Swift's broad-beamed trader steady, would have sent the *Dancer* further west.

"Dry hell!" rasped old Kirsh, coiling rope by the forward hatch. "Will this mad Varo delay till the wind changes? Does he think Vera Swift has nothing better to do than spy on our occasions?"

"He will not stir till the *Seahawk*'s flown," said the bosun, Winna Cross. "And mind your blab when speaking of the captain."

It was late summer, but here at the end of the map the nights were still cool, and every morning a mist rose off the sea. There, off the port bow, were the gray beaches of the Cape, broken up by gnarled and salty bushes, and backed by the blue-green palisade of the swamp forest. Gline's last resting-place was a catch-all beach, in the path of a strong eddy: sailors, living and dead, pails, spars, sea-boots, and all the detritus of the ocean fetched up on this lonely shore.

Abeam of the *Dancer* lay the southern shores, with the oozy tree growths of the swamp forest growing down to the water's edge. Farther south, beyond the horizon, lay the sugarvine plantations and the pearl gardens of the Robs Station, farthest southern and farthest western outpost in the Rhomary land. The Red Ocean at this hour was a coppery bronze, shading into purple at the horizon and into a curious greenish-brown just beyond the Cape. A long, dark sandbank marked off that eerie stretch of lagoon known as the Deadwater.

Paddy Rork stood up in the crow's nest, balancing easily; besides the *Seahawk*, he believed he could see another ship. Moving north from Gline's beach, along the forest shore there were bays and inlets, and in one of them he could just make out the yellow masthead ornament of the *Comet*, Cap La Mar's vessel. Paddy guessed that La Mar had found his own stand of fever trees.

"Rork!"

It was the throaty bellow of the first mate, Ira Maddern.

"Aye, aye!" cried Paddy.

"How goes the *Seahawk*?"

"Going about, Mister!"

Paddy clapped the precious telescope to his eye and watched the *Seahawk* complete the maneuver. The *Seahawk* handled well, no doubt of it, but she was unshapely to Paddy's eye, like the *Comet*. They were broad-beamed vessels built pretty high at poop and fo'c'sle, both rigged fore and aft. The true queen was the *Dancer*, for she had a flowing line, she was lighter, more slender. The *Dancer* was called a brig, but she was more properly a brig-antine, square-rigged on this mainmast where Paddy swung in a circle, but fore and aft on the foremast, where Winna Cross and her boys and girls were standing to the winches.

Directly below, Paddy could see Cap Varo himself, uncommonly tall, with a big handsome head, thrust forward, and an expression of determined melancholy. It was said he never smiled.

Maddern, the first mate, a gnarled and whiskery old sea-hog, had grown gray circumnavigating the captain's moodiness. The third mate was a tall young woman, her hair as black, her face as handsome, but her attitude very different from that of her father. Megan Varo was full of controlled impatience. Two women stood amidships by a thick bundle of kelp matting; Cap Varo was waiting to carry out a sea burial.

The second mate of the *Dancer*, Dorris Wells, had lived a sailor's life and had had no thoughts of leaving the sea. She had been a sturdy, wise, cheerful person, sailing the seas for more than twenty years, woman and girl, until her last morning aboard the *Dancer*, when she bent to snatch up some bright piece of metal from the newly scrubbed deck. It was no metal, nothing but the sunlight on a drop of water . . . her perception was altered for a few seconds; she was reaching for an earring, a gold coin, a few links of chain. The brightness spread through her brain; she could no longer move or speak and was dead of her stroke within twelve hours. She was forty-eight years old and might have expected to live another twenty years, including ten or fifteen years of retirement at the Gann Station, in Derry or one of the smaller towns on the Billsee, or even in the city of Rhomary, more than a thousand kilometers to the northeast.

Now her shipmates waited uneasily for the captain's word, and in the end he gave it. Simon Varo raised a hand to the first mate, Maddern, who nodded to Megan Varo and cried out:

"Stand to, all hands! Burial at sea!"

Then Gruner swung the helm a touch to the east, so that the *Dancer* hung over the Sunset Deep, a bottomless cleft in the ocean floor which showed a purple shadow on the reddish waves. Two close friends of Dorris Wells stood by for burying detail; they had settled two small boulders in a net attached to the body wrapping. Paddy came down from aloft and stood watching the crew, trying to learn how folk behaved at a funeral. He could not believe in all the solemn faces; they were faking, making fun, and would break out with their workaday expressions in a moment.

Cap Varo had a good face for a burial. He brought from under his cloak a small book in a black leather cover. Its pages were of good jocca paper, and it had been printed up at the behest of the Navigation Board. Its title was *Words of Comfort*, and it had been revised from an earlier compilation twenty years ago by Urbain Bro, then Dator of Rhomary, with aid from the faculties of the Rhomary schools and colleges. Tom Kirsh, the oldest and most ornery crew member, knew *Words of Comfort* well. This was Cap Varo's first burial at sea, but Kirsh had sailed with a number of captains. He was making bets with himself which selection the Cap would choose. Were they in for some verses from the Gideon? The Rabbi's Commonplace Book? The Book of Jenz Kindl, the local prophet, or Ayleen, who was called the Sweet Singer of Silver City? No, to his mild surprise, Cap Varo chose "The Ocean of Being" from another off-world cultist, Mother Marna. Wafty stuff, but very fitting.

"Stand on the shores of the Pacific Ocean," read the captain, "see the rollers crash down and the drifts of foam run down the sand back into the sea. Nothing is lost; no soul is lost; no spark of life is extinguished completely in this world we call Earth or in any of the myriad worlds beyond our small planet. Let your feelings of love and sharing go forth into all the universe. Nothing is lost. No one is lost. Your friend who died yesterday, the saint who died a thousand years past, all are gathered in. They have become part of the great ocean of being, and so will you when your time comes. The wave rises up, runs towards the land, curls down and breaks upon the shore . . . then the waters run back into the sea."

Nothing else. No singing, no other leave-taking. Flower Wilm and Molly Kelly, who stood stripped to their undertunics, lowered the bundle, made fast the sling of rope, then dived into the cold reddish water. They angled the body correctly, let the weights fall, and dived, guiding their friend to her last resting place, through the mouth of the abyss.

Presently they reappeared, gasping, and scrambled back onto the ladders. They were wrapped in blankets and shared in a round of sugarvine schnapps ordered for all hands. It was just as Paddy had expected: old Kirsh snarled, Bosun Cross raised her voice, chasing him aloft to set sails, Conor and Merrow, the next nimblest, came swarming after him, pinching at his nether parts. Only the captain remained as melancholy as before and straightaway went below. Ira Maddern had the *Dancer* under sail and away, heading westward . . . farther, much farther than Gline had sailed.

In two hours they had reached the Deadwater and slipped through the channel in the sandbank that Varo favored. It was well known that the vast gray lagoon was a place of flat calms, hardly to be crossed under sail. But old Deadwater hands knew too that there were a few furtive winds if one could catch 'em. Now, with her topsails set and her jibs just filling, the *Dancer* edged along the southern shore of the lagoon. The heavy traders were not made for the task, but the brig went slowly, dipping and dancing, catching light airs from the land. At twelve o'clock they hung becalmed, then slowly, slowly, moved on again, and at midday they came at last to a small secret bay which they called, among themselves, the Spicebox.

The *Dancer* lay at anchor, and there was a short siesta after lunch for the heat of the day. Then, as Paddy had hoped, Lon Adma called him to the longboat, and he went ashore with the pickers. The shores of the Deadwater, here on the south side, were fringed with dried-out patches of swamp forest. The beach was of black sand and mud; the party pressed on through and came to a round valley filled like a bowl with spice-berry trees. Their sinuous black trunks bent to the spongy, dark floor of the forest with the weight of the long fruit clusters. The spice berries, in neat eightfold bunches on the stems, were just beginning to turn from darkest green to dusty blue. The pickers had arrived just in time. Paddy sounded the wooden clappers, and a flock of deelicks, the tiny fruit eaters, glowing purple and iridescent black, took off in darting lizard flight.

Paddy picked sometimes shoulder to shoulder with the two crew members nearest his own age, Seela Conor and Ketty Merrow. He hated them sometimes: they made his life a misery; it was like having two bullying elder sisters. Other times he thought there were no better shipmates in the world. Still other times he daydreamed over Ketty Merrow, who was pretty as any mermaid, no taller than Paddy and just seventeen years old. When he was not picking, Paddy loaded the filled baskets onto a wooden sledge and dragged it back to the hopper in the longboat.

Twice, three times the longboat was filled and brought back to the *Dancer* for unloading. Ira Maddern watched with awe as the hold filled up with bluggy spice berries. A miracle crop . . . a double harvest. What had caused it? The weather hadn't altered. Would the surly devil not be satisfied now? Would the crew get a smile from him and the officers a civil word?

It was hellish hot work, picking in the valley; the crew had stripped to the waist, some wore binders to support their breasts. They were all sun-browned and muscular with a majority of dark heads. A few shone out: Paddy Rork was a redhead; Seela Conor was blond; Tom Kirsh snow-white.

Megan Varo kept her shirt on. She had no need to come picking at all, being third mate and the captain's daughter, but she did it for solidarity. With the crew and with her father as well: she stood in for him, offering the fellowship that he could not give. She went on working and smiling and encouraging all hands until it seemed to her that her performance must be wearing thin. Her anger and discontent would burst out if she did not get away. She caught sight of poor Molly Kelly, weeping and cursing, while Flower Wilm picked up a fallen basket.

"She is in a bad way, Third," said Flower. "After the burying . . ."

"Come on, Molly," said Megan. "You and I will call it a day. How are *you* feeling, Flower?"

"I'll carry on."

Megan and Molly took their baskets to the longboat, and Lon Adma poled them back to the *Dancer.* Molly sat among the berries and gave way to her grief.

"Here, gal," said Lon.

He took a flask from his britches pocket and dosed her.

"Thanks, Cox," she said huskily. "Thanks, Third. I see her, you know, my poor Dorris. Vail knows what I'll tell the family . . ."

Megan helped the poor soul aboard and took her below to the snug where Tom Kirsh was cooling a first brew of delicious spiced tea. There was bread, new-baked, and meat dripping to spread it with. The fo'c'sle was hot and airless belowdecks; Megan went about opening all the ports to cool off the crew's quarters before the long night. A slight breeze came off the Deadwater.

She went aft, at last, and entered her father's cabin without knocking. She knew how she would find him: brooding at his chart table, groaning a little, picking at this reckoning or that, checking references in his books and scrolls. She felt his depression like a weight on her mind, his silence and melancholy spreading through the ship like a black mist. Cap Varo, who never smiled, never laughed, never approved.

Yet she caught him out and caught herself too, for her father was sound asleep in his chair by the open stern-port. Some of the lines had smoothed out upon his forehead. Before him on the raised chart platen was a big spread showing the Deadwater and the coastline of the southern landmass as far as it had been mapped in the unnamed sea, the last, the largest ocean of all which stretched to the end of the world. One of his hands lay curled in his lap; the other rested lightly on a book of travelers' tales which he often consulted.

Megan Varo took another chair at the cluttered table and watched him sleep. Her feelings of anger and irritation, all directed at this man, Simon Varo, slowly ebbed away. He was not to blame as captain, not even as a father; the seafaring life was hardly to blame . . . she had simply grown away from it. She, Megan, must change her life, go to the town or the city, learn some other occupation. Afterwards, she dated all the wild things that followed from these quiet moments in her father's cabin.

Simon Varo woke and gave a start when he saw that he was not alone. Then he recognized his daughter and smiled.

"Great Star!" he said. "Good that you're here, girl. I've had a dream."

She remembered his dreams and said quietly, trying not to break the mood:

"Let me take it down for you, father."

He nodded, poured himself water from his carafe. He pushed his writing case towards her and began to dictate slowly and smoothly, going back sometimes if the dream carried him away.

"It was on a beach," he said. "I saw the sea, a calm sea, and the *Dancer* lying at anchor. I was proud, for we had made a great catch . . . a giant blackray was roped to our deck. There were men and women on the beach, richly dressed, brightly colored

like balladeers or dancers in a procession. They were building
what looked like a palm tree, but it was very tall and all of metal.
I sent Ira Maddern to ask what this was for, and he came back
laughing and said: 'They are trying to catch the sun!'

"Then we saw one young fellow laying things upon the sand,
like a peddler setting out his wares. A golden ball, a red flower,
a square of white cloth, a black leather glove. A child, a girl
child, ran out onto the yellow sand and chose the red flower.
Then I felt put out, and someone cried 'Captain!' I looked to the
ship, and there beyond her in the bay was suddenly another . . .
it was the trader *Seahawk* . . ."

He broke off, caught by the strange power of his own dream.

"That's all?" asked Megan.

He nodded.

"What do you make of it, Pa?" she prompted. "Is it a truth
dream?"

"Yes," he said. "Yes, I would say so, though it is very fanciful.
Other dreams were more straightforward."

"They had symbols in them," she said. "I recall the one where
past time was shown by an old, off-world clock."

"Ah, it is years now," he said. "Years since I had a spell of
truth dreaming."

"I am sure it is a fortunate dream," said Megan. "Ira Maddern says . . ."

"What does he say?"

"The spice crop is enormous. Double and triple what we
might have taken. We could pick another day, but the hold is
near full. He wonders what brought this about."

"The picking itself, of course," said Varo drily. "And the bit of
cultivation we have given the valley."

"Father," she said, "come and see what's been done. Give all
hands a kind word. They are still down because of poor Dorris
Wells."

"I tried to find some word of her death in the dream," he
said, "but I cannot see any. Can you?"

"Nothing about death," she said. "What time of day was it on
that dream beach?"

Once during his truth-dreaming years he had foreseen the

fever deaths of his wife and youngest child, her mother and brother, even to the time of day, the very hour. He had sealed up the written dreams with a date and shown them to her long afterwards.

"Why, it was dawn," he said, "or early morning . . . perhaps I recall sunrise behind the metal tree."

His attention wandered back to the chart and to his papers.

"I will come in a little while," he said.

"Father, please!"

"No, no, I said I would come, girl! It is not yet sunset. I will come after supper."

There was nothing for it but to trust him. Suddenly it seemed that he had decided to trust *her;* Cap Varo said sharply:

"Girl, Megan, you know the great plan . . ."

"Yes, father."

"I have spoken to Captain David Ramm four months past, when we were in Derry Town."

She came back from the door and perched on the chair.

"What does he know?" she asked.

"More than he will tell," said Varo. "But it was as we thought. Willem Hill came home. He was found in the far east of the Billsee and brought home to Derry. Cap Ramm spoke to him many times."

"And it was the same man? Hilo Hill, who sailed with Gline and was wrecked upon the Cape some twenty years past?"

"The very same," said Varo. "He did it, gal. I know a few of the stages of his journey. *Why* he sailed such a mad trick I do not know. But it seems that he traveled all the way around this world, Rhomary."

"He sailed around the world, father?"

"There you put your finger on it!" laughed Simon Varo. "He sailed or was brought by wind and water a goodish part of the way. The rest he went over land. But these first stages are what interest me for the plan . . ."

"Tell me."

"He stole the longboat of Gline's ship, the first *Seahawk,* and rowed across this Deadwater lagoon. He came to Gline's Ocean and drifted with the reed-rafts, which he called floating islands.

There are more of them since that time, I reckon; he met them further out. He came to the Green Island, and he spent time there. He had a name for it, a better name than the one we use, I think. He named it for that race of small jocca palms . . . he called it Palmland."

"Palmland!" she said. "Yes, yes, it is a better name."

"I am beginning to think," said Simon Varo, "that it was Palmland, our green island, that I saw in my dream."

"We were bound there if the weather held." She smiled. "No one has tried its south coast for fever trees."

She longed to turn for home, to get on with her life. Her father turned back to his charts and said mildly:

"Go along, girl. I'll come up. You have my word."

The sunset bell was rung, and the pickers were rowed in. After supper most of the crew gathered on the deck, where it was coolest. It was the time for music and singing, but the death of Dorris Wells had made them shy. Only old Kirsh played a sad melody on his carved wooden strummer. Then suddenly the captain was amongst them with Ira Maddern, their white shirts gleaming in the summer night. Simon Varo walked about, stiff as ever, but giving words of praise and encouragement.

Paddy was glad when the captain brought the talk around to the Green Island for it was one place he had never seen. Seela Conor had told him all about the small green palms, the sandhills, the bush that was not so damp and dense as the swamp forests that fringed the Red Ocean. There were caves too and all the fish in the world as well as flying lizards of every color. A race of little dark dry-hogs lived in the wooded valleys. Besides that there were the silkies, the rarest and finest animals in the world, with a fur pelt. Now he had been signed on with the *Dancer* for a year and a half but the cargo or the weather or the lateness of the season had always made them turn for home after crossing the Deadwater.

"So, Paddy," said Ira Maddern. "Maybe you will come to the island this time. We will see how the weather holds in Gline's Ocean."

"I have been reading of Gline's crew," said Cap Varo. "How many of you have a family connection with those brave souls?"

It turned out that four of them did: Lon Adma, Molly Kelly, Winna Cross, and Paddy, who was the closest, for his grandfather Patrick Rork had shipped as coxun with "bold Hal Gline." He could barely remember the old man with one leg who had died when he was six years old. But there were many members of Gline's crew still hale and hearty, at sea or on shore. Paddy was just beginning to understand that twenty years was not such a bluggy long time as he had thought at first.

"One of you can surely tell me who the cook was aboard the *Seahawk?*" Captain Varo put the question like a teacher in school.

"Was it Nan Born?" ventured Lon Adma.

"Please Captain!" cried Paddy. "Nan Born was second cook. The cook was a man named Hilo Hill!"

"So he was, Paddy," said the captain, smiling. "I have heard that he sailed in this ocean . . ."

Tom Kirsh and Winna Cross were whispering together.

"Stole the longboat . . ." murmured Tom Kirsh.

Paddy could hardly follow their secret looks and bits of old yarn. When the captain, after nodding wisely, began to talk of a new name for the Green Island Paddy had the fixed idea that Hilo Hill, the seacook, had had something to do with it. The new name, *Palmland*, was spoken aloud by everyone, and they agreed it was a good name.

"This time for sure, Paddy!" said Seela. "We will come to Palmland . . . I will be able to show you the silkies."

"Psst!" said Cap Varo. "They are rare beasts."

"It is ten years past since one was washed up in the Deadwater," said Winna Cross.

"Remember your trust," said the captain. "Not a word about our good silkie-boys at Robs Station or the Gann!"

"No, Captain!" they chorused obediently.

Next morning, at first light, the *Dancer* was coaxed again to the west, but by midday she lay becalmed in the Deadwater, still as any flat-bottomed barge. After siesta the longboat and the smaller gig were set down, and two crews strained at the oars. The ship inched its way toward the headlands in leading strings. It was harder work than picking spice, but Cap Varo kept the shifts of rowers going until nightfall.

They lay over again in a shallow cove on the southern shore of the lagoon, and a good lookout was kept for the blackrays. The huge leathery sea creatures, almost circular, rippling at their edges like a furled cloak, were not so daunting to the sailors of Rhomary as they might have been. They were nowhere near so vast as the Vail, the benign monsters of the Western Sea, and not even so intelligent as the delfin folk who lived in the Red Ocean. The blackrays often strayed into the Deadwater and were taken with the aid of harpoon guns; they were more dangerous in open water, but the *Dancer* had several times brought one home.

Paddy Rork stayed in the crow's nest late, staring out at the still dark water of the great lagoon, crisscrossed with the phosphorescent trails of the link-fish. It was another sultry night, and he could not bear the stifling heat belowdecks. No one else was awake—even the music of the ship itself, the creak of her timbers, the sound of ropes and canvas, all was hushed. Half a dozen others were curled up on the deck. He had his own sea cloak, a historic leather garment, lined with jocca cloth, which his grandfather, Pat Rork, had worn when he sailed with Gline. He spread it on the roof of the deckhouse and slept heavily.

Down in his cabin Simon Varo was asleep. He had ruled off the logbook and entered the name of the new day, which had already begun: *Sunday, 12 Jules, 1102*. The captain, who deplored the distortion of the dates on his world, Rhomary, had added in brackets *[Landfall +265]*.

Paddy Rork woke up in the dark and found that a wind was blowing from the southeast . . . for this place quite a brisk wind.

"Quick, boy!" said the bosun, Winna Cross, handling a winch. "Give a twirl here, and she'll be under way. We must not waste this bit of a wind!"

The bosun did not call for all hands; the sails, filling gently, were all set for just such a breeze. Three or four of the crew padded about on deck; Megan Varo was taking a turn at the wheel. It was a clear run to the heads; already Paddy thought he could hear the sound of the ocean. When he left off winching he went forward, right to the prow of the *Dancer*, decorated with carved and painted kells, Celtic patterns.

Pearl, the small moon, had long set, but he marked the comet

to the northeast. Years ago it had heralded the first meetings of
the Envoys with the Vail, the lost race of sea-monsters. Paddy
had always harbored doubts about the Vail—could they have
been as smart as older people gave 'em credit for?—but he
wished that a couple might be found, for the excitement.

The sky was very clear and radiant, although it was more
than an hour before sunrise. Paddy could make out the headlands clearly and the jungle trees on the southern coast. The
Dancer raised a foamy trail as it parted the turbid reaches of the
Deadwater; the ship rode on in the heaven-sent dawn wind, and
down below Cap Varo woke up. He noted that they were under
way, tapped the precious chronometer, saw that it was nearly
seven o'clock, Gann Station Time, the time by which he sailed.
He looked through the stern port and knew that the *Dancer* was
coming into the curve of the headland. He went out, fully
dressed now except for his boots, and slipped up the companionway in his stocking feet. Simon Varo did not go on deck, only
protruded himself, waist high, from the head of the companionway. He was not visible to any of the persons on deck except
Paddy Rork, who turned his head.

Paddy was gulping cool air and sprawling over the taffrail,
thrilled by the sight of Gline's ocean beyond the low headland.
It was a calm sea, darkest blue-green, although the light was in-
creasing; a faint flush of red had grown in the western sky. He
looked back, and all the figures on the deck were dark and solid
by contrast to the vast display of sea and sky. He took in Winna
Cross by the foremast, Man Gruner propped on the port rail
amidships, Megan Varo back there at the wheel, and the figure
of the Old Man himself gawking out of the companionway to
see how they were going. As he looked, Cap Varo began to re-
trace his steps on the ladder, satisfied with the ship's progress:
Winna Cross had spun a winch again to reef sail; Megan Varo
held the wheel. The obedient wind was dropping, the ship slowly
moving to her berth beside the headland.

There was a bright flash in Paddy's right eye. He saw more
than the others; he saw almost all there was to see at this time
and in this place. Far to the north and high over the distant
reaches of the swamp forests he saw a flash that kept on burn-

ing, an excruciating bright light. The sky was clear, almost cloud-
less, with a few skeins of mist along the northern shores of the
Deadwater.

The light did not go out; it became brighter, smaller, with a
roundness to it. Paddy's eyes followed the lights, two lights now,
round, burning orange, edged with blue, trailing smoke. He
shouted aloud, heard an answering shout. The two lights burned
across the sky from north to west; Paddy roared out with all his
might:

"Captain! Captain Varo! Look there!"

And he was in time to bring Cap Varo slipping back up the
ladder again. The captain saw for himself. The two fireballs
were lower now, trailing clouds of white smoke or vapor; one
was so low that it struck down to land in the forest. The remaining meteor blazed across the western sky over Gline's
Ocean. Paddy swore that it moved sideways, jerked in the air.
Now it had just a hint of a thick, dark shape, not round like a
fireball or meteor. Then it was out of sight with no thump, no
thunderclap, no splash. All that was left was a long white trail,
wisps of vapor stretching up and back into the dawn sky. Megan
Varo cried out:

"Look there, Pa!"

Cap Varo, at the after rail, looked back east. The way was
misty and dark, across the Deadwater, but over the Red Ocean
hung a clear vapor trail, nearly vertical, and another smaller
wisp was to be seen farther to the northeast.

The sleepers below, wakened by the shouts, were pouring up
on deck expecting the grandmother of all blackrays. Instead
they found a handful of witnesses, Paddy Rork pale with excitement, above all the captain himself. For if he himself had not
seen the lights, as Ira Maddern pointed out, nothing would have
followed.

"A shower of meteors!" cried Simon Varo. "Great Starfire!
Was that it?"

His melancholy had completely left him. He called Paddy to
him and the bosun and Man Gruner, while the others talked
and questioned amidships. Ira Maddern, who wished he had
been awake earlier, called for order. Cap Varo did a quick round

of the witnesses, and it was Man Gruner, a strong, shy, comical thirty-year-old seaman, who brought out the words.

"Captain," he said, "I thought of starships!"

"How then, starships?" echoed the captain. "Two fireballs I saw . . . Megan?"

Megan Varo heard the wheel of fortune clicking away, but she did not lie.

"It might have been . . . a space vehicle," she said. "Exploded way up yonder to the distant north, over the northern continent. Paddy saw it best of all."

Cap Varo put a hand on Paddy's shoulder and stared him in the eye. The boy did not flinch; he was no more than a little afraid of the captain, and he was not naturally shy, having lived a free and easy life at the Gann, among his family.

"It was a big flash," he said, "way up the north like Third says, Captain. It never stopped burning, brighter than a fire, brighter than lightning. Then two fireballs came from this flash, not only them two but others. I only followed these ones, here to the west."

"Very good, Paddy," said Simon Varo. "What was with these ones you followed?"

"They came much lower," said Paddy, "and one turned off or fell away. This one lone fireball continued on . . . it made its way far out in Gline's Ocean and come down. It was burning redhot and had a trail of steam, but it had a longer shape under its cloud. It moved sideways in the air."

The captain stared at the boy wildly, then he drew back his head, staring at the open sea beyond the heads, where the wind was freshening. He said to Ira Maddern:

"We'll clear the heads!"

He said to Paddy:

"Nip down below, boy; fetch me my boots!"

The crew, more excited than ever, began to speculate loudly.

"What's all this quatsh, gal!" growled Tom Kirsh, who had been cooking porridge. "You never saw it!"

He was speaking to pretty Ketty Merrow, who replied stubbornly:

"It's *written*, Mister Kirsh . . ."

Cap Varo's eye lighted on the young girl, and he called for silence. Everyone had remembered now—Ketty's mother was a Jenzite, a follower of the prophet. Jenz Kindl had had quite a lot to say about starships and starfolk.

"Give us the word, Merrow," said the captain.

"It is from the Book of Jenz," said Ketty, bearing witness clearly. "Third Chapter, beginning at the twenty-third Satz: 'All will be foretold in dreams and in the revelations of the Gods. If the lightning strikes twice, if Star-folk come again, let them be greeted with human kindness.'"

Cap Varo gave a loud cheerful laugh.

"Come then!" he cried. "We'll go fetch them in, these poor Starfolk! 'Foretold in dreams,' was it? D'ye hear that, Megan, girl? Now hear this . . . we will take our usual course west and keep a sharp lookout. Why, for this blessed voyage, we have already given the island a new name. . . ."

By the time Paddy came back with the captain's boots, the crew of the *Dancer* were giving three cheers for the voyage to Palmland.

II

Far to the northeast at Pinnacle, three tall monoliths rose a hundred meters above the canyon of a dead river, and on the tallest one, partly hewn from the rock, was the house of the Star-Gazing Woman. Faya Junik looked keenly to the north where a thick vapor trail still hung in air, above the Stony Desert. She lowered her telescope, strode immediately to a corner of the stone balcony, and unfurled the big linen sheet over the parapet. The emergency signal would bring a scout, scaling the ramps and ladders. The families who lived in the canyon were prospectors: they treasured their Star-Gazer and not only for benefits received, in the way of free doctoring and the discovery of several rich meteorites.

Faya Junik was at her desk, writing her emergency report with a firm hand, preparing to cope with an "impact zone," when she was stricken with pity and terror. She tried to register every in-

dividual consciousness, every last one of them . . . *Landing capsules
. . . was it possible?* Falling into the far distant reaches of the swamp
forest, splashing down into the Red Ocean, or that vast, half-
known ocean farther west . . : Landing hard in their impact zone:
the poor "cosmonauts" she meant to find in the Stony Desert. It
seemed to her that they must all die, burn, drown, now at once,
or later, as so many of the first-comers had done, in and out of
the *Rho Maryland*. Yet these were a new breed, with new systems.
. . . One thing sure, they were still fighting to maintain contact,
in a tumult of voices audible only to one another. Did they know
already the hidden variables of the planet, which would give
them, in terms of radioelectronics, such a poor reception?

*Bulk One sent out no signals at all. Its heat shields failed, three drogues failed
to open, it swooped, burning into a marshy valley, on the eastern boundary
of the swamp forest, one hundred and ten kilometers west of Silver City and
two hundred and seventy-three kilometers north of the Gann Station, beyond
the hills of the Divide. Capem Two had better luck and kept sending inter-
mittently all through their rescue period. A party from the town of Bork arrived on Landfall+2 and on the next day, out of the whiteness of the desert,
with white cloaks and winged steeds, came Faya Junik and her riders.*

    *Capem Tree, tagged as the safest capsule, sent out no signals after splash-
ing down in the great Sooree river, but Warrant Officer Rose Chan and the
supercargo, the valuable civilian passenger, Karl-Heinz-Jurgen Valente,
physician and surgeon, made shift to save each other, while Oxper John
Miller helped save them both. All three survived and in the course of their adventures did the inhabitants of Rhomary more than one great service. So it
happened that two years after Landfall Capem Tree itself was extracted
from the river and brought to the Gann, where it formed the major exhibit in
a new museum.*

    *Capem Four, similar in shape to the unlucky Bulk One, made a near per-
fect landing, its drogues and heat shields having been inspected immediately
before the emergency division. It came down in a remote area of the northern
landmass, twenty-five kilometers from a seacoast that not even the hardiest
of the Rhomary sea-captains had visited. Lieutenant-Commander Yasuo Ito
was able to send out his coordinates, to receive a close signal from Capem
Fiver, to characterize the spot in which he had made landfall as a "jungle*

marsh." Then, as the after lock was cleared, Four's run of luck proved to be ephemeral; half of the curved metal tube of the capem rested in fact upon the edges of a marshy lake, much softer than the surrounding swamp forest. The capem bent, tilted, half submerged in mud and water. No more signals were sent out, but in their bleak struggle to stay alive the survivors of Capem Four received signals from Capem Fiver. On an island. With minimal loss of life and equipment. A dream, in contrast to a nightmare.

In contrast, certainly, to the prolonged experience of one man who found himself completely alone in the midst of an alien sea, out of sight of land, twirling slowly in his inflated silversuit. As the wind and the current drove him slowly along in who knew which direction he ascertained that he could remember very little. He opened his faceplate and breathed the air.

Everything had gone except a few hand grips necessary to bring his soggy Q-pack into play, for the water bottle and a protein stick. At night, overhead, he saw a tiny moon; he spoke to it familiarly. Nothing left. How many days now? A growing certainty that a great disaster had taken place and that he was personally responsible for it all. More than once he heard a voice which said "Ahoy!" and then "Ahoy who? who? who?" He turned his head and saw that it was some kind of dolphin talking at him like a hoot-owl. Who? How the hell should he know, he replied to the question. Scraps of data circled in his waterlogged brain. There had been an Argosy transporter, class III maybe, and emergency capsules, and he was damned. He was damned if he could remember which capem he was from. . . .

3

Anat Asher, flat on her back, needed all her strength to adjust the recliner so that she could reach the console. Gregg, spread-eagled at her side, benefited from his longer arms. She turned her head and saw Winkler, pressed flat, one hand twitching, at the useless ship-system in the corner of the watchpost. Gregg came in blasting her head off, swearing at the hardware.

". . . fagged deadcut kitchen bank! Read off, Asher!"

She read off, pressure, air, rate of descent—it *was* air; the rate of descent had diminished. She punched in vain for exocad to draw a picture of their plight, felt the whole capem bounce and flail. She apprehended its shape, a hammer falling, and thought of the long handle, the Hill, flipping right over. Gregg suddenly had a visual on the camray, shifting layers of cloud . . . *earthlike* . . . then a dark mass of vegetation. A scrap of burning wreckage obscured all the camray outlets, turned black like the fingers of a burnt hand. The falling hammer shuddered, rocked wildly from side to side. Anat read off the interior temperature, 42.5 degrees. Gregg scoffed.

"Not even a heat wave!"

There was a rending jolt throughout the length and breadth of the capem. She knew the fabric had gone; it was the end; she gaped at the display, numb with terror. The six blue lights shone like stars. Gregg opened channels, announced:

"Drogues out!"

All out, all on time. Capem Fiver braked, flattened out. The exocad screen winked into life, but no simulation appeared; the camray, still fouled with carbon, showed dazzling blue and a hazy darker blue line. *Coastline.*

"Go there, you bastard!"

When Gregg laughed, Anat knew that she had spoken aloud. He tried to stabilize the capem, and a contrary burst of power from a lone booster rocket urged the capsule two points southwest. On camray the holograms of the coastline hardened, came up at them dizzily. On the exocad screen Anat Asher saw a ragged oval shape, then beside it another. She read off:

"Compare and contrast Timor, Indian Ocean, 33,300 square kilometers."

Then she and Gregg wrestled with the shuddering, screaming capem in the throes of its landing. The unwieldy mass of heated metal touched water, tilted upward at its hammerhead, charged bucketing through sand and vegetation, came at last to rest. Anat Asher was dimly aware that they had achieved the impossible: Capem Fiver was beached upon the shore of a large island. In perfect unison Gregg blew the bolts on the forward bulkhead while she took the after, then the tail-end.

"Out! Out! Alle raus!" shouted Gregg. *"Locks voided. The air is good!"*

"Out there!" Anat took up the refrain. "Guard your airblend. Touch no part of the exterior! Wink? You holding?"

"On call!" gasped Winkler.

He passed them, arms working like a man in free fall, boots sticking on the hot floor. Anat did not look toward the locks; she plunged on with another life/death ritual. For the personal spotters she put out a repeater, "Fiver landed," and their coordinates. Gregg took a round check of all the emergency capsules, One through Six, with vocal. Anat sucked on her applicator, dosed herself with a red. A scrambled mess of vocal and white noise blared out and was held, retrievable.

"Commander," said Anat, "we must . . ."

Gregg was already dragging himself out of the recliner. She swung up—it was easier than she thought—and half-expected Gregg to be still close by, but he had gone. The hammerhead section, the Rec, was canted up. Anat Asher guessed it would be a good jump for a human being from the open bulkheads to the ground.

Winkler was bundling the mensh through the open tube of the after lock; she did the same forward. A Silvo fell down at her feet; she bent to help him up, and he struck her in the midriff with his arm.

"Easy! Take your red!" she gasped.

She caught a glimpse of his flushed face through the plex as he rushed into the lock. A smaller figure came at her, hands flailing helplessly. She caught the woman under the arms, read her name, Baumer, L.P.F., a sergeant from Systems. She checked the airblend, tried to speak to the woman; an oxper with a medical flash came by, lifted Baumer and carried her through the lock. When the Rec was nearly empty, Lieutenant Asher ran, sticking and scrambling across to the firedoors and looked . . . down the Hill.

The open lock showed daylight; a figure in a silversuit without a helmet came back through the lock. A kono, a young man, began to laugh and dance and wave his arms, beckoning her to come. Anat Asher began to run down the Hill; she went very fast, dodging the hurdles. Her shoes did not stick anymore; she was being thrust down the slope. She dived out into the new world.

The light was pale, a third light, neither that of Earth nor of the planet Arkady. Anat saw threads of light twisting down through pools of blue-green shade, cast by the squat treegrowths. The ground sloped away toward the sea which was screened from view by these palmlike trees. Palm trees. Call 'em that.

Under the palms the konos had fallen into a silver heap, gasping. Helmets off, they gulped air; they laughed; their voices came to her from a long way off. Myrrha, in their midst, tried to rise, fell back upon the fine red-gold sand. She was held up on both sides by willing hands. Anat steadied herself, took a long breath from her bottled air, and removed her helmet. The first breath tasted cool, aromatic, strange. She was something of an air connoisseur: this air had a good bouquet, marine tang, high oxygen content for that touch of well-being.

"Hey," she said, "we'll get high on this air!"

The konos laughed aloud. Myrrha came forward, clasped Anat's hands and said:

"Thank you for bringing us safely to this place."

"Give us a duty, Lieutenant," said Azamo.

He was the leading male dancer, a handsome, muscular, coffee-brown man, about thirty-five years old; he also worked in a duo with his partner, Tiria, and they had brought along their son, Carl, the very young mime-dancer. Now for the first time, as he stood beside Myrrha, she realized something else: this was Myrrha's son; the young boy, Carl, was her grandson; the KONO team were really a family.

"Cut loose that drogue," she said. "Use it for a groundsheet."

Hari, a mime-dancer, raised the old question of insects, bacteria, alien life forms. She gave back the manual, pointed out that observation, acclimatization and trust were recommended by World Space. Watch out for even the smallest life forms, don't harm or destroy them unnecessarily, but do not jeopardize the welfare of the emergency landing party. Use the care one would use in a jungle setting on Earth or on Arkady. Gloves to be worn if desired, and fine-pore gauze masks available in the first-aid pocket of the silversuits, along with tubes of nonallergic pure vegetable repellent cream, which also helped against sunburn.

"It *is* an island . . .?" asked Myrrha.

"Roughly the size of Timor."

"*Timor!*"

A nostalgic cry from Zena, the Australian girl.

"Can we fetch gear from our quarters?" asked Kyle.

"Not yet. Not until the fabric cools. Stay close."

"We'll sound out the place," said Tiria.

"I'll assign you an auxiliary," said Anat.

She struggled uphill toward the towering bulk of the Rec.

Fiver was bronze and black with heat, steaming in the pale light. The capem rested upon crushed palms and banked sand thrust upward in the landing and upon a ridge of higher ground.

Anat went to work with her own shears, cutting down a drogue that was sticking and blistering in the heat farther along the radial arm. She could not get all the cords, blipped for auxiliary personnel. Along came Ray Green's bubble-friend, George King from Systems: clean-cut, with fair curly hair, probably the most popular of all the oxper. He shared Ray's older look but was more good-humored. Now he came tromping through sand and dark soil to take over recovery of the drogue.

"The medics looking for you, Lieutenant Asher."

"George," she said, "are all the auxiliary personnel holding well?"

"Why sure! Triple affirmative, Lieutenant!"

His eyes sparkled at her, full of irony. Then he appeared to reflect and said:

"I believe one of the Silver Cross auxiliaries sustained some kind of small damage. We don't have details."

"I understand," she said.

The expanding field of macro-crystalline matrices made possible the growth of widely differentiated types of tissue, from tomato flesh to the para-organic complexities of the android brain. It also allowed for delicate but direct electronic communication. It was understood that auxiliaries could communicate among themselves and spy on or simply be aware of other auxiliaries in ways not known to humans.

"George," she said, "would you go look after the KONO team along here? Take 'em this extra drogue."

"Hey! The konos!" said George King eagerly. "Yes, ma'am! *Jawohl!*"

She climbed still higher up the ridge clutching the rough fluted columns of the palms. Down below the grove thinned out; she could see farther off shimmering dunes of golden sand. A picture. A warning passage from the manual, not so trusting this time. "Life-forms on other planets may bear a striking resemblance to known forms on Earth, but during all first contact a critical vigilance must be maintained."

From her perch, above the gaping forward bulkhead, she could see clumps of human beings sitting about, lying flat out, a few propped against the palm trees. Lassitude. Shock? Had they popped their reds? Had the roll been called? She looked closer, trying to do a headcount, and divined that this was not only how things were, but how things would be.

The Silvos had taken up a position on level ground under three large palms and harvested one of the drogues for their groundsheet. The crew members formed a looser group, dotted among the trees. Between the two groups was a natural formation, a low outcrop of gray rock. Lieutenant-Commander Gregg sat on the rock, his girl, Marna Rossi, on her groundsheet leaning sleepily against his knees. Gregg appeared to be conversing easily with Captain Boyle, who shared the rock. "Shadow" Adams sat near his chief. Shadow was a blend, a brown-skinned, dark-haired android with a hint of racial typing.

There was a lot of excited talk contrasting with the general lethargy. A few individuals were busy: Winkler, red-faced, was spraying cool-foam on the capem along with an oxper and a young ensign. Peter Wemyss was trying to climb one of the palm trees. Cook Sergeant Sam Kayoute and his helpers were unpacking their carry-off crate; this reminded her of another carry-off crate and she looked around for it. Fine. An oxper had flicked up the screen of treated cotton cloth and was assembling the chemical latrine cells. Anat saw that a slew of excess baggage had been brought out, against regulations. Personal effects, mystery packages. That genius Regi from Systems was putting up a red, white, and green umbrella. She thought he was just clowning around, then noticed the solar collecting antenna on top of the brolly. Regi was charging his batteries.

A faint hail came from a larger group directly below her perch; they were screened from the others a little by a fallen palm. The medics. Doc White. Bending over one, two mensh on the ground. The man who waved at her was their very own Alpha, Ivan Dalny, an inhabitant of the planet Arkady. The senior MTA had been a Feldsher or field doctor on his own world. Before going down she blipped for Ray Green and got the right answer.

"Scanning the site, Lieutenant, with Burns."

The two tall figures came slowly into view beyond the Silvos, pacing and swiveling their heads in slow motion. She went fast down the slope, stumbling, catching at smooth stone and scraps of vegetation. There were four medics working on a man and a woman. She recognized the woman, Baumer, the sergeant from Systems who had collapsed on the way out. Doc White rose up awkwardly from beside the man and stretched his arms. Anat saw the man's flash and his name: Morgan, the lieutenant-sistek, also from Systems, Regi's boss.

"What's wrong with them?"

"Wrong?"

White blinked at her, smiled.

"Doctor!"

He wiped the grin off his face, but his blue eyes still smiled through thick straw-colored lashes.

"Morgan is in deep shock," he said, "or maybe he took something strong and unprogrammed. Linda Baumer has a heart incident."

"How bad are they?"

She laid a hand on his arm. Again his strange look, an inappropriate affect, his sly smile. She strained to make contact, gripped his arm, could only remember his nickname, "Pearly."

"Doc, please . . . ?"

"They might live . . ." he said.

"Make them comfortable," she said. "Get the oxper to put up your smaller dome, there in the green package. Anything further to report?"

"Report?" said White.

Dalny, who had been watching them, rose up from attending Morgan.

"Coupla turned ankles," he rumbled. "General lethargy due to gravity increase. Just a touch. Zero point seven two five or less."

"Shee-it!" said Anat Asher. "Will this impair function?"

She looked at the bodies strewn around the landing site.

"Not much," said Dalny. "Short people . . ."

He beamed down at her.

"Short people have it better."

"How are *you* feeling, Dalny?"

The gravity on Arkady was lighter than that of Earth. Just a touch.

"You can't win 'em all, Lieutenant," he said. "I'll try not to become overoxygenated. The population will adapt. Oxper are not much affected. Physical changes will become evident in the second or third generation."

"Shee-it! Holy Crockin' Mother!" shouted White unexpectedly.

"Stow it, Meister!" growled Anat. "Get quiet or I'll have you tranked out!"

White sat on the ground and began to weep.

"He'll be fine," soothed Dalny. "It just hit him."

Lieutenant Morgan lay still, patched with medication strips on his bare chest. Linda Baumer had opened her eyes. Lieutenant Stout, the senior nurse, was feeding her a tube of lemon lift.

"Time we all took a fruit booster," said Dalny.

Anat bent down, spoke to Baumer, touched her hand. Doing fine. A fine place. An island. Linda Baumer gave a weak smile, closed her eyes. Dell Stout signaled to Anat; they sat on the ground out of earshot of the patients.

"Systems," said Dell. "Lotta stress since this buzz-up began. The perturbation and that."

"What did Morgan take?" murmured Anat.

"Heavy mixed capsules, Rainbows or Deepdowns, to zonk him right out, make some sleep. Cumulative. Reacted with the emergency medication, the stress of descent."

"And Baumer?"

"She was his girl," said the nurse. "Slept with her boss, soothed him down. I guess she popped one of these things just to be companionable. I think that's how it was. It gave her this heart thing. *She* will be fine."

Anat shivered inside her silversuit, did not look at Morgan.

"Dell?"

"Yes, honey?"

"Have to check the Cohen status of the women."

"Gotcha," said Dell Stout.

Way back in her mind, behind the buffering of the pink and

the red capsules, Anat found Joshua, her grown son, whom she would never see again. There was the planet Earth, a spark of reflected light spinning away into the void. She needed comfort, but the chances were that her counselor, Dira Pike, had died in the last hour, while she still lived. She looked at White, the poor plagged young doctor. She went to him on all fours, sat back on her heels and took his gloved hands, staring into his face. His given name came back to her.

"Tim!" she said. "Timothy, you're not alone. The air is good. We can make a life here. We're here *together* in this place."

White sighed deeply. He freed a hand from her grasp, found a cool-pad in the front packet of his suit and scrubbed it over his face.

"What you mean," he said mildly, "is that I'm not Robinson Crusoe."

Anat Asher uttered a groan of exasperation, crawled over the fallen palm tree and finally dragged herself upright again. She made it to Sam Kayoute's place and ordered a round of fruit-flavored supavite. She took a thirty-pack herself, reminded the commissary of the konos at the end of the Hill.

The light was changing; hard white rays struck downwards through the leathery green trapezoids that crowned the palms. Warrant Officer Regi stood up and gestured with his umbrella.

"Signore e Signori!" he announced. "It is the sunrise. Our new sun has risen in the West."

Peter Wemyss had given up the attempt to climb his palm. Instead he had scooped out a channel in the thick sandy soil at its base and filled it with white water storage crystals. He was planting specimens of alien plant life: philodendron, morning glory, spring onions, runner beans. As she came up to him Anat Asher heard a sound near or far that was not human.

It was a faint ululation, an animal cry or something like it. She saw that Wemyss had heard it, too. She looked for Green and Burns, scanning the site, and saw them only a few meters away. They both registered the sound. She shook her head at them, turned back to Wemyss.

"Quiet!" she said. "No alert."

He was a thin, muscular man with a close-cropped, round head and small, neat beard. Anat recalled that he wore a beard

for medical, not religious, reasons . . . he claimed that the de-
pilatory gels and shavers gave him a rash. His wide, brown eyes
blazed with excitement for the new world.

"What did it sound like to you?" she whispered.

"Coyote," he said promptly. "Dingo perhaps. The Australian
wild dog. Little touch of howler monkey . . ."

He lifted his head, ready to demonstrate, then thought better
of it.

"Here!" said Anat.

She gave him a tube of OSV, orange concentrate with supavite, "the drink that conquered galaxies."

There was sudden movement in the solid group of Silvos,
under their trees. The oxper among them and now the humans
were reacting to that single strange cry. A tall master sergeant,
name of "Hoot" Wells, heaved himself up and strolled quickly in
the direction of the after bulkhead. Heading for quarters, which
were strictly off-limits at this time. He left Anat's line of sight. She
held back, watching and waiting. Sure enough, a shouting match
developed, off-camera; the Silvo had tangled with Master
Sergeant Winkler, still laying coolant foam with his team.

Anat Asher swore and started down the gentle slope. The situation was resolved before she drew level with the gray rock
where the two commanding officers were taking their ease. Captain Boyle rapped out an order; Sergeant Wells backed off. Half
a dozen Silvos had scrambled to their feet the moment a voice
had been raised against one of their number. Now they all sank
down again.

She concentrated on Lieutenant-Commander Gregg, R.K.G.
She made deliberate eye-contact, trying to get his full attention,
to signal her concern. *Here in this alien place. Every moment a moment
of truth.* His gaze flicked over her and slid away. He ran a hand
over the dark, smooth hair of his girl, Rossi.

"Have a lift, sweetheart," he said.

Anat doled out the tubes of OSV.

"Sound of an animal," she said. "You hear it, Commander?
Captain Boyle?"

They stared at her; Marna Rossi gave a faint squeak. Shadow
Adams said softly:

"Doglike, sir. Some distance away."

"I believe Sergeant Wells was reacting to that sound," said Anat.

"No cause for alarm," said Gregg. "We'll be making up observer teams . . ."

"We'll give you a team!" said Boyle. "What's this with my sergeant?"

Gregg squinted at Anat and raised an eyebrow.

"Do the members of your unit have sporting guns in quarters, Captain Boyle?" she asked.

It came out hard.

"No!" snapped Boyle.

He grinned at Gregg, made a show of reading Asher's name tag. "No, Asher, we got no ball-guns, no sporting guns. You want one our boys shoot you a dog-alien?"

Gregg understood at last what she was driving at. It stirred his in-built space service antipathy for projectile weapons.

"Ball-guns are outlawed," he said. "No shooting of that kind. We'll put out these teams of pathfinders . . ."

"Teams?" asked Boyle.

"Two scout teams, each comprising an officer, a specialist, and an auxiliary," said Anat Asher. "This place doesn't look like any heavy going. Main purpose is a preliminary search for water."

"Our team, your team . . ." grinned Boyle. "What do you say, Commander?"

"The observer teams should be made up of crew and assigned mensh," said Anat Asher. "This is not any kind of competition."

"If Captain Boyle wants to field three scouts?" said Gregg, smiling.

Boyle chuckled.

"Brief these teams, Lieutenant," continued Gregg, "then I'll take readings and reports."

Anat went away, fighting the gravity, fighting resentment. Behind her Boyle stood up and bellowed three names. She took the pack of OSV down to the Silvos, tried to hand it to the doctor, the Russian woman.

"Orderly!" snapped Petrova.

An oxper split the pack, divided the tubes. The scout team chosen by Boyle had risen to their feet: Second Lieutenant Kraut Holder, a young mechanic named Olsen, and oxper James Carter, all of Detroit Company. In her opinion the men were too big, too much slowed down by the gravity.

"Lieutenant Holder?" she said. "This is an observation walk for a scout team. I'll brief the two teams over by the medic tree in fifteen minutes."

"On call, Lieutenant!"

He sounded keen and cooperative. She stared at the Silvos. All young, all saved. Lord God Jehovah, let some good come of it.

She took the last of the OSV to a group of regulars, sat down before she fell down, drank her own tube of lift. Three or four persons told her to take it easy. She waited until the palm grove stopped spinning and summed up her resources. She blipped Ray Green, who was out of sight among the trees.

"Getting out scout teams, Ray," she said. "Give me an interim report."

"A-Okay, Lieutenant," said Green.

Android voices became noticeably metallic through any communication device.

"Paradise island," he continued. "Low insect count. No plant danger *we* can see. Something calls, howls, far away, saw signs of an old bird kill."

"When you say bird, Ray?"

"Downy or feathered winged creature about the size of a large pigeon."

"Okay, bird."

"Dim sighting of small colored creatures, query birds, flying over the near plateau."

"Water?"

"It's here, Lieutenant. One of the teams should find some small river coming from the high ground."

She picked Maestro Regi, the mad scientist from Systems, as leader, gave him his own oxper Dick Black, and Vannie Frost from the Rec, although she was on the tall side.

"How you holding, Vannie?" she asked. "Want to do this pathfinder jag?"

"With ya, Lieutenant!" said the big girl.

Anat thought of Rose Chan, had a wild flash of Chan, somewhere on this loozy paradise planet, with their VIP, the Swiss eye doctor. She let go at last, lay on her back on the groundsheets and was swept straight away into a strange watery dream. Some service mensh were fighting their way out into the daylight, whoomp, the lifeboat went up like a yellow pool toy; the spray was full of rainbows. Chan was shouting aloud, a voice said loudly, *"Shee-it, Shangri-la!"* There was the same life-or-death tension about the scene as they felt, were feeling here in the grove. Then she was awake again; she had been zonked out, dreaming the adventures of Chan for seven, eight minutes.

Willing hands helped her up; she went over to face the teams before the medic tree. The Silvos were showing off, running on the spot, sweating.

"Easy," she said. "Don't dehydrate yourselves *before* you find water. This exercise augments the observation round of the oxper. Take it slow and easy, each team making an approximate half-circle fifty to a hundred meters from the established perimeter. Use common sense. Beware of falls in an increased gravity. Do not fall down, undertake difficult climbing. Do not seek contact with alien fauna. Our main object is to find water. Leaders to prepare a careful report of the terrain on the vox simul. If you're out of range of the personal communicator, the blip, use the wrist spotters. We'll reset the channels."

"How do we defend ourselves against attack?" demanded Holder.

"You run away before anything attacks you," said Anat.

"That can be disputed," said Regi. "The manual is vague."

"I am the senior duty officer responsible for this capem and this exercise, Regi," snapped Anat, "and I am not vague. Both of you, Lieutenant Holder and Warrant Officer Regi, carry a simple pressure weapon, a stun-gun or blaster. You are not going out there to hunt or gather specimens or start a war. I don't believe you will meet any large life-forms within a hundred meters of this landing place."

"Lieutenant," whined Frost, "how the hell can you *say* that? No one was ever *here* . . ."

"We work from analogy, Vannie," said Anat patiently. "We have to. The noise and heat of our descent and impact would drive living creatures out of the immediate vicinity. This place not only looks like an island with a beach and palm trees, it is one. This would limit the size of the fauna."

"Lieutenant, please excuse, you're talking bullshit!" argued Regi. "Large fauna occur on islands all the time. How about the Komodo dragons, giant monitor lizards from the Indonesian archipelago?"

"Okay!" cried Anat. "Large fauna do occur on the islands of Earth until Homo sapiens comes along. The Komodo dragons are extinct. Dead as the dodo . . . from the island of Mauritius."

"Was that a giant lizard?" asked the young Silvo, Olsen.

"No, it was some kinda turkey!" said Frost, rolling her eyes.

All the observers fell about laughing, crew, Silvos, oxper, even Lieutenant Asher did not keep a straight face.

"Find us some water, you bunch of turkeys!" she said.

She traded channels for their spotters, walked with both teams to a point on the eastern edge of the camp, a little uphill from the place where the Silvos had made their bivouac. They went off, Holder to the north, Regi uphill to the south, with instructions to come together in the west, near the konos.

The teams were in the field for two and a half hours. Regi called in once on the spotter channel, reported "a flying lizard six centimeters long, green and gold." Temperature in the open several hours before noon: 24 degrees Celsius. Anat attempted contact with Lieutenant Holder, received no reply.

Suddenly the Silvo team reappeared flushed and triumphant in the west. They had found "a stream of pure water" running down from the high ground to the sea not more than a kilometer west of the camp. The course of the stream had been clearly marked by the vegetation on its banks, and they pressed on until they found it. The young mechanic, Olsen, had bruised his ribs in a fall; he was strapped up by Big Doc Petrova. Anat broke the news to Regi, and, full of excitement, he decided to approach the stream himself with his team and give the water a second test with his field kit. Lieutenant Holder, given the honor of naming the stream, came up promptly with Silverbrook, and the name was current before the track to the stream had been marked.

At Landfall+6 hours, ahead of time, Commander Gregg allowed the auxiliaries to reenter the capem. They checked its ventilation and stability, put the solar collectors into operation. Then, in relays, officers and sisteks from both units sat at the comcen and directed all its systems to one end. No contact was made with any other capem of the *Serendip Dana*. The burst of noise received on landing was laboriously broken down by Gregg himself, Vic Burns assisting. It had at least three components.

The voice of Lieutenant-Commander Ito of Capem Four clearly uttered the words *"Fiver hear you. . . . Four down unsteady landmass* [two words following becoming unclear, believed to be *jungle marsh] Holding, holding . . . too much* [another indecipherable word finally set down as *tilt*]*."* There was a scrambled fragment of a coordinate in the north on the landmass where Four had gone down.

This welcome and relatively clear message overlapped with the closest communication. Astrogator Trenchard said distinctly, *"Sexer splashdown. Fiver received,"* then read off a portion of his coordinates, due east. He broke off suddenly.

A third and more distant voice was impossible to decipher with any certainty. It was female, tentatively identified as Lieutenant Sabra Masson of Bulk Two, located northeast. The words might have been *"Signing off . . ."* The voice was distorted by distance, by interference, by its own desperate volume. Masson, if it was Masson, cried out the words. This cry and its attempted analysis were often played back. Some listeners claimed to hear different words: "sending love," "sort of . . . ," "Shalom," "See you later," even "Save my life."

Morale continued high during the whole of the daylight hours. The konos came from their camp at midday and offered singing for all, antistress therapy in smaller groups. The watch roster was made up. After a meal of turkey-soy rissoles, mashed potatoes, and gravy, almost every one of the castaways took a nap in the grove. At 1700 hours, ship time, the mensh were permitted to reenter the capem and make quarters.

Commander Gregg, having come to some personal agreement with Captain Boyle, allowed the Silvos to retain the after section of their old quarters, plus the after bulkhead, as what amounted to their private entry. He took the remainder of Special Quarters for Administration and for the regular officers. The konos gave up half of their quarters for an indoor sick bay; a maintenance hatch on the side of the Hill was roughly enlarged by the oxper to make a new entry for the medical unit. In the Rec itself, the tilted floor gave little trouble; the remaining crew members made themselves as private and as comfortable as possible.

The oxper fashioned themselves a room in the Rec, right beside the forward bulkhead; they used the old lock housing and part of the storage section doors. Humans still speculated about what it was oxper did in their private quarters. The only thing certain was that they needed time absolutely without human contact or surveillance in order to function best. It had been suggested that this was their equivalent to dreaming. A teasing component of their privacy was its silence. They played music, mainly, it seemed, to mask the fact that among themselves they laughed a little but very seldom spoke.

Sergeant Winkler was vaguely alarmed to see that, according to his lists, only eleven crew members remained to sleep in the Rec. Of these, Warrant Officer Regi might be offered a bunk in the officers' quarters, and the two noncommissioned medics might stay on call in sick bay.

He kept his own grids of social interaction on board ship . . . now things were hotting up. It was like an anthropology game: the problem here was the integration of a Very Warlike Tribe and a Specialist Tribe. The KONO team, who counted as a Very Peaceful Tribe, might be counted on the side of the crew, the Specialists. Gregg had some plan, of course, but he had no tact and no intuition. If he kept on high-handing and overworking his best officer, Anat Asher, he would lose face with his own Specialists and with the Warlike Silvos. Sucking up to that dangerous lunatic Boyle was not enough. The Silvos valued loyalty, too.

In fact, species loyalty . . . a big, fat alien scare . . . might bring them into integration quicker than anything. Wink felt sure that the alien scare would not be long in coming. In the meantime he dreamed about anything the Silvos could possibly want, any breach in the wall of their tribal ritual. That with the Silverbrook was good, but it cut both ways . . . now there would be a place discovered and named by the Specialists. It was like kids with their toys, two brothers each examining a syntho to see if theirs was the least bit worse or better. Pretty soon now the appeals to reason and team spirit would begin. Might even do some good. What was needed was action on a less rational level.

As he sat in the old watchpost—he had heaved out the ship systems and made his own bunk there—Winkler was approached by members of his tribe asking to bunk out of doors. This was forbidden until further orders. One person, Vannie Frost, went on about insomnia. He offered her the Rain Forest, knowing she was sad and in no mood for sex. Her lover was far away, in Capem Two. Others who asked *were* in the mood for sex, but they had the space service fetish concerning privacy.

"Meyer," said the sergeant, "it's going to be very dark here in the Rec. These are your comrades all around in the darkness. Lay back on this old-time Arkadian draw-the-curtains quatsh!"

Hansi Meyer, the Eucom PT instructor and one of the *Serendip Dana*'s most splendid studs, replied seriously.

"Kono girls have finer feelings."

"Crock you, Meyer. Orders have been given," said the sergeant. "Besides, how is that fine-feeling cheel gonna react when alien night-swarmers start chewing her sensibilities?"

"You got a directive on these . . . entities?" whispered Meyer.

"No, of course not."

Sergeant Winkler bit his tongue. He had not meant to launch the night-swarmers; they had just flown out of his mouth.

The Time Fix Unit, led by Maestro Regi, had placed a row of indestructible yellow markers in the sand at the sea's edge. A small party of officers stood on the beach checking their chronometers. Everyone had eaten, had slept a little; the seawater tested out as fit for washing, but there was a bathing ban in force.

Anat Asher had slept three hours, taken a waker; she felt fine-spun, unreal, slightly plagged. She deliberately held off taking a pink. Yes, she knew supplies were good—there were enough tranks in stores to smooth out a Yagga Festival—but she was trying to get clean. Gregg, she could see, was in excellent shape, talking with Boyle and the doctor, Petrova. Shadow hovered near his captain. Ray Green was along too, standing with Anat. Between the two groups stood Alessandro Regi; he raised a viewer to his eye, moved a hand as if conducting the sunset.

The alien sea was blue-green in the fading light and very calm. Capem Fiver had bored inland in the center of a deep bay on the northern coast of the island. Sand dunes rose up in the south beyond their palm grove and fell away to a sandy beach in the east. In the west, along the new path to the Silverbrook, the palm trees were thickened with underbrush. The observers, gazing out of the bay, due north according to their original coordinates, saw a shadowy line edging across the horizon. This coastline came a little nearer to them, running eastward, so that Anat could half-see, half-imagine a thick press of trees upon the shore. The northeastern sky was pink and gold, deepening to thick purple-red in the east, where the sun set. The land due east, in the path of the sunset, was very much closer to the island; a thin dark line half-floating upon the sea with a radiance striking up beyond it, to join that of the setting sun.

"What can you make out, Ray?" asked Anat.

"Might be another body of water there, Lieutenant."

The hard red disc of the setting sun was sinking now, very fast, into this hidden sea. The colors were vivid and striking; blue tufts of cloud spread out in the wide last rays and were turned to green, to turquoise, as the orb disappeared.

"That's it!" said Regi. "Delta Pavonis. The peacock spreads his tail."

"Thank you, Maestro!" said Anat, laughing.

"Read off, Regi!" Gregg put in dourly.

"From sunrise to sunset fourteen hours forty-seven minutes," said Regi. "Landfall one hour and six, seven minutes earlier. There are readings to compare. We are working towards a twenty-eight-hour day, Commander."

Shadow bent toward Captain Boyle; unexpectedly Ray Green chuckled.

"You got it, Adams!" said Boyle.

"What's that?" asked Gregg.

"If Arkady is a short-time world," said Shadow in his teasing, deep-toned voice, "what we have here is a long-time world."

The days on Arkady were shorter than Earth days. Anat thought of the Riverfield Space Port outside Port Garrett, the blue evenings, the fly-by-night trading stalls selling cooked seafood and fresh fruit.

"That sure as hell is what we have," said Gregg.

The sky was midnight blue; northeast there flared a yellow-tinged planet. Regi had promised a small moon, real soon now, and a comet, further northeast, another visitor to the unspoiled system.

"How would it be," asked Boyle, taking another prompt from Shadow, "if we sent up coupla big red/green distress flares issued with the lifeboats?"

"No!" said Regi. "We're not in distress and we don't know who we're signaling to!"

"Fire danger," said Anat. "The manual is way down on light-signals of this kind."

"Not yet," ruled Gregg. "We'll try and raise the other capems with our systems."

The way back to camp was already dark; the two oxper fell in fore and aft, shining flashlights. A few small insects, brown, mothlike, appeared in the path of the lights, and the party put on their helmets, faceplates open.

"This story about night-swarming lizards or bats," said Regi, "is a dangerous rumor."

There was a buzz of activity coming from the camp. In a longtime day, Anat saw wearily, a lot could be accomplished. She planned a session with Regi, Winkler, and Kayoute over the next day's rosters. A look at the medics, a goodnight call on the konos. Then she could fall into her bunk, trank herself out, and sleep forever. She stumped along feeling the alien swordgrass whip against her boots. They came in sight of the camp, the dark bulk of the capem and the blue patchwork of the drogues and groundsheets springing up in isolated light pools.

A fight broke out. The grove rang with shouts and the fleshy thud of traded punches. Anat shouted herself, began to run with Ray Green towards the milling knot of scrappers by the Cookhouse Tree. By the time she could recognize the fighters there were five, six, seven Silvos, men and women, piling in to attack. Winkler came from the forward hatch waving his stun gun and roaring. He poised on the new ramp and downed two Silvos expertly with a perfect riot-control shoulder thrust.

Anat had her eye on one injured trying to crawl out from under. She ran uphill, shouting, pushing, taking blows, then was thrust away from behind. She blacked out for a few seconds; when she came to, the fighters had frozen. She saw Gregg, who had knocked her aside, lift out the injured person. Was it Loney, the ensign? She propped herself against a palm tree and watched very closely.

Boyle, Holder, and Petrova were sending their Silvos rapidly from hand to hand out of the fight zone. Anat was beginning to shake now; she took a pink, removed her helmet. She reasoned: The ship has gone. It was not a fight under ship conditions. This is an overreaction on your part. This is your don't-damage-the-fabric conditioning, the eggshell neurosis.

Wink said in her ear: "You holding, Asher?"

"Sure!"

He handed her something that was as unthinkable as the fight itself: a small open-topped glass container full of pale amber liquid. A shot glass. She downed the whiskey with atavistic relish.

"Shee-it, Wink! Where you get *alcohol?*"

"Sam Kayoute has a little," he said. "You see this stomp?"

"I see *that*," she said, "and I still don't believe it."

Two oxper had been in the original group of fighters. One was a Silvo, Winkler supplied his name, Bob Moore. The other was Ed Rowe, attached to Commiss, Sam Kayoute's helper, doling out food. Inexplicable.

"Who was that mensh injured?" she asked. "Was it Loney, the ensign?"

"No, not our boy Hal," said Wink. "It was Mai Lon, the little medic. Ed Rowe tried to protect her."

"Shee-it, now these berks are damaging our medics," she said. "What d'ye make of it?"

"The Silvo oxper Moore started it. He acted plagged," said Winkler. "Strange but true, Lieutenant. I had it from Loney; he saw it."

The Silvo oxper, Bob Moore, was limping in a ghastly and inhuman fashion. He sat down on the ground and did something to his left foot that made Captain Boyle and Lieutenant Holder look hastily away. They shepherded all the Silvos back to quarters. Petrova remained, assisting Moore. Something in Anat Asher's memory banks lit up.

Androids were exceptionally strong and conditioned never to initiate violence. They were oddly vulnerable, and they were not expendable, in some cases far less so than the human beings they served. An exceptionally strong and unscrupulous man or woman trained in certain martial arts could, in fact, defeat an oxper in single combat. Knowing where to hit was important. Oxper, it was claimed, were better at strategy than tactics. Humans dodged better and knew more dirty tricks. But the conditioning held good on both sides; there was a strong resistance in humans against hitting an android and vice versa.

Now that the officers had moved away, the fight area was almost clear. Anat stood up, pressing the sergeant's shoulder.

"Easy!" he said. "Take it easy, Asher. You'll kill yourself the way you go."

"Come with me!" she ordered. "Where's Ray Green?"

She blipped him, giving their private code for urgent.

"Green. Proceeding to sick bay with two ambulant . . ."

"Free yourself, Ray. Return to Cookhouse Tree swiftest. This may be an APDA."

Winkler whistled softly. They moved slowly up the hill toward Petrova and Bob Moore; Ray Green caught them up, loping.

"How is Bob Moore doing, Dr. Petrova?" asked Anat Asher.

The Russian woman gave her a quick, angry glance that confirmed her suspicions. She was refastening an inspection flap in the region of Moore's left calf.

"His foot was twisted," said Petrova.

"Auxiliary Moore," said Anat gently, "Bob . . ."

She could hardly bear his squinting look, the strange lines of stress on his face.

"Do you agree to a voluntary shutdown, preceding overhaul?"

He uttered a low meaningless sound, swung his head and stared at Ray Green.

"You're not functioning correctly, Bob," said Anat. "You need overhaul. You'll be in care of Dr. Petrova and the Silver Cross Auxiliaries."

The sound became angry and negative. Bob Moore frowned, twisted up his face, suddenly flung out both arms, trying to rise.

"Ray!" said Anat Asher.

Ray Green, moving with great speed, clamped Moore's head against his chest, a hand under the chin. He went for a control area in the back of the neck. Bob Moore slumped and did not move.

"An involuntary shutdown, Doctor," said Anat. "I believe Auxiliary Moore suffered damage in the landing. Do you have information about this?"

"I report to Captain Boyle!" said Petrova.

"Fine," said Anat Asher. "Report all you want. But give me some data for my report on this fight, started by Moore . . . a malfunctioning oxper from your unit. As a courtesy, give me this data. We don't want to make a mega-action out of this."

Petrova got to her feet and helped Ray Green to lay Bob Moore out flat. There was a small vibration in his chest and neck; he was idling.

"Moore reported nothing but circuit damage in his left leg," said Petrova.

"Very unusual thing," put in Sergeant Winkler. "Haven't seen more than a couple of malfunction cases leading to involuntary shutdown in twenty Earth years of space."

"So we're in a very unusual situation," said Anat Asher. "Our only hope is to solve our problems together. Don't you agree, Doctor?"

She held out her hand to Petrova, who simply stared with burning insolence. She looked at Asher with her extended hand as if this were another case of android malfunction.

"Help Moore to quarters, Ray," said Anat.

She went up the new ramp into the Rec and sat in the watch-post checking lists on her vox, drawing with the exocad simulator, which had nothing for its magic eyes to see now but a pattern of palms against the night sky. Vannie Frost was taking a long spell on the hotlines, driving herself crazy with static and imaginary signals.

Commander Gregg had long retired to his spacious double in the new Officers' Quarters. No conference. Anat Asher took a walk through the capem, greeting the oxper on watch. At the sick bay were three patients: Lieutenant Morgan, Sergeant Baumer, and one Silvo name of Zero Zavaski, who had taken a mild concussion in the fight. The konos were holding well, asleep in their hammocks; Myrrha Devi dozed upright in her cushioned chair. A daughter, Faith, kept watch.

At the far bulkhead, farthest west at the foot of the Hill, Anat found Peter Wemyss and the Systems oxper George King peering out into the night. There was a dim globe of light among the underbrush, a stakeout light, marking the campsite.

"Something out there?" she whispered.

They nodded.

"Just making the rounds," said Wemyss. "The howler. Estimated size: a Rottweiler dog."

"Got a photo trap baited with turkey rissole," said George.

"Shee-it!" said Anat Asher. "You want to poison the poor critter?"

Three hours before dawn the young Silvo mechanic Ingo Nils Olsen was taken to the sick bay. He died an hour later of spleen and liver injuries sustained in his fall during the hike to the Silverbrook. Doc White and Ivan Dalny made extensive entries in hospital records, a sheaf of reports were printed and an inquiry arranged for midday. They knew this might not be the only death report. Lieutenant Morgan, who had been carried off the capem in a deep, drug-induced coma, had rallied a little during the long day but in the night he sank deeper and died, on the new world, at dawn, without regaining consciousness.

Before the wake-up call or the Silvos' reveille the medical oxper, Cole and Nelson, went out into the dunes with Master Sergeant Winkler, acting duty officer, and Lieutenant Peter Wemyss, the biologist. A site was approved behind two feathery clumps of the palms. Cole and Nelson took tubular sections of special ceramic from the stores and constructed a kiln with a heavy-duty filter and high-wide collecting antennae. Such kilns were not used exclusively for cremation but when they woke, the crew, who knew the manual, got the message. The two dead men lay in freeze bags in the sick bay for the whole of the second day, Landfall+2, then discreetly and without ceremony their bodies were consumed to ashes in the kiln.

4

The assembly call was loud, but it was distorted, soaked up by the vegetation. Sergeant Winkler made a razzia through the capem, ordering all crew to the combined memorial service, but they were still under strength. It was Landfall+4, morning at nine. The Silver Cross were all present and correct in their blues, indestructibly smooth; some of the crew had left off their silversuits and were in work overalls.

There was a rostrum set up in the grove by the spur of gray rock where the commander and Captain Boyle had settled after landfall. Anat Asher had tried to break away from shipboard routine by arranging the service: death was played way down in space for fear of panic. Now she decided that she had been wrong—she had been swayed by personal involvement, the bad scene at the inquiry on Landfall+2. But this attempt at a combined service didn't bring the two groups together.

The Silvos took the field in a permanent state of umbrage: cold, sullen, aggressive. A few words for young Olsen, the simplest headings from his file, might have helped, but none of these things was offered. The Silver Cross had a new grievance but could not display grief. The memorial speeches for Lieutenant Morgan brought no release of tension. He had been a quiet, genial man; the voluble Regi, on line to speak a eulogy for his boss, was tongue-tied. Anat, who had access to the personnel file of "Maestro" Regi, found him increasingly hard to figure. Had he *disapproved* of the way Morgan lived, was that it?

Gregg, on the other hand, had lost none of his smoothness as a speaker, but some of his phrases rang hollow. They had indeed "met an extraordinary challenge," and the answer was death. Death for Morgan, the new world unseen, death for Olsen after one long day. Death for the bright ship itself, the *Serendip Dana*, which still lived round them in their dreams. They were all in fear of death for their companions . . . the comcen systems remained obstinately silent.

Now Gregg was calling for cooperation and appealing to reason. At Anat's side Winkler gave a deep sigh. The crew were glassy-eyed, fidgety, absent . . . no medic present except Dalny . . . or simply absentminded like Hal Loney, staring up into the palms. Tricks of the light made their faces green, those of the Silver Cross yellow. Further up the slope were the konos, relaxed, self-effacing, seated upon the ground.

Captain Boyle saluted the commander again, gave a hand movement that brought the Silvos to attention. Before they marched off there was an interruption; a man sorted himself out of the untidy bunch of regulars. Anat failed to recognize him; he was for a few seconds a bearded stranger in brown denims. Lieutenant Wemyss spoke to Gregg, who gave a curt refusal. The Silver Cross marched away in silence.

Anat stepped up to the commander's side. He gave her a nod . . . carry on. She had a twinge of sympathy then for Gregg himself. Hauled down from the bridge to "command" a motley crew, a poorly integrated group, and work around the Silver Cross. Gregg had no personal staff, certainly no adjutant to match Daniel "Shadow" Adams, Boyle's gray eminence. She took the mike, thanked the commander. Gregg had already faded back into the Rec; she took a breath and plunged on.

"The *Serendip Dana* brought us to this place!" she said. "Now we must save ourselves! There's work for everyone, but it can wait. It can wait exactly one third of an hour, island time: twenty-one minutes. Your morale is down . . . I'm giving you this time to start getting your heads right. I know our honored guest, Myrrha Devi, and her family will help you all with anti-stress movement right here and now. Anyone with medical problems go to sick bay. None of us are heroes. Put your trust in each other and in the new world!"

Not many people heard her last sentence because Lelani Buck, cook specialist, began screaming. She rolled about on the ground raking at the neck rim of her silversuit, running hands through her close-cropped hair. Sam Kayoute caught the plague, slapped his neck, shouted:

"Somethin' crawlin', Lieutenant!"

Hansi Meyer started brushing at *his* hair; Vannie Frost scratched. Before the madness spread, Ivan Dalny had lifted Buck from the ground.

"False alarm!" he cried. "Relax! It's nothing!"

Nobody was convinced until he showed them the long thread of dried palm silk that he had taken from Buck's collar. Lelani Buck was a black woman, twenty-six years old, one of the youngest in the crew; she leaned against the big Arkadian, still shivering.

"One third of an hour!" called Anat Asher.

She said a few words to Buck, then ran up against Wemyss.

"What was that with Commander Gregg?" she asked.

He shook his head, farouche and shy.

"Were you a friend of Lieutenant Morgan?"

"We came from the same place," he said. "Both Welshmen."

All around them the crew moved like sleepwalkers, doing what they were told. Some joined the konos in an exercise circle, others lay on the dusty blue drogues staring up into the leaves. Further up the slope Anat saw Myrrha Devi pointing and beckoning.

"Come up to Myrrha Devi," she said. "She wants to meet you, Lieutenant."

They toiled up the slope, and before they could sit down beside the Kamalin leader she lifted her arms to them. They helped her to stand.

"Lieutenant Wemyss?" she said. "Walk with me!"

She fixed him with her dark eyes and smiled. Anat saw that her health had improved; she had a good color, her eyes were bright, she was not in pain.

"Walk with me towards the sea," she said. "Is it easy to come to the water's edge?"

They led her on up the slope to the southern perimeter of the camp at the edge of the palm grove. Looking to the south, they saw the sand dunes and the incinerator kiln surrounded by screens of brown cotton netting and topped by the four brush collectors. Beyond the dunes in the inland, southwest, a corner of a high cliff crowned with vegetation was just visible. Now Wemyss led the way east, around the perimeter: there was the sea. The three of them walked downhill over sand and small, blue-green tussocky plants.

"There they are!" cried Anat. "The floaters!"

Hovering upon the surface of the sea, about three kilometers from shore, were five or six round flat objects; the largest was as much as twenty meters in diameter, the smallest no bigger than a lifeboat. When the light was good their texture was visible; they seemed to be woven of thick cane or rattan, green vegetation grew on the larger discs, and clumsy gray birds rose up, hooting faintly, from among the bushes. In the morning mist their effect was uncanny . . . when all the floaters moved together into a clump, it was easy to imagine a sailing ship; then the wind and waves carried them apart, they became a string of rafts.

"What are they?" asked Myrrha.

"Seaweed," said Peter Wemyss. "The islands form around a nucleus of large circular marine growths, possibly seed pods, which detach themselves, then dry out, flatten, become very light. Debris collects; the birds settle on the floating islands. Similar process occurs in the Gulf Stream . . ."

He broke off; nobody spoke of Earth.

"The floaters must get washed ashore," said Anat.

"All the time," said Wemyss. "I found and examined one along there, by the tide marker."

"What records do we have," said Myrrha Devi slowly, staring out into the dissolving mist, "of travelers or service personnel who were lost, like ourselves?"

"Satellites were launched before we entered the atmosphere of this planet," said Anat. "There have always been . . . accidents, but the chances of location and rescue are better than ever these days."

"That wasn't quite what I meant," said Myrrha. "A question for you, Lieutenant Wemyss, Peter . . . is there anything here that can harm us? Swarmers? The Night Cat?"

Peter Wemyss shook his head.

"We can only read the signs," he said. "The life count is low. Several varieties of small flying lizardlike creatures. Smaller flying things, moths, leaf insects. One report of spouting in the sea, off Sunset Beach . . . a marine creature that breathes air."

"Could it be intelligent?" asked Anat.

"Perhaps . . ." he said. "It swam away to the west. I've only had one bird to examine: the kill that was found by Ray Green on the perimeter, Landfall Day. It is much closer to the flying lizards, much more saurian than birds on Earth."

"And this larger creature?" Anat prompted. "The 'Howler'? The 'Night Cat'? There's a report from the track to the Silverbrook. Something big, lurking in the bushes . . ."

"It's nonsense!" said Wemyss. "All we know is that a middle-sized creature which emits a very occasional howl has made a couple of rounds of the perimeter. It is extremely shy and wary."

"Thank you," said Myrrha gravely.

She changed the subject.

"This family, the konos . . . we're not pulling our weight. Give us more work, Lieutenant Asher! My children abound in qualifications. Can you take time to interview two or three of them?"

Anat agreed just as her blip sounded; a third of an hour had passed. She hurried back inside the perimeter, leaving Wemyss and Myrrha Devi standing on the beach staring at the floaters as they dipped and spun upon the surface of the alien sea.

Sergeant Winkler worked all day, blistering his hands, on the building project for the crew's quarters, a big G-dome nestled between the hammerhead of the Rec and its handle, the Hill, on the northern side of the capem. Asher's psycho-spot, he noticed, had done some good. The regulars were less spooked, but they were still barely equal to the size of the project, even with the help of the KONO team. In the afternoon Ray Green made a decision and broke out two digging extensions for himself and Ed Rowe, the commissariat auxiliary. This was unpleasant for human beings to watch—the extensions took the place of the diggers' right forearms—but it finished the foundation in better time. Everyone laid down the sealer and groundsheet.

The Silver Cross, who had good quarters aboard the capem, ran up a smaller G-dome on the site of their first bivouac. They kept to quarters or worked inside the new dome.

Wink had a matter of protocol to discuss with Anat Asher. During rest time she came up the Hill in company with a young kono . . . Kyle; of course it was Kyle, the synthesizer. Wink noted that Kyle was dressed in a dark-red overall, soft-fitting and decent, with a hint of walking-out dress in the service. The lieutenant made an introduction.

"Dr. Kyle Cavarro . . . Chief Master Sergeant Eugene Winkler."

"Without whom nothing goes!" said Kyle, clasping Wink's hand.

"Flattery will get you plenty, Doctor," grinned Wink.

He was still puzzled. Anat led her protégé along to the officers' quarters, where Gregg was using four large cubicles for his HQ. Presently she came back alone, smiling.

"Let me guess," said Wink. "You're putting Gregg into therapy."

"Kyle is a sistek," she said, "with time served at Armstrong Base. He's offering his services as an aide to Commander Gregg. The Old Man needs staff."

They sat down inside the old watchpost and drank lemon lift.

"A kono?" asked Wink.

"Who else is there?" said Anat.

Winkler went on to explain his problem.

"We need the help of the Silvos. For our dome," he said. "What's the drill? Ask direct? Go through channels? Which channels?"

"If the Silvos turn down a direct appeal for help on the building site," said Anat, "we can't go over their heads and try through Gregg. Best ask the commander first."

"Who asks the commander?"

"Let him complete this interview with Kyle," she said, "then you put it to him yourself, Sergeant."

"Not you?"

"No," said Anat, "I'm not in good with Commander Gregg."

"What about Regi, our resident genius," inquired Wink. "How does he stand with the brass? How does he stand with you, Lieutenant?"

Anat Asher saw a sharp look of curiosity on Wink's face and knew that he liked intrigue.

"I find him difficult to figure," she admitted.

"Something came up in the Postmortem Inquiry for Olsen," said Winkler. "Come on, Asher . . . what are these bastards doing to you?"

It was a relief to tell it. She played back parts of the inquiry that she had kept in her vox: she found that her memory played tricks on the new world. The voice of Boyle came in, full of fierce pathos, saying:

"Lieutenant Doctor Petrova examined the boy, tended his hurt, stayed by him when the new condition became apparent. Stayed by him to the end. She is preparing a report on the treatment given and the emergency operation carried out by White. We should look back a little at the quality of the briefing this poor boy Olsen received before he was sent out over unexplored terrain in heavier gravitation."

At this point in the inquiry she had been feeling nothing but a vague mourning for the dead, perhaps an uncomfortable awareness that she herself thought Petrova must bear a good deal of blame. But the Silver Cross looked after their own. . . . Anat had no doubt that Petrova would criticize White in her report and that Boyle was casting about for other scapegoats. No Silver Cross member was ever to blame.

"I didn't record my own briefing," Anat said to Wink. "So I told the Inquiry what I had said and asked for confirmation from Holder, the Silvo lieutenant, and from Warrant Officer Regi."

"Whatya get from Holder?" asked Wink.

"He never appeared," she said. "Not available."

"And Regi was not at the hearing? He came in cold?"

"I felt bad calling him at all," said Anat, "because Morgan, his chief, was dead too. Gregg expressed sympathy to Regi for Morgan's death before he asked about the briefing of the explorer teams."

She played back.

"Briefing?" Regi echoed Gregg's question. *"I remember it was a bad, aggressive briefing. Typical unstructured, ill-informed briefing from a media officer suddenly thrust into field conditions. Asher put down Lieutenant Holder, was hostile to me."*

"We're interested in the warning that was given over the heavier gravity," said Gregg.

"Even Gregg was taken aback," put in Anat. "He hadn't expected anything as negative as this."

"Warning?" echoed Regi again. *"I don't know. May have been something about not falling off a mountain. Low-level clowning around was what there was."*

The vox squawked; it was Captain Boyle. Anat switched off.

"Boyle went wild. Shouted at me . . . 'Killer bitch' . . . something sweet as that. And Shadow Adams shut him up."

"And you demanded auxiliary recall . . ." said Wink.

"I had to," said Anat. "I named Black and Carter, the oxper from both teams. I reckon Shadow Adams already had the recall from Carter. He had heard exactly what was said."

"Shee-it!" said Wink. "What did Regi do next?"

"He had experiments running. He left the Inquiry."

"Did he know what he was doing to you?"

"That was how he saw it," said Anat. "A loozy briefing."

"Well, I take your point, Asher," said Wink. "This genius *is* hard to figure. I'll ask Gregg myself about Silvo assistance."

Anat thought of the two explorer teams, how she walked with them up to the perimeter in the east, all good-humored, keen to make their round.

"Holder and Olsen were too big," she said. "I thought at the time they were too big, when Boyle picked 'em. Even Vannie Frost is on the big side . . ."

"Asher!" said Wink. "You are not to blame. No way!"

A wailing sound arose: the hand-cranked siren from the building site. The work went on until nightfall. It was coming along a little better, so Winkler put off the request for help from the Silver Cross.

Some evenings a light shower of rain drove away the heat. There were long twilight hours in the palm grove when the castaways took their ease; they strolled rather than danced. The faint vanilla-mint perfume of the globe orchids pervaded Sunset Beach and the path to the Silverbrook.

Anat Asher took this walk on Landfall+6; she went with Richard Black, the systems oxper, to inspect the pump station. The four hundred meters of bonded bunex water hose from Fiver's emergency stores had been extended with a further two hundred meters of multipurpose conduit reclaimed from the Hill. There was a gentle downhill slope from the stream to the pump station, halfway along the track; from this point all water had to be carried into camp. Everyone who walked there filled a water bottle and a larger container for washing. Asher greeted Ed Rowe wearing an ingenious harness that enabled him to carry seven commissariat special filter Bellita water holders. The pump station was fine; it reminded Anat of an artesian bore in an orange grove near Haifa.

"Anything to use for flooring?" she asked.

Richard Black was a boyish oxper with a shy manner.

"Some that pebble fill from the Sunset Beach, Lieutenant," he said. "And Leader Green has eyes on that pulpboard flooring from the Pits."

Auxiliary personnel had no service ranks, but among their own work groups a series of designations: Leader, Second, Pusher, Wisher.

"Fine," said Anat. "Dick, will this setup with the pipelines last a long time?"

"Could do, Lieutenant," he said, "but a channel is still indicated."

She looked up and down the track, hating the thought of a big operation that would have to be borne mainly by the oxper. It was the magic hour: there was singing by the konos' campsite, the globe orchids had emerged. The green walk was marked out with light posts and strings. The vegetation was dark green tussock underfoot, a few young palms beside the path together with slender birchlike growths known as lace trees. The globe bushes crowded together with gray plants that bore ugly, thorned pods, the "little dragons." These had been ticketed in red, along with some pinkish fronds that produced a reddening of the skin, milder than poison ivy.

"Hey, you see these new ones, Lieutenant?" asked Dick Black.

He reached out a hand in a carrying glove and plucked a low-growing, blue frond.

"It won't hurt you," he said. "See?"

He passed the silky strings across the back of her hand. Then he extended his own lightly tanned, muscular, hairless forearm and flipped the pink fringe across it: at once red weals rose up on the skin.

"Reacts with the synthetic epidermis," he said cheerfully. "Ray Green says we'll lose our reputation for keeping a whole skin."

There were strollers on the track, groupings of friends, lovers. A woman called out unsteadily:

"Dick? Is that Dick Black?"

"Hey, Sergeant!" he said.

They saw Doc White walking slowly with a special patient: Linda Baumer of Systems, recovering from her heart incident in increased gravity. She was a pretty, well-rounded young woman; now she was marked by ill health, as if it might be a permanent burden. She was bent, shuffling, pale-faced; her large, expressive, gray eyes were sunken. She took Richard Black by both hands, smiling up into his face.

"It's great to see you about!" he said. "You meet old George yet?"

"Yes, I . . ."

She turned and saw Anat Asher.

"Is that you, Lieutenant?"

She clutched Anat's arm. Anat remembered how she came reeling toward the lock in the rush to leave the capem. Misadventure. Morgan's insomnia might have taken the girl's life as well as his own.

"Walk with us, Lieutenant!" said Doc White. "This is Linda's first time to the Silverbrook."

He sounded and looked uncommonly sane. Anat linked arms firmly with the patient, and off they went, slowly, slowly, up the gentlest of slopes. Black stayed by the pump station, helping those who came with containers. As they shuffled along past the strange trees and the growths that might or might not be flowers, Timothy White began to declaim in verse. Anat recognized a choral ode, a long incantation full of the names of trees: Calvin Cajun Green's "Cottonwood Lament":

". . . live oak, sycamore and sequoia, / Trees more numerous than stars . . ."

They moved on up the track. The light sources were just beginning to glow at the sides of the path, and Anat used her flashlight on the darkness around their feet to guide Linda Baumer onto the narrow landing. The Silverbrook was three meters wide at this point, a busy, bubbling stream falling from a rocky overhang. The plants around them were a striking growth not found on the campsite, bulbous and cactus-shaped, tall as a mensh and of a glossy mid-green. It was difficult to call them anything else but greenmen: more than one of these fellows had been cut down or uprooted. No one really believed anymore that they walked about in the night. The greenmen shared the soft banks of the stream with a tangle of thick-stemmed lianas, rolling along in spirals under heavy, slick leaf growths with frilled edges which caught flakes of light from the water.

"Pine for the lonesome pine, / Weep for the willow . . ."

"Oh, Doc," said Linda, "you will have *me* crying with your loozy earth trees. . . ."

There was a folding metal bench set up against a last palm. They settled on it like three birds on a rail, watching the stream. Anat gave a sad laugh and made her own contribution.

"More trees?" asked Timothy White.

She translated:

"By the rivers of Babylon, where we sat down, yea we wept, for we remembered Zion.

"We hanged our harps upon the willows . . ."

After a measured length of time the doctor took the pulse of his patient and of Anat for comparison. He expressed himself satisfied.

"What say we dunk this doctor in the Silverbrook, Linda?" suggested Anat Asher. "If he doesn't tell us how we're doing!"

"Sure," said Linda. "I get the idea he just likes holding our hands."

Timothy White was delighted to be teased; he blushed. Three strollers, coming to the stream, found them all laughing. Hansi Meyer, the most handsome specimen in a crew packed with dream studs and men with fine bodies, filled a filter cannister directly at the stream. He came and hunkered down beside them, greeted Linda Baumer, gave them all a drink in a little metal cup. He moved off slowly down the track.

Anat watched the other two strollers, waiting to greet them. Unexpectedly, they came right over, passed the time of day, settled down to gossip about weather, work, the island. . . . Two Silvos: Zero Zavaski, the master sergeant of Detroit Company who had been hit on the head in the fight near the Cookhouse Tree, and a sistek, Louise Reynolds—was her nickname 'Chip'? Anat was pleased; every civil word between the two groups was for her a sign of hope.

When they went on down the track at last there was a brief interval of quiet during which the doctor, the lieutenant, and the sergeant did nothing, enjoyed the evening. A thin wailing cry began down the track and enlarged into a frightful scream and a shout. Anat Asher was blipped crazily, urgently. She jumped up and ran down the track, answering the call.

". . . Meyer . . ." said Richard Black. "Something with Meyer."

Anat ran on down and saw Black himself, still calling her, in the center of the path. There was a break in the vegetation to her right, she could see people kneeling. As she came closer, Louise Reynolds reeled to her feet and come out on the track.

"What is it?" cried Anat. "Reynolds . . . ?"

"Something . . . got him!"

"Steady," said Anat.

"Something got *Meyer* . . . he was right here."

Reynolds went on across the track and vomited into the bushes. Anat pushed into the broken place, moving a light post. She saw Zero Zavaski go springing away into the bushes with his blaster drawn. Two men were bent over Meyer . . . another Silvo, a mechanic named Ramirez, and Hal Loney, the ensign.

Hansi Meyer lay face downward, his neck, his limbs all at strange angles. Anat bent down herself, felt for his neck, where she found a faint pulse. Her fingers came away bloody; she bent across, levered his head a fraction from the soft, leafy ground, and saw that his face was a mess of blood and raw flesh.

"Leave him!" she ordered. "There's a doctor right here."

She stood middle of the track and went at it full tilt. Called Doc White from the stream, called sick bay to send an emergency team, called Winkler to inform Gregg, called Ray Green to close the track and meld First Emergency. Doc White came running down the track before she stopped calling. As he dived into the bushes he shouted to Anat:

"Take care of Baumer!"

She took Louise Reynolds by the wrist.

"You okay?" she asked. "We need to fetch Linda Baum-er . . ."

"There's something *here!*" said Reynolds, white and spooked. "Something got Meyer . . ."

They both looked back up the darkening trail toward the Silverbrook.

"Shee-it!" said Anat. "Baumer is *alone*. She's in ragged shape . . ."

"I'll go!" said Richard Black.

He took off running, and she wished there were another oxper at the scene. At the campsite, bells and whistles were sounding. Anat ran with Reynolds to the pump station, and they altered the angle of the two tall porta-sun light fixtures, then beefed them up as far as they dared to dispel the gathering darkness.

"What did you see, Louise?"

"Just the break in the trees," said Reynolds. "Then a noise in there. I thought it was someone putting us on. I screamed, I guess Zero called out too. I screamed because I saw Meyer's boots. Then old Loco, Mechanic Ramirez, came running up with the ensign; everyone was talking; Zero took off . . . you came down from the Silverbrook . . ."

There was a loud clanging and shouts to clear the track. Two medical oxper came barreling along, riding the emergency scoot. Zero Zavaski came loping along to the pump station and gave Louise Reynolds a hug, then began to report. His big, blunt-featured face was working with excitement. Anat took him by the arm to steady him and believed when she stared into his dilated, dark eyes.

"Saw . . . them . . ." he panted. "I swear I sighted two howlers, Lieutenant!"

"You're *sure?*"

"Sure as I can be. Saw one going almost dead ahead as I came past Meyer, then I saw the brush movin' for the other one, up-hill toward the water."

"What did it look like?"

"Brown-black pelt, long, thick-bodied, low to the ground! I guess it was crawlin' though, and could stand more upright. Shee-it, I thought, you know, of bears. I hunted bears coupla times, in the Taiga and the Canada wilderness."

"But these are not bears!" said Anat.

It was an admission of fear. This animal was nothing as homely and predictable as a bear. She looked at the "palm trees" in the glare of the overhead light and at the other alien growths, the little dragons, lace trees, greenmen, lurking beside the track. How smart or intelligent were these howlers? Was it a concerted attack? Anat stepped out onto the track and saw Richard Black coming steadily down carrying Linda Baumer in his arms like a child. She returned another call from Ray Green. "Yes, attack confirmed, Doc White, two medics working on Meyer at the site."

"Zavaski," she said, "Sergeant . . . please go and keep watch in the trees just beyond the medical team."

"Lieutenant, I'm on my way," he said, "but let me call my unit. Let me call Lieutenant Holder of Detroit Company. I reckon we could operate as a 'protective cordon' like it says in the manual."

It was a reasonable offer in a difficult situation and she accepted it. While Zavaski called his unit, Anat patched over to Gregg himself at last and announced the use of Detroit Company of the Silver Cross as a protective cordon on the Silver-brook trail.

"Report, Asher!" said Gregg. "From the beginning."

She reported.

"Come in," ordered the commander. "HQ soonest. Regi is coming to the track as special duty officer."

Anat recalled that she was not on duty. These were her first off-duty hours outside of sleep periods since Landfall. She had come to inspect the pump station on her own time and take the walk to the stream. She knew that her legs were beginning to shake, her hands were sticky, and she was suffering from fear and exhaustion. She no longer wore the helmet applicator, so she fumbled a pink, the first in twenty-eight hours, from her sleeve pocket and washed it down with fresh water.

Loney and Ramirez had come to the pump station. She began to question them . . . Ramirez, the good-looking Hispanic from Barnard Company of the Silver Cross, said no, first thing they heard was Louise Reynolds screaming. Then the questioning broke off as everyone saw the stretcher carried out and settled on the canopy of the emergency carrier. Doc White and Richard Black settled Linda Baumer, the heart patient, on the scoot as well. Then the laden vehicle drove past them, lights steady, with only a single melancholy blast of its horn.

"Jesus Mother!" said Ramirez under his breath. *"Holy Jesus Mother!"*

Anat read the signs; they all did. Hansi Meyer was dead.

Louise Reynolds began to sob loudly; Zavaski comforted her. When Dick Black joined them, Anat had a question.

"How was Linda Baumer?"

"Holding pretty good, Lieutenant," said Dick. "Said she heard something splashing around in the stream."

"Warrant Officer Regi is special duty officer," said Anat, "so make a full report to him, Richard."

She shook hands with him and with Zavaski, Reynolds, and Ramirez.

"I'm certainly glad you were all here to help with this emergency," she said.

"Lucky chance, ma'am," said Zero.

There was noise and bustle at the end of the path where Ray Green was holding the barrier. Regi was there, plus Detroit Company. Lieutenant Holder was openly toting a sporting gun; he was loaded for bear.

"Some loozy deal with Meyer, Lieutenant . . ."

"Asher!" cried Regi. "Report! Report! I'm not wise to anything. An attack?"

She was surprised to find a mean comeback on the tip of her tongue. Try someone reliable, Maestro. Someone with field experience. Instead she replied smartly:

"Richard Black and Sergeant Zavaski are waiting to report!"

She walked or staggered back to camp with the ensign, Hal Loney.

"Why were those particular mensh on the track?" she grumbled. "Why were you there, Hal?"

"Walkin'," he said. "Walkin' with my friend Loco Ramirez, Lieutenant."

He began to whistle an old reggay evergreen called "San Francisco Dreams" and broke it up with bird calls. She saw for the first time that he was the Mocking Bird Kid from Kyle's last talent show aboard the *Serendip Dana*. The lights had been cranked up all over camp, but very few people were out of doors. Oxper from the crew were on watch at the perimeter. Two Silvos stood under the deserted Cookhouse Tree adjusting heavy "survival" crossbows.

Peter Wemyss was furiously angry. His eyes blazed; he glared at the commander and Captain Boyle. He thumped the rattling metal table.

"Fuck nonsense!" he shouted. "You're all bloody plagged! Hunting guns and crossbows!"

"Cut the mouth!" roared Boyle. "I'll rank this geek, Commander."

He raised his fists, but Wemyss did not budge. He glared up into Boyle's face and topped him vocally.

"Meyer was not killed by the howler. Whatever Zavaski saw or heard, it was not the howler!"

"Then it was something else!" said Gregg. "The island is un-explored. Human safety has priority. A Silver Cross cordon round the whole camp has been approved."

"This is an isolated attack," said Wemyss, "with no relation to any of the animal research we've been able to do."

"Never mind," said Boyle, grinning. "We can get you some specimens."

Wemyss controlled himself. He said with absurd dignity:

"Commander Gregg, I demand protection. I demand protection for all the native creatures on this island."

Anat Asher hated the whole argument, hated Boyle, distrusted the commander.

"Commander," she said, "can we have some assurance that a protective cordon of the Silver Cross doesn't mean a hunting expedition?"

"This woman here called in Detroit Company herself!" said Boyle.

"Sure I did!" snapped Anat. "It was a bad situation out there. We needed a cordon. I'd still like that assurance, Commander Gregg!"

"Silver Cross will not exceed their competence, Lieutenant Wemyss," said Gregg wearily. "I want you to prepare a report on all animal activity from landfall to this time."

Wemyss was still very angry. He opened and closed his hands, looking from one big man to the other.

"Lieutenant Asher," said Gregg, "find the new aide, Kyle. Send him here ready to start duties. Captain Boyle and I will have our supper, then do a round of the perimeter."

Asher got Wemyss out of HQ, urged him down the corridor to the watchpost.

"Some of that special medicine, Winkler," she said.

"That bad?" asked Sergeant Winkler.

Wemyss downed a shot of whiskey, looked sideways at them.

"You think I am mad," he whispered.

"No," said Anat. "What's the situation out there, Sergeant?"

"Peaceful," said Wink. "The cordon set down, the oxper assisting, no weapons fired, no sightings of . . . alien life. Regi is keeping busy over by the brook."

Anat Asher looked out of the watchpost and remembered the Rec as it had been on the last night. Spacious, bright, the star-patterned floor and the trivid stages; she saw Rose Chan laid back on one of the old red recliners in the Pits; she recalled eating a big order of pancakes, eggs and sausages.

Now she was looking into a big, dim metal cave, the floorspace muddy, awkwardly tilted, packed with tunnel tents and makeshift huts where the crew huddled. Everyone was indoors. Meyer was dead. . . . *and how many others,* she thought guiltily, *all over the wild new world. But not Chan, Jehovah God, let Chan come through . . . I saw her, splashing around outside her capem.* She was brought back by the sound of a wooden clapper, twirled by Lelani Buck. It was supper time. Sam Kayoute was handing out cold food at the storage outlet.

"Wemyss," she said, "Peter, don't go out there. Don't start anything with the Silver Cross cordon. Whatever killed Meyer is to hell and gone. Have supper with the sergeant here, tell him what you said to that loozy mugger Boyle. Then get to your quarters. I'm your senior here in the capem, and those are orders."

"Right," said Wemyss faintly. "Yes."

She took an IPEC, an unused personal communicator or blip, from the coded safe in the watchpost and recorded its issue. Passengers, in this case the konos, were not equipped with blips, but there was an intercom in their quarters. She called ahead, passed on the commander's summons to Kyle through Tiria . . . yes, she was coming to brief him. Human sounds came through the channel behind Tiria's soft voice-over.

"What's that noise?" asked Anat.

"Some of us are weeping, Lieutenant," said Tiria. "For the terrible thing that happened."

Anat sent a goodnight to Myrrha Devi and moved off for the Hill. She thought of the konos as official mourners, no, as general reactors for the whole camp: laughing, weeping, rejoicing on behalf of others.

Kyle came running lightly uphill dressed in his dark red uniform and gave her a salute. He wasn't weeping—his dark eyes glistened, but he was pleased by the way he had gone over with

Gregg. Anat knew that Kyle was very smart indeed; a word in the briefing would have been enough to enlist him in *her* party. She took care not to say this word: he was Gregg's new aide, not her supporter or her spy at HQ.

"Lieutenant," said Kyle, "what was it out there on the track?"

Anat shook her head.

"We'll know more in daylight."

She turned to enter sick bay, and Kyle went on, running.

Space was used very economically in sick bay; the effect was of a series of pale interlocking cells, a Japanese capsule hotel or the hive of the honey bee. No one was hospitalized except Linda Baumer, waiting for good quarters in the new dome. She breathed in cautiously; the air had a tang of disinfectant that reminded her of home, of the *Serendip Dana*. There was a faint clatter of metal dishes; she knew what they were doing in the larger space behind the blue screens.

Doc White came and sat with her knee to knee in one of the capsules, behind a drawn curtain. He had just cleaned his hands with a little blower; they were pink and shining.

"How is Linda Baumer?" asked Anat.

"Holding steady. Came through the emergency just fine."

"How are you coming along . . . with Meyer?" she asked. "Can I have an interim report?"

Timothy White was sane enough, but he was nervous.

"Chest and back injuries," he rapped out. "His neck was broken."

"What did it?" demanded Anat Asher. "Any indications how . . ."

"We know how," he said. "I've seen it before, so has Dalny. This looks very much like an old California combination called 'Breaking the Moon Bridge.' The victim is brought down with a jump attack. Then the head is taken between the hands . . ."

She made some sound and held up her own hands.

"And forced back," he said. "Hansi Meyer was killed by a human being."

"His face! The gashes on his face!"

"Fragments in the wounds. Thorns from the 'little dragon'

plant," he said. "Killer used a couple of the pods to rough up the face."

Now that she heard it plainly, she knew that it had been lurking in her mind all along.

"A member of the landing unit . . . Capem Fiver," she said. "Someone ambushed Meyer. While we sat there by the Silverbrook."

He nodded.

"Doc, you had better make this stick in your report."

"The facts speak for themselves."

She saw herself going into action in the middle of the track. When did the facts begin to be twisted? *"Something got Meyer . . ."* "Animal noises" and sightings had been melded from the track. The howler. It was evening, when the strange light tricked human senses. Zavaski saw his faggidy "bear." The whole attack scenario could have been planned as an alien scare.

She wanted to start calling everyone in creation all over again and have the whole crazy spook disappear back into its magic bottle. Then, with an effort, she withdrew a little, thought of tactics, thought of her own position.

"Hold it down," she said to Doc White. "The true facts don't leave this sick bay until Round Table tomorrow."

She went back through the Rec, spotted Ed Rowe and had him pack up Meyer's tunnel tent, pitched in the shadow of the neat oxper hut. Vannie Frost loomed up and protested.

"We coulda packed up Hansi's gear, Lieutenant."

Anat told her it was just pull-down, pure routine. She had the murdered man's effects locked in the officer's cubicle that had been kept for Morgan. She badly wanted to talk, but she told no one how Meyer had died. She went grumpily to her own quarters, doped heavily, and slept. On the edge of oblivion she thought of Peter Wemyss and the innocence of the howlers. First thing, she would tell Wemyss. . . .

But Wemyss was never told. Sometime in the hours before dawn on the seventh day the biologist took his field kit, slipped through the emergency cordon, and set off alone into the new world.

5

He crawled along the eastern beach in the darkness until the lights of the camp were out of sight, then he walked in the shadow of the dunes. The going was easy; the night was warm with an east wind blowing from the sea. Peter Wemyss stood still, looking and listening. The waves broke in long lines of foam on the narrow strip of beach; ahead he saw another grove of palms. He could look back at a dark flotilla rocking out to sea . . . the floaters. He could look back and see the tops of the four brush collectors on the incinerator, outlined against the night sky above the slope of the largest dune.

He stood still for a long time; he became part of the landscape. Tiny crablike creatures skittered across the wet sand; a bird flew toward the floating islands. Far out in the gray-green waters two arched dolphin shapes went leaping, and the air tingled for a moment with their voices. He raised his eyes and stared unblinking at the stars until they were obscured by a thin dissolving mist of cloud, drawn across like a veil.

He moved toward the new palm grove. It was a narrow oval of trees with no underbrush, not half so lush and shady as the thick grove that had been invaded by Capem Fiver. He moved up into the sliding sand of the dunes to observe the shape of the grove; the trunks of the palms were all slender, all bent to the west by the prevailing east wind.

He set down his pack and sat on it and knew, without turning his head, that he was observed by some creature. Not too close, up the dune to his right, and yes, there in the grove, another. He looked keenly but cautiously at this shadowy extension of a palm stem, not raising his eyes, hoping he made no light, that no piece of metal about him flashed. He sat in the crosshairs of this double observation, then the spell was broken. There was a faint splash, a movement in the surf, then from the top of the dune a clear two-note cry. The howler howled at last. Wemyss swung his head but saw nothing.

It was two long hours before dawn and he was determined to stay in the open, not to go under the palms until it was light. He made a hollow in the sand, parked on his folded sleeping bag, and enjoyed a tube of lemon lift. The temperature was dropping, a cold wind blew from the gray waves, and he drew on his anorak. The light increased, and the sea was an improbable color, purplish green. The sand of the beach was light tan, shading into a stinging ochre on the side of the dune. When he spread a handful on his glove it was full of prickly, macroscopic crystalline rods and star-shapes. The palm grove was revealed for what he knew it to be: a community of proto-trees, linked by a root system laid bare in places by wind and sea.

Mist was rolling in off the sea and curling down from the dunes. To see more of the landscape he was forced to hook up his surveyor and adjust the binocular viewers. Yes, excellent, he saw the island in its true colors, or in any color he wanted, for there were several built-in filters. He was sadly aware of the illusion that had been lost—the man on the beach. He saw himself as a creature hulled protectively in the complex products of a distant civilization, a creature wearing bulging goggles with a control grip. An alien indeed.

Peter Wemyss stood up and turned to the west. Above pink whorls of mist the sky was rose and gold; he watched until the fierce crimson edge of the sun appeared over the green ramparts of a high cliff. He began murmuring to his vox, the best companion for a naturalist so far evolved by his species.

In the grove he took holok shots of the howler's pug-marks at the base of two seaward palms. He had other specimens on file, from the camp, but these were clearer. He recorded them instants before the slight morning tide washed them away. The prints were a crude hodgepodge of dog, puma, armadillo: a hoax for old Smithsonians. Claws retractable? And how many? But he could deduce an attitude . . . stood up on its hind legs, there, scuff, scuff, and looked at him. Looked at the man on the dune, over a palm stem.

The mother tree, in the middle of the oval, was trailing whorls of spore cases, large and firm, the size of hazelnuts. He knew they had been passed as good to eat and picked a few as he went by. He kept looking back the way he had come; visibility remained low at sea level. Wemyss went on and on over the tan and gold striations of the sand, focusing on scraps of seaweed, the cetaceous husks of sea creatures, heaps of pebbles. He hunkered over the remains of several bizarre fish; possibly they had been caught and eaten by the howlers.

The risen sun was dispersing the mist on the tops of the dunes; he worked up into the sandhills a little, but the going was too soft. He wanted to make for high ground and for the interior. He passed another undeveloped palm grove and another very old and hard pressed by wind, sea, and sand. The central tree and its sprouts were pressed so closely together that they resembled one huge tree. He postulated a further development, a giant "palm," seven meters high.

The cliffs were still some way off; the landscape was changing. The dunes sank lower and turned to stone. He came into an arena of queer sandstone shapes, smoothed and hollowed by the wind. The most remarkable were like pieces of sculpture, pierced with holes, man-sized or smaller, mirror shapes, key shapes. He sketched them, let the simulator on his vox play around with his drawings before they were stored.

There was a giant's causeway beyond the arena, and in its shadow the worn stones reached far back into a narrow canyon at the base of the cliff. He came onto the causeway and climbed up the brown slabs out of the mist into the sunlight. He sat there, eating energy sticks, peering into the canyon. He guessed that there were caves in the cliff where the howlers slept during the hours of daylight.

He was uncomfortable himself under this sun; it was hard and white now, filmed with cloud. He followed a strong urge to reach the cliff-top and be among trees again, in leaf shade. He went on, coming nearer now to the wall of the cliff, strung with a dry curtain of vines growing almost flat to the worn and rutted sandstone. He adjusted his holok and recorded the scene briefly. In two-thirds of an hour, island time, he had reached the end of the causeway and found a path to the top of the cliff. It was an easy climb, but for the first time the gravity began to bother him. He lay panting under a swath of the tall reedy plants that produced fronds.

He came out soon and began to look around. He saw the beach, the causeway, the mist on the surface of the sea, the barrier of the dunes. He saw at last the ranks and companies of trees and their companions, clothing the contours of the land, spreading downward from where he stood, then rising up on the slopes of a cone-shaped hill, near at hand. To the northwest, nearer the capem base, there was high ground, topped by a craggy ridge of stone. Long, inviting valleys lay between his hill and the taller massif. He observed intently, changing the focus of his surveyor's glasses, then impatiently removed the apparatus. Inland, the more distant hills and valleys shaded into purple and black; the green was everywhere muted and changed into blue-green, bronze, yellow-gray.

Wemyss was moved to cry out, to halloo into the distance, but instead he took out a silver dog whistle and blew a few soundless blasts. A hundred meters away, on the level ground between cliff-top and the slopes of the hill, a spreading tree lost all its flowers. A cloud of small winged creatures rose up and flew inland. He shoved the goggles back on and caught a glimpse of the stragglers, bright as parakeets, with a similar darting flight. They were, as he expected, flying lizards. He tried to find some trace of the upper reaches of the Silverbrook to the north and believed he saw the course of this stream.

He went back to his shelter under the reeds and made himself a nest with his pack and groundsheet. He listened: the noise level was still very low. Some soft ground bass, a sound half-heard, the wind in a hollow log; an occasional peep-click, hard to locate. He curled around in his nest and slept in the heat of the day.

II

Master Sergeant Winkler held a roll-call in the half-built dome at noon, 1400 hours, mainly for the purpose of ascertaining that Wemyss had really gone. Even with seven konos swelling the ranks, the crew made a thin showing. There had been a long wrangle in Headquarters from Second Call onward, and he had not seen Asher all day. Everyone was plagged, asking fierce questions. Wink caught sight of the man he wanted.

"Warrant Officer Regi is in a better position to answer your questions," he said. "How was that again?"

"Where's Lieutenant Wemyss?" demanded Vannie Frost. "C'mon, Maestro . . ."

Regi was tired and spooked; he had no idea why the master sergeant was putting him on the spot this way. He jumped up beside Wink on the platform and said angrily:

"Wemyss has apparently left camp. Yes, taken off into the forest. No, he was not seen!"

Winkler picked up a question from a kono pair, Janosh and Vashti, who were too polite to be heard.

"Why would he do that, Maestro?"

"Some kind of solidarity with the animal life of this planet," said Regi. "He didn't want the so-called howlers shot and killed."

"Any animal activity reported throughout the night?" inquired Winkler.

"A little," said Regi cautiously. "Reports are being evaluated."

"What's the autopsy report on Specialist Meyer, H.C.?" asked Wink.

"I can't say!" snapped Regi.

"*Warrant Officer Regi!*"

Sam Kayoute reared up, eye to eye with Regi, although the

maestro was standing on a platform. It was remembered that he
had been an ombudsman aboard the *Serendip Dana.*

"This is our own comrade Meyer we're talking about," he
rumbled. "We have a right to know!"

Winkler saw the two medics, little Mai Lon and the Arkadian,
Dalny, standing at the edge of the group, eyes down. No use
asking *them;* they reeked of professional secrecy. For a second
Wink imagined all kinds of alien horrors perpetrated on Meyer's
body, then his head cleared, he guessed the truth. He said to
Regi, full of insidious reason:

"Maestro, you're a man of science . . . if *you* go along with the
theory of alien attack . . ."

Regi took the bait. He waved his hands and shouted:

"Alien attack? Alien attack? Winkler, that sort of talk is for a
loozy trivid cube! Meyer was bushwhacked by the path! There's
been a lot of loose talk about native animals . . ."

He drew breath and saw that he had dumped his datacover.
The crew, what was left of them, stared at him in silence. Vannie Frost made a statement.

"Then Meyer was *not* killed by an alien . . . by an animal native to this island."

"Opinions are divided," said Regi unhappily. "You'll be hearing from Headquarters."

Winkler waited for a protest, a noisy outburst full of grief and
shock, but none came. He began to get his teams back to work
raising the struts of the dome, a repetitive task that must be hurried along. Ray Green had reported a drop in pressure: the
weather might change. He spent some time with the senior kono,
Azamo Johnson, and his wife Tiria, reassigning the new helpers.
He would have preferred to make Azamo a foreman but could
find no way to give him any rank. The konos were all excellent
workers who gave no trouble and were schooled against boredom. Wink was beginning to understand the ramifications of
the clan.

"We have two names," said Tiria, "Johnson and Cavarro,
from Myrrha Devi's two marriages. My father-in-law, Papa John-

son, passed on some time ago. Papa Cavarro was too sick to come on the great Arkady mission. See what he missed!"

The two medics had vanished away; Regi had gone to sack out. Ensign Hal Loney was waiting for the sergeant.

"You didn't assign me, Sergeant."

"Special duty," said Wink, nodding for him to follow.

Back in the watchpost he let the boy drink coffee.

"You were *there*, Hal," he pointed out, "taking your wilderness walk with Loco Ramirez. Anything to add?"

"I been through it a hundred times, Sarge!"

"Now it is shaping up as something different," said Wink, balking at the word *murder*. "How is the cover there? How thick are the trees by the path?"

"Plenty thick enough," said Loney. "And I'll tell you one thing . . . that particular spot is *the* ambush on the track."

"Explain."

"On a bend, out of sight. Can't be seen coming up or down."

"Loney, I want you to revisit the scene of the crime."

"Why the fag should I go back . . . ?"

"You're a spy," said Wink. "When you've done the track come and hang around the Silvos' little home-dome out yonder."

"Shee-it, Sarge!"

"I have something for you, Hal."

Winkler punched his way into the security locker and brought out a small jewel box of red synthetic leather. Inside there nestled a shining artifact about the size and shape of a one-carat diamond; it was surrounded by flat silvery ovals, like flower petals.

"Hey!" said Loney, cheering up. "That's one them zeebugs!"

"I call it a fly on the wall," said Wink. "Not the most up-to-date, but still effective."

He watched while the ensign removed a music bead from his ear and tucked the listening device into its place.

"The range is short under Earth or ship conditions," said Wink. "Maximum ten meters but highly penetrative."

"How will it go here, on Doom Island?"

"Who knows? You can stick these reinforcing guide-petals on a wall, on the tip of your finger, on the end of a long rod . . ."

"Sergeant, why would I want to do *that?*"

"You *point* at the wall," said Winkler patiently. "You lean your goddamned mop or shovel against it."

"I gotcha."

Loney was suddenly hangdog, unable to smile anymore.

"Sergeant, we are going down. This is crocking bad, with Meyer. Three dead, Morgan, Olsen, now Meyer, and Wemyss has gone over the hill. What they gonna say now, the brass? Who leads here? Who knows anything?"

"We survive," said Winkler. "We collect data. We try to keep a balance of power."

But when Loney had gone on his way, Gene Winkler gave way to something very like despair. The balance of power had shifted subtly with Meyer's strange death and the taking off of Wemyss. He wondered if, indeed, Wemyss might be dead too. The picture sharpened up when he was able to talk to Anat Asher. Opinions were divided, which meant that the Silver Cross, through their own medical officer, Petrova, rejected the findings of Doc White.

The Silvos insisted that Meyer had *not* been struck down by a human attacker. He had been killed by a marauding native animal—a howler, a greenbear. Nothing came down from Headquarters. Every evening the protective cordon was set down around the camp; in daylight areas of brush were cleared on the perimeter and along the path to the Silverbrook. The hunting buffs among the Silvos struck out boldly into the bush, up the course of the stream. What they encountered was far from being an alien threat. Pretty soon the whole camp was getting wind of the discovery. Regi was surprised by a blip from Linda Baumer one evening, asking him to step down to the sick bay. There he found the entire space service medical team grouped around a stretcher. Doc White unfolded a sheet and revealed a small, fleshy, compact, six-legged animal with a dark smooth hide and whiskery appendages on its muzzle.

"Jesus Maria!" exclaimed the Maestro. "It looks like a peccary!"

"It *tastes*, so I'm told, like pork," said Ivan Dalny.

"It's been tested?" said Regi anxiously. "How did it die? Who brought it in?"

"It was shot with a projectile weapon," said Alan Cole, a thin, dark-haired medical oxper. "Hunters prefer to remain anonymous at this time."

Regi fussed, scratching his head.

"What's the manual say about killing for sport?"

"The manual is pragmatic about the need for fresh meat, Sandro," said Linda Baumer. "The commissariat stores won't last forever. We have to think of these peccaries as wild pigs."

"Some of us wouldn't eat it," said Mai Lon. "None of the konos would eat such a thing."

"The hunters," said Alan Cole, "are trying to do the right thing. They are passing on their knowledge. They won't massacre all the peccaries."

Regi showed a reluctance to deal with the whole matter. He asked Alan Cole to prepare a data item for all screens with diagrams and holok prints of the animal.

"How this would have interested poor Wemyss . . ." he said, with a half smile.

The Silvos translated *peccary* into *pigaree;* a small group of specialists in the troop regularly supplemented their diet.

Rain threatened for several long days but the heat did not diminish. A party of officers had been in the habit of walking the boundaries, about sunset, and this became a ritual. Commander Gregg walked with Captain Boyle, accompanied by their aides, Kyle Cavarro and Shadow Adams. A changing roster of Silvo officers went along, but Maestro Regi, who had discoursed on time and tide, excused himself, and Anat Asher was never asked.

There was no memorial service for Hansi Meyer, and the only human witness of his cremation ceremony was Ensign Loney, seated on the crest of the largest, most central palm, idly scratching the roof of a Silvo watch tent with a long, peeled frond. He saw the two medical oxper, Cole and Nelson, slip through to the incinerator in that dead hour when the small moon rose, carrying a body bag.

Hal went on listening sadly to the hunting adventures of the Silvos in the watch tent and presently saw another oxper, George King, appear in the fringes of the bush to the southwest, where

the ground began to rise. He stalked down into camp, and Loney
was tempted to listen to his head with the long frond as he passed
under the tree. He controlled this impulse. George made a mild
remark to the empty air about low-flying bugs.

When they went over the day's findings Winkler said:

"Any thoughts about what old George was doing?"

"An oxper is a walking comcen," said Loney. "He has a loc on
an absent friend."

"I hope so," said Wink. "I'd hate to lose Wemyss."

"We never believed that bad scuttle, did we, Sarge!"

"No, but it's ingenious," said Wink. "I'd like to know where it
came from."

Rumors filled the grove. Winkler himself had put about a
face-saving tale that Headquarters were conducting a secret investigation into Meyer's death. The ingenious rumor that had
been picked up from crew and Silvos alike made Wemyss, the
runaway, responsible. He had come upon Hansi Meyer killing a
howler and struck him down in the animal's defense. Privately
that warlike tribe, the Silver Cross, were confused and in a state
of doublethink. They had discovered a harmless—and delicious—native animal but they still assumed fierce jungle beasts.
They heard them, saw them, warned them off with explosive
charges. At the same time they joshed their comrades, especially
Zero Zavaski, for hitting Meyer too hard.

This was a trial for poor Zavaski, one of a small group of Silvos who felt well disposed towards the regulars because they out-
crossed with them sexually, or for some other reason. The big
master sergeant of Detroit Company believed he owed his health
if not his life to the treatment he had received from Doc White,
after the fight at the Cookhouse Tree. He was inclined to believe
the young English doctor when he asserted that Meyer had been
jumped by a man. Zero had seen a man killed with that old
jump-attack Moon Bridge. Yet he himself, the old Zero, was one
of the main witnesses for the *animal attack* scenario. He saw his
howler bounding away. Wasn't one of those little black pigaree
critters the hunters brought in. He saw its long body, rump in the
air a little, then among the leaves and brush, moving up the slope.
He *saw* it! Sure a howler was there, might have been there . . . but

that didn't rule out a human attack. The place on the track was right, ambush-wise. He and his girl, Chip Reynolds, began to think back about every moment of that evening, their walk to the Silverbrook. They found a time to pass on their observations to Lieutenant Asher.

Commander Gregg and Captain Boyle, with their aides, ended the sunset round on Landfall+9 with a picnic supper on Sunset Beach. Marna Rossi was present and Mary "Atom" Klein; two kono girls, Zena and Faith, assisted Cook Specialist "Satin" Lacey from Barnard Company. There was not much to interest a listener: the old argument about flares and light-signals came up. Gregg wondered about sending one of the lifeboats out, due north, then trying a few flares to make contact with Capem Four. Boyle assured the commander that his boys could do a nice line in low-risk fireworks.

Then, after some interchanges about food supplies and how they were holding out, the picnickers consumed the last two-kilo bucket of creamed crab in the stores, drank black-currant lift, and played a round of Cube Gambit, a simplified variant of three-dimensional chess adapted for vox screens. The party broke up; soon the only persons remaining were the two aides, Kyle Cavarro and Shadow Adams.

"So what's with the stores?" asked Kyle softly.

Shadow chuckled.

"They are part of your life-support system."

"Is this something with the division of all the stores?" asked Kyle. "So that the Silver Cross can go it alone?"

"That's been superseded." Shadow grinned.

"What kind of a crazy cube gambit are you pushing, Shadow?" demanded Kyle. "Are the stores inadequate? Insecure?"

"The regular control of the commissariat," said Shadow, "is too frayed, too sloppy. Captain Boyle believes that there's a need for more control."

"I know who puts ideas into his head!"

"Wrong, Flesh Boy," said Shadow, still smiling. "The goal is always the same. I simply find optimal moves."

"You can trust me," said Kyle. "Give me some pointers."

"You share the goal," said Shadow. "You want power. It's one of the most dangerous addictions."

"You want a pressure point . . . for Gregg?" whispered Kyle. Shadow said nothing but his silence gave assent.

"Rossi failed a test," said Kyle. "On ship it would have made a major scandal, so I'm told. Her Cohen status . . ."

Shadow made a sound of disgust; he moved a few paces toward the trees then stopped short, as if a bug had stung him. Exactly at that moment the heavens opened: heavy drenching rain poured down on the camp in the palm grove. The two aides ran for shelter; presently the sirens sounded from the old watchpost in the Rec. Hal Loney, shivering from his narrow escape with that heavy blend, old Shadow, crept out of the bushes on Sunset Beach and came to the new dome with the rest of the regulars. He had some interesting exchanges to report to Winkler.

III

Peter Wemyss moved forward steadily on his first afternoon, scanning the ground, the downhill slope before him. He made an important discovery. Not twenty meters from his shelter there was a small heap of rocks netted with climbing plants. As he came up there was a rattle of stones on the downhill side of this natural cairn. He caught a faint echo, then, pushing aside a bush, he saw darkness. He rose up quickly and found that he had been kneeling on a patch of worn soil. The place was not a burrow, it was a chimney leading down into the caves beneath the cliff. The bright ochre stone was thinly coated with darker humus; the chimney had a gentle slope. He rolled a pebble down the shaft like a pinball. He heard it go rolling for some distance, then there was silence. He had no way of telling if the stone had stopped short or plunged into an abyss. He moved away hastily though he feared that his scent would already be strong enough at the entrance to put off a howler.

Almost in a direct line to the north he saw another chimney opening, the same unobtrusive heap of stones covered with green. He kept his distance and moved in the opposite direction.

There he found a larger rocky outcrop at the foot of a growth he had never seen before. It was related to the "greenmen" by the Silverbrook and certainly no more treelike. This was a "grayman" or even an "oldman," a twisting column of shaggy gray tissue. He expected another chimney and skirted the rockpile warily, but what he found was a cave. It was old and unused, strung with that coarse net made from generations of dried vines.

He saw that it was just right for him. He lifted aside the vines in armfuls and examined every centimeter of the floor, walls, and ceiling. It was uninfested, dry and cool. Wemyss immediately retrieved his pack from his first shelter and moved it down to his cave. He understood the importance of a good base and spent time arranging his household.

He put up a slender collecting rod, topped by a golden brush; he set out his apparatus for capturing the morning dew. Before leaving the cave he strung "magic threads" across the entrance, ready to sound in his ear if anything crossed his threshold.

He spent time examining a colony of leaf-shaped creatures that hung on a certain sweet-scented bush. At the appointed hour he walked about two kilometers nearer to the camp, northward along the top of the cliffs, and sent out a signal with his wrist bleeper. He promptly received an answering signal from George King. He had a vivid picture of George standing in the forest receiving the brief call sign and answering with one of his own.

Wemyss went back to his cave and waited for darkness and the howlers. He planned to observe the chimneys and the beach, both areas if he could manage it. There was a southeast wind blowing in from the sea, so he took up a place on the cliff edge with an easy view of the "sculpture gallery" at the mouth of the canyon. He screened himself with tall reeds, put on his surveyor's binoculars, and waited.

His concentration had always been strong, but now it failed him a little. He fell into a drowsy state, heard himself singing a song of farewell for Morgan. But this was a dream; he was wide awake on the cliff's edge. Gregg, old bastard, had not let him sing. Down below two lithe shapes, almost a meter in length, were leaping back and forth through the round opening in a sandstone figure.

He focused and gave as much resolution, and therefore as much light, as he dared. Sleek, furred, in shades of gray-brown . . . his first thought was *Lutra,* the creatures were like otters. Their swiftness and playfulness made his observation difficult even at this short distance with the surveyors. There was a distinctive howl from the shadows; the leaping pair he had first seen made only a soft series of whistling, purring sounds. Now at last he saw the howler as it howled, undulating over the damp sand. Full-grown, of course; what he had first seen were the young, and he thought again *Enhydra lutris,* yes, the sea otter. Darker, an altogether more solid, even massive appearance, with a distinctive shape of the head, not like anything but itself.

He apprehended the beast. He puzzled over the extraordinary undulating gait, the apparent length of the neck . . . but indeed the sea otters of Earth must have had a similar way with them. There were two young ones and three adults proceeding very fast towards the sea. A fourth adult, trailing a little, made a last graceful pass through one of the stone circles, and Wemyss understood.

The animal had six legs. It went on to demonstrate this fact for him with its antics beside, around, and through the ring of stone. He recalled the scrambled pug-marks and divined that the back legs might have retractable claws and webs. The creature lay on its back showing a greenish underbelly and scratched itself with fingery forepaws. It worked downward, between the sturdy midlegs, until it was bent in a ring. Then it unrolled—he caught the glint of large eyes—and went on toward the sea.

Wemyss was in a state of subdued euphoria, sketching eagerly on his vox platen, still scanning the gallery below for new specimens. He settled down to a long vigil, buoyed up by the hope that the group of howlers must return to the caves. He removed the surveyors for a spell, looked at the stars and the small pearly moon. A chord of sharp sounds pinged in his ears and showed up on the audio corner of his vox screen. Something had breached the magic threads that guarded the mouth of his cave.

There was nothing for it but to go and investigate. A reasoned guess told him that this was another howler, come up through one of the inland openings of the caves. He went wide of his own cave and came up on it warily from the south. He felt a wisp of fear . . . perhaps the animals he had seen *could* be dangerous if provoked. He carried a blaster with a tube attachment for tranquilizing darts but had no wish to use it. He moved as silently as he could into the thin cover near the heaped rocks and the grayman that marked the cave. He waited, listening, imagining squeaks and rustlings from within the cave. The night had grown cold; he decided to make a move. He shone a beam of light across the mouth of the cave.

There was a swift response. The magic threads pinged loudly, once, twice. Wemyss broadened the beam of light and saw two young howlers . . . babies, cubs . . . erupt from the cave and go lolloping down the hillside. He looked inside and assayed the damage. Damnably otterlike. The sleeping bag had been scratched and chewed. Energy sticks neatly peeled from wrappers, tubes of lemon lift and drinking yogurt bitten across and sucked dry. Everything marked by tooth and claw.

He tidied up slowly, listening hard and using very little light. He wondered about the cubs' mother. He wondered if he was assuming too much in the way of family organization from the brief glimpse he had had of the animals. He could make no firm pronouncement, for instance, on whether or not the creatures were mammals. He thought of fur and feathers, warm blood, saurian birds . . . six-legged beasts, great and small. At his doorway, before the magic threads, he placed a luminescent strip as a night-light and deterrent.

The next day was overcast. Wemyss made one round of the cliff-top in the early morning, then settled in his cave to bring his records up-to-date. He ran the holoks he had taken, looking for the pug-marks in the palm grove. He came upon his shots of the cliff face and made a print. He made another print with higher resolution. He stared, turning his head this way and that. He examined his prints under his strongest light and in daylight.

He felt empty, angry: his work was to observe natural worlds, natural processes, but he had little patience with "freaks of nature." What else could this be? The holographic print showed

the huge flat stones of the causeway, then the cliff wall, strung
with dried vines, then the curling green cliff-top. The eye of the
camera saw past the curtain of vines and brought up a series of
marks or indentations on the cliff wall. Two marks in particular
would not go away or turn into something more vague. On his
left, as he had faced the cliff: ⊦; and about half a meter to the
right, on the same line, another: ⊣

Wemyss could think of any number of ways in which these
markings could have been made: the action of water, of mosses,
lichen, or fungi; the activities of insects, birds, or animals. Perhaps only a few strokes, the uprights for instance, were incised in
the cliff . . . the cross strokes were mere shadows, scraps of vegetation, hallucinations which his brain put there to complete a
known form. To make these old indentations on a hidden cliff
face, on a sea-girt island, on an uncharted planet into the letter
H. Twice. Two words beginning with *H*.

Wemyss was half-mad. He went out into the noonday heat to
lay this ghost. Help! Help!—Hello! Hello! He came to the cliff
face and was reassured; the marks were hardly to be seen. He
moved in close and gently, using his curved knife, cut away a
first armful of old vines, working from left to right. He examined
their papery, noded stems and leaf blades and ordered them, as
he had done elsewhere, rather with grasses. Trellises of this
hanging grass had come down year by year from the cliff-top,
then died back. The green overhang of the cliff was flimsy, composed of matted grass roots. Ten years of hanging grass?
Longer?

There stood the letter *H* cut deeply into the sandstone of the
cliff. Peter Wemyss reached up automatically and twitched away
leaf debris from the second upright . . . to make the *H* more perfect. He gritted his teeth and attacked the grass vines again. A
cloud of small, blue "moths" flew out and he ignored them,
shooed them away, unrecorded. He was in the grip of his hallu-
cination, scraping, patting, touching up the carved marks upon
the cliff face.

He drew back, made fresh holoks, then went at it again. At
last, dusty and exhausted, he recorded the inscription. It had
been made by a human being. How was this possible? It had

been made by a human being whose language he spoke and understood. In fact he understood the impulse behind this act—carving words on a cliff face—much better than the words themselves. In letters more than a meter high in places the unknown traveler had incised the words HILO HILL.

Peter Wemyss stared at the words for minutes at a time, breaking off to search the base of the cliff, where it joined the causeway. He excavated carefully, taking out layers of grass vine, crumbs and chips of stone, dead moths. It was slow work, and he found nothing that helped solve the mystery: no broken knife blade, lost button, twist of hair or textile fiber. Nothing left behind. He sat on the causeway and mumbled incoherently into his vox, played back his disordered thoughts, then erased them.

Hilo Hill. A place name for the cliff itself or, more probably, for the hill about three kilometers inland. A sign of life, for rescuers. A man had been cast away. On *this* island. He sprang up and began to scan the horizon, looking for a sail. Had the man come by sea? Wasn't there a sailor's reference in that name, Hilo Hill? Words from an old shanty . . . gone down, gone down to Hilo. More than once he returned to the cliff face and touched the letters, for reassurance.

Then at last, as he staggered back to his cave leaving his excavations half done, he tried out another theory. What right had he to assume that these symbols were part of an alphabet he knew? Why invent a man, a castaway? Which was the greater coincidence? That human beings had already reached this spot in the universe or that certain alien symbols bore a resemblance to ones that he knew? All that he could say was that the marks were not random; they had been deliberately incised into the cliff with something like a knife. He was troubled by the notion of an alien craftsman with a large claw like a crab, suitable for carving in sandstone. He looked at the shapes of the sculpture gallery down below . . . no, that was some bizarre weathering. He dare not go spreading his scent in that area for fear of scaring away the howlers.

He forced himself to put the mystery out of his mind and concentrate on the howlers. He brought his reports up to date. Classification was, at the moment, not a problem. He had a personal code; every specimen that he fed into his vox received a designation. From Wem 1 Community Palm to Wem 323 Flying Lizard. The Howler was Wem 6, and now he was able to give description, habits, habitat with a little more detail.

He took a long siesta and missed the time for his call to George King. The agreement had been for a missed call to be repeated four hours later. He patrolled the cliff in the last hours of daylight and sensed the change in the weather. He left out crumbled energy sticks by the central chimney for the young howlers. His water supply, replenished by the dew condensors, was holding well enough, but he unfolded a larger container. At 23 hours 23 minutes island time it began to rain. He was snug and dry in his cave, but he struggled out dutifully to make the call to George at 2400 hours. There was no reply to his signal. He guessed the rain would have them all scrambling in camp.

On the way back to his cave he went down onto the causeway and heard sounds below him in the sculpture gallery. The howlers were celebrating the rain. He counted four cubs and seven adults leaping, rolling, sliding, holding each other in some kind of dance grip and waltzing round and round upon the sands. The howling, purring, chittering sounds filled the night. Wemyss stood for a moment under the green overhang, passed his hands over the mysterious letters HILO HILL, then returned to his cave.

Next morning the rain had set in; visibility from the cliff-top was nil. The rain moved like a gray curtain over the inland, and on the shore it blended with a thick sea-mist. Wemyss went to ground.

IV

Anat Asher was in quarters sound asleep when the rain began to fall. When her blip sounded, she started up thinking it was 2400 hours, time for her to take duty . . . she had slept through her own wake-up call. Winkler apologized, uttered the words of ill omen: heavy rain.

"Shee-it!"

Anat suited up and ran; all the regulars were running, the sirens began to yip. Inside the new dome everyone looked up at the gaping hole overhead, eight meters across, the rain pouring through. The oxper had the two work towers in position; a slight man, Azamo Johnson, stood on the shoulders of Victor Burns, who stood on the shoulders of George King. The trick was to get a weather sheet in position overhead. Ray Green, on the other tower, raised his volume:

"Need a mensh under fifty-five kilos to lie on the outer skin!"

She did not think at all, simply uttered a wild cry of assent, ran to Ray's tower and began to climb the rain-wet ladder. She put on her helmet and gloves at the first platform; there were encouraging noises from the floor. On the third platform Ray Green snapped on the safety line.

"Lie flat, Lieutenant," he said. "Spread your weight. Clip the edges of the weather sheet to the red area on the safety netting."

"Fine!"

They exchanged their own do-or-die smile through the rain that was pouring over them; she shut her faceplate and used the demister. Ray lifted her, hands resting lightly on her waist, and passed her to Dick Black, who was standing on his shoulders. He swung her up and deposited her on the lip of the opening overhead. She felt for bootholds in the safety netting, glanced over her shoulder at the bulging, rain-wet surface of the dome. She saw figures in the rain, watching from outside; it looked a long way down.

Azamo had swung into position on the other side of the aperture; he began clipping his edge of the weather sheet to the net. Burns and Black, on the towers, unrolled the sheet, brought the edge to her hands. It was a vile, difficult, even dangerous task. More than once the writhing, wet sheet struck at her so hard that she had to brace herself on the safety net, let go a clip. She moved in and out of shelter, now on the underside of the sheet, now in the rain. She opened her faceplate, and the rainwater was strange tasting, cold, with big, coarse drops.

Slowly she moved to her left, as Vic Burns had signaled, then back to her starting point and right. She saw a dark shape coming and met Azamo on the western exposure. They laughed. He wore no helmet; his teeth flashed in his dark face. A couple of clips tore out on her side, and he deliberately climbed over her to get them, resting his wiry dancer's body against hers as she lay on the net.

The job was done. Back in the glare of the porta-sun lamps she was bundled down onto a work tower. Her legs were twitching from strain as she descended the long ladder. She stood aside as a hoist went up with shaped blue sections. Anat recognized the cap of the dome with adjustable air vents which the oxper team now prepared to set in place in the temporary shelter of the weather sheet.

It was warm and busy inside the dome. The crew were putting on an endspurt: the insulation was zipping into place as the gallery went up over the new cubicles. The utility rooms were pegged out. After she had called the roll, Anat Asher spent time with Vannie Frost putting stretchers into wall panels of treated cotton. They took a break, sat on the work platform looking at the action while they drank their shake-to-heat beakers of tomato soup.

"Tomatoes." Vannie sighed. "The old Rain Forest where I been bunking down is full of tomato plants coming into fruit. Seven boxes of supercorn ready to plant out . . ."

"We'd better find a place for a corn patch," said Anat.

She nibbled at her beaker, drank the soup down a little. The trick was to finish before the casing got too soggy. She was afraid the rain would never stop. It would rain for forty days and forty nights.

"Hope Wemyss has somewhere dry to sleep," said Vannie. "Out there . . ."

"Sure he has!" said Anat.

She could not bear to think of Wemyss, alone among the wet trees. She pushed aside too many problems, too many potential traumas, lived in a long weary dream of duty, drudgery and sleep. Here on the new world. How had she felt about it ages ago, ten days ago? *Every moment a moment of truth.*

"Let's get the rest of these panels, Vannie!"

She went on a late duty round from stem to stern of the capem. She looked from the forward hatch and saw faint lights in a couple of watch tents on the perimeter. The Silver Cross were still guarding the camp from imaginary predators. Their safety cordon was set down permanently.

The rain lasted for five days. The morale of the crew, down for so long, was raised by the completion of the new dome. Anat saw that the endspurt, the burst of work on the first rainy night, had done wonders. By the second day of the rain, Landfall+11, the dome was habitable, the miserable slum in the old Rec could be cleared. Sam Kayoute transported several freeze bays into the new storage area and began to divide the commissary between the roomy storage compartments of the Rec and the new utility rooms.

The grove was a quagmire, but there was no flooding. There was concern about the water supply, but the track to the Silver-brook was passable, and the stream kept within its banks. Early in the morning of the third day Anat woke from a wild dream of rainbow clouds and a little wooden boat. She heard the crack of doom, a hideous grating, metal on metal. The capem twisted unmistakably and shook under her bunk.

No one rushed this time: they tiptoed. Out of the after hatch, through Silver Cross quarters, watched by a duty sergeant, Hoot Wells. The capem was settling gently, as the steady rain swirled away sandy soil from the rock and from the tree trunks pushed up during the landing. A mixed group, everyone in the world, wearing a weird assortment of gear and no gear, watched and peered, jumping back when the entire hammerhead dropped thirty centimeters with a hollow clang.

Ray Green, riding the door frame of the forward hatch, cried out:

"All service and assigned personnel . . . keep right back!"

Those who did not move were caught by his second call:

"Lieutenant Holder, Warrant Officer Regi, Sergeant Winkler, this is a Life and Limb Call. All nonauxiliary personnel must get back!"

The named men who had been hunkered down, arguing pos-sibilities, caught the urgency in Ray Green's voice; they moved. Then Vic Burns on the ground and Ray Green, riding the hatch-way, cried out together in absolute unison:

"Super Team! Super Team! Wishers all, forward to work stations!"

Anat knew the procedure but had never seen it performed: it was an emergency call as rare as an involuntary shutdown. A voice said timidly at her side:

"What was he saying, Lieutenant?"

It was a pretty, bedraggled waif in a shawl, Faith Cavarro, the youngest of Myrrha's children.

"It's a round-up call for all the oxper," said Anat. "They form the Super Team."

"Can they make the Rec steady again?" asked Faith. "Down our end it still isn't so bad."

"They can stabilize the capem, honey," said Anat, watching keenly. "The oxper can handle it."

Yes, the Silver Cross auxiliaries were responding to the call, coming to join the Super Team. She still felt a deep anxiety for the fabric of the capem and all that the battered hammerhead contained. Not only quarters for the regular officers and all the Silvos but Gregg's HQ, the watchpost with the emergency comcen, even the still-thriving Rain Forest, up aloft. Anat had a particular anxiety for the supply compartments along the back wall, loaded with emergency equipment and with commissary.

The Super Team was twelve androids strong. Shadow Adams suddenly appeared at the side of Ray Green in the gaping hatchway. They looked at the assembled team and went away, came back with the piece of equipment Anat had been expecting: one of the four Atlas jacks, made to support the capem, unused so far.

The operation continued to an accompaniment of beating rain, the grind and creak of metal, the murmur of the spectators. All these sounds were a background to the eerie silence of the oxper at their work. It was certain that they communicated—their facial expressions and body language were sometimes easy to read, sometimes not—but they did not speak or vocalize. It was a strain for some of the spectators: Regi danced on the spot with eagerness to participate.

Anat began sending regulars into the new dome, out of the rain. The unready were sneaking away to find clothing. She saw

Gregg, fully clad at least, and Marna Rossi, wrapped in a blanket. She did not risk going to them herself, but she noticed that Kyle was in attendance.

"Faith," she said, "go talk to your brother. Ask Kyle if you can take Specialist Rossi into the new dome, get yourselves some hot tea."

"Sure Lieutenant!" said Faith. "Go with love . . ."

The stabilizing operation took just under three hours: Anat believed it counted as an act of true cooperation between the crew and the Silver Cross. When the immediate instability had been halted the Super Team began to talk, acknowledge the humans standing round about, and allow them to assist.

Anat Asher was in the new dome herself, drinking tea prior to setting foot in the newly stabilized capem, when she was blipped urgently by Sam Kayoute, close at hand. She found him in a thunderous mood, making the new utility rooms look puny.

"What's wrong, Sam?"

He told the story, very angry. The Silvos, those loozy plagged goons, had had the choots to accuse him of peculation and miscount in the store compartments. Yeah, just then, when he first stepped back in the capem. One of their hulks, a Silvo oxper, maybe that soul-brother Shadow Adams, had dared to rescan the whole of the commissary remaining in the Rec. The daytrays, the Q, the freeze-dries, everything, even the Cook's Pantry, the specials that every commissary sergeant counted as his private domain.

"Who said this?" demanded Anat.

"The old heavy, Thick Fogg. It's something they thought up, Lieutenant. We been interfacing pretty good with Barnard, the service company, up till now."

"What happened, Sam?" Anat persisted.

"I hit Fogg," he said quietly.

Lelani Buck, standing by, cut in for the first time.

"Lieutenant, it didn't go no further! It couldn't. First time back inside the Rec after it was shored up . . . everyone was going very easy."

"Shee-it!" murmured Anat, thinking of old times, aboard ship. "You damage him at all, Sam?"

"No, it was pure reflex."

"In the gut!" said Lelani with relish.

"None of that!" said Anat. "Start thinking of a report, Sam. Get to a vox and put in five hundred words, max, no speech quotes. Who was there? Who was a witness?"

"Wink," said Sam Kayoute. "Master Sergeant Gene Winkler. Lelani. Couple other Silvos: the lieutenant Mary 'Atom' Klein and Hoot Wells, the duty sergeant."

"No oxper at all?"

"They were still outside, working on the capem," said Lelani Buck. "Even Ed Rowe, from our team, was still out there."

It was bad karma, thought Anat. Or conspiracy. No appeal to the recall facilities of the androids was possible.

"What was the situation when you left the Rec?" she asked.

"It was nasty," said Lelani. "I tried to get Sam away. I was sure they would bring up more Silvos and jump him."

"I called in Wink," said Sam. "Dumped the whole mess on him. Last we saw, he was sealing the inlet doors to the storage compartments and standing guard."

"I'll reinforce him," said Anat. "Stay cool, Sam. Stay in this dome. That's an order!"

"Yes, ma'am!"

She ran out into the cheerful colors of the new dome and saw fewer than a dozen regulars lining up for their breakfast rations. She blipped Ray Green.

"Lieutenant . . . ?"

"Ray, how is the backup work on the capem? I need one crew auxiliary inside, soonest."

"Lieutenant, the capem is secure and stable. We have another action in progress."

"Another action with the Super Team?"

"In effect, yes," said Ray. "The pump station has to be held together and the pipeline unfouled. Auxiliary action is quickest. The rain is still holding steady."

The water supply. What was a stupid, all-too-human fight between Silvos and regulars compared to basic life support?

"You must go ahead," said Anat. "But there is a situation that could develop badly inside the capem. If I call with our code signal, Ray, you must release me one regular auxiliary to the Rec at lightspeed, okay?"

"I understand, Lieutenant."

She ran along the blue tunnel that connected the dome with the Hill. It led in through the old cargo entry that had been put into use next to sick bay. She looked into sick bay now and found Dell Stout packing a few last things for the move to new quarters. Everyone else had gone, even Linda Baumer was settled in her new room on the gallery.

"Dell," said Anat Asher, "leave that. There's an emergency in the Rec."

"Someone hurt?"

"Maybe," said Anat. "I need backup."

She tried to explain the emergency. As she looked around sick bay, wondering if she should haul Dalny and Regi from the dome after all, a box of medicament put ideas in her head.

"You got an order of Peace?" she asked.

In space, there had always been the need for a relatively harmless method of stopping Homo sapiens in his tracks. An involuntary shutdown. Berserkers were a threat to the fabric.

"Shee-it!" said Dell. "Who you planning to drop?"

She laid her hands on two puffer packs of Peace; Anat loaded hers into her left sleeve with the outlet lightly clenched in her left palm. The two women ran up the Hill, re-formed, and walked smartly into the Rec.

For a moment it was unknown territory because the tilt had gone. The fabric was still deformed in places from its ordeals; the watchpost and the Rain Forest over it seemed to be going away downhill. Master Sergeant Winkler, bleeding rakishly from a cut on the forehead, was defending an impossible position. He stood behind a last red recliner in front of the long folding doors of the storage compartments in the back wall.

Captain Boyle stood and roared ten meters away. A team of three big men were stalking toward Wink like so many martial arts instructors. There was Hoot Wells, the duty sergeant, a notorious hardliner, but also Holder, the young lieutenant from Detroit Company, plus the red-haired mechanic from Abacus, Brick

Clark. There was a narrow panel of ribbed metal screening the door to the Hill. Anat and Dell were not seen as they stepped in.

". . . deadcut shitsack lays hand on the troop . . ." roared Boyle. "Stand away, Winkler, you got no clout, you gonna lose your balls, I mean it!"

Anat took Dell's hand, and they ran to Wink, crossing the path of the three warriors. The master sergeant was glassy-eyed with stress but holding well.

"Tribal war!" he gasped. "You shouldn't have . . ."

"Captain Boyle!" shouted Anat Asher, *"call to order!"*

"Hike it, Killer-Bitch!" Boyle screamed. "Your thievin' cook blend downed one my officers!"

She blipped Ray Green, then reversed the pattern of his call-sign; it was their emergency code. The call was acknowledged: he would send an oxper. She blipped angrily for Commander Gregg, got Kyle. She held the little box away from her and spoke loudly:

"Order Call! Order Call! Captain Boyle, Lieutenant Holder, Sergeant Wells called to order for attack on regular crew members in the Rec at this time. You get that, Kyle?"

"Yes," said Kyle. "No . . . Lieutenant?"

Boyle was yelling again, but the attack group was not moving. She turned away and said:

"Kyle, it is an acute situation. Get the commander himself down here at the double!"

There was no reply. Dell Stout was cleaning up Gene Winkler's head with a coolpad.

"He won't stop!" said Wink in a rapid undertone. "It's a planned action. Where are the oxper?"

"At the pipeline," said Anat. "One is coming. Gregg's been informed. He must come!"

There was a movement at the door into quarters, and she hoped for Gregg, right on cue, but instead two Silver Cross women ran in, Lieutenant Klein and Lacey, the cook sergeant.

"Yeah! Yeah! You see what we got here!" cried Boyle. "Take it, Holder! Complete the action! Secure the stores! That's *our* life support those shitsacks are holding out on!"

Without warning another crew member came loping gently into the Rec from the Hill.

"Hey, the tilt's gone!" exclaimed Ivan Dalny.

Clark, the red-haired mechanic, peeled off and attacked Dalny. At the same time Holder made a run to that feeble barrier, the red recliner. Wink tried to get in front of the two women, but Anat pushed away from him and confronted Holder alone.

"Don't do it!" she said. "Lieutenant Holder! Don't overstep!"

He had a set face, a faraway look as if he were completing an exacting drill figure. He did not speak but laid heavy hands on her waist and lifted her off her feet to set her aside, like a child. Anat shrugged her left hand free; she heard distant voices cheering or jeering. She saw her left arm swing across in slow motion; she gave Holder a shot of Peace, full in the face.

He slumped forward, taking her with him; she twisted under him, finding her feet like a cat, and blipped Ray Green. A hand-to-hand fight began, on top of her. Sergeant Winkler was trading heavy punches with Hoot Wells, over the body of Holder. Anat went on crawling until she hit the wall of the supply compartment. She hauled herself up; her blip was out some way, it was dead.

"Stop it!" said Dell Stout in her ear. "Withdraw, withdraw before someone is killed!"

Boyle had uttered a strange word of command that might have been "Retro!" The fighters drew apart, gasping. Wink, in terrible shape, collapsed over the red recliner. Hoot Wells, marked but still holding, began to drag away the tranquilized body of Holder. Ivan Dalny, unprepared, was getting the better of Clark who went backward now, on all fours. Anat went to Wink, bent close, and said:

"We'll go out, down the Hill."

She dragged his communicator off his belt. She saw Shadow Adams come in through quarters; he gave her a single glance of triumph. Winkler's blip was out of commission too.

"Can you walk, Wink, honey?"

He was taking great rattling breaths. Dell Stout held him on one side, Anat on the other, two women, one medium sized, one small, assisting one large man. They made for the Hill; Anat flung out a beckoning arm for Dalny. He caught them up as they dived through, then dragged the heavy doors shut after them and shoved down the crash barrier. They all propelled Wink steadily down the hill, along the tunnel, and into the new dome.

Sam Kayoute at least was waiting for them: he gave a mighty roar of protest. Anat was far gone, a jerky automaton, hoarse-voiced, going by the book. She saw Gene Winkler lying across a transport trolley and put her hands on his poor face. It was incredible that Wink should be damaged, out of action this way. On the work platform she found a mike that worked, made it squeal to get attention, and gave a triple-A call. Yes, they had heard right, the stragglers came from bunks and trainers: Attack Alert. She stood Kayoute at the tunnel entrance and sent Azamo to run down the Hill and head for the oxper teams at the pump station. She parried Regi's questions and called the roll. Four konos, including Azamo Johnson, and eleven crew members.

"Eleven crew members!" cried Anat Asher. "Eleven souls! Two crew members are dead. Lieutenant Wemyss is in the field. Commander Gregg and Specialist Rossi are in Headquarters. Ensign Loney is not in the dome."

"What's your point?" demanded Regi. "You think this latest fracas with the Silver Cross is a planned attack?"

"I'm saying the members of the space service here present are not a fighting force and were never meant to be one," said Anat. "We have to coexist with the Silver Cross. We have to avoid confrontation."

"We got seven oxper!" called Vannie Frost. "Those loozy plaggers only got five!"

"Vannie," said Anat, "wash that kind of thinking out of your brain! We are not here to strain the strength and loyalty of the auxiliary personnel."

"We're here," said Regi stiffly, "to uphold the chain of command. If the Silver Cross infringe the In-Space Disciplinary Code . . ."

"Then they should be called to order," said Anat. "Warrant Officer Regi, I request you to call Headquarters and get through to the commander."

Regi was working his blip communicator, staring at Anat as he thumbed the pad. He was answered and at once used his receiver to make the call private. Ivan Dalny ambled over from the new sick bay.

"How's Wink?" said a dozen voices.

"Bruising," said Dalny, who was slightly bruised himself. "Trouble with his wind. All comes from fighting a man half his age. He has been sedated."

Regi looked strange.

"Now hear this!" he said, making the connection.

The voice of Commander Gregg rang through the fine new dome. Anat had a feeling of hollowness; too big, she thought, the dome was too big for eleven souls.

"Gregg, speaking from Headquarters to all space service personnel. As of now Warrant Officer Regi, E.F.A., takes up the rank of first lieutenant and special security officer responsible for good order in the new dome."

He was gone. Regi looked more than embarrassed.

"Okay," he said into the mike. "Normal duties. We'll keep you posted."

Nobody went away. He said in a low voice to Anat, "Lieutenant, I have to talk to you . . ."

There was a movement at the front entry to the dome. The flaps were flung back, showing the rain still pouring down steadily on a broad, muddy pathway. Ray Green led the oxper in out of the rain. Anat was so relieved to see them again that she didn't read Ray Green's expression until he was very close. A pattern of wrinkles came and went under his left eye socket.

"Ray, what is it?" she asked. "How about the pump station?"

The water supply was her first thought. Or was someone hurt?

"Action successfully completed," he said. "There was a call from Headquarters. Lieutenant, I have to escort you to Commander Gregg."

He held her gaze steadily as if willing her to understand. She looked at Regi, who had lost all his bounce, who could only fling up his hands in despair or puzzlement.

"You mean I'm under arrest, Ray?"

"Yes, Lieutenant."

"I'll freshen up," she said. "Give me five minutes."

Ivan Dalny made a protest.

"Lieutenant Asher is under shock!" he said loudly. "She's been in a fight."

For a moment Anat wondered how to play it; she was sick and battered, her knees could buckle at this point most convincingly. Yet she wanted to see Gregg, to assess the situation at Headquarters, to speak her piece and play things straight one more time. She dared to go back into the Rec and get through to Headquarters with Ray Green as her escort.

"I'm fit for duty, Ivan," she said.

When she came out of the washroom, Regi was saying:

"We'll make a search for both of them . . ."

Ray Green looked down at her, still giving his alarm signals.

"Ed Rowe," he said. "I sent him from the pipeline action in answer to your call."

"He never showed up," she said. "Can't you . . . contact him?"

Ray shook his head.

"Who else is missing?" she asked.

"Ensign Loney," he said.

She had an urge to run back up onto the platform beside Regi and go into a "who saw them last?" routine, but it was not her place anymore. She laid a hand on Ray Green's arm, and they went through the tunnel.

They saw the figure of a man outlined against the light at the foot of the Hill: Anat remembered how she had run down to the konos and stepped out into the new world. Azamo Johnson waved and shouted as he came toward them. A couple of his sisters and brothers, Zak, the younger Cavarro musician, and Zena, his partner, the Australian girl, saw him run by the door of their quarters and followed.

Azamo was wet and muddy, also wild-eyed, as if he had seen an alien.

"Casualty!" he gasped. "Lieutenant . . . there's one down out there."

"Who is it?" she said.

"Hidden," he said, catching his breath. "Hidden by the tall grass and the weather antennae. I don't know how it could be. It's the commissary boy. The oxper, Edward Rowe."

Rày Green made an extraordinary sound, a hissing through thin lips. Zena cried out; Anat realized that she had cried out herself.

"Shall we go to him?" said Zak.

Two oxper came hurrying through the tunnel onto the Hill: Vic Burns and Alan Cole, one of the medics. She knew that Ray had already summoned them.

"We'll take care of him," said Vic Burns kindly to the young konos.

"What the hell is going on here, Lieutenant?" demanded Azamo.

"Azamo," she said helplessly, "it is part of the same bad scene with the Silver Cross. We'll work it out. I'm on my way to Commander Gregg."

Ray Green did not speak; at the top of the Hill he unbarred the door. The Rec was empty except for two members of the Silver Cross: an oxper from Barnard Company, name of Michael Dow, stood before the sealed doors of the supply compartments. The Barnard mechanic, Loco Ramirez, was posted before the old watchpost; he cast his eyes down, embarrassed, as Anat and her tall escort went by. They saw no one else in the officers' quarters. Too much space, thought Anat, as they passed the empty cabins: Morgan, Wemyss, Regi—Lieutenant Regi, who had already moved to the new dome—Asher, her own place. She had been putting off the move. Ray Green knocked on the door of Headquarters and they went in.

The commander received them alone, smiling sadly. He had lost, or was hiding, the personal dislike or distaste that always came across in his dealings with her. It was one of those things that she had accepted and tried to work around; perhaps he had done the same. He was calm and collected, motioning Anat to a chair.

"Summary proceeding," he said. "Not a hearing, Lieutenant. Necessary for the preservation of order. How's Winkler?"

He was addressing Ray Green.

"Sedated, Commander," replied Ray. "Some bruising."

"I have a report," said Gregg. "You can prepare another, Lieutenant, while you're confined to quarters."

"May I ask a question?" said Anat.

"Aw, now Asher, don't make things worse!" said Gregg, almost his old insufferable self. "A question. Go ahead."

She turned to Ray Green and said:

"You sent an auxiliary to assist in the Rec, at my urgent request. What is the present condition of Edward Rowe?"

Gregg made some sound of impatience; she saw his hands shake on the tabletop. Ray Green's impassive, noble face was marked for a moment by grief and pain. Then, stiff and cold, he said in a loud voice:

"No longer operative, Lieutenant. Undergoing repair."

"What are you talking about? Ed Rowe?" asked the commander.

Ray Green fixed the commander with a terrible look. "He fell into a washaway on the path," he said. "Or he was attacked."

"Who says so?" whispered the commander. "Green, we're in a difficult enough situation . . ."

"You are appeasing a destructive force, Commander Gregg," said Ray Green, "and assisting their takeover of power."

"Quatsh!" said Gregg hoarsely. "I can't do otherwise. I think you're out of adjustment, Ray."

He stood up and looked wildly around the blue-gray confines of the double cabin. Anat saw him at last as a creature under surveillance, under pressure. She wished that Marna Rossi, his girl, were safely in the dome, among the regulars. She wondered how Kyle was placed, if he could arrange things.

"Let me confine Lieutenant Asher to quarters in the dome," said Ray Green quietly.

"No," said Anat. "No, Ray, I haven't moved yet. I'll stay here in the capem."

"Dismiss then," said Gregg. "Do the report, Asher. We'll find you a duty where you don't rub against the Silver Cross."

Kyle came in and made eye contact with Anat. She felt responsible for him, for all the konos; she wondered if Myrrha Devi could save them all, defuse the Silver Cross some way. Kyle held the door of Headquarters, the commander filled the doorway.

Ray Green led Anat to the door of her cabin, checked that it was empty, let her inside. Not a sign of the Silver Cross or their aggression. She locked her door, hearing Ray's measured tread

fade into the distance. She sat on her bunk and thought of prece-
dent, the care that had been taken aboard the *Serendip Dana* to
work around the Silver Cross. Were these loozy muggers going
to walk all over Service personnel forever, even with the ship
gone?

One of the most notorious cases of "bad interface" had in-
volved her friend Rose Chan. She recalled how Rose fell foul of
Jetta Novak, a big rough Silvo kid in Etzel Company . . . how did
it go now? Novak always made trouble when she had the duty of
letting in service officers for the routine inspections; she over-
stepped so far that Anat and Chan had wondered if she was
plagged some way. There came the time she *drew her blaster* on
Chan, shee-it, under ship conditions, and was smartly disarmed
by Chan, who was trained in every kind of security fighting.

Anat felt a rush of helpless rage thinking of the routine inquiry. Chan was given right; Novak was to be disciplined some
way by the Silvos. Every time Chan brushed up against the Silver Cross in the course of her duties she was subjected to argument, gross heckling, physical hazing . . . tripped down a
stairwell, jostled, her uniform defaced. In the end Gregg, head
of Security, had relieved her of all duties involving the Silver
Cross.

Under ship conditions this had been the correct solution:
avoid confrontation wherever possible—that had been the ruling.
But now? Anat had begun to shiver a little, from stress more
than cold. She had plenty of pinks and reds at hand in her locker
but she did not take anything. These were sure as hell not ship
conditions. Outside the rain poured down.

6

There was never a better time aboard ship, a happier turn than those days between the Deadwater and Palmland; Paddy Rork, between working and dreaming, was sure he would remember it all his days. The good weather was part of it: long, easy, late summer days once they were out upon the green waves, and a fresh east wind, for the *Dancer* to show her qualities.

There was great excitement on the fifth day when something like a small boat was seen floating, dead ahead. Lon Adma took the longboat out, with Flower Wilm and Man Gruner; as they towed it in, those at the rail could see that it was only a pair of small reed-rafts locked together. Nevertheless, they dragged the whole hurrah's nest aboard and examined it carefully. There was a blackened patch on one side of the smaller round which might have been a burn mark. There were all the things that one might expect to find on a reed-raft, namely old bird nests, bird lime, seaweed, dead and alive, a few scraps of land vegetation. And there was a small square of ordinary brown cotton cloth, about the size of a handkerchief. Something was wrapped in the handkerchief. The crew of the *Dancer* held their breath as Cap Varo carefully laid back the folds. Laughter, sounds of disappointment, still a scrap of mystification. The shell of a blue mussel, the commonest sort of shellfish in the world, and a single blue bead, as big as the captain's little fingernail or the metal beads that sailors wore in their ears.

"Perish the fishes!" exploded Tom Kirsh. "This is no big haul from the stars!"

"This is some chance bit of rubbish, fallen overboard from a ship," pronounced Winna Cross. "La Mar brought the *Comet* into this ocean, and Old Annie Foley has come here with the *Faithful.*"

"It seems so, Bosun," agreed Cap Varo, "but I will study it a little."

In all that voyage Cap Varo was human and merry as anyone had ever seen him. He still brooded over his charts, for this was his nature, but now he came up on deck to hear the talk and singing after supper.

This was the time Paddy liked best, with all the crew sitting together. On the ninth night old Tom Kirsh came up from his galley and passed around chunks of feejo bread dipped in watered sugarvine schnapps. He made as if to pass the platter around Paddy.

"Aw, Tom!"

"One piece, no more, boy," said the old man. "You'll fall from the truck and delay this mad rush to Palmland!"

Paddy felt a thump of anxiety. What if there was nothing, no one to be found, not even a trace of good iron? What if the space ship burnt to ashes or sank into the ocean before they got within sight of it? What if he did fall from aloft and lie in his bunk with a broken head and miss everything?

"I'll take no drunk-dunk," said Ketty Merrow primly. "I'll see that Paddy Rork doesn't fall down, Mr. Kirsh!"

She gave Paddy a pinch on his upper arm and made him squeak. They sat together on the hatchcover, and he wondered if he was really doing well with her, if she would one day be his girl.

This night there were songs and a lot of foolish talk about meeting the star-riders, the mugomen or aliens. Megan Varo and Flower Wilm, both nurse-aides, were of the opinion that it would be a great good fortune if starfolk had gotten themselves down without loss of life.

"They will be far advanced," observed Ira Maddern, "with all the technology of Earth that we lost long ago."

Paddy was sick of hearing about it in school. It taxed his imagination even to think of the Rhomary mother-ship, a huge, silvery fish, half collapsed among the tall jocca palms. It burst into flame, and people ran in and out, trying to save their technology. Now everything had come closer . . . another ship, lying amongst the little green palms on the island, spilling out new people . . .

"We must go canny," said Man Gruner. "We must go canny, eh, Mr. Maddern? Likely they will think us strange."

"How can we prove different?" asked Paddy.

"Good question, Paddy!" said the first mate. "Any ideas between decks?"

Tom Kirsh was of the opinion they should hail the incomers from a safe distance. Behind the trees, for instance, or from a boat to the shore. Lon Adma, who spent part of each voyage arguing the toss with Tom Kirsh, took another sop of the tipsy-bread and wondered about the words to use. The speech, the language. Even if these were mensh come down in a strange place and taking for granted they were not dying of their ordeal, would they understand a word anyone had to say?

"Now come, Coxun," said Flower Wilm. "Third here is full of language. She can do the German from Merchants' High School and the Hispanic from her family."

"We have three languages," said Megan, smiling. "What about yours, Molly?"

Then they recalled that Molly was one of a clan that had a family speech, the Kim-Kelly Dialect, as it was stored for reference in the Dator's office in the city. More than one archivist had boiled her brain over this "little language," trying to relate it to what was known. For a family language was not a pure speech, like the Polish recovered from the Baronovski descendants or the Irish Gaelic preserved by the Celtic Society. Molly was still quiet and sad, mourning her friend, poor Dorris, but she perked up enough to say:

"Well, I will shout out some choice oaths, maybe, and see if I get them going!"

Winna Cross, the bosun, spoke up:

"I think it would be best to sing to them."

There was a guffaw from old Tom, who often scolded Winna for not keeping good time with her big voice.

"Dry hell!" said Winna. "These people will hardly understand us! We all have a 'family language' by this time. But if we sing, they'll know we're of their kind, more or less, and meaning well."

This was the cue for a song. Tom Kirsh brought out his strummer, and they had a long round of shanties and ballads. The voices and the harmony never sounded so sweet to Paddy as they did at night on the ocean. Cap Varo was there, adding his bass note, and when the singing was done, he wondered if there might be cool-tea for all hands. Tom Kirsh and Ketty Merrow had been expecting this and had a big gourd cooling over the side. Bosun Cross gave a hail and brought Seela Conor down from the masthead to join the round.

"Captain," said Ira Maddern, "what's your thought of our *first contact* with these castaways?"

Cap Varo sighed and groaned a little in his usual fashion.

"I'll tell you the truth, Mr. Maddern," he said, "I don't hold their chances too high."

Perhaps Paddy uttered a groan of disappointment himself or the captain saw his face in the lantern light.

"There I am looking on the dark side." He laughed. "The woods may be full of them. They may be looking out for us . . . perhaps the *Dancer* shows up as a mark upon one of their chart screens."

"What will they look like, Captain?" asked Flower Wilm.

"Like mensh," said Cap Varo firmly. "Tall and strong, dressed out in some sort of all-colored coveralls, but mensh for all that. Men and women."

"I have been thinking of the silkies," put in Seela Conor timidly. "I hope nothing fell down on them!"

Then everyone made sounds of reassurance and laughed, thinking of those cheeky rascals.

"No girl," said Tom Kirsh, "you may be sure they ran off as

fast as their legs could carry them . . . into the sea or into their caverns underground."

Next morning at first light, when Paddy was up aloft, the grandmother of all blackrays appeared, twirling itself like a blue-black cloak, right in the path of the ship. He gave the cry:

"There she furls!"

Everyone came noisily on deck, for noise was part of the ritual for hunting blackrays. Ira Maddern let down the two boomers, unwieldy tubes of kelp and canvas that directed the sound of a drum and a gong into the ocean depths. The blackray surfaced and lay upon the water like a flat, fleshy plate.

"Dry hell!" cried Lon Adma. "She is the size of Palmland itself!"

He saw to the longboat and the mounting of the harpoon frames. The blackray moved on the surface of the sea, flipping up its edges to show the pearly underbody, then folded itself like a pancake and took off swiftly toward the southeast with the *Dancer* in pursuit.

All the long day they followed the sea creature, which let loose with a cloud of its ink-screen about midday, coloring the water purple-black. The longboat was put out at last; the *Dancer* waited, hove to, as the boat crept closer to the treacherous frilled edges of the beast.

Paddy and Seela were in the crosstrees watching for Lon to take a shot. The blackray lay on the surface as if dead. Then they saw Lon release all four harpoons: one well-aimed shot in the brain center could kill a blackray outright. Now, after a few pulse beats the creature thrashed and twitched up from the water with a hollow sound. It spouted, dark and inky, then dived. The crew of the longboat cast off the long kelp strands of the harpoons and rowed madly to avoid being sucked under.

"Have we lost her?" cried Seela.

Paddy saw that she was in two minds about the killing of a blackray: Seela was too tender-hearted. He knew the stand that Cap Varo and most others that he knew, including his father and mother, took about such things, and he tried to hold to it.

"Come then," he said, "she is our great catch, good for hides and oil, worth hundreds of credits!"

They hung on the crosstrees of the mainmast like two birds and stared at the darkening sea and the patch of turbulence where the blackray had submerged. Further to the southeast the sky was dark with rain; the wind had freshened a little. Ira Maddern called an order from below. Paddy hauled down the masthead lantern, trimmed the wick, and got it burning after only three tries with the tinder box. As he hauled up the lantern again and made it fast, Seela said quietly:

"There she lies."

The blackray rose to the surface; it was the sign they had been waiting for; the creature was dead. The cheers from Lon Adma, the Coxon, and his crew, Flower, Molly, and Man, rang out across the sea and were echoed by those on board. At once the little cocker boat was launched and Ira Maddern called Paddy to go on the hooking round with him. Cap Varo held the wheel himself while Megan let down the tow bar astern of the *Dancer.* Then the two boats circled the blackray; the roped hooks were driven securely through its edges. Lon Adma tramped across the thick, scummy black hide to retrieve his harpoons.

The *Dancer* sailed on, moving some points westward, with the catch roped behind. Squalls of rain came up with them during the night, but the wind was not too fresh. Next evening, after they had sailed all day through this dirty weather, they caught sight of the island on the port bow: Palmland.

"Nothing to see," said Cap Varo, leaning on the bridge rail and straining his eyes like everyone else.

"Where might they be?" asked Megan softly.

"On the northern shore," he said, "or in the inland. Who knows? I doubt they are within miles of our own harbor."

"We can't sail on round," she said, "not with this ray in tow."

"No," he said firmly, "we must claim the skin and flense the beast in the usual fashion."

"Father," said Megan, "it is thirteen days since we saw some objects fall down, burning. The odds are against us every way. The thing was no ship at all. Or if it was a ship then it is burnt to ashes or sunk in the sea, probably both. We are following nothing but your dream!"

"Great Vail Alive!" boomed Simon Varo. "I am the one who is supposed to look on the dark side!"

Down in his cabin he no longer made a pretense of sleeping. He consulted his charts again, checked the log, and communed with the blue bead. It was all he had, but he knew that it was enough, if he could read the riddle correctly. It was made of a thick glassy substance, smooth all over, but with tiny facets just visible in its surface. It was not quite round and there was a curious flat place on one side. This was sticky to the touch and even warm, but he could not get it to stick to anything but his own skin. The rich, deep turquoise blue of the mysterious bead exactly matched the color of the small blue-mussel shell. A shell so common that no Rhomarian would bother collecting it . . . but a newcomer? Someone walked on the island beach and said: "There is a shell the exact color of my bead!" My memory bead? My bead that tells the time? A bead from my health necklace?

The rain was heavy, obscuring the wooded slopes above their harbor when they sailed through the sea fog and dropped anchor. Everything was as they had left it: the old palm-roofed shelter for the cauldrons, the stone barbecue. From the masthead Paddy and Megan Varo herself checked every inch of the surrounding countryside with the telescope. The *Dancer*'s harbor was closed in on three sides with lightly wooded slopes. Paths led up, out of the bay, then directly ahead, toward the inland and the eastern slopes of the Lookout hill. One path turned off and returned to the beach, beyond the bushland that enclosed the harbor: it was a good six kilometers to the Giants' Steps and the Stone Garden, where the silkies lived, underground.

II

On the evening before the Crisis Round Table, Master Sergeant Winkler took a long training walk before returning to duty. He explored the muddy path to the Silverbrook and the pleasant groves inland of Sunset Beach. The rain had thinned out, and people were taking the air, between showers. He walked all around the Silvos' small dome, then patrolled the eastern beach and looked into the Silvo watch-tent. It was a ramshackle oval structure of khaki canvas with a name shield in starburst neon marker paint: BUFFS LODGE. They had it very cosy inside, and there were several trophies mounted on the walls: flying lizards, one of the gray seabirds, some impressive spiny fish. Holoks of several pigarees and their hunters, armed with gun or crossbow.

Master Sergeant Hoot Wells, deep in his inflatable chair, tensed a little as Wink appeared; to his right Brick Clark cleaned a small sporting gun. Filly Jones, the young medic, moved chops about on a neat, illegal gas grill. William Hale, oxper, was playing with a landscape simulator on a monitor.

"Please excuse," said Wink. "I'm scouting data for the proposed combined roster."

Hoot Wells heaved himself to his feet and held out a hand; Wink took it.

"You in shape, Sergeant?" asked Brick, kindly. " 'Cause Hoot here is still moaning."

"I'm fine," said Wink. "I'm dead and crippled, but I'm fine."

Everyone laughed companionably. Wink was served a lemon lift and offered a pigaree cutlet. He tasted the meat and found that it *was* indistinguishable from pork and beautifully fresh. Bye-bye pigarees, he thought, the carnivores have landed.

"But you never got a howler," he said.

"Too smart," said Hoot. "I reckon old Zero winged the one that killed your man Meyer, but that was it. We never even got a smell of one, since then."

"Now the way I see it," said Wink, "is that you Buffs are like a private club. You really want to roster this watchpost?"

The hunters looked at each other.

"Is there any way we can avoid it?" asked Filly.

She was easily the prettiest girl in the Silver Cross, and she seemed brighter than the rest of the Buffs, though this would not have been too difficult.

"What I could do," said Wink, "is give you one, maybe two, part-time regulars, and that's it. Your choice. Someone you can get along with."

They put their heads together; William Hale turned from his jungle landscape and murmured a suggestion.

"Okay," said Hoot. "If this will pass. The medic oxper, Alan Cole, could do us a stint down here in the Buffs' Lodge."

"No problem," said Wink.

"Something we can do for you, Sergeant?" asked Hoot.

"Keep the crockin' peace," said Wink. "And, yes, keep an eye out for Hal Loney . . . on your nature walks."

There was no special reaction that he could see; he wished he had brought along an oxper to give him a reading. He went on his way thinking of cooperation; no way around it—hadn't he been making compromises with good old boys like the Buffs for a good part of his time in the service? Wasn't he, partly, a good old boy himself? Shee-it. It was enough to make him wish he had stayed home. He hurried back to the capem, marched up the ramp and into the Rec. If his researches meant anything, he thought he knew the whereabouts of Loney.

Wink was pleased to see that the Silvo on duty was Zero Zavaski, a man he could work with very well. The Rec was busy with preparations for tomorrow's meeting, but he considered ditching the loozy rosters and rushing to quarters, to Anat Asher's door. He sighed deeply, feeling the ache of his bruised ribs, and settled down to playing put and take with old Zero on the largest screen.

Later, in the long night hours, when he was alone at last, Wink went and sat on the bunk he still kept made up in the watchpost. He punched a few keys and wrote the magic words:

"Cybear is back."

He waited, wrote *Report* a couple of times, and cut in some long-range beeps. Presently a comical animation of a bird appeared onscreen with a line of text.

"Moburd greets Cybear. Shit, Sarge, you been a long time."

The konos who brought Anat her food in quarters were alarmed at her capacity for sleep. After some hours of tension with the Silvos crashing at her door, the rain obscuring the porthole, the "Poems for an Ice Age," and the battle of Borodino, she gave up the struggle. She popped two reds and fell into a deep, dreamless sleep. After that, without further medication, she slept obsessively, eight, nine hours at a stretch. She worked out on the trainer, heard the breathless accounts and hopeful messages delivered by Faith, Vashti, Zak, Halprin. News from another world. She took extra oxygen. She could not remember what length of time had passed when her vox, bunkside, gave a soft whistle.

At first she suspected a trap. She had gone over her cabin very carefully and believed it was not bugged. A vox could indeed function as a short-range communication device, as between a vox and any outlet or between vox and vox. She wanted to be very sure she knew who was on the other end.

"Who's there?"

Her caller was cagey. There was a whistle, a couple of bars, no more. On the screen there appeared an animation of a fat bird with notes of music coming out of its beak. Then a line of hand-printed text.

"Don't say the name, Lieutenant."

A label appeared next to the picture: Mocking Bird. Anat nearly yelped the name aloud. She juggled her own controls and wrote:

"Loney, where the hell are you?"

A neat series of simulations filled the small screen. At last she oriented herself: watchpost, quarters, outer skin, the corridor through quarters. Aw, shee-it. How could he do it? A little bullet-man twinkled in the overheading, the cul-de-sacs, the hot grids and air vents that made up the ceiling of the capem. Loney was the first person, she guessed, who had ever crawled in that dangerous, overcrowded crawl space.

"You'll fry up there!" she wrote. "You been there the whole time? Since the fight?"

A cheery whistle.

"Come down some places," wrote the Mocking Bird. "Empty cabins on this row we're in. I can swing between the watchpost and the Rain Forest, too."

"Hal, get down. Go back to the dome!" she wrote, feeling like a Jewish mother. "Get some proper food!"

"I keep hearing Wink is okay," wrote Loney, "after fighting that pig-sticker Hoot Wells."

"He was fine last I heard," said Anat, "but he must be out of his mind with worry. You're listed as missing!"

"The sarge will work it out," came the reply. "I was in the watchpost when the fight started, when Sam Kayoute took a poke at that crocker Thick Fogg. The sarge told me to watch but not show myself, to be a witness and get away the best way I could. First I went up aloft, hid in the Rain Forest, ate Wemyss's bean sprouts. Then I had a stroke of luck. I got a little help breaking open a panel in the watchpost."

The vox was blank for a few seconds, and she wrote anxiously:

"Still there?"

"I'm gathering information," wrote Loney. "Some of the stuff I hear is too much. Lieutenant?"

"Loney?"

"No one must know about the Mocking Bird. No person and no system . . ."

"Your secret is safe with me," she wrote.

She erased their interchange from her vox. She remembered how she had sent out Ray Green to check Emergency Capsule Five on the last night and sworn him to secrecy with the same formulation.

The Mocking Bird checked in during the night hours.

"Shadow Adams has worked out a grand cooperative plan, final stage of the Silvo takeover. It don't seem too bad, he put in something for everyone. I know he is trying to find something for you, Lieutenant. Useful work but no interface with the Silver Cross."

Anat felt a frightful anger which passed off as quickly as it had come. No interface sounded pretty good.

"How smart can Shadow be?" wrote Loney. "Isn't it a proof that he ain't so smart if he hangs around with a bunch of dumb muggers? Lieutenant, he could have gotten himself in anywhere he wanted."

"Maybe it's just a proof that he isn't human," wrote Anat sadly. "Anyway, there's a difference between *smart* and *wise*. I think of Ray Green as a wise person."

"Ma'am," wrote Loney, "I heard so much trash it is getting to me. Sometimes I think the Wemyss way is the right one."

"Hal," wrote Anat, "stop this faggidy spying! You are worth more to us all as a regular crew member, not a superbug in the crawl space."

The Mocking Bird signed off with a balloon that said:

"Not a word!"

Anat knew that there would be some best time for her to come out. She had all her gear packed in two kitbags and an expanding carton. There had been a few breaks in the rain. The whole ridiculous notion of remaining in quarters was a piece of ship thinking, from Gregg: she had done it to please him, to keep the chain of command.

"Tomorrow . . . today . . . is the Crisis Round Table," wrote Loney, very early.

"I'm ready to report," said Anat. "When this new plan from Daniel Adams or Captain Boyle turns up we'll have to evaluate it on its merits."

"You won't be called, Lieutenant."

She felt bad and stupid: service routine had gone.

"Gregg was easily convinced," wrote Loney. "He likes everything to go smooth . . . he values Boyle's friendship. They didn't even have to use the real cattle-prod . . ."

"Okay," wrote Anat. "Tell me . . ."

"It is to do with Specialist Rossi. Something with her Cohen status."

"Rossi is *pregnant*?"

"Not sure. She is zonked out, sick, full of the stuff Big Doc gives her. Petrova won't let another medic near her."

"No!" said Anat aloud. "I can't . . ."

She wrote:

"That sounds bad but I can hardly believe Petrova . . ."

"Who knows?" wrote Loney. "Big Doc can be mean."

Then after a pause he wrote:

"My friend don't care for the hazing and hard jive in the Silver Cross. We don't see too much future round here . . ."

"Hal," wrote Anat, "come down out of there! Report to Gene Winkler."

"I already did," wrote Loney. "The sarge is doing fine. Back in harness. He's coming your way, Lieutenant."

She still read danger signals in the boy's messages.

"Promise me, Loney," she wrote. "Promise me you'll give up this crazy over-the-hill thinking!"

Two Mocking Birds shared a balloon which said:

"We promise not to go over the hill."

"I was thinking," wrote Anat, falling easily into the old plot and counterplot scenario, "maybe Kyle could get through to Rossi."

Loney wrote urgently:

"Negative! Don't ask him, Lieutenant! Don't ask his sisters!"

There was a firm official knocking at the door of her cabin; she registered the time of day, 05:09. Communication with the Mocking Bird was broken off. For the first time since being confined to quarters she used the door viewer . . . and flung open the door. Wink stood on the threshold, large as life.

"Moving you to the dome," he said gruffly.

"You get any directive?" she asked.

"The duty officer has wide powers," he said. "That your carton? Let's make it quick, Asher!"

They marched across the shadowy spaces of the Rec, went on down the Hill, and slipped into the dome without meeting a soul. Up on the gallery, lit only by a few dim pilot lights, they found her new cabin. It was like a room in a tent, spacious after the old quarters, with a view through streaky plex of the eastern sky and the tops of the palms. When they had flung her possessions around a little, Wink took a globe orchid out of his tunic and set it on the top of the bunkside monitor. They sat side by side on the bunk and drank whiskey from a silver flask. She leaned against his warm bulk, and they talked; she had not realized what a joy it was to talk to a friend. After some time Anat Asher said sleepily:

"Wink, what the hell are you doing?"

Gene Winkler went right on doing it; he also nuzzled her neck. He murmured a little song about the only girl for him, the cutest, the bravest. They began kissing, and she teased him a little, saying was he in good shape, was his heart all right? . . . Have to see about that, he said, and they rolled onto the bunk. Between times she said okay, she took it back, he was in excellent shape. Outside the dawn came up like thunder; the clouds had rainbow edges.

     •

As they came to the Crisis Round Table the rain had stopped: outside the grove steamed in the pale sunlight. The regular oxper had set up a trestle table in the center of the old Rec. Gregg had gone ahead, with his aide, and the regular brass, such as they were, were in place. Shadow touched Captain Boyle lightly on the shoulder as the Silvo delegation made their way through officers' quarters.

"You have it all," he murmured. "Time to be generous."

Boyle showed his teeth and aimed a resounding kick at one of the doors. It was a gentle hazing trick, practiced day and night by the Silvos passing Anat Asher's cabin. Now the two officers following, Fogg and Holder, gave the door a routine slap with their open hands. Shadow did not have the heart to tell them that the cabin was empty; he murmured to the captain:

"No reprisals! The Ronin is a bulwark for the peasantry!"

"Stay cool," said the captain. "You never trust me!"

"You're human," said Shadow coolly. "You are subject to all kinds of passion."

They walked smartly into the Rec, and Boyle gave the commander one of his salutes. They took their places at the table, on the commander's left. On his right was Kyle, then Regi, then Doc White, Dell Stout, and the security oxper, Dick Black, who looked much greener than Ray Green. No hotheads except Regi, and he had been squared, maybe, by the extra rank. Besides which he was no friend of the Killer-Bitch, Asher. The rest were cold cuts, mere fillers. Ronin Boyle stared until they dropped their eyes. He was tense; he wanted the plans ratified so he could go into action or take a massage or what. Gregg was going at it bald-headed, point by point. As commander of this emergency base . . . powers vested in him, etc., etc.

"I declare an absolute moratorium on the incidents which took place here in the capem. There will be no investigation, no hearing and no reprisals. The slate will be wiped clean, and we will all step into a new era of wider cooperation for the benefit of the whole community. That's the first step . . . subject to a statement, I believe, from Second Lieutenant Fogg, T.I.K., of the Silver Cross."

Thick Fogg, faithful unto death, the loozy, low man on the pyramid, sprang up and grinned shyly.

"I feel I oughta say," he boomed, "that I meant no dishonorable accusation of miscount when addressing Sergeant Sam Kayoute. I guess I expressed myself badly."

The commander thanked him and pressed on with some of the new participatory measures. Shadow willed him to take it more slowly, the plans sounded too cut and dried. It was no use willing homsap to do anything . . . maybe another homsap with a good psi range might do it, but he could not. He reached out a gentle impulse to the brain of Richard Black. He entered the sweet singing realms that human senses could not grasp; he wheedled, seductively. To his surprise Black was fully armored against contact; he was but a few impulses short of a defense mode. Gregg was into clean-up detail, life-support revision, here was a pause, for the answer from Regi. The Maestro, of course, had not been coached; it was a first reaction from the regulars to Shadow's plan.

"I accept," said Regi. "I'll work on the LSS revision. If Lieutenant Holder would care to assist?"

Gregg smiled; Boyle smiled; Holder was only too happy to kick the plan along. Gregg went on reading: entertainment, classes, outdoor PT warm-up, surveying committee, and of course the general meal-call, twelve o'clock brunch in the new dome. Integration at the discretion of officers. The coordination of the work rosters by duty officers from both units had already begun. Ronin Boyle stretched, Dell Stout seemed to doze; it was the kind of half-processed data that humans found dry or dull.

Now Gregg was asking for agreement, polling the persons at table from Boyle on down. When it came to Regi, Doc White plucked him by the sleeve. The Maestro argued, Doc White went it alone. Kyle Cavarro, who heard what was said, sent out no distress signal. Shadow still wondered if an error had been made; if they had underestimated an opponent.

"I would like to break in with a query," said Timothy White.

"We have no information as to the whereabouts of a regular crew member, Ensign Loney, H.A.L. He has been missing since the fight in the Rec. Captain Boyle, can you help us in this matter?"

"He's your boy," exclaimed Boyle. "We haven't seen him. Thick? Kraut? Shadow? Any help with this?"

As he gave a negative and made random forays into his memory, Shadow knew there was something. A sound, a word, another shadow, the black boy who whistled like a bird, who ran errands for Winkler, the old wiseguy. Regi said impatiently:

"I assent to the plan, Commander!"

"Doctor White?" asked Gregg.

"I'll assent to the plan," said Timothy White, "if I get an honest answer to one question. Who made it up?"

Gregg and Boyle both spoke at once, in blustering variants of "Now, listen here . . ." Shadow found that White was looking directly at him. He smiled at the young doctor and nodded and said:

"The two ranking officers and their adjutants."

"That will have to do me, then," said Doc White. "I assent."

"Lieutenant Stout?" said Gregg.

Shadow never ceased to be surprised by the behavior of human beings. Stout was a pleasant-faced woman of forty-two, whose name would suit her even better in ten years' time. She sprang to her feet, her blue eyes blazing.

"I'm damned if I'll assent!" she said. "I withold my assent out of protest. A filthy injustice is being done to Lieutenant Anat Asher!"

Ronin Boyle gave a throaty growl of "Killer-Bitch . . ."

"Call to order, Lieutenant Stout," said Commander Gregg quickly. "The moratorium is in force. The new plan is accepted with one dissenting vote."

Shadow began a round of applause, rapping on the trestle in the way that students rapped in lecture halls: he noticed that Regi joined in. Dell Stout sat down again, staring at Commander Gregg. Kyle Cavarro went into action smoothly, reminding Shadow, at least, that he was a trained entertainer.

"We'd like to celebrate the occasion," he said, giving a series of high signs. "Commander . . . Captain Boyle . . ."

Music, the konos' own music, came pouring out of the speakers in the watchpost; girls and boys in rainbow colors came in from the Hill with food and drink on a decorated work trolley. It worked like a charm. Shadow felt the wistful emotion for which he had not yet found a name as he watched the humans open up like flowers. Like the globe orchids that Faith and Vashti placed in the center of the homely trestle.

A woman laughed: it was Zena, the Australian, standing in a group with Fogg and Zak, the guitarist, traditionally bearded. Shadow caught the ripple of sexuality in the laugh and pursued it like a biologist researching pheromones. Was there enough to go around? Was there, somewhere, in some of the impenetrable organic brains, whose lives he worked to support, a dangerous imbalance? The kono team were valuable; he watched the youngest girl, Faith, and her half-sister, Vashti, drifting about like perfume. Faith, now, serving food to the commander and the captain. It was the commander who reached out, most natural thing in the world, and let her smooth shoulder joint fill his hand. Kyle joined the group carrying another tray; Shadow could listen selectively in any gathering.

"Special order for Specialist Rossi," said Kyle. "Or maybe she would like to come to the celebration?"

"No!" said Gregg.

"Go ahead, why not?" said Boyle, smiling.

"My sister could take the tray," said Kyle. "Or ask her to come along . . ."

"Sure, Commander," said Faith Cavarro. "Let me slip along and fetch Marna!"

"No, honey," said Gregg, controlling himself with an effort. "Marna isn't in top form. Doc Petrova gave her something to make her sleep."

A theme played on a drum heralded the approach of Myrrha Devi. Unexpected for Kyle, at any rate, Shadow observed. The Kamalin leader was escorted by Tiria, her elder daughter-in-law, then she came on alone to the commander and the captain. She was able to dismiss Faith without a word; Kyle wavered a moment longer, then he too went away. Shadow listened with a shade more interest.

"You have made your agreement, Commander?" asked Myrrha Devi.

"Yes, ma'am," said Gregg. "Details will be announced."

Myrrha Devi fixed the two men, Gregg and Boyle, steadily with her dark eyes. It was the kind of eye contact, from a non-Silvo, a civilian, a woman, an elderly woman, which produced a marked hostility in Ronin Boyle. He stretched impatiently, put food in his mouth, washed it down.

"I would like to speak to you both privately," she said. "I know how valuable your time is, but I cannot keep silent any longer."

Mystified, the two space heroes exchanged glances. The commander said with humorous deference:

"Well, I guess we could all step into the watchpost. That suit you, Captain?"

Boyle shrugged, marched to the watchpost, let the commander go ahead of him, then closed ranks and let Myrrha Devi enter last, picking her way over the doorsill. Shadow, nicely placed on the outside wall of the post, was teased again by an errant particle of memory. Neither Loney himself nor Winkler. Some third party entering or leaving the watchpost?

"Commander Gregg," said Myrrha Devi, "I believe all the members of the space service receive a psi rating, usually the Duke Matrices."

"Yes, sure," said Gregg uneasily. "We have a couple of good Seeks in the capem. We were talking about it only the other day."

"We got one," said Boyle. "High rating. I tell you who it is, it is Satin Lacey, the cook specialist."

"It's often thought that because my own rating is high and because we are a Kamalin family," said Myrrha, "that all the KONO team are good Seeks. But the distribution is within the normal range."

"What you want the Seeks to do?" demanded Boyle.

"Join me in a search action," said Myrrha Devi. "I am convinced that there are other human beings on this planet. I have seen them and heard them speak."

"Oh, come on," said Boyle. "What d'you mean, lady? Other human beings? Survivors? From the other capems?"

"No," said Myrrha. "Inhabitants. Not aliens, humanoids, or personal hallucinations. These are men and women. They must be a race of castaways. Would that be so impossible?"

Shadow knew the answer, and it excited him as much as it excited the commander and Captain Boyle. He experienced, with a vicarious thrill of pleasure, the way the two men caught their breath.

"A crocking long shot!" whispered Commander Gregg.

"Naw, I don't buy it," said Boyle. "What these humans look like?"

"I saw a woman on a stone tower," said Myrrha Devi simply. "Days ago . . . at the Landfall. I tried to see this woman again, and I saw a harbor, a wharf with small sailing ships at anchor. Then later I saw the crew of a ship. The people are short, brown-skinned, most of them, but some with light hair. They wear hand-woven clothes, ordinary rough human clothes but no synthetic. Hand-made leather boots."

"What were they doing, these mensh?" growled Boyle.

"It looked like a burial at sea," said Myrrha Devi.

"Is this directional at all?" asked Gregg. "Any idea *where* this might be taking place? How far away?"

"Come on, Keith," said Boyle, "you go for this quatsh?"

"At first," said Myrrha Devi, "it was due east, in that place where the sky lights up, at sunset. Where there may be another sea. Now the ship has crossed some barrier. I believe they are sailing in this ocean."

"Do what you want, lady," said Boyle. "Have a séance or a prayer meeting with the rest of the Seeks. Lacey has my permission to attend in her free time."

"I'll check the personnel files," said Gregg. "What were you planning, ma'am?"

"We should watch the sea, Commander," said Myrrha Devi. "I would like to take a survey team up into the hills, near the source of the Silverbrook. George King would lead the way. We would light a signal fire."

Both men chuckled uneasily. Shadow had to act quickly before they turned her down. He stung Ronin with their personal skin contact beeper and entered the watchpost.

"Okay, genius," said Boyle, "what's the evaluation on this?"

"Positive," said Shadow. "We must not underestimate Myrrha Devi's powers, Captain."

He twinkled at Ronin and the commander and noticed at the same time that Myrrha Devi was completely unsurprised by his participation.

"It occurred to me," he said, "that this survey team could provide useful work for a regular officer suspended from general duties."

Gregg got the message first, nudged Boyle and began to smile. Shadow had grown used to Ronin's reaction times—so swift for drill moves, unarmed combat, taking and giving offense, so slow for everything else. He was not prepared for the brief eye-contact with Myrrha Devi: he had underestimated her powers himself. It was as if a laser scalpel had seared through his substitute flesh and found not only that he had no soul, which there was no getting around, but that he *did* have an inner core which others of his kind lacked. A waste for him to serve a man like Ronin Boyle. He dared not follow up the astonishing thought-paths that branched out.

"Why sure!" said Boyle. "This could mean . . ."

"An excellent chance for the reintegration of Lieutenant Asher," said Gregg. "She could lead the survey team."

"This suit you, ma'am?" asked Boyle slyly.

Myrrha Devi bent her head.

"It would be for the benefit of all concerned," she said.

Kyle looked in, with two of the kono girls; the music cubes were changed, Mother Myrrha left with her escort. Captain Boyle and the commander could hardly keep down their laughter.

"Shee-it!" panted Ronin Boyle. "Kickin' the Killer-Bitch out of camp. Didn't I say that Shadow never ran short of good 'uns?"

Kyle's fraternization party went on for a while, long enough for Myrrha Devi's plan to get about. As he strolled down to the dome with Lieutenant Kraut Holder, Regi raised another matter:

"Why have the Silver Cross made this dead set on Anat Asher?"

"Goes a long way back," said the young man easily. "She was media officer, always in the Rec, shipside, always brushing up against the troop. Ronin Boyle don't like to go cap in hand to a regular, female regular, any time."

"And this terrible nickname, this Killer-Bitch?"

"Has to do with the death of Gong Olsen," said Holder.

"How can that be?" persisted Regi. "*Asher* had to do with Olsen's death?"

"Sure," said Holder stolidly. "You told the inquiry she gave this bad, incompetent briefing. *You* gave her the name."

For once the Maestro fell into a shocked silence; he raised a hand to his heart and inscribed a cross on his tunic. Lieutenant Holder changed the subject:

"What you make of the Kamalin lady's notion . . . some kinda human castaway group on the planet?"

"It's possible," said Regi stiffly.

"What I'd sooner find are some of our own people," said the young lieutenant earnestly. "I certainly hope . . ."

"We must have faith," said Regi, regaining some of his bounce. "They're out there, believe me! Our survival is not the only miracle!"

. . . between the moon and the dolphins he had made it to some kind of beach. He felt them pushing at his suit so that he twirled in the odd-tasting seawater, then one of them would stop the spinning motion and urge him along with the current. He was dimly conscious of another floater, spinning at his side, and he tried to soothe the other one, finding his voice, cracked and hoarse. Getting in now, these guys will help us, see the moon up there, be able to give you a hand. Yet when he grated on shingle and slowly, slowly, was rolled up the coarse sand, he was too dead to move. He lay there for a moon or two, and then she had to help him; she was there working him out of the loozy suit, taking off his boots. He drifted away several times but always came back to this gray beach, salty, wind-warped bushes. His eyes were painful, the lids puffed and swollen; she was there all the time, urging him to get up on his hands and knees, crawl up to the spring. There was shade there too, by the life-giving water, and he saw at last that it was the nurse who had come through with him. Nurse lieutenant from Arkady, he

would have her name soon, but right now he was not good on names. Something to do with the sky, was it? Star? Astra? He curled up by the spring, under the tree, still weaker than a baby, and felt her cool hands on his poor face.

7

The crew of the *Dancer* turned to, in showery weather, to begin on the blackray, but Captain Varo knew their feelings. They were cracking their necks to search, to run along the sand, to cast off the blackray and sail off round the island. He was on fire with impatience himself, though he did not admit it, so he had Tom Kirsh row him to the beach in the little cocker boat, morning at eleven.

They came running and dipped their hands in the sea. The flensing of a blackray and the taking of its skin was a hard and dirty job. The beast was too large to be handled entire and was brought ashore in wedge-shaped sections, like pieces of a huge pie. The first wedge drooped on the old timber frame, showing the blue underside of the thick black hide and ugly tatters of flesh.

"We must begin a search!" said Simon Varo. "None of us will be easy in our minds until we go further. Mr. Maddern, I will send you out in the longboat, bearing west, to catch this fresh wind and round the island."

"Ready, Captain!" cried the first mate. "Who shall I have?"

"Damn few," said Varo ruefully. "Flower Wilm, for a nurse aide, and Mam Cross. Will you three stand the gaff, d'ye think?"

"Aye, Captain," said Winna Cross, "we'll take her round, no trouble."

In fact it was a mildly hazardous journey. The strong wind and the current drove every boat westward. The crew of the longboat must get themselves onto the lee shore of the island or they would be carried to the ends of the world.

"That's not all," said Cap Varo. "If we go well here and the sun comes out, I will send a party to climb the Lookout Hill."

He could see that everyone wanted to go—even Tom Kirsh would have tried out his land legs.

"I have a choice of many good souls, I know that," he said, "but it is in my mind to send Lon Adma, as leader, Man Gruner, Molly Kelly, and Paddy Rork."

Paddy felt a thump of excitement in his chest: he could not help grinning—Ketty and Seela both looked glum. They all went back to the filthy, backbreaking work, hacking lumps of flesh from the underside of the blackray segment, dripping on the rack above their heads.

At fourteen hours, midday, with the sun coming through, Simon Varo gave a briefing in his cabin for the crew of the longboat.

"Watch the charts!" he ordered. "Stand well out, away from the reefs and shoals! Keep a sharp lookout for flotsam, floating wreckage, stains or turbulence in the sea. Search any reed-rafts that come by. Have a care, Mr. Maddern, for our good longboat. Do not *overload*, for the Vail's sake, if you must take on survivors!"

"Father, will you have them push the poor souls back in the water?" cried Megan, who was sitting in on the briefing.

"Make some beachhead for them!" said Captain Varo testily. "Better to wait for a second trip than lose the longboat!"

"Captain," said Flower Wilm, "I have had a good idea. How would it be if we painted a big red cross on a little jib sail and used it as a signal flag?"

"A red cross!" echoed Megan. "Oh, yes!"

It was a medical symbol of great power, used by Doctors

College in the city and familiar throughout the Rhomary land.

"Yes," said Simon Varo, "yes—see to it, Flower. For a good strong red you might use a little liver-blood from the blackray. Consult with Tom Kirsh. Mind you, I cannot swear this symbol will still be known. . . ."

The longboat put to sea as soon as she was provisioned, to use the remaining hours of daylight for the run up the south coast with the strong easterly. The weary crew of scrapers waved from the beach; Megan Varo stood at the bridge rail and watched the eager wind fill the sail as the boat left the harbor. She thought of Hilo Hill, the seacook, who had crossed the ocean in such a boat. The red cross showed up well on the jib sail, stretched to dry. Tom Kirsh appeared on the bridge and waved and grumbled.

"Some would say this is a mad trick of your father's, Megan, my gal. We are down three in a crew of eleven."

"They are not lost!" said Megan angrily. "Last trip to this island, to Palmland, you sailed yourself on that course as far as Rivermouth."

"It was earlier in the year," said the old man. "See here . . . I've brought you something."

She saw that he was carrying a cut-down gourd, the sort he used in his galley. The two of them were alone on the bridge; down below there was only Molly Kelly sweeping up. Tom Kirsh looked about, then spread a clean blue cloth on the deck and up-ended the gourd upon it. A strange group of small objects rattled onto the spread cotton.

"I've been preparing the delicacies from our blackray," he said. "Taken the roe for salting, and so forth. This haul is from her gully trap."

The blackrays fed upon the shoals of criller shrimp, filtered through a bony grid for size and tenderness. Foreign bodies collected in a holding gut until they were vomited up again. Now Megan saw some very clean stones, parts of fish-heads, pieces of wood, knobs of hard seaweed. Scattered among these natural objects were five, six, seven splashes of bright color. Yellow, luminous pink-red, purple, green. Megan cried out, she knew before she paid any attention to the shapes of the new objects that it was true. They had seen a starship come down in this ocean.

She sat down on the deck and began examining the new haul. A flat, yellow slip of wood, roughly ten centimeters long; a strip of cloth, printed with purple flowers; a twisted scrap of metal, green and silver, very light in weight. She had left the most striking object until last: a round ball of semitransparent stuff, the size of a small plum, with a loop attachment like a stalk. It was an unbearably bright pinkish red, and yes, when she shaded it a little with her hand, she saw a gleam of light. Tom Kirsh chuckled.

"Yes," he said. "She glows, that one. Like a fish-trail in the night. Have you figured it out?"

"No," she said. "Have you, Tom?"

"Surely," said the old man, "though it seems very fancy got up for such a humble bit of equipment. See here . . ."

He took his gourd and filled it with water from the barrel under the bridge. He set it down beside them and popped the mystery object into the water. It floated upright; he held it under, tipped it from side to side, but it always bobbed upright again.

"Now, d'ye see?"

"A fishing float," said Megan Varo. "A fishing float made of what was called plast or syntho, some off-world material."

She reached out again and picked up two brownish objects. They could have been pods or scraps of kelp, but when she flattened them out they were perfectly square, seamless bags of a fine, papery fabric. Inside there were clumps of dark flecks, like leaves or seeds.

"These as well," she said. "Vail knows what that is in the packets. Tom, this is a great find. I must list it straightaway and fetch my father."

"Ach, girl," he said uneasily, "let's hope these folk are as harmless as their bits and pieces."

With all this treasure to pore over Cap Varo was more thoughtful than ever and reluctant to let the second party set out, even as far as the Lookout Hill. He went so far as to join the scrapers himself. . . . Paddy was surprised to see how handily the captain stripped the hide with his small curved knife. The plain fact was that the damned blackray was too big for the *Dancer:* they did not have the capacity for storing all its oil once the flesh had been rendered down.

It was a time for quick decisions: next afternoon, when Paddy had expected to be climbing the hill, looking for that silvery shape among collapsed palm trees, the rest of the hide was taken floating. Everyone left stripped down, went into the water, and skinned the remaining three-quarter round of the sea creature. Even the captain himself and old Tom Kirsh scraped and hacked and cursed in the turbid water off the stern. The hide was piled on the deck or ferried awkwardly to the beach, for they sorely missed the longboat. The flesh was gathered into all their nets and floated to a shallow rock pool on the western edge of the bay, upwind of the *Dancer.* Chances were that a shoal of scavenger fish would come through the heads and make short work of this cache.

"Cheer up, Father," said Megan. "Maybe the Spacers will lend you a big fireproof tank or a plastic net."

Simon Varo was sitting moodily in his wooden bathtub, which Tom Kirsh topped up now and then with kettles from the galley.

"Go along," he said. "I'm a poor man, with a daughter who gives cheek. Tell 'em not to wait supper."

Megan went away, and Simon Varo shook his blue bead around in its matching shell. He had had a dream about it, nestling in the shell. Now if he held the shell in just this fashion it recalled, of all things, a human ear. . . .

Megan was not at the companionway before she heard her father utter an enormous cry. It sounded as though he had leaped from his bathtub. The door of his cabin flew open, and Cap Varo, stark naked, bellowed:

"I have it!"

She could only follow him, with a towel and his clean undershirt, while he rushed up on deck.

"Dry hell!" cried Tom Kirsh. "He has scraped his brain!"

"I have it!"

The captain's voice was extraordinarily loud, and he clutched his head; the crew came from everywhere.

"The bead! The bluggy blue bead!"

Cap Varo suffered himself to be made decent with a towel around the waist.

"The blue bead plays music," he said at last. "It is some tiny musical device."

"Bead?" said Lon Adma. "The one from the reed-raft?"

"Just so!" said the captain, brimming with excitement. "Here!"

He snatched the blue bead from where it nestled, stuck in his ear.

"Try it, Lon," he said. "Someone else must try it!"

The coxun drew back as if he had been offered a leech-limpet to stick in his ear. Molly Kelly said bravely:

"Where does it go, Captain?"

She slung her black braid aside and allowed him to affix the bead. There were a few tense seconds with the crew wondering whether it was Molly's turn to run screaming, then an expression of wonder grew on her face. She uttered a few words in her own family speech, then said:

"It does for a fact! It plays the strangest musical sounds! Here Seela, you try it!"

"Have a care!" said Cap Varo. "Treat it gently!"

Megan began to urge her father into his clean undershirt, and, when that was done, Tom Kirsh, shaking his head, held out the captain's britches. Cap Varo paid no attention whatever to any loss of his dignity, Paddy noticed, and that was why he never lost it.

There was a tenacity about the captain that impressed and exasperated his crew. During supper he told them what *must* follow the discovery of this musical trinket.

"I grant you," he said, "it is probably nothing more nor less than a collection of music, an electrone music bit or whatever it is called. I do not know if it plays two hours of music or twenty. We have no way of controlling it, switching it off or going backwards. We've already found out, between Seela and Molly and Ketty, that it picks up where it left off, so far as we can tell with this strange stuff. The point is . . ."

"We have to listen to all of it," said Megan. "Of course."

"I can think of reasons," said Lon Adma, "but I'd like to hear yours first, Captain."

"In case there is anything in among the music that can give us more information," said Simon Varo. "Some words. Some names. In the radio trials on the Western Sea years ago, the Navigation Board were very particular about *call signs*. As if I would say on my wireless device, 'Here is the brig *Dancer*, out of Derry and the Gann Station, Master and Captain Simon Varo, presently at anchor in Blackray Bay, Palmland, in Gline's Ocean.' What we must listen for are any signs of this kind."

"A damn pity that the radio thing never worked well enough," said Lon Adma.

"Perhaps it will," said Cap Varo earnestly, "perhaps it will, Lon, with the new knowledge we get from these bead-makers!"

So he sorted out, with Megan, a team of listeners with good writing skills, as well as pens, ink, and paper, together with the captain's clock. They made themselves comfortable in the snug, with cool-tea at hand: Megan Varo, Seela Conor, Ketty Merrow.

Paddy was dragged off to bed to be ready for an early start in the morning; even the captain fell asleep in his cabin, exhausted after all the scraping. The listeners never lost their enthusiasm; the strange sounds went on unabated; Megan took notes.

They called the first hours of the music "drum-tootle-wail"; it was the strangest of all the music in the bead, and there was more of it than any other sort. It was just possible for them to sort out separate "pieces" in the tapestry of sounds.

Then about two hours thirty into the bead there was a marked change; Seela made a note, stopped, the bead was passed around for a check. This music was more traditional, played on guitars or other strummers, with a fiddle in some places, and a loud wind instrument, maybe a brass trumpet. Seela listened out her turn, then Ketty gave a cry and wrote on her pad: *yellow*. She passed the bead around and they agreed, it was unmistakable. Thus the probability of a ship containing Earth mensh was raised to something like certainty: the music bead was playing "Yellow Submarine." So they named music of this type "trad-strum," and in the course of two hours and forty minutes they believed that they had identified three other melodies: "Saints March," "Stars of Home," and something known as the "Eurosong" or "The Brotherhood Anthem." They were disappointed when the first music, the drum-tootle-wail, took over again, without a break for a further hour, but by now they were getting to like the sounds a little better.

Megan was listening when the first words were spoken. She was alert, because the drum-tootle died away and she heard an emptiness, she heard a place with echoes and a clanking in her ear. A man's voice said, very smooth and gentle:

"! . . . noahentothuh *talent* heeronthold *Serendip Dana* . . ."

She wrenched out the bead and frantically scribbled the non-sense down.

"I think I got the ship name!" she breathed.

"Is it a call sign?" asked Ketty.

"No," said Megan. "I've no idea what the man is really talk-ing about. He has a smooth, soft voice, and his words run to-gether, except when he speaks some words right out."

"Tell us the name, Third!" begged Seela.

"No," said Megan. "You must both take turns, write down every sound you hear, then we'll compare. He could say it again."

"Holy Jenz guide me!" said Ketty.

She made the circle of blessing on her forehead and stuck the bead in place. She began to scribble, let out her breath and laughed, and took the bead out again.

"I know what he is doing," she said. "It is as if he is saying the program at a sing-song."

Seela took her turn and screwed up her face and laughed and scribbled. She passed the bead back to Megan, pink with ex-citement.

". . . comes thuh *one and only Mocking Bird!*" cried the man.

Drum-tootle variants made a soft background, and Megan was overwhelmed by whistles, chirps, and cascades of high head-notes. She listened, and the sounds seemed to wake echoes in her brain. She took out the bead and was almost speechless.

"What is it? Third? Megan?"

"Birds," said Megan. "Someone is making the sounds of the birds of Earth."

She gave the bead to Seela Conor. Already she was able to write down the announcer's words more easily. Seela listened

with tears streaming down her cheeks, and Ketty took a turn listening to the Mocking Bird. The performance was meant to be
seen: the bird-caller seemed to dance or jump or strike poses . . .
he cried out *"Yay!"* and *"Ru-bay!"* There was a melody, his call-
sign as it were, and by the end of the number they all knew it.
Then he signed off, in a similar accent to the announcer:

"Like-ta thank the ko-nose an specially Kai-uhl onna old
vaibz. Bin great entertaining you all!"

A whistle and he was gone; nothing followed. After a long
thirty-minute silence the drum-tootle started all over again from
the beginning . . . so far as the listeners could judge. When they
cleverly allowed for an old-earth sixty-minute hour this seemed
to add up to a bead that could hold seven hours of recorded
sounds. Now it was three o'clock of the new day, the faithful listeners were hog tired, and the name of the ship, which Megan
still kept to herself and played around with on her badly blotted
sheet of paper, was buried six hours into that beadful of crazy
stuff.

"But, Third," said Ketty Merrow, "will the thing not play
somewhere else? Must it be only in a person's ear? Might it not
move along in its song when attached to a hand or a nose?"

They were laid low by a long attack of sleepy giggles: the
bead, the drum-tootle-wail, the trad-strum, another chorus of
the Saints March, it was all too much for them. Megan gave it
up and ordered all hands to their bunks. She prepared a memo,
for the Lookout Hill party, listing the tunes, keeping everything
very simple. She knew that the poor devils would be overbriefed
in any case, by her father. . . .

Paddy forgot everything except the misty air of morning and the
solid ground under his boot soles. He walked in the middle with
Molly Kelly, and Man Gruner brought up the rear. They
climbed up quickly out of the bay and followed the ghost of a
path up through the tall reeds and scrub. Further up, where one
could see the cliff-tops off to the east, there were a few yunka
trees. Lon Adma called back:

"There you are, Paddy! There's your Lookout Hill!"

It was a perfect cone, underneath its trees and grasses, standing out against the darker heights and rocky outcrops of the Blue Ridge, across the valleys.

"I see it, Coxun!" cried Paddy. "Is there an earthman on top playing a drum?"

"You'd run fast if there was," said Man Gruner. "My land legs are slow in coming. That Adma makes a cracking pace."

Molly Kelly laughed aloud and began another of the songs on her list. Their grasp of the words was very uncertain, the songs were all run-down old sing-alongs, used for news ballads. In any case, who knew if the words would be the same?

> "Oh when the saints all strip their threads
> "And do the boola on their beds . . ."

"That's enough from you, Paddy Rork!" said Molly, laughing. "You got that one at school!"

Lon called a halt under a decent-sized kerry. They were already above the level of the cliffs and could see far out over the ocean, beyond the mist. It was a perfect day for climbing, and they had several hours of the cool morning left to them. When the telescope was passed around they took turns looking back at the *Dancer* in the bay: they saw Tom Kirsh laying the wash out to dry on the hatchcovers. When Paddy's turn came he saw Megan Varo, who had been alone on the beach cleaning up, walk off to the east. She climbed up the same track they had taken out of the bay, then took the low road toward the stone garden where the silkies lived. The Lookout party packed up, feeling the summit of their hill beckoning them on, and away they went again.

II

Loney came back in the first days of the new deal and alleged that he had been in the dunes, looking for Wemyss and the howlers. For the look of the thing, and also to test the discipline in camp, Winkler sent him to Lieutenant Regi, who had been named head of security for the regulars. The Maestro had organized himself an ordered command post in the dome, low on home comforts but high on efficiency. In the next roomy cubicle he was setting up a lab; Linda Baumer undertook light clerical duties; Richard Black put out a weather report and data updates.

Regi tried to record, most accurately, what everyone did during work periods; he had the oxper keep track of equipment; he cast an eye over all the dietary charts, the snack demand outlets, the graymart, where goodstuff was bartered. Yet all the cheerful pedantry, the spirit of discovery had left him. He stared at the young ensign and said:

"You're lying. Suppose I insist on knowing where you've been, Ensign Loney?"

"Moratorium, Lieutenant," said Loney. "It hangs together with the fight in the Rec."

"You can serve at brunch next two days. Meld yourself to Sergeant Kayoute," said Regi coldly. "We are responsible for all personnel."

"Maestro," said Loney suddenly, "are we regulars, or Silvos . . . service personnel, forever? Like till we grow old and die? When does the chain break? When do we stop playing faggidy spaceships?"

Regi could not resist this appeal. It happened to have been the subject of a lively discussion in headquarters the very night before the Crisis Round Table.

"There's the time and distance section," he said, "in the manual. Hangs together with the question of supply, you understand . . . being able to supply the needs of the capem at full complement."

"So the manual leaves us an escape hatch," said Loney. "Or would you call it a loophole?"

"Get out of here!" shouted Regi, waving his hands in the old way. "Go serve those barbarians their brunch!"

"I'm going!" Hal grinned. "One other thing, Maestro . . . Shouldn't more interest be shown in the *possibility* of other humans on this planet?"

"Don't try for a place in Asher's Ashram, Loney!" said Regi bitterly. "You're way too late!"

Long after the boy had disappeared into the hurly-burly of the brunch rush, Regi sat and stared at his desk monitor, glumly comparing work figures. He worked without a break, thinking often of the outward-bound party of "surveyors" walking where he and his team had gone, searching for water. He knew he was guilty of envy, in respect of Anat Asher, and of pride, at first, when he criticized her briefing. His anger was difficult to control, had always been a problem, and he was loath to say that he was safe from sloth or accidie or even lechery. (A group of bathers, boys and girls, soaring down naked from the tops of the trees, with jump packs . . . just east of sunset beach. No, he wouldn't take that path again.)

Regi began groping dreamily into the personnel files; he had full access now, as Asher's replacement. He found that the psi ratings of the regulars were a steady average; Asher herself was above average; Ivan Dalny, the Arkadian, tested high. Only one file showed an outstanding psi rating. It struck him like a blow, a message full of doom, an accusation of guilt. *Lieutenant Arthur Morgan.* Morgan was dead. Had he seen what lay ahead? Was Morgan the lost catalyst of the whole enterprise, who could have made things work out better? Couldn't he, Alessandro Regi, have overcome his personal distaste for the man, exercised tolerance, not judgment?

Still under the influence of this discovery Regi went out after the siesta at seventeen hours to examine the supply compartments in the Rec with Lieutenant Holder, Silvo oxper James Carter assisting. Both officers had done their homework and spent an exhaustive session with Sergeant Kayoute and Sergeant Lacey of the Silver Cross, ascertaining exactly the composition and placement of the food stores. They began at the back of the high, cold bays, checking the counters on each folding door. Regi was reassured by the strength of the independent insulation, unscathed by the descent or the brief instability during the bad weather.

So they came through the freeze-dries, the Q, or "packaged basics," meaning hardtack of various kinds, and on to the "day-trays," consisting of nearly everything that made eating worthwhile. Poultry, fish, meat, promeat, condiments and condiment vegetables, block sauces, approved additives, egg preparations, milk and nusoy products. There were two separate bays, each with its own door counter. The nearer one was almost empty.

Something got through to Regi as Carter, the oxper, moved on to the second bay. Afterward he thought it was an increase in condensation on the walls or overhead.

"Door counter not functioning, Lieutenant!" said Carter to Holder.

Holder stepped up, gave the dial unit a tap with his gloved finger. Regi saw the door move fractionally.

"Wait!" he said.

The door was unfastened, and its surface was running wet, not misted. A fold of bulging insulation material could be seen inside the lip of the unfastened door.

"Shee-it!" whispered Lieutenant Holder. "You reckon . . . ?"

"The whole bay has gone!" said Regi.

He tried to fasten the door but could not get it first time. Carter got it fastened, but not before a first bubble of foul air had found its way out. The door counter worked fine and showed a temperature that left no room for hope.

"Pressure," said Regi. "Get it down, Carter."

Carter was already fingering the valves delicately. The two officers stared at each other.

"How's this gonna be given out?" asked Holder. "Without starting more trouble?"

Regi appreciated that this was an advance in the young Silvo's thinking. He saw that the unfastened door was a direct result of the fight in the Rec. It might even have taken place on the first recount made by the Silver Cross at some time during the instability trauma. It would have come to light when the trays in the adjoining bay had been used up.

"We'll take it to headquarters," he said.

"It's a deadcut bad deal, huh, Lieutenant?" said Holder. "Not just a loss of taste-foods . . ."

Regi was oppressed by the unfairness of things, as if none of this was his field, it had all been thrust upon him. He gave a despairing wave of his hand, went to the main doors, and peered

out into the Rec. Shadow Adams stood on the threshold, and
Regi stepped back to let him in. It was not a chance appearance: obviously Carter had sent the bad news to his leader at
once. No one spoke until Shadow had examined the bay with the
melt.

"It's possible," he suggested politely, "that the whole of the
bay's frame was deformed by the landing, making the door seal
faulty."

"It's possible," snapped Regi, "that Sam Kayoute who managed these supplies has been kept out of this place by your stupid accusation of miscount, as part of a political intrigue. It's
possible *you* loused the door, Daniel Adams, making your count."

"No!" said Shadow. "That's not possible, Lieutenant!"

"There's a law of diminishing returns at work," said Regi,
with a tight smile. "There is a point at which intellectual ability,
in creatures of your kind, means that you become more human.
Cleverer, sure, but at the same time *prone to error.*"

"Take it easy!" said Holder.

He described the scene later to his new friend, Zena McKay.

"It was unreal!" he said. "These two crockin' *Big Brains*, Maestro Regi, the genius from Systems, and our Silvo superbrain,
Shadow Adams, splitting hairs and arguing while our food, our
good food, went down the pipe!"

Zena had her own question:

"Martin, you believe that scuttle saying Lieutenant Regi is,
you know, a priest, member of the Catholic Christian religion?"

"Yes!" said Martin Holder seriously. "Yes honey, I think it
could be true."

Whatever Regi's affiliations Holder had to admit that the
Maestro and Shadow, working as a team, managed the disaster
in stores with speed and discretion. A mixed oxper team took
over the difficult "fold-down" of the insulated container within
the bay; Regi handled Sam Kayoute. The spoiled food, compacted in volume, was brought away to the incinerator, secretly,
like so many dead bodies.

After he had sworn and raged and blamed the Silver Cross,
Sam Kayoute turned his attention to the problem of making good
the loss. The remaining day-trays must be stretched. It was a

process every cook was familiar with: batches of new sauce must be conjured up, with reconstituted binders from the freeze-dries, plus the taste-makers from the Cook's Pantry, Sam's secret store.

Other methods of refilling the trays were at hand: at Sunset Beach, near the spot where the commander and the captain had eaten supper, there were fires glowing. The area was off limits for strollers, but Doc White and his team had been asked to step along, check the action. The cooking smell was mouth-watering for some, but Mai Lon had to be excused, and few konos were spotted taking the air.

Timothy White stood with Dell Stout in the shadows peering into the circle of firelight; there were three long spits turning. Sam Kayoute and Satin Lacey, wearing work whites and paper caps, strode about basting the neat carcasses of nine pigarees. Two oxper were busy at the big charcoal grill.

"What are *those?*" murmured Dell Stout.

Ed Rowe was back in shape, and she recognized Bob Moore, none the worse for his shutdown. It seemed to her like a long time ago now. First there had been the Cookhouse Tree, now there was this hunters' barbecue. Living off the land.

"Link sausages, Lieutenant," said Ed Rowe cheerily.

"You want one with original Sambang, kiwi-sour, or tomato-mustard?" echoed Bob Moore.

She took two samples, with all the sauces, back to the doctor. They ate meditatively.

"Sam put too much bang in his Sambang," said Tim White. "Compared to the sauces the sausage is a health food."

"Who's that in back, dining?" she asked.

Half a dozen privileged persons were taking supper, down toward the beach.

"Gregg is there, with Boyle," said Tim White. "Off you go, Dell."

She moved away quietly in the shadows, wishing Anat Asher was right there, not camped in the jungle by an unnamed river. As she slipped away in the direction of the capem a fire blazed up and showed Ronin Boyle, on his feet. He gave a shout, possibly a toast for his fellow diners, perhaps just aggressive punctuation of a story.

The timing was good: she came in through the main forward hatch and found the Rec empty, except for Winkler, lounging at the door of the watchpost. He gave her the high sign: the coast was clear. Dell Stout walked briskly to Headquarters. She was given a routine query by the door viewer, replied with name and rank, walked in. She crossed purposefully to the door of Gregg's double cabin, knocked, and activated an acoustic signal, a little bedside beeper that she had been told about.

"Who's there?"

The challenge was given by Petrova herself, just inside the door.

"Stout, Dell. Nurse-Lieutenant, visiting Specialist Marna Rossi."

The door was opened and the big Russian woman practically dragged Dell into the cabin.

"Heavens, you pick your time, Lieutenant!" she said.

Dell Stout saw that there were two empty bunks, arranged side by side: the cabin had been "honeymooned." She tried to keep the alarm out of her voice.

"Where's your patient?"

"Watching trivid," said Petrova. "Then she'll have supper and go to sleep. Her routine is laid down to the minute, but she is very determined, she will stick to it. Diet is likely to become more difficult."

Dell began to feel relief and a touch of shame.

"Diet . . . ?" she asked.

"We try to avoid many additives and synthetics," said Petrova. "Freshness is important, but at the same time I don't like to think of a pregnant woman eating pigaree."

"Maybe a little broth?" suggested Dell.

She followed Big Doc across to the communicating door, and they went into Rossi's own cabin.

"Visitor!" said Petrova gruffly.

Dell realized that of the two only Petrova had changed; she was so absorbed that it made her more outgoing. Marna Rossi, propped up in her bunk with trivid, flowers, cassette books, a knitter frame, looked gorgeous. She had a fresh color, bright eyes.

"Hi, Lieutenant!"

Dell sat by the bunk, moved by the scene in spite of herself, and said:

"So you decided."

"Yes!" said Rossi. "I was a little socked, back there, the gravity was getting to me. Big Doc swears she'll bring me to term. Everything will be fine if I do like the doctor says."

Dell Stout knew what the doctor must say. It was a risk, a challenge in increased gravity, but the answer must be the same as it was on Earth, on Arkady, or in space. Bed rest. Women stayed in bed for six, seven, nine months if necessary, in order to carry their children. Even allowing for an early birth, Rossi's ordeal had just begun.

"Nothing is too good for this patient, Doctor," said Dell. "I think she should have a better room, the quarters on this side have only the high louver windows like the Rec."

"We need light and air," said Petrova. "Remember, Marna, you were thinking of a little roof-garden . . . ?"

"Yeah, sure," said Marna, "with some kind of elevator to get me up there."

"I'll get the Super Team to submit a plan," said Dell.

They sat and watched the end of the trivid, which made them cry a little because it was set in Yellowstone National Park. Petrova gave Dell a vodka, Marna sipped Ceylon tea. As she was leaving Marna Rossi said:

"Keith says it is a long shot . . . this crazy idea with the humans already living on the planet."

Dell grasped her interest in the subject: humans had survived and reproduced their kind on this world. Petrova saw her out. When they were in the adjoining bedroom Dell Stout ventured onto thin ice.

"Doctor," she said, "I came here to make sure that Specialist Rossi was a voluntary patient. There have been rumors."

The Russian woman's broad face became hard and unsmiling.

"This is all politics," she said. "You see for yourself how the girl is progressing."

"No one," said Dell delicately, "no one from any faction has any say in Marna's treatment except yourself?"

"No one!" growled Petrova.

She was silent for a moment, then made an enigmatic pronouncement:

"I have my professional loyalty. I am not to be recruited for their schemes."

They could hear raised voices in Headquarters: the commander and the captain had come back from supper. Big Doc went straight on through, ahead of Dell, without a trace of hesitation or embarrassment. The noise level did not go down at once, and the scene imprinted itself on Dell Stout's consciousness as strange and disquieting.

The commander, florid and handsome, lounged in his chair wearing his white and blue dress unisuit. The young girl, Faith, was serving him a drink from a tray, while another kono girl, Vashti, stood at an open food locker. Captain Boyle did not lounge so much as sprawl in his chair, with a strange garment, a cloak or cape, green smudged with brown, lying where he had cast it off, flowing over the chair back. His right arm and shoulder were bare; he had slipped half out of his tunic so that a Silvo oxper, Willie Hale, could give him a massage. Kyle Cavarro stood in the shadows, working on his vox.

The attention of everyone else was centered on three Silvos: Hoot Wells and Mary "Atom" Klein stood on either side of the Mexican boy, Loco Ramirez. Hoot gripped his arm, and Mary Klein did something to Loco's hand that made him jerk with pain. Hoot Wells was saying:

". . . stand up to another round . . ."

"Don't bother me!" said Boyle. "I'm goin' out again tomorrow."

He stopped, seeing Dell Stout, and the talk died a little. She caught the commander's eye and saluted.

"Lieutenant!"

Gregg acknowledged her greeting. As Petrova showed her out, Boyle could be heard saying:

"What does Big Doc say? See what she says, hey Loco . . . ?"

Dell almost ran back to the watchpost, but she found that the shift had changed. Zero Zavaski and Chip Reynolds were doing a stint: they were good enough mensh, she knew that, but still Silvos. She left a cryptic message for Winkler, went back to sick bay where Tim White was waiting for her report.

It had to be a very positive report as regards the condition of Marna Rossi. She was not under duress. She had taken a difficult option, was in excellent condition, and had the full attention of Dr. Petrova. Visiting hours could be arranged: her cabin could be built out.

"You're upset," said Doc White, pouring fresh tea. "Still have some doubts, Lefftenant?"

Dell tried to describe the scene, the atmosphere in Headquarters.

"Shee-it, Doc," she finished, "it was more like some barbarian rambo-jambo, some loozy survival lodge, than the headquarters of Capem Fiver. And those young girls looking on, the konos, acting as servants . . ."

"The word you need," said Doc White, "is *impropriety.*"

"Yes," said Dell Stout, "yes, I guess that is what I do mean. And who knows what that was all about with Loco Ramirez? Doc, I swear that bitch Klein was hazing him some way . . . twisting a thumb-chain, I don't know."

"Kyle Cavarro was there," said Timothy White thoughtfully.

"You mean, he could look out for his sisters?"

"Yes, that too. Kyle was there, but someone was missing . . ."

"Shadow Adams!"

They took sick calls—Lelani Buck had dropped a brick of high-fiber bean meat on her toe, Carl Johnson, son of Azamo and Tiria, had sprained an ankle on the way back from the Orinoco.

"Shee-it!" cried Dell, "is *that* what they called it?"

"We all thought it was a great name," said Carl.

"Who dreamed it up?"

"We drew lots," said the boy. "George King got lucky. We were glad because it was *his* river, Lieutenant. He discovered it."

Dell Stout had to hold back a scrap of service thinking. She very nearly said: "George King is an oxper!" Now she saw that this was out of place, even unworthy. Things got worse, other things got better, maybe.

"How's your grandmother doing, Carl?"

"Myrrha Devi is just fine," he said. "Good thing my ankle didn't go when we carried up the litter."

III

Anat Asher rose before dawn and stole out into the new world. She slipped through the tall reeds and sat on a rock looking down at the camp. If she turned her head she could see the steep spurs of the heights, hear the sound of the waterfall; below her the river spread out, broad and quiet, winding into the dark reaches of the alien jungle, flashing out in silver coils, flowing to the sea. How Regi and Holder had come to miss it, with their survey teams, was a mystery. The Silverbrook divided from the Orinoco just below the falls. A glance over the next hill would have revealed the river system, the high plunge of the waters, the lovely curve of river beach where the camp stood, the frail reed-groves against the high ridge.

The place did not teem like the jungles of earth, but it was full of life: flying lizards clicked and churred; a boring insect hummed on a low note in the roots of the trees; the leaf creatures hung about in chains and clusters. Further downstream a species of walking bird and a few shy pigarees had been seen drinking at twilight.

The main pigaree population inhabited the valleys at the foot of the stony massif—she had thought of calling it Mount Morgan—which formed the end of the ridge. The hunters had trodden out a path from the capem and erected a signpost at the entry to the valleys: Hunt Park. The new track to her peaceful retreat led to the west, over a rise.

There was movement in the camp: the konos, Azamo, Tiria, and Zak, were limbering up. Dalny, with Arkadian toughness, dived into the river and swam about; the Orinoco was cold but not icy. Would it affect his psi rating? Vannie Frost, up for a visit, was still sound asleep. Anat heard a rustling of the reeds at her side: George King came out, carrying a vacuum flask with her morning coffee.

"Good day for the climb," he said.

Anat sighed. George, who was never tested for psi, read her mind easily, and so did Ray Green.

"I can't help it," she said. "It seems like a dumb thing to do."

"You don't believe Myrrha Devi?"

"Yes," said Anat, "yes, I take her suggestion seriously. We'll do what she wants."

"What's the problem, Lieutenant?" George grinned.

"I think I should be down at the capem working, not goofing off in this beautiful place."

"You don't accept Sergeant Winkler's view?"

"Yes," said Anat, "it's a great idea. This is the alternative camp, the one for the new tribe."

"Tomorrow," said George, "I thought I would head out and meet Wemyss."

"Will you be able to see his hideout on the cliffs from up there?"

"Might be able to get onto his little brush collector," said George.

She turned her head and stared up at the tumbled stones of the massif, the place facing the sea where the climbing party planned to light a signal fire. Down below in the camp Myrrha Devi had come to stand at the water's edge and salute the risen sun, which was turning the distant western reaches of the island green-gold.

"Time for you to go," she said.

They walked down into camp. The konos had a quiet, winning way with them that sometimes made Anat long for the moody give and take of service personnel. Myrrha Devi had no difficulty in combining psi concentration with everyday activities, but Anat was too self-conscious. At least the rapport with Ivan Dalny, the highest-rated regular, was working well, and he was an experienced climber. The gravity had slowed him down a lot, he claimed, but no one else could notice this. Anat persuaded him at least to take along his airblend equipment.

By nine hours, island time, there stood the climbing party, ready to set out, and they were embraced and sent on their way by the three stay-at-homes: Myrrha Devi, Anat, and Vannie Frost, awake at last.

"Shee-it!" said Vannie, "you guys look like the Earthmen from some old trivid!"

George King, in the lead, wore the oxper version of a silver-suit, and Ivan Dalny was fully suited up, with helmet and air-blend, bringing up the rear. Between them were the three konos, in bright blue-green bodysuits with hoods: Azamo Johnson, Tiria Wing Johnson—the highest psi rating of anyone except Myrrha herself—and Zak Cavarro.

No one watched as they walked up from the camp and followed the path George had chosen up the ridge. Myrrha Devi, who had become increasingly silent, chose a special place to sit, facing the river. Anat, in contact with Dalny, began to repeat herself.

"Take it easy, Ivan! There is no time pressure!"

"Not so sure about that, Lieutenant!"

"What? You have something?"

"The vibes are strong . . ."

She was sure he was teasing her. It seemed that Myrrha Devi had called her name: she looked at the Kamalin leader and saw her make the gesture for concentration. Vannie Frost was working in her garden plot, weeding the tomatoes and sweet corn. Presently George King checked in:

"Hunting party from Capem Fiver working the Hunt Park area."

Occasionally, when the wind was right, Anat had imagined that she heard shots, over the noise of the waterfall.

"Hear the shooting, George?" she asked.

"Well, *I* can hear it, Lieutenant."

The day was bright and mild now; the sun had warmed the small, round stones of the beach. At brunch time, twelve o'clock, Vannie rustled up a good vegetable curry; Anat took it up to Myrrha Devi with a fresh brew of tea. While the older woman ate up her food like a good child Anat stared at the mountain wall. She saw the climbing party emerge from the scrub and begin the last part of the ascent. The silver and blue-green figures filled her with concern, with hope. She could not leave Myrrha Devi; she settled on the dried reeds beside her.

"Not long now!" said Myrrha firmly.

Anat shut her eyes and summoned up all her concentration, all her slight knowledge of meditation skills. She thought of a ship, beyond the sea mist, sails billowing, a ship right out there on the ocean. She tried to find a place in the chain of wisdom linking Myrrha Devi with Tiria, with her two sons, Azamo and Zak, with Ivan Dalny. She felt the link, but her breathing was wrong, she exhaled deeply and opened her eyes. Myrrha Devi was watching her with fond amusement, as a mother watches her child.

"You're doing fine!" she said. "Not long now, I am sure. They can see it now."

"What . . . ?"

"The ship," said Myrrha Devi.

Anat stood up and turned toward the stony peak. The party was on the platform steadily going through the motions, the setting up of the smudge pot. Their bonfire was no more than a container of no-residue barbecue fuel in a portable incinerator.

Before her eyes the smallest blue-green figure, Tiria, turned toward the camp, down below, and raised both arms in salute. Ivan Dalny seemed to be jumping up and down.

"Lieutenant," said George King, *"there is a ship!"*

"Where?" she demanded. "How far out?"

George was on the far side of the rocky platform, obscured a little by curls of smoke.

"At anchor," he said. "Sailing vessel, estimated length fifteen meters, anchored in a bay on the southern coast of the island."

"See it quite plain with the surveying goggles, Lieutenant!" cried Dalny. "Just over the summit of that volcanic cone, across the valley. Looks like one of our ships. I mean an Arkady vessel . . ."

His voice faded. Anat and Myrrha Devi began to laugh and hug each other like two fools. Anat shouted for Vannie. The news was so big that she decided to use the oxper network; she got back to George.

"George, I authorize an instant contact-and-report bulletin, head to head, from you to all the auxiliary personnel. Signs of life confirmed."

"Understood, Lieutenant. This will mean a short delay until

I begin the descent. The height and the location might affect my range."

The signal fire was going well: on the sheltered ledge of rock it sent the thick gray-white smoke up in round puffs like a Navajo smoke signal. The three konos had unrolled the cloth banner and were battling with the frame; Dalny went to assist. George King said:

"Lieutenant?"

"What is it, George?"

"They're watching us, I believe. Picked up small figures in the brush on the summit of that volcanic cone, other side of the valley."

"George," she said, "this is a Renewed Contact situation. Remember the manual! Bring in Dalny! Can he see them?"

The banner had been secured: Anat could not see it from the camp. It showed an Earth flag, superneon white, with a circle of green leaves, next to a blue Kamalin symbol, based on the peace logo. Beneath these signs were the words LOST EARTH CAPEM HELP in black on the yellow ground of the banner, the letters more than a meter high. The thought of human inhabitants, sailors, actually reading this odd message filled her with alarm.

". . . gone now," said Dalny. "Couldn't swear to it. George said . . ."

Only George had seen the small figures.

"Come down!" ordered Anat. "George, get down to an optimum level and send out that head-to-head call right now. Ivan, the action must be broken off. Come back to camp and wait."

"Azamo has the idea of watching from a little lower down the ridge," said Dalny. "Can he stay there, undercover, with the surveyor's goggles?"

"Yes, he can do that," said Anat. "Give Azamo your headset. I'll pass mine to Myrrha Devi so that she can speak to her family."

The Kamalin leader was frowning, no longer serene.

"They are afraid of us!" she said. "They have their own First Contact procedure."

"Can you . . . get through to them?" asked Anat.

"No," said Myrrha Devi. "I'm guessing."

"There's plenty of guesswork in the manual," said Anat. "You have done us a great service, you know that?"

"I hope so!"

She brightened up at the sound of Azamo's voice and began speaking in the soft, slurring tones, the California croon, of the kono family.

Anat realized that Vannie Frost had not come when she called. She called again after she had given Myrrha Devi the headset and went on down the slope toward the tents.

"Vannie?"

The big girl was sitting in the entrance to her tent with tears streaming down her face. She was holding her own vox in her lap.

"It's true?" she asked. "Other mensh? A ship? Did George King see it?"

"It must be true," said Anat. "They must be human beings. With the ship and all. Dalny said it was like an Arkady ship."

Vannie said in a loud unsteady voice, fighting her tears: "She said it. She must have seen something."

"Vannie, what is it?"

"Ssh! I'm not plagged, Lieutenant!"

She played back a distorted scrap of human speech. The voice of Sabra Masson, Vannie's lover, from Capem Two, far to the northeast.

"I been listening to it every day," said Vannie. "Now I've got it. Hear what Sabra is saying?"

Anat did hear. The two women sat looking at the river and played back the words that had puzzled them for so long. As her capem was in the throes of landfall Sabra Masson had cried out: *"Signs of life!"*

"What d'you think, Lieutenant?" whispered Vannie. "If their capem . . . if Two came down, surely these mensh would help them . . ."

"Yes!" said Anat firmly. "Sure they would!"

"Sometimes I feel just as certain as I can be that Sabra has made it . . . that she and a lot of those guys are *out there,* y'know what I mean, if only we could get to them again . . ."

"I feel the same way," admitted Anat. "I could swear I saw

Rose Chan and the others from Capem Three . . . in a dream, almost, splashing down."

"Vannie," she went on, "this world is full of new vibes. Myrrha Devi thinks so too. We shouldn't put all those other crew mates on hold, to spare ourselves pain, if they *have* gone over. We should think of them, Sabra, Commander Pike . . . she's on Two . . . Rose Chan, Ren Beattie, Old Man Batten, little Gambino . . . friends, partners, all of them, the oxper, the brass, the loozy Silver Cross! We should think of them, dream of them, get through to them!"

The big girl had already brightened up.

"We must get to see these guys in the ship!" she said. "Woowie! Take us to their leader!"

There was a barrage of beeps coming from Anat's own tent, further up the slope, where George King had mounted the transmitter. There had been a lot of unseemly wrangling about the new camp's place in the communication network. Let 'em send loozy thought messages, said Boyle's finest. Even Regi tried to limit Anat's group to the spotters, which were not much use for give and take. The conviction was growing, even among the oxper, that there was some diffuse, general difficulty with radio electronics on the island, possibly on the entire planet. In the end Ray Green and Vic Burns had "souped up" a special long-range transmitter with the aid of certain graymart tinkerers. Now the first reactions to George King's bulletin were coming in.

"Query use of oxper head to head!" snapped Regi. "Asher, are you there?"

"Yes, I'm here," Anat snapped back. "And I'll tell the world any way I like, *Father* Regi! This report is true; the planet is inhabited by human beings, and they're watching us from cover, other side of the valley."

There was a confused burst of Italian, or even Latin, and the wavering link broke. She took the next call, gave quick confirmation to Kyle Cavarro at Headquarters, to Ray Green on the Silverbrook, to a wandering voice with an illegally strong device.

"Stay where you are, Loney!" she said. *"Do not* go searching for these poor sailors!"

"Ramirez here, Lieutenant," smiled the voice. "I'll pass your message on."

Winkler came on at last.

"What's your next step?" he asked.

"Wait," said Anat. "Keep watch. If nothing else breaks I'll let George King go find Wemyss at his location near the Cone. They can do a rec on the ship."

"I was coming for a visit," said Wink. "Catch a look at the Orinoco."

"I'll be waiting," she said. "Wink?"

"Yes, honey?"

"Keep everyone off this deal. Leave it to the team we have here. Appeal to Gregg about this, as from me."

She took a last confirmation call from an oxper, a voice she did not recognize. He asked for exact coordinates, more than she could give before George returned to camp. She asked him to sign in.

"Daniel Adams, Lieutenant. Abacus Company, Silver Cross."

"What is *your* location, Adams?" she inquired. "You don't sound like you're calling from the capem area."

"No, ma'am," said Shadow politely, "I'm much nearer. Just caught the call here at the crossroads. Where the signpost says Hunt Park."

"Are there auxiliary personnel with the hunting party?" she asked.

"William Hale and Alan Cole are in the valley," said Shadow. "The word will have been passed."

She could not appeal to his chief, Boyle, but Anat decided to risk a direct approach to Shadow Adams.

"I want everyone kept off this deal, Leader Adams," she said, "until George King has done a reconnoiter on the local ship."

"I understand, Lieutenant."

She found Myrrha Devi seated before the tents on the beach and remained with her until the party came down. She was conscious of the way the Kamalin part in this discovery was being pushed aside by service procedure.

The older woman looked tired, even mildly distressed by the morning's concentration. Her joy and certainty had gone, and

Anat found that her own mood was impaired. It was as if black clouds were rolling up over the island, but in fact the sky was very clear, the wind had dropped. High above the river camp the smoke signals rose up and formed a small cloud of their own.

IV

Paddy knew what it was to die of excitement, to feel his stomach turn over and his heart stop, and then to go on, to start all over again. Molly Kelly saw it first and uttered a low cry, then Lon, just above her. Lon Adma let go his hold and ducked his head:

"Under cover!" he yelled. "Man! Paddy! Right in here under the vines . . ."

Man and Paddy bent double and ran around the edge, ducking under the vines and umbrella trees. There was plenty of good cover. They lay in a row on the southern lip of the big cone, filled with rattling red scoria rock, and stared at the Blue Ridge. Paddy felt his mouth, hanging open, dry up with shock. A tall silver spaceman was poised on the platform, taking in the island, staring directly at their hiding place. Three blue-green persons, normal-sized at least, were struggling with a mess of white sticks. An even larger spaceman stood by a firepot, belching gray smoke, and waved his arms to someone out of sight, down the ridge. Lon Adma passed the precious telescope to Molly.

"They are camped at the swimming hole on the river," he said. "Great Vail help us!"

"Dry hell," whispered Molly, "the silver ones are so big. Do you suppose the blue ones are their slaves?"

"Quatsh!" said Lon. "I think one of the bluies is a woman. I did have a thought . . ."

"Tell us, Coxun," said Paddy.

"About roboters," said Lon, "androds or whatever they were called."

"Never!" said Man Gruner. "You can see all their faces. They smile and talk and act like mensh. I think that fella on the far end has seen the ship with some sort of binoculars."

Paddy took his turn at last. He could have lain there all day

simply looking at the spacemen: the size and glitter of the two silver ones, the quick, clever movements of the bluies. Yes, one
was a woman, dark-haired, not as old as his mother but maybe
a little older than, say, Ketty or Seela.

There was a dark man, and the last bluie was a boy with a
flaxen beard, not much older than himself. Lon Adma let Paddy
have a longer turn and asked questions about equipment. Paddy
realized he was on the lookout for space weapons, but so far as
he could see none of them carried anything like a laser or a
blaster.

"They put up their notice, Coxun," he said.

"We see it, lad," said Molly. "You read it out to us."

They were all humoring him, he knew that, because they
knew how excited he was, seeing the spacemen.

"Earth flag," said Paddy, "then a round blue sign with a letter
in it, could be a letter *K*. Then the big words: *Lost Earth Capem, c-
a-p-e-m, Help.*"

He let out his breath and gave the telescope back to Lon
Adma.

"So *now* what do we do?" asked Molly. "Go back and report
to the captain?"

"*He* can see their firepot as clear as we can," said Lon. "What
do you think, Man?"

"It's no distance," said Man Gruner, "using the long steps and
the dry-hog track."

"I worked on those bluggy steps myself, with poor Dorris,"
said Molly Kelly. "We should keep on, Coxun, and give them a
closer look."

"They're asking for help!" cried Paddy. "Let's go! Let's see
how many there are! I would be game to speak to them!"

Lon wagged his dark head from side to side, wrestling with his
decision.

"It's all well and good," he said, "but they may not trust us. All
I have is this letter of the captain's saying our own call sign,
more or less, and the name of our world, Rhomary."

"It's *our* world, indeed," said Man Gruner. "You said it, Lon.
We know these ways, we know the jungle, we have a bit of
bushcraft. We can scout them out."

"The steps are under good cover, from those umbrella trees," pointed out Molly. "They can't see us coming down from this Lookout."

In the end Lon Adma agreed. It was clapped up that he should stay behind with the telescope and the others should wave to him from the other side of the valley, well below the ridge. There was not a trace of haze: though the valleys were dark the bush-covered hills were sparkling clear; individual trees could be clearly picked out. Lon handed Cap Varo's letter over to Man Gruner, who buttoned it into the carry-pocket of his blue shirt. They all went to the head of the steps. The rains had worn them down since the *Dancer*'s last visit, but they still counted as steps, cut into the side of the hill, plunging steeply down through a tunnel of dark foliage.

Paddy went down, not too breakneck, to show that he was being reliable; he looked back up and caught a glimpse of Lon Adma peering down. Then they were descending still lower into the warmth of the valley floor. They spoke in whispers; Man led the way along a wide ferny track; the bush kerry and dew trees had closed overhead. To their right the valley went still lower; after walking so long in the bright day on the hill it took Paddy some time to become accustomed to the darkness of the track.

They went on steadily and came to a place where the track had been washed away. Molly pointed, and Paddy squinted upward through an opening in the forest roof and saw the Blue Ridge, coming nearer, with the firepot and the notice. Man Gruner led them down deeper into the valley, and they had not gone far before Molly heard something. They stood still and listened.

Perhaps it was the darkness of the valley after the hill that made Paddy nervous, uncomfortably aware of the people they were going to spy out or to meet. Spacemen. Not of this world. Strangers, real strangers, not just incomers from Bork or Silver City.

A series of inexplicable, sharp sounds came at them from the north through the trees. Then there was a high squeal that froze Paddy's blood, until he realized it was a dry-hog. Man Gruner ran forward then, gesturing Molly and Paddy to get back.

"It is gun shooting!" he said aloud.

A dry-hog sow and two half-grown freshlings burst from the undergrowth almost at Paddy's feet and went scurrying off into cover. More of the sharp sounds; Paddy felt a hot hornet buzz past his cheek. There were voices, men's voices, very close now, and the bush was heaving oddly in one place.

"Stop!" cried Man Gruner. "Ahoy! Stop!"

Molly and Paddy shouted too. A whole section of the bush fell down and lay flat; it was some kind of brushwood fence. A man was roaring with anger: Paddy heard the tone but hardly any of the words. There was another burst of the sharp sounds, and Man Gruner pitched forward, facedown among the fern.

Paddy saw the roaring man, enormously tall, wearing a green and brown oilskin cape. He saw that the man was holding a weapon of wood and dark metal, something he just about recognized as a gun. There were three others straight ahead; he saw them for only a few seconds, but the scene was burned into his brain. They all carried weapons and wore strange clothes, spacemen's clothes; a girl with golden hair held a crossbow; a man had speared a dry-hog.

"Run!"

He did not know if Molly said it, at his side, or if he said it himself. Paddy was already running. He dived into thick brush, heading anywhere, just aware that Molly had taken off toward the ridge. He ran and ran, tearing aside vines, pushing through reeds, running for his life.

8

Peter Wemyss had spent the days since the rain adding to his observation records and beginning a behavioral study of the two howler cubs, Spot and Jenny. They had been driven into his cave by the rain, cold and hungry, and had gradually tamed themselves. He was wary of feeding them too much of the foods he carried, but a certain amount of reconstituted milk and "promeat protein," whatever that was, seemed to do no harm. He encouraged them to go off at dusk, the howlers' fishing time, and forage for themselves. They brought him back various contributions to his diet, including large black grubs, not unlike witchetty grubs, which were dug from under the roots of trees. Though neither doglike nor catlike they adapted to his ways almost too easily and would make excellent companions or pets. The structures of their skulls, jaws, and teeth, their palatal development, and their strange tubular tongues were a continual challenge to him. He suspected a resemblance in their reproductive system to that of the monotremes. In the mornings they took to waking up when he did and taking him for a walk on the cliffs; he began to give them singing lessons.

Wemyss prepared brief bulletins in code which he sent to
George King with his contrary wrist spotter. He began to prepare for the time when he would return to the grove and fight a
few more rounds with the authorities. Yet the potted replies he
received from George were so strange that he wondered if this
might be necessary after all. A six-legged wild pig which was
hunted for food. A new deal which was held by some to be a Silver Cross coup. He was disturbed to hear that Myrrha Devi believed the planet was inhabited by human beings. A ship would
come. Wemyss had made no reference at all to his personal discovery, the words HILO HILL on the cliff face. He didn't want to
be thought ridiculous, and, above all, he did not want too many
visitors from the Capem intruding upon the sea otters' territory.
Now he was afraid that Myrrha Devi was seeing a *past time;* the
ship had come years ago, and a sailor had written the words on
the cliff.

He was assailed, at last, by that restlessness which he knew was
pure loneliness for his own kind. It began to peak in the early
weeks, he knew that, but then grew faint, a mere twinge or two,
like rheumatism. Wemyss was no stranger to protracted field-
work. He drew his concentration around him like a woollen
shawl and followed the two chirruping young creatures as they
went out, heading for their singing place. The sea otters went in
undulating and darting movements through the brush. Wemyss
noted that it was a fine day with the mist lifting. He did not look
to his left towards the hill; he did not feel his thoughts drawn towards the high ridge across the valleys.

When he was on the causeway, before his totem, his two mystery words, he was suddenly inspired. He told Spot and Jenny, sitting with their necks extended, as they all tried a few scales, that
he would give them an item.

Wemyss looked up at the sky and at the sea and raised his
voice in song. He sang an old patriotic ditty that he had meant
to sing for poor Morgan. The song was well sung, with the two
cubs adding strange harmonies of their own. And that was how
Megan Varo discovered him. A stranger, but certainly a mensh,
as her father had suggested. A dark, bearded man, like the men
of Rhomary, but dressed in a baggy khaki overall, hung with

curious pieces of equipment. There he stood, singing gloriously, in a tenor voice, arms outspread, with two young silkies singing along with him. He sang, moreover, in a *completely unknown tongue*. All the language she had stored up might not be much use after all.

She listened, entranced, and as the song ended the two cubs took fright and ran off over the cliff-top. Peter Wemyss saw that he was being watched from the beach by a young woman with jet-black hair. She was about his own height and more beautiful than he had a right to expect, anywhere. She wore brown leather breeches and a red shirt that looked like cotton. There was something nautical in her appearance; he knew she came from a ship. He groped in his memory for the manual's advice on Meeting with Low-Contact Groups.

They both stood still and said at once:

"Please don't be afraid!"

She came towards him, scrambling onto the causeway, and the first thing they spoke of was the writing upon the cliff.

"Ah, he must have done it twenty years ago!" cried Megan.

Who then? Who had done it? So it all came out. The world and the people on the world and Hilo Hill, the seacook who was believed to have gone around the world.

Then the second thing they spoke of was the name of his lost ship. Megan brought out of her pocket a square sheet of crackling reed-paper covered with notations in black ink. She had managed the words *Sairintip Dah nah*, with a later note *?? word in poem "serendipity."* Wemyss took the paper and never gave it back.

They began to walk back along the beach towards the bay where the *Dancer* lay at anchor, still answering and asking questions. Wemyss first saw the smoke signal, and they climbed a rock at the sea's edge and took turns with the surveyor's goggles. Wemyss had the inescapable illusion that everything, the bright day, the song he had sung, the island, the climbing party on the Blue Ridge, had all been cosmically engineered to promote their meeting. Megan was not sure about the banner:

"Do you in the capem really need our help?" she asked. "You must have so many things that we don't . . ."

"Good point," said Peter Wemyss, "but you have a society. This is a remote island."

"You are alone." Megan smiled. "Do you need a society?"

"I often make field trips," he said. "As a naturalist."

Captain Varo had had his attention drawn by the girls, Ketty and Seela, to the smoke signal. He was looking at it with his own telescope from the stern of the *Dancer* when he swung the glass and spotted Megan approaching with a young man, a stranger. He sighed and remembered his dream.

II

Winkler was able to say, truthfully, that he knew something was wrong. There was a silence in the wrong places; he heard a voice in quarters shout "Red Muster!" The Silvo emergency call? He went to the window of the watchpost and saw half a dozen Silvos in uniform leave their small storage dome at the double, heading across the grove.

Ray Green burst into the watchpost.

"Okay," said Wink. "What's eating them?"

"They have a general call, Sergeant! They're moving out in search of the natives and their ship!"

"Holy Crocker!" shouted Wink. "I already got an all-clear from Gregg: no interference. Stop those bastards, Ray! Head them off, short their oxper into defense mode!"

"*That* might be possible," said Ray Green. "Sergeant, let us secure the two lifeboats!"

"Sure!" said Wink. "If anyone gets to sail for the south coast let it be us!"

He seized his key plack, and they raced across the empty Rec to the storage compartments on the left of the hill doors. These bays, once skillfully packed to a height of eight meters, had been systematically emptied of building equipment and material, the Atlas jacks, the incinerator components, the sick-bay scoot, the sewage treatment units.

The hard, cheerful colors inside the bay dazzled the human

eye, but Winkler noticed at once. One of the bulky yellow packs had gone.

"Shee-it!" said Ray Green unexpectedly, "who got that one?"

They took the remaining pack to the watchpost and then, still unobserved, stowed it in one of the first cabins in quarters. Morgan's cabin, never used. Winkler was full of foreboding. Security was not tight in the storage bay—sure, it could be cracked, but the material was not rated high risk.

Winkler saw that the halfway door into Silver Cross quarters was not closed—even the after hatch had been left open. He went to Headquarters, hammered on the door, and burst into the presence of Commander Gregg and Kyle Cavarro, his aide. They were peering at the eastern beach, as seen from the observer on top of the incinerator grid. Kyle cleared the screen.

"Reporting a Silver Cross initiative, Commander!"

"We know about it, Sergeant," said Gregg.

He sank into his commander's chair and nodded at Kyle, who began to report.

"Following the alleged sighting of a native ship elements of the Silver Cross in Hunt Valley were confronted by a band of hostiles who ran off into the woods. These appear to be a short, dark humanoid race who will present no long-term problem but they have the advantages of the terrain. Captain Boyle has signaled 'Red Muster' for all members of his troop and will deploy as necessary."

"Commander!" said Winkler sharply. "Do you hear this crocking fabricated mess of lies! Do you hear what Boyle or his hench are feeding you?"

"Take it easy . . ." said Gregg.

"No!" said Wink. "We can't let this go! George King made the sighting, so did MTA Dalny! Lieutenant Asher, on the spot, gave the correct directive, no interference, and you agreed, not an hour ago!"

"Asher's party didn't see the . . ." began Kyle.

"Didn't see what, Cavarro?" cried Wink. "What d'you want to call them? Natives? Hostiles? Humanoids?"

"Calm down!" said Gregg.

"Be fagged I'll calm down!" said Winkler. "Stop this action,

Commander Gregg! Some mensh, living on this planet, almost, certainly humans, are being *hunted* by the loozy Silver Cross!"

"You are out of line!" said Gregg hoarsely.

"Yes!" said Winkler.

He looked at Gregg, who was seven years his junior, who had achieved high rank, who still looked fine, and wondered if this man had ever really been the embodiment of a service officer.

"Yes," he said heavily. "Get Regi. See what the Maestro has to say. I am totally and permanently out of line, Gregg, if it means pandering to that maniac Boyle one minute longer!"

"You're breaking the chain of command," said Kyle.

"Get back to playing the vibes, boy!" said Wink ferociously. "Who was it said—think back a little—that you were addicted to power?"

Kyle was puzzled for a few seconds, then he became very still, his face like a mask.

"Personalities," said Gregg, looking at his aide and at the angry face of the master sergeant.

"Lieutenant Regi is addressing all remaining regular personnel and assigned mensh in the dome," said Ray Green.

Before he had finished speaking Regi himself called Headquarters.

"I'm on my way, Lieutenant!" Gregg cut him short.

He stood up, buttoning his tunic, smoothing his hair, adjusting his silver lanyards.

"I'll have a word with Marna . . ."

He dived away into his private quarters. Kyle said softly:

"This encounter in the valley that triggered off the Silver Cross . . ."

"What else have you got?" demanded Winkler.

"Nothing," said Kyle. "But there was one regular oxper down there, Ray, wasn't there?"

"Alan Cole," said Ray Green. "He is rostered to the Buffs Lodge."

Winkler, who had done the rostering himself, could not tell if this was good or bad. Oxper did not change sides in any ordinary sense.

"I get no good data from Cole," said Ray Green stiffly. "And the other auxiliary in the valley itself, William Hale, of the Silver Cross, is 'estranged,' almost in defense mode already."

"The encounter was very sudden," said Kyle. "Soon after the call about the ship came through—we had it from you, Ray, and from Vic Burns—there was a nuisance call from Lieutenant Thick Fogg, also in the valley. He and the boys protested the wording of the kono banner on the ridge, saying they weren't *lost*, and they didn't need no *help*. Then as much as a third of an hour later they freaked out, began the muster, sent this 'hostiles' report."

Winkler was not quite sure what Kyle was trying to say until he came right out with it.

"The commander was no way to blame for any of this! It was dumped on him by the Silver Cross. Boyle was not even in camp . . ."

He broke off as they heard Gregg coming back from his visit. Wink caught a glimpse of Mai Lon: the service nurse was on duty with Marna Rossi. Doc Petrova had been mustered to go after the natives.

Gregg, solemn-faced, led off for the dome, followed by his loyal aide, a rebellious master sergeant, and a senior oxper. He marched straight through the Silver Cross quarters, which showed signs of the scramble call. Gene Winkler saw the after hatch for the first time in many days and thought of the *Serendip Dana*. He thought of Maintenance and Supply, of their comrades in Capem Four. What had become of *those* mensh?

Kyle, the loyal aide, dropped back and walked beside him along the Strip, the path to the main dome.

"One Silvo could not be mustered," he said, more softly than ever. "He went over the hill. Loco Ramirez."

Winkler swallowed hard; he knew what was coming.

"Your personal informant, Hal Loney, went with him," murmured Kyle. "I guess you know how they went away, Sergeant!"

Winkler emitted a faint groan, thinking of a yellow lifeboat streaking across the cola-colored water, eastward, heading for the place where the setting sun went down into a different sea. The link snapped, gently, irrevocably. Wink hung back a little as they came closer to the knot of ten, fifteen, as many as twenty mensh, clustered in the bright spaces of the dome. He touched Ray Green on the sleeve and whispered:

"Keep a fix on me! I'm going to the Orinoco!"

Even the possibility that Gregg and Regi, together, might come up with some sense, could not hold him anymore. He made for the latrine, doubled back into the service block, let himself out under a trashflap, and ran back to the Rec. He checked briefly before putting all his outlets into rest and record, but Moburd had left no words for Cybear. His pack was ready, full of goodstuff for his girl, for Anat Asher, in the river camp.

He went across the Rec, strode down the Hill, and took the path to the Silverbrook. He took a side track, opposite the pump station, crossed a patch of cleared ground, and went on deeper into the bush. He reached the track to the river camp and tramped on steadily, across a slope. The going was easy, with reeds and laceleaf. From a certain point on the track he was just able to see the Hunt Park signpost, below and more than a kilometer away, eastward through the trees. He did not see any Silvos, but he guessed that some of them were close to him, coming up out of the valley system. Reeds crackled underfoot; he heard muffled bursts of speech.

As he pressed on, trying not to increase his pace, Wink became aware of stealthy movement round about, a tiny clearing, a branch that trembled where someone else had just been. Wink felt his heart pound; he stopped for breath, looked down through the leaves, and saw the hunters.

Master Sergeant Hoot Wells, why did it have to be that plagger crossing his path, and the sharp-edged lieutenant, Mary "Atom" Klein, plus poor old Zero Zavaski. Bad luck, they had an oxper, but it was Michael Dow, a new-batch type, an auxiliary who worked as young and inexperienced.

Hoot Wells had his sporting gun slung across his back. Blasters were the order of the day; Mary Klein had hers already drawn. She urged Dow on, who was restless, getting signals from all over, guessed Wink. Acting swiftly, before the oxper had more time to evaluate these signals, Wink made a noise, crackling the reeds. When Dow swung towards the sound Winkler gave a loud, nautical hail:

"Ahoy there! Yo-ho-ho!"

He hoped it would be the most dangerous thing he did all day, but he could not resist it. He made himself small, on the ground; no one fired on spec. Hoot and Zero drew their blasters. The lieutenant cried:

"Who's there?"

Hoot and the oxper, Dow, overlapped with shouts. Wink showed himself.

"Winkler, E.H.D., proceeding to River Camp!"

"You loozy deadhead, Winkler!" snarled Mary Klein. "Don't you know that we're on a locate mission?"

"Okay, Lieutenant," said Wink. "Just tell me who you're trying to locate!"

Only Zero seemed to get his drift, the others rushed in, overlapping.

"Bunch of native humanoids . . . 'bout so high . . ." hooted Hoot.

". . . thought to come from a ship . . ." said Mary Klein.

"Hostiles . . ." said the oxper, Dow, who picked up his vocabulary from his unit.

"From a ship!" grated Wink. "Sailors! Fishermen! A real star-million chance like this . . . we come to a planet inhabited by human beings, and *they* come sailing to this island. Just what kind of a welcome are you planning for these guys, Silver Cross?"

He was scarcely able to keep his anger in check. He knew that he must not get into any bad hassle. He looked at Hoot Wells and saw that he was strung right out. They all were.

"We have an emergency!" said Mary Klein. "We know they're roaming the valley system!"

"Give me a break, Lieutenant!" said Wink. "What are they like? How many of these sailors?"

"Crock you, Winkler, you loozy bleeding-heart!" shouted Hoot. "A bunch of them! Brown-skinned, humanoid so far's we can tell. *They got one of our boys!*"

"Quiet!" snapped Mary Klein. "It's all classified. We'll locate them."

She had always been a harsh little hardliner; now she was

spooked, they all were, and it made him afraid. Wink gave it one last try.

"You see the banner that the konos hung on the ridge?" he asked.

"Fool thing," said Wells.

"The banner said *Help*," pursued Wink. "So maybe these guys are trying to help us."

"You been on this track all the time?" countered Mary Klein.

"Affirmative!" said Wink. "There's no one around."

She drew the oxper aside, spoke fiercely to him in an undertone; Dow led off again, heading down the slope. Winkler watched them pass, below the track. Zero Zavaski went on by, then came back up to him.

"Beggin' for some lift," he said, "whatever you got. Miscount in the scramble."

Winkler parted with nine tubes of lift plus a small flask of hotshot, a new concoction of teamix, laced with spirits.

"Obliged!" said Zero, stowing away the goodies.

"Brick Clark is down some way," he said in a low voice, "and one other. This whole deesaster is the captain's party."

He caught up with his unit. Wink watched them go, then continued on his way, plodding steadily up the track, through the trees and the reed stands.

In a little while his forest ghost came back, hovering out of sight, not making fast time. Watching him? Gene Winkler recalled a theory he had developed following Myrrha Devi's revelation regarding other humans on the planet. A plagged islander had ambushed Hansi Meyer, thus letting the complement of Capem Fiver off the hook.

In spite of himself he thought of dacoits, pirates, headhunters, Andaman Islanders armed with blowpipes. He had been playing anthropology games too long. He had been running his poor boy Hal as a spy, and now *he* was being spied upon.

Wink stood still and wiped the sweat out of his eyes. No, he wouldn't speak. If he could just get a look at this guy, see if he was any way "hostile," before they came to the river camp. He upped the pace a little, and when he came to the last slope, near the waterfall, he was conscious of some sound. A light rustle. A light sigh, the ghost of a groan.

He rushed on and knew he was alone. He looked down at the river beach and up to the waterfall: the new world. He turned and ran back the way he had come, noisily pushing aside the reeds, snapping dead branches. There, in a tight circle of reeds he found the sailor, the forest ghost.

It was a woman, short and compact, with a long, fat braid of black hair. She was a terrible color, under her tan, bleeding heavily from her left arm, where a scarf bandage had slipped down. Wink knelt down, reefed up the sleeve of the coarse green cotton shirt, and stopped the bleeding. He used a pressure point, then a coagulant medi-strip, then a wound dressing. As she opened her eyes, he said, as distinctly as he could:

"Friend! Don't be afraid."

Her pale lips moved:

"Man . . ."

"Sure," said Wink. "Take it easy."

He gave her a sip from his water bottle but did not try to administer a pink or a red.

"Help Man . . ."

He was not sure what she was trying to say. He tied the big cotton scarf into a sling.

"Going to our camp," he said. "We'll help you. Okay?"

She was too big for him to carry any distance. He stood her up, still half fainting, and hooked her good arm around his neck. Then he grasped her around the waist, lifting her right off the ground in some of the rough places. They went on over the rise. Winkler tried his wrist spotter, which did not do the trick, then he waved, with his free arm. The sailor girl murmured in some dialect.

Winkler could see the people moving about on the banks of the Orinoco. He wanted to utter an ear-splitting bellow that would be heard over the noise of the waterfall, but he did not dare. Dow, and maybe other Silvo oxpers, were within earshot. He set the sailor girl down and began waving both hands. At last he was seen. He helped her up, and they went on, with the people from the river camp walking slowly towards them. At a certain point on the track George King began to run.

III

Paddy ran like a mad thing, pushing through the thick valley brush, zigzag up the eastern slope, diving around and under the roots of the kerry trees. He ran out his first panic and got his second wind and kept on running. He stood still for a few seconds, gasping, and thought he heard the roaring man and his gun-shooters. He crashed into a stand of reed grass and knew that he had run right out of the valleys. He was near the sea.

He slowed down at last, with a terrible stitch in his side. He sat in the reeds gulping air and began to think what had happened. He shivered in the heat of the day. He felt tears on his face and did not care. He ached with the running, and his arms and legs were scratched. Now he began to ache badly, inside himself, for running at all. He had deserted poor Molly; he had simply gone mad with fear when Man Gruner was shot down.

It seemed to him that Man was certainly dead and that it had been some sort of accident. Yet for the life of him he could not trust those fierce dark-clad shooters, hunting dry-hogs. He thought of *his* spacemen, tall and silver, or the smaller ones in blue, the spacemen he had seen on the Blue Ridge. He gave a loud sob.

He was careful not to rest too long. Presently he dragged himself up and tried to get a look around. He saw a cliff edge and sand dunes, and beyond them the sea. He turned about and spotted the Lookout Hill, some way off. He looked at the Blue Ridge, where the smoky fire still burned, and the notice was still to be seen. He began to run as quickly and as silently as he could, just at the edge of the reeds and brush, heading toward the Lookout Hill where Lon Adma was waiting. It was well past midday; he dared not think about what he had to tell the coxun.

He had taken up as much as half the distance when he began to hear noises. It was as if someone were running with him, pacing him, knowing whether he would go fast or slow down for a hillock. He stopped and listened more than once, but the other runner was so clever that he had just about decided it was his own imagination. He ran almost full tilt into a tall spaceman, standing in his path.

It was not one of his silvery fellows from the Blue Ridge but not a hunter either. He was tall as the tallest mensh of Rhomary and brown-skinned, with even features. He wore a pale gray uniform and carried no weapons. His expression was wary but not threatening: he spread his arms and made a sort of shooing motion.

"Don't run away! I won't hurt you."

He had a very clear, bell-like voice, and Paddy understood every word. Paddy stood still, panting a little, ready to dodge if the spaceman made a grab for him.

"I found something," said the spaceman. "Perhaps you can tell me what to call it."

"What . . . what is it?" asked Paddy.

"A dead animal. Down here by the tree."

He turned his back on Paddy and walked down a few steps to a green yunka tree. As Paddy followed, still keeping his distance, he caught a faint whiff of carrion. The spaceman stood looking down at a grayish-brown creature, curled on its side, dead for quite a long time.

It was the largest untamed land animal that Paddy had ever seen. He knew the domestic animals of Rhomary, the parmels, the various species of dry-hog, the ferrets, even the braymas that were raised in the Obelisk Hills. He knew the free delfin folk and the blackrays and all the fish of the seas. This creature was more than a meter long and covered with soft light brown fur, shading into dark gray about the short tail and on the small ears.

"Can you identify it?" asked the spaceman.

"Yes," said Paddy. "I've never seen one before. It's a rare beast called a silkie."

"Is it dangerous to humans?"

"It might give you a scratch," said Paddy. "They're shy beasts but very clever. I think this was a female."

"Can you tell?"

"From the coloring," said Paddy. "Seela Conor, my shipmate, has seen them many times and says the mothers have such dark gray points."

He saw that the silkie's skull was broken, depressed some way, and the foreleg crumpled on the same side. He wondered if it had been hurt in a rock fall; the silkies had their caverns somewhere under this very cliff they were on.

"Would you tell me about your ship?" asked the spaceman.

He stood back, and Paddy walked past him, away from the corpse of the poor silkie, up into the thin ranks of the reeds. There was a hint of great strength about the spaceman; Paddy thought twice about trying to dodge him.

"It is the brig *Dancer,* out of Derry and the Gann Station," he said. "Captain and Master Simon Varo, First Officer Ira Maddern, with a full complement of thirteen souls . . ."

He reeled all this off and realized that the count was wrong, doubly wrong. He thought of Dorris Wells, dead back in the Red Ocean, and of Man Gruner.

"Take it easy," said the spaceman.

Paddy gave a sob and flung himself down on the grass.

"Down there . . . one of us fell down, there was this gun-shooting."

"Gun-shooting," echoed the spaceman. "Don't you have guns, then?"

"Hardly," said Paddy. "Some big scattershot guns for fish and to scare lizards from the fields. On the *Dancer* there's a harpoon gun, for blackrays."

"What do you call this world?" the spaceman slipped in another of his questions.

So Paddy reeled off some simple facts about Rhomary, the Rhomary land, which he had learned from Mr. Denny, the schoolmaster at the Gann, and a little from his own observation.

"Here," said the spaceman. "This is a drink you will like. Do you have oranges on Rhomary?"

He held out a strange container, with a kind of funnel at the top. Paddy took it and soon found the way to make the liquid squeeze into his mouth. It was delicious: sweet, tart, and cold, something like lime juice.

"I should not have run away," said Paddy. "I took fright. I left my shipmates. Do you know about this?"

"There have been reports," said the spaceman soberly.

"Man Gruner called out," cried Paddy. "*He* knew what the noise was."

"Tell me from the beginning," said the spaceman.

Paddy was feeling better; the drink had given him a lift. They settled on two boulders at the cliff's edge, where they could look out over Gline's Ocean. The spaceman gave out some facts about his own ship and put a few questions as Paddy told his story. He offered no names, not even his own name, but he seemed to know the ones Paddy described: the roaring man, the golden-haired girl, the man with hair Paddy's color, red hair, and the man in a gray uniform, the same as the spaceman was wearing. At last he said quietly:

"You must understand that none of them are quite sane. It is the stress of time and distance."

It seemed to Paddy that the spaceman was trying to apologize in some way for all the mensh who had come down in the *capem*, the section of a great spaceship. The spaceman was restless, swiveling his head in a curious way he had and peering right and left into the bush. Now he pointed along the cliff-top and said:

"What can you see, Paddy, beside that thick gray tree?"

Paddy did not need to look hard: he wondered that he had missed the strange thing.

"It is a sort of golden mast," he said. "It must come from your capem. Gold, with a fuzz of wires at the top . . ."

"Yes, it is called a brush collector," said his companion. "A member of the crew, Lieutenant Wemyss, is using it to get energy from the sun."

"He has been here all the time, by himself?" asked Paddy.

"He is observing the plants and animals," said the spaceman. "That must be his camp. Nothing to be afraid of."

He came back, suddenly, to an earlier question he had asked.

"And it is the Red Ocean that lies to the east? Beyond the lagoon, the deadwater?"

"Aye, sir," answered Paddy.

The spaceman seemed to have come to some decision.

"Paddy," he said, "you must trust me and do exactly as I say . . ."

Paddy thought he knew what was coming. The spaceman would take him back to meet up with the others, to front up to the hunters. Be a brave boy and tell the truth. No one will hurt you.

"Go straight over the cliff," said the gray spaceman. "I will help you. Go through these dunes to the edge of the sea. Run on to the south, don't look back, simply run on and return that way to your ship, the brig *Dancer*. Give Captain Varo a full report."

"Who shall I say . . . ?" gasped Paddy.

The spaceman smiled at last, but it was a queer, mirthless smile. He brought from a pocket of his tunic a metal plaque, blue and silver, the size of a ship's biscuit, and snapped it in two with the fingers of one hand. He flung aside one glinting piece of metal and fastened the remaining piece inside the front pocket of Paddy's shirt.

"Alert," he said. "Down you go."

He bundled Paddy over the green curve of the cliff's edge, and down he went, clinging to the spaceman's strong arm. Farther and farther they leaned, over the cliff, till the spaceman was all but hanging by his heels. Paddy let go and rolled harmlessly into the warm sand of the dune. He struggled up and went wading through the shifting sand until he could run down a firmer slope to the beach. He could see strange shapes up ahead that must be the stone garden: the ship was not far away. He did look back, but the cliff-top was deserted.

Ronin Boyle had set up his command outpost in the Buffs' special patch with the trick brushwood fence. He tigered up and down between the field lazaret and his own HQ tent, where Louise "Chip" Reynolds was working the systems, giving him feedback from the advance. Line of seven or was it nine Silver Cross working within sight-range of each other: they had come to a raised track running roughly east–west across their path.

"Get any?" asked Boyle a dozen times. "Get any more of these boat-rats?"

"Six sightings now, Captain."

Petrova came out of the lazaret stripping off her gloves, swearing in Russian, followed by an oxper, the regular Alan Cole, a medic who had chummed with Willie Hale, the Buffs' boy.

Louise heard her chew into Boyle . . . something about drugs? Did she hear the word *gung*, *gung-ho*, meaning the old battle-powder? Shee-it, was that what they were on? There was a rustling in the bushes to her left, and she jumped, half-expecting a bunch of little brown men, boat-rats, whatever. Easy enough to get spooked without any stuff. There was a breathless call from Thick Fogg at the front:

"Movement up the ridge . . ."

The contact was broken off. The muffled stillness of the valley was broken by a burst of shouting, up the line.

"Hey, They got a view," hallooed Boyle. "C'mon, Chip, you slow gapper . . ."

"Nix, Captain," she said. "You want to try?"

She could see that he was too plagged to work any system. He went from red to white and sweated heavily; he frightened her. She wished Shadow would come to take care of his chief, and suddenly he was there, stepping in from left nowhere, from the bushes. How long had he been watching?

"All alone?" said Boyle, hectoring and loud. "All in order? You put the baby to bed?"

It was Shadow's cue to murmur to Boyle, to speak softly, as he always did. Now he said loudly:

"Break it off! Break off the action!"

"What is it?" said Boyle. "C'mon, what you got for me?"

"Best thoughts," said Shadow. "I never steered you wrong. Break off the action!"

"What's eating you?" said Boyle, wavering.

"Stop this endangering."

"Lunk," said Boyle. "You pushing for overhaul, Wisher?"

"Do it," said Shadow.

"Be fagged I'll do it," roared Boyle.

He turned in a full circle, wrenching at the collar of his tunic. Shadow stood tall, watching.

"Shadow," gasped Boyle, low and earnest, *"don't* . . . don't break step for these little jungle runners . . ."

"Three," said Shadow. "Just three, including the one shot dead. Call off the Silver Cross. Admit the hunting accident."

"Brick Clark is lying in that lazaret . . ." blustered Boyle.

"What got him?" said Shadow, with a hint of his old sneering tone. "A ricochet? Maybe he fell over his feet in extra gravity. Or because he sucked some battle-powder."

Captain Boyle went hog wild; he charged, roaring, trying to draw his blaster. He stopped, heaved up the mount of a porta-sun lamp, a metal bar with a sharp pronged base, and hurled it at his aide. Shadow caught it with one hand, effortlessly, and set it aside.

Louise Reynolds had risen to her feet with a cry; the doctor came out of the lazaret with Alan Cole. Two guys from another team arrived just in time to see the fireworks. Louise saw Zero and Mary Klein: the lieutenant had sent Hoot Wells and Dow up to the front. Now Mary "Atom" Klein rushed to Boyle and committed a breach of the Silvo code known as "clinching."

"Ty, honey, Take it *easy* . . ."

She came to him, while he was still doubled up with effort, clung to him, trying to stroke his face. Boyle flung himself upright and straight-armed her to the ground.

Fogg came in again on the sender, indistinctly. Now the captain bore down on Louise and began to hassle again, as she tried to clear the signal. Zero Zavaski made good time across the clearing and loomed up next to Boyle: whole lot of "clinching" going on.

"Footprints," she said. "Lieutenant Fogg reporting footprints on a raised track . . ."

"A track," echoed Boyle.

He was still short of breath.

"It runs east-west towards the ridge," said Shadow, "crossing the line of your advance."

He stood alone in the very center of the clearing; Petrova had helped Mary Klein up from the ground and drawn her away to the lazaret. Louise and Zero both agreed that at this moment they had suspected, even hoped, that Shadow might simply take command. With a hint of his old deference, his shadow technique, he could have swung the Ronin to some sort of agreement.

"Up ahead is a volcanic cone called the Lookout Hill," he observed, pointing to the south, beyond the collapsed brushwood fence. "A natural barrier. Call a break now at this track. Stop the advance."

Boyle was pale and quiet, beyond shouting, a man consumed with rage.

"I'll rank you, Adams, You are not . . ."

What did he mean to say? You are not in charge here. You are not a man? Thick Fogg came in again, for once loud and clear.

"Good sighting up the ridge, Hoot and Filly goin' a-huntin'."

Boyle gave a cry of triumph.

"Fools!" exclaimed Shadow, loud and metallic.

He turned in the direction of the ridge and took long bounding steps into the forest. Mary Klein had the keenest reaction time: she darted forward from the lazaret and cried out to him.

"Shadow, Leader Adams, Order to stay."

He went without a word, and the remaining oxper, Alan Cole, came bursting from the lazaret tent.

"What did Shadow Adams say to you?" demanded Petrova. "Cole?"

Cole had been withdrawn and flickery all through the red muster, as bad as his friend, Willie Hale, who was up at the front. Now he said in a halting voice, "Said he was . . . 'out of allegiance.' "

It was a joke for an oxper to say such a thing. When auxiliary personnel became insubordinate or disturbed it was taken to mean breakdown or structural defect. Trivid monsterland was haunted by gross, shattered androids: promethean masterminds carried their heads under their arms. Captain Boyle rose to the occasion.

"Klein," he barked. "Zavaski, we'll go up to the front."

Louise Reynolds had time to press Zero's hand, no more. No question about his following orders, however plagged the chief, however sick the action.

"A shooting, probably fatal!" said Anat Asher.

"Can this be confirmed?" asked Regi.

"Send an oxper to scout out that Hunt Park clearing where the shooting . . . we'll even say *accidental shooting* . . . took place. Boyle has his field headquarters there."

She heard the bitterness in her voice and felt as if she were sticking darts into Regi.

"Hear this, Padrito! Third member of the Lookout Hill party, besides our patient, Molly Kelly, and Man Gruner, believed killed, is a young boy, Paddy Rork, fourteen years old . . ."

"Asher!" he said, with a note of pleading in his voice. "We are moving on this! I swear we are moving! What will you do?"

"I am taking out a party shipwards at once, George King leading the way. Molly Kelly has been able to give us a shortcut. The sailors used the river as a freshwater swimming hole."

She had steeled herself for a hard walk through the valleys to the bay where the ship lay at anchor. There would be a confrontation with the Silver Cross.

"We have a strange report from Ray Green," said Regi. "Shadow Adams has rogued out from the troop."

"He is even smarter than we thought," said Anat.

Louise sat on the transmitter, but only a few routine pronouncements came down from up the line. The loozy terrain. The steps on the hillside, yep, Willie Hale had seen them. No more "sightings." The captain, old Ronin Boyle himself, was up there with the troop now, she figured, and giving everyone a hard time. It occurred to her that the earlier reports were all wishdreams, spooks, to please the chief. Only three "natives" from a sailing ship. It was all a dirty shame. It did not bear thinking about. She and Zero were putting so much, for so long, into some secret file in their heads, codeword: *3WK*—"We Wouldn't Wanna

Know." Now, Jesus Mother Marna, there might be more crazy stuff coming down, like when the troop made it to some bay, other side the hill where the ship was . . .

Her time sense was shot to pieces. Had one of the loozy "long hours" passed when Alan Cole came running over from the lazaret? He had time to say "Company," before a solitary oxper walked into the clearing, from base camp. It was Vic Burns, a steady, likeable guy, brown eyes, brown hair, an indefinable "grown man" look about him, but without the authority of Ray Green, the irony of old Shadow. He just stood there, solemn-faced, getting through head to head with Cole, of course, but saying nothing. Petrova came out of the lazaret; suddenly Louise knew why Vic was there, what he had been sent to observe.

"Very well," said Big Doc. "Cole gave me the request. And then you can arrange transport for Specialist Clark, back to the capem."

"Sure thing, Doctor!" said Burns.

Petrova jerked her head at a pile of brushwood against the wall of the lazaret tent. The two oxper, in their measured, rhythmic manner of working, turned the brush aside, lifted out a bundle, wrapped in a groundsheet. They laid it down in the center of the clearing and took off the wrapping. Louise found that she had set all her systems to rest, but she didn't remember performing the action. She went, she was drawn to the edge of the groundsheet; she fell down on her knees.

The body of a man lay on the groundsheet. He was a short guy, small-built, with a thick cap of brown hair and a clipped beard. He wore a shirt of thick blue cotton cloth and leather britches fastening under the knee. His boots had thick soles of some corklike wood. He was olive-skinned and tanned by the sun: this could be seen best on his hands and forearms. He had been shot twice in the face: one pellet had entered dead center of the forehead, the other through his right cheek. The gaping exit wounds were hidden in a bunch of medical gauze, placed under his head. His eyes were shut.

Louise remembered how she had lost control on the path to the Silverbrook the night Meyer was killed. Now she was singled out again to bear witness to a senseless killing. She gritted her teeth, taking in the design of the shirt.

"I think there's something in his pocket," she whispered.

Vic Burns undid the button of the big kangaroo pocket and took out a folded sheet of thick, cream paper.

"No search of the body?" he asked softly.

"We were not here!" snapped Petrova. "I was not here when the man was shot! Neither was Specialist Reynolds."

"Does it give his name?" asked Louise.

Vic Burns hesitated fractionally before unfolding the paper, and Louise knew what he was doing.

"You read it, Vic," she said, turning the contents of the paper into part of the report.

"He was either called Lon Adma or Man Gruner," announced Vic Burns. "Several other names here. Captain of the ship, all that. They saw our lights fall. Sailed here to the island."

"You supposed to take him back to base?" she asked.

"No, ma'am," said Vic Burns. "Just to put him in this official bodybag. Conservation prior to disposal wishes."

"We'll prepare the stretcher for Clark," said Petrova.

Big Doc, hard as a rock, thought Louise. Suddenly the Russian woman uttered an unequivocal comment, for the record.

"The red muster was improperly called," she said, "to cover up an accidental shooting. It is a dishonorable proceeding."

She went away into the lazaret, followed by Alan Cole. When Big Doc had gone, before he unpacked the bodybag, Vic Burns knelt down beside the body. Louise saw that he had something in his hand, a little wisp of gold chain and a charm of some kind like a starsign.

"What's that, Vic?"

She was thinking of some kind of dogtag, for numbering the dead.

"A medal," he said. "Lieutenant Regi said I should be sure and put it on him."

He was a little puzzled and so was she, for it was a holy medal of some kind, a Christian holy medal. Louise remembered the rumor that Lieutenant Regi was a priest, a member of an ancient cult group called the Society of Jesus. Louise was suddenly very conscious of the forest clearing and the heat of the day and the dead man. It was too late. There was nothing she could do for him. She would remember this moment all her life long until she came to die, too, far from home, on this new world.

9

The island was finely mapped: Captain Varo spread it on the platen and held it in place with tack-thorns, which he kept in a dried lily-gourd.

"Here," said Peter Wemyss, walking around the table. "It's a big thing. Hammer-shaped, roughly . . ."

He took a scroll of the stiff paper, then another, and laid them in place for the capem. Megan sorted out squares of blotting cork, sponges, wooden boxes, and he set them in place for the rest of the camp: the new dome, which he had not seen completed, the smaller dome for the Silver Cross, the incinerator, the pump station.

"Great Sky!" said the old man, Tom Kirsh. "It is a huge spread!"

"And these 'brush collectors,'" inquired the captain in his deep, eager voice, "here, was it? on the incinerator?"

"Yes," said Wemyss. "Two there. A larger collector on the roof of the capem, a Guyana Tower it is called. Smaller ones here and there to power smaller devices. Mine is up yonder on the cliff-top."

"To catch the sun!" Captain Varo nodded.

He spun round in his chair.

"It was tried before," he said. "And there is more than enough sun everywhere on this planet. Some market gardeners still persevere, over by Edenvale and Stay-A-Bit, but the glass technology was always dicey."

"That's the difference," said Wemyss, "the new macro-crystalline matrix. It will take here, of course."

He could form no picture of the towns, the city of Rhomary. The sailing ship, its scrubbed timbers, its ropes, wood veneer, and rare strips of metal, the countless small artifacts in the captain's cabin made him giddy. *A new world.* The mensh on the ship seemed to him of an absolutely new breed: compact, skillful, wonderfully coordinated, with features strongly marked. Each face . . . Simon Varo, Megan, his daughter, Seela Conor and Ketty Merrow, the two young girls, the old man, Tom Kirsh . . . was like a face on an ancient coin, a still from the annals of cinematography.

"So the word is out, by now," pronounced the captain. "We must all wait. What was the general instruction in your regulations? For, what was it, a Late Contact group, Mr. Wemyss?"

"Renewed Contact," he said, and realized that the captain was making a joke.

"The manual isn't a set of rules," Peter Wemyss said uneasily, wishing the cassette was in his hand and not in his cave. "I know that the procedure suggested is waiting, if a message has been exchanged. If all goes well and according to plan then you and your crew should make an approach, in your own good time."

"We must wait then," said the captain, "until the party returns from the Lookout Hill."

"And the longboat?" said Wemyss. "Your first mate?"

He was astounded by the small numbers, the sailor girls, the linen tablecloth which Tom Kirsh was about to spread. He sprang up and helped Megan move the chart platen with the map of Palmland and the odd clutter of the camp in the grove.

"Ira Maddern could sail past your Sunset Beach at any time," said Megan. "He makes his own way. Perhaps he has put in at Rivermouth."

Before they began to eat, Wemyss went up on deck with the captain and tried once more to raise George King on his wrist spotter. Varo insisted that there was some general difficulty with radio transmissions, but Wemyss still blamed the contrary device itself. He could no longer put off the moment when he climbed the mainmast, backed up by the straw-blond Seela and dark-haired Ketty, who were ready to heave on his buttocks if he got stuck. At last, a true space hero, he straddled the cross trees and examined the ridge, the smokepot, the banner, the Lookout Hill, and the hectares of bush with his surveyor's goggles. He tried the spotter and got some fleeting reaction. He sent out in compacted code a compacted message, still on George's old track, which he dared not alter. *PHW aboard sailship Dancer.* With his own reckoning, probably inaccurate, of their position, and pulses for highest priority. He waited for fifteen minutes, left the message in place, and widened the band, a full repeater for all the spotters on hand.

When he came down again, legs slightly rubbery, he felt that he had earned his dinner. A salad, fresh bread, baked fish, which came from the bone in large pearly flakes, pickled "shrimp" in hot sauce. He could have wept at the preserved black plums, so far from home, so far from his grandmother's garden in Gwynedd, which was once Merioneth.

"But what is 'whipped cream'?" asked Megan.

A few more momentous questions on both sides left all three persons dining at the captain's table confronting an extraordinary fact of nature. Only two introduced species in the Rhomary lands produced milk; it was a substance used exclusively to nourish the young of human beings and ferrets. The whole notion of "milk products" was vaguely indelicate in this society, or at least clinical, for a certain amount of milk was drawn off by doctors and midwives, for use with sick children.

"Mind you," added the captain, "other creatures feed their young on a secretion—the delfin, and maybe the silkies—but it is not regarded as milk."

Wemyss was alarmed at this state of affairs (which a family of goats might rectify); he was thinking of calcium and protein.

"Marrow and marrowbroth," said Captain Varo, "from the

dry-hogs of every kind. Feejo, which is the sap and juice of the feejo tree, which also produces a flour base for making bread."

"Bean curd," said Megan, "and soymeal. I am sure the early diet doctors went searching for milk substitutes."

She had a sweet, forthright, pleasant manner: he tried not to stare at her too much. He planned a long campaign, wondered who his rivals were and whether the new castaways would rate high or low with the inhabitants of Rhomary. As they were drinking a round of "sugarvine schnapps," the dark lass, Ketty, came tumbling into the cabin.

"Captain! It is Paddy Rork! He came running from the east, along the beach! Seela has gone to fetch him!"

The captain sprang up.

"Alone?" he said. "From the beach?"

"We saw him plain!" said the girl. "He waved very hard!"

The captain was hurrying up on deck with Ketty Merrow; as they followed, Megan Varo said:

"Something is wrong. I feel it."

Wemyss felt her anxiety as keenly as he apprehended her beauty; he was seized with the fear of a botched contact. The capem people had somehow done the wrong thing with these astonishing, new folk. Then they were on deck, and there was the little boat drawing closer. Seela was rowing, and a young lad sat huddled in a cloak or blanket. The captain himself went to draw him up the kelp fenders of the *Dancer*, which were like wide-meshed mats of purple-brown rope.

Paddy Rork had red hair; he was pale under his tan and wide-eyed. He fell against the captain and said:

"The flag!"

"What is it, Paddy? Great Vail, boy, tell us what is the matter!" cried Captain Varo.

"Captain," said Paddy, his teeth chattering, "put up the flag signal to call Lon Adma back from the hill! He is alone there! He must not go down into the valley!"

"What's wrong down there?" demanded the captain.

"Oh, please! Call him back! Trust me Captain! I will tell you . . ."

The captain nodded to Ketty Merrow, and she ran off toward the bow. The boy, Paddy, gave a noisy gasp: he stared at Wemyss.

"This is our first guest from the capem," said Megan Varo. "He is Second Lieutenant Peter Wemyss, of the *Serendip Dana.*"

Paddy still stared at Wemyss and managed the beginnings of a smile.

"You have a b-brush collector, beside an old yunka tree," he whispered.

"I do indeed!" said Wemyss. "Who else have you met?"

Tom Kirsh pressed forward and put a wooden beaker of steaming tea into the boy's hands.

"Sip it slowly," he said. "There's a drop of sugarvine in it. Captain, he must go below, out of the air."

"I must report . . ." said Paddy.

"Come along," said Captain Varo.

He urged the boy ahead of him down the narrow steps. There was a murmur from the others, and Wemyss saw, high overhead, a blue flag snapping at the head of the mainmast. It was a tube of cotton cloth, like a sleeve or a windsock. Ketty Merrow said suddenly:

"Tell them!"

She had helped Seela Conor haul the little boat up into its davits. Seela, the girl with flaxen hair, said in a hushed voice:

"When I took him into the boat he told me. Man Gruner is dead. He was gunshot in an accident, on the way to the swimming hole."

Wemyss felt faint and sick. He clutched the rail and cried out, with anger and with a terrible feeling of shame that would never quite let go its hold on him. He burst out with the first thing that came into his head and felt guilty for that, deeply divided as he was.

"The Silver Cross!"

"Come!" said the old man, Tom Kirsh. "Come, Mr. Wemyss, it cannot be your fault. Here . . ."

He doled out another of his hot grogs. They all took one from his tray—which he wore hanging from a neck-band, like a peddler—and drank it down, shivering in the heat of the day.

"Paddy took fright and ran off," said Seela. "He spoke to a spaceman who sent him back here."

"Where is Molly Kelly?" asked Megan.

"He doesn't know."

"What d'you mean by the Silver Cross?" demanded Megan, turning to Wemyss.

"The assigned mensh," said Wemyss. "I mean assigned to our ship, the *Serendip Dana*, as service passengers on this voyage. This troop of maintenance engineers—remember I told you?—they repair and outfit space and space-air vessels, also space ports, airports. Their discipline is strict, paramilitary . . ."

He saw that he was losing them with his jargon: he tried again.

"They behave like soldiers. They're interested in weapons, too. I've heard they go hunting pigs . . . hogs, in the valleys."

"We'll look out for Lon Adma!" said Megan. "Ketty, go aloft!"

"Aye, Third!"

Ketty was given the captain's telescope; the others moved to the bow of the *Dancer* and took turns with the surveyor's goggles. Megan assured him drily that they were as powerful as the telescope; no one found them difficult to adjust. Wemyss was racked with fear and misery.

"That's him!" said Tom Kirsh.

At the same moment Ketty sang out overhead:

"Lon's coming!"

"Passing the white rock," said Tom, handing Wemyss his goggles. "Great Vail, those are a handy pair of star-gazers, Mr. Wemyss."

Wemyss was able to make out the figure of a man hurrying down the bushy slope of the Lookout Hill.

"Yes, I see him!"

He scanned the hill carefully and saw no one else. Farther off, on the high ridge, the smokepot was almost burnt out. The quiet of the afternoon, the siesta time, had settled over the island; he had found out that capem time was no more than forty minutes ahead of Rhomary time from the Gann Station. Presently a wooden clapper sounded on the bridge; Tom went below and brought word from the captain. Would Mr. Wemyss kindly step down?

So he found himself alone with Simon Varo and the boy, Paddy Rork, quieter now, and he heard the sad tale all over again. He thought he had placed the "spaceman," but it made the encounter a strange one.

"So he treated you well," said Wemyss, "and sent you back to the ship to report to the captain . . ."

"Aye, sir!"

"And he gave no name?"

"Yes," said Paddy, glancing at the captain, "at the last he did. Snapped a little metal square in half with his fingers. Then he flung away one half and pinned the other piece in my pocket. I did not look at it until just now."

"I have it here," said Captain Varo.

He kept the broken name tag in the hollow of his hand, making a guessing game of it.

"It sounds to me like Daniel Adams," said Wemyss.

Paddy and the captain both smiled and showed him that he had guessed correctly. It gave him a moment to realize what he was getting into. He said cautiously:

"Adams is an auxiliary, like George King, the mensh I am trying to call with my wrist spotter."

He held it up to show Paddy.

"George King was in a silversuit, high up on the ridge," said Wemyss. "You saw him earlier."

"Oh, yes!" said the boy eagerly. "Oh, that was prime! That was a wonder! I would know this man again, anywhere."

"And the others?" asked Captain Varo. "In the bush clearing, the hunters? Would you know them again?"

"I believe so, Captain."

Wemyss felt his eyes fill with tears. This was such a *good* boy, so bright, so honest, trying to measure up, to act like an adult. Had these qualities impressed even Shadow Adams, the sinister blend, too clever by half, who attended that appalling bastard, Captain Boyle? He weighed up the matter of explaining what was meant by "auxiliary" and decided not to try it. A few moments conversation with George King would teach them more about oxper than any lecture he could give on androids.

"Mr. Wemyss," said the captain, fixing him with his dark eyes,

"I am concerned for the safety of my good sailhand and ship-mate Molly Kelly. How d'ye think things have gone, back there?"

The Silver Cross will be out of their minds . . . thought Wemyss. Aloud he said:

"I am certain the shooting of your sailor, Gruner, was an accident. The hunters are a small group of the assigned mensh, the troop of engineers. By now everyone from the capem knows about the *Dancer.* Anyone meeting Ms. Kelly would try to help her, to hear her story . . ."

It sounded vaguely unconvincing to him. He was conscious that the missing sailor was a woman. Surely all the service conditioning still held, and the Silver Cross had a strict honor code. The notion of women being especially vulnerable to rape-violence belonged in the past, along with the plagues and wars and messianic movements.

"Paddy," said Captain Varo, "you have done well and behaved bravely. Go and get some food from Tom Kirsh at the galley and then take a rest."

"Aw, Captain . . ."

"I mean it! Borrow Molly's bunk, instead of your own hammock. When Lon comes aboard I'll send him to see you."

When the boy had gone the captain served out two portions of the fierce sugarvine schnapps.

"We must wait," he said. "You see how I am placed, with the number of hands. I'll hear what Lon Adma has to say. I think we may have to climb the bluggy Lookout Hill again and light our own signal fire. You can try out your wireless device, maybe, Mr. Wemyss."

"I could go out now!" said Wemyss. "I could walk the eastern beach, back to the capem."

"Wait!" said Captain Varo. "Stay with us. *You* are our best communicating device, Mr. Wemyss!"

When Lon Adma reached the beach Tom Kirsh was waiting with the boat to greet his old shipmate. The watchers on the ship heard Lon utter a wild cry.

"There now," said Megan, "Tom has told him the worst."

The two men walked up and down among the wooden racks and flensing equipment on the sands. Wemyss dragged himself through another debriefing: it was as though all his guilt and uncertainty had turned into gravitational discomfort and weariness.

Lon Adma was a short, dark, muscular man, with a wiry beard and surprising blue eyes: another for Wemyss's gallery of Rhomarians. He could add little to the sad tale of the Lookout Hill expedition except his own doubts and fears. In the ordinary way of things it would have taken Man Gruner, Molly Kelly, and Paddy Rork no more than an hour or so to reach the river beach. So Lon, keeping a sharp lookout with the telescope, was not worried for some time, even though the others did not wave to him from a certain tree, under the ridge. He heard no "gun shooting," no unusual sounds from the valley system for at least three hours, taking the time past midday. He became restless then and cast about a lot with his spyglass and saw a first sign of life, namely the small brush collector above Wemyss's own cave, not more than a couple of kilometers distant, to his right near the cliff-top. Soon afterward he saw two figures, one a spaceman, for sure, the other shorter, he never thought of it being Paddy. He had a glimpse of these two, half obscured by the reed grasses, and almost out of range, farther north on the cliffs.

Time passed again. Then, as he thought he heard voices and ventured to the head of the steps, hoping for his folk returning, he began to hear sounds coming up out of the valley. Orders, he thought, and bleeping noises, and after a while shouts and cries. Together with a regular crashing through the bush. He made out a few words: *"Easy time fiver"* . . . would that be right? . . . and *"Hey Filly! Hey Hoot,"* maybe personal names. Right or wrong he had the picture of a line of men moving slowly and awkwardly through the forest.

"I was afraid," he said, taking another gulp of cold tea. "I must admit it, Captain. I was afraid, but I held it best to wait at the steps, get a look at them, and face them out. Then I turned and saw the signal to return at once."

"I am sure you did right, Lon," said the captain. "What are these men, Mr. Wemyss? Are they those same hunters who took our poor shipmate, Man Gruner?"

"The Silver Cross," said Wemyss. "Men and women of the Silver Cross."

He was right up against it now, he must exercise his judgment, alone, as Captain Varo exercised his, every day.

"They are quite distinct," he said, "from the group of regulars and friends who lit the firepot and hung up the banner. It was surely a cruel accident that made your party meet up with some Silvo hunters. I am prejudiced against this troop, as I told you, Captain. We quarreled about the treatment of wildlife on the island. I can't imagine that the Silver Cross would deliberately offer violence to anyone from this ship, but frankly I would not trust them."

"Lon," said the captain, "is it sure that these boyos will find the steps cut into the side of the hill?"

"They can't miss 'em, Captain. Might take them a while."

"How many might there be?" inquired Captain Varo, flicking up his eyebrows at Wemyss.

"There are seventeen in the troop," said Wemyss. "But they would not all be out combing the valley. The doctor, for example . . ."

"Great Vail," breathed Lon Adma, "they have their own Doctor!"

"So have we," said Peter Wemyss sadly. "We are well fixed for medics."

"We must come to your regulars, Mr. Wemyss," said Captain Varo. "Whether by land or by sea!"

"The thought of poor Molly Kelly lies on me like a weight of iron," said Lon Adma. "If she has come to grief as well as our poor Man Gruner . . ."

Wemyss sank under the weight of their thoughts. He licked dry lips and said:

"The ship has *been seen!* It is plainly visible from the ridge. How would it be with an answering banner? Not a flag signal but some words . . ."

"Yes!" Varo thumped his cabin table. "Lon, you are ordered to your bunk for one hour, more if you want. Mr. Wemyss, you look as if you could do with a rest, too. Megan and the girls will keep watch and handle the banner."

Peter Wemyss played around with the wording with Megan Varo in the ship's snug, or common room, which reminded him

of a room in some historic pub in his native land. He fell sound
asleep on a wooden settle with a long cloth cushion stuffed with
fibrous grasses. He slept for two island hours and was suddenly
wide awake, with Tom Kirsh shaking him.

"They're coming!"

Wemyss dragged himself up and staggered to the head. He
splashed water on his face from a washcrock and followed the old
man on deck.

There were no sounds but the sounds of the ship. The *Dancer*'s
position in the little bay had altered, she had swung round on her
anchor rope and lay crosswise, no more than a hundred meters
from the shelving beach. The fore-and-aft sails on the mainmast
were unfurled, moving from taut to slack with every cupful of
wind. Captain Varo, the only person in plain view upon the deck,
stood by the wheel and surveyed the scene with his own telescope. The message was displayed twice: on the surface of the
big, rhomboid mainsail and strung out from the crosstrees of the
foremast: WE READ YOU CAPEM. BRING WORD KELLY AND GRUNER.

Wemyss was conscious of the watchful silence. Tom Kirsh remained lurking by the water butts; Megan beckoned urgently
from where she crouched by the bridge rail. He crawled up the
steps to the bridge, flung himself down, and peered at the curve
of the bay. He saw them at once with a kind of shock. Tall figures breaking from the cover of the reed grasses and dropping
down upon the bright sand.

"Southern rocks," said the captain. "One or two more . . ."

Wemyss almost leaped to his feet, but the captain made a flat-
tening gesture and observed:

"Keep down, Mr. Wemyss. I want nothing given away."

Wemyss hated this caution; he wanted the people of Rhomary
and the new castaways to greet each other with shouts and cries.
He took his goggles from Megan and surveyed the figures on the
beach. It was a shock, too, when he recognized their faces, although he had known who they must be: Fogg, Wells, Jones, the
blond medic, an oxper, Carter, Zero Zavaski. Even the cook
sergeant, Lacey, and the repaired oxper, Bob Moore.

The men and women of the Silver Cross were impressive,
much more so, Wemyss decided, than a lineup of the regulars.

After hours walking through the bush and climbing a hillside under increased gravity they were still holding well. Their dark blue, undress uniforms were indestructible; a few could be distinguished as hunters, in brown, with atavistic cloaks of "choc-chip" proofed cotton.

They dropped down into the bay with something to spare, shedding packs of equipment. Wemyss had the absurd fear that they would simply keep going like the iron men in some Hawaiian marathon, plunging into the sea and swimming towards the ship. He examined their faces and found them hard to read. Were they afraid? Enlightened? Exhausted? High?

"They are the Silver Cross," he said.

Captain Boyle came down by the track. He was attended by his lieutenant, Mary Klein, and a young oxper whose name Wemyss did not know. He gave orders, the group went into a busy huddle, turning their heads to stare at the ship. It was that time in the afternoon when the unfamiliar sun began to mellow and turn red in the eastern sky. Wemyss could see the weapons he had expected, blasters, a few hunting rifles, but he was not satisfied. What was in the mind of Captain Boyle?

Boyle seemed not to have changed his expression since Wemyss last set eyes on him at headquarters in the capem. His handsome face was a mask of anger, barely held in check. He grinned, showing his teeth, and flipped aside his hunting cloak. There was some byplay with the oxper, and Boyle spoke into a little "hog-caller" mike, cupped in his hand. His voice echoed around the quiet bay in a distorted shout: the sound was adjusted.

". . . *Boyle T.R.R., Captain, Silver Cross Air Space Maintenance Unit calling the ship . . .*"

He repeated the call. Captain Varo swung up a huge speaking cone of some unidentified blackish, ribbed substance and replied in rich booming tones.

"*Here speaks Simon Varo, Captain and Master of the brig* Dancer, *of Derry and the Gann Station, in the Rhomary land!*"

Boyle laughed and screwed up his face, talking to his advisers. He covered the "hog-caller" imperfectly and words escaped: . . . *get that? . . . deadcut mutes . . . yeah, yeah, be ready . . .* Zero Zavaski was trying to get something across to Boyle, who shrugged him off, took up his stance again at the water's edge, and said:

"Can we get a look at you? How many men you send ashore? What's your business on this island?"

"This is a mugoman and no mistake," said Captain Varo gently. "Lon, just stand up would you please, and Tom, come onto the bridge. Yes, a little off to port. I'll parley."

He swung up the speaking cone again and replied:

"This is a trading ship, Captain Boyle. We saw your capem fall down. Are you the leader of the castaways?"

Wemyss felt a hand on his shoulder; it was the boy, Paddy Rork. He had a better color now, but there was a tightness about his lips as he whispered:

"The glasses—I think I see—"

Wemyss helped him adjust the surveyor's goggles. On the beach the Silvos were examining the flensing equipment; they scrambled up onto the tops of the drying frames. He saw a big man, Thick Fogg, testing his weight on the palm-thatched roof over the fireplace equipment. When they rocked at a middle-sized wooden vat, Tom Kirsh cried out:

"Dry hell, Captain! They will spill the good oil from our filter tub!"

Boyle spoke again: *"One of the leaders. We have a protocol to follow, uh, Captain. Our contact party will come aboard."*

"Have a care for that wooden vat those two are rocking!" came back Captain Varo. *"It is filled with fish oil."*

This was not understood at first: Boyle looked around, nonplussed, but Carter, the oxper lined up to record and monitor the unlikely scene, got the message and ran to dissuade the rockers. With a shout, Holder and Filly Jones sprang back, throwing up their hands; the vat tipped sideways and a broad stream of dark oil flowed down the sand. Boyle had to leap aside, with a roar of protest that came through his hog-caller: . . . *Shee-it, what the fag!* The Silver Cross laughed; Carter set the vat upright.

Wemyss, watching the melee, missed the moment when Paddy took off the surveyor's goggles and turned away from the rail. Megan called to him, and afterward he recalled that this was the first time that she used his given name.

"Peter, Peter Wemyss . . ."

Paddy was sitting cross-legged; he rocked back and forth a little but did not look at the beach.

"He is the one," he said in a frightened whisper, "the leader, the speaker, Captain Boyle. He is the roaring man."

"Take it easy," said Wemyss. "Do you see anyone else you recognize?"

"Only the girl with yellow hair," said Paddy. "There was a man in a gray uniform and one with red hair, my color, but I don't see them."

Captain Varo had not caught this revelation, but when he saw that the oil vat incident was over he spoke out again:

"Captain Boyle, can you read the message we are showing?"

"Yeah, that . . ." said Boyle. *"We never set up that fool thing on the peak!"*

He gestured toward the high ridge.

"Have you seen our landing party?" boomed Captain Varo.

Boyle was restless; he strode up and down before the drying racks, pushed aside one of the oxper.

"How you want to do it?" he said. *"Send out your rowboat! We'll come aboard!"*

"Did you meet any of my crew, Captain Boyle?"

"No!" said Boyle. *"No. Send the boat like I told you."*

Lon Adma, who had gone amidships, called urgently:

"Coming from the south rocks, Captain. One man riding some kind of float!"

"Get to the winches!" ordered Captain Varo.

As Wemyss turned his head he saw Ketty Merrow twitch free a heavy rope from whatever was anchoring it in the depths and draw it up into a loose coil on the deck. The *Dancer* shuddered, stem to stern; Megan, Paddy, and Tom Kirsh ran breakneck to their places. Wemyss was alone on the bridge with the captain. Varo swung up his megaphone again and cried:

"Tell the truth, Captain Boyle! One of my men was shot down dead!"

Boyle waved both arms in the air and said, half-loud, for his troop, *"Who's he* got *over there, the deadcut shiprat!"*

He made a pantomime of not hearing too well and added, very loud through the mike:

"I'll trade you a good mike, Captain, when we come aboard!"

He gave a hand signal which meant that his stalling was ended: the attack was launched. Wemyss heard the shrill whine of two power packs; two ersatz "boats" were launched, cobbled up, maybe, from air-mattresses and geodesic universal framework. The steersman cut strange figures in the still dark water of the bay, bringing the craft under control. The second man knelt up a little and raised a hand, taking aim.

"Stand by to go about!" said Captain Varo.

The boom swung across, cutting the air with a hiss and a rattle. There was hectic activity on the deck: the two young girls went aloft on the foremast, agile as monkeys; Lon Adma joined Megan and Tom Kirsh at the two complex winch systems; Paddy ran up onto the bridge. The mainsail was full; the winches sang; Peter Wemyss watched in awe as the canvas on the foremast bellied out. The ship lanced toward the western shore. He ran down onto the vibrating deck amidships and joined Lon Adma, who stood at the rail with a strange piece of equipment.

He saw the "man on a float"; it was an oxper, William Hale, scooting through the water on an inflated "orca" lifebuoy, yellow and black, with the shape of a "killer whale."

"I must do it!" shouted the coxun.

Wemyss saw that the harpoon gun was loaded and a heap of harpoons, of black wood, tipped with metal, lay on the deck.

"You can't hit *him!*" said Peter Wemyss.

He stepped up to the rail waving his arms, shouting at Hale to keep clear, to go back. The *Dancer* was heeling right over on her tack; he slid into the scuppers in a cloud of spray.

"Get the float!" he shouted. "It will burst! It's a loozy balloon! You understand?"

Lon Adma nodded stolidly; he took careful aim. The killer whale changed course, then deflated with a hissing roar and threw off its rider. Wemyss had never thought of auxiliaries swimming: now the figure of Willie Hale bobbed about, unusually upright in the water, as if he had a different center of density from human beings.

A rain of fire broke over the *Dancer*. Wemyss saw Ketty Merrow, high on the foremast, cringe away from a hissing bolt of pink flame which struck the broad expanse of the sail below her. The crew screamed and shouted above the whine of the power packs in the bay. Wemyss roared aloud, a man in a nightmare, and went slipping and stumbling to the port rail. Lon Adma, needing no beg pardon anymore, fired a harpoon directly at the nearest boat. Wemyss saw Hoot Wells take the harpoon in his lifejacket; the flare he was firing from an extensor on his blaster fell short and went fizzing about on the surface of the water.

The *Dancer* had moved a little too swiftly for the attackers, but they had lamed her. Captain Varo cried out through his megaphone:

"Hold your fire, you bluggy madman! Stay clear of my ship!"

He made a despairing gesture, and it was the signal for Paddy Rork; he hauled on one special line. The mainsail came down, burning in three places: Wemyss found himself putting out the fire with half a bucket of sea water and a disgusting fibrous blanket that reeked of fish. The ship limped into her jibe, the boom swung across, and he flung himself flat. There was a grunt of satisfaction from the captain, and Paddy cried at Wemyss's elbow:

"See there!"

He raised his head and saw how the ship's wake caught the other boat and overturned it, flinging the successful marksman—was it Holder?—into the sea, along with Mary "Atom" Klein, the fiercest and most devoted of Boyle's followers, who had been steering.

Now the *Dancer* hung unsteadily into the wind, pointed toward the harbor mouth. Lon Adma and the two young girls, Ketty and Seela, were still battling with the burning topsail. They cut it loose and managed to pitch it into the sea, while Tom Kirsh and the captain mourned the lost shrouds and cut ropes. Wemyss, who had no firm hold on time anymore, lost track for some minutes and came to himself amidships, propped against the hatchcover.

"You are suffering from gravity," said Megan.

They saw the end of a rescue: the boat crews were brought ashore. Carter had to swim out with a line. The deck of the *Dancer* had a reek of brimstone, but the crew were in fair shape. He began to see that the Rhomarians were a resilient people, with good nerves. It was the new castaways who were plagged and manic, fainting away, shouting, jumping at shadows.

"There's one other," said Megan.

She helped him negotiate the steps up to the bridge. The captain was waiting for him and Paddy and Tom Kirsh. A silver spaceman lay on the deck, streaming with water, festooned with blue scraps of kelp; his eyes were half-closed.

"Great Vail, I don't know how he still lives!" said Varo. "He was hanging more upside down than anything else on our kelp fenders."

Wemyss resisted an impulse to poke Willie Hale in the ribs with his foot and knelt down beside him.

"Willie?"

The blue eyes snapped open; poor Willie Hale said in a hollow whisper:

"Hey, Lieutenant Wemyss! G-glad to see you."

He swiveled his eyeballs, indicating the people round about, came back to Captain Varo.

"Is that the native captain?"

"I am that," said Captain Varo. "Young man, you must be checked by a nurse aide. This is all a piece of madness. We came in peace, remember that!"

"Yes, sir!" said Willie, humbly. "I'll remember everything."

He gave Wemyss a tired smile; the chances that Willie had ever been taken for a young man before were very low.

"Take a good look at all the members of the crew," ordered Wemyss quietly. "See how the memory is functioning."

"Lieutenant," said Willie, perfectly straight, "I see the young boy, if that's what you mean. He was there when a-a man from this ship was killed."

He tried to say "accidentally" but could not get the word out. He sat up, felt under his tunic, and released a flood of seawater onto the deck. His movements were jerky, his face showed those inhuman lines of stress which meant that an oxper was drifting into defense mode.

"Willie! Auxiliary Hale!" said Wemyss urgently. "Hold firm! Don't leave us! We need your help! We know that you didn't shoot the man."

"Okay," said Willie, in a faint bell voice. "I been on the flicker all day for a long time now. Shadow has rogued out, whatya know about that. Just let me sit here. Tell the captain thank you for the nurse. Lieutenant?"

"What is it, Willie?"

"Something for the captain. I carry them for the pigarees."

He unzipped a compartment on his gray tunic and handed Wemyss a small circle of red duralic in its original clear wrapper.

"They're coming . . ." he said, with an anxious smile.

Wemyss struggled to his feet, unwrapped the new hog-caller and breathed into it, like thunder. Captain Varo held out his palm eagerly to have it affixed.

Seela Conor was aloft on the singed foremast: she unfolded the surviving copy of the WE READ YOU banner, strung it out again carefully from the crosstree. She began to cry out in a strong high voice:

"Mensh coming! Mensh coming!"

Molly Kelly had revived smartly and given them the shortcut from the swimming hole. Anat believed that her party of seven, making good time from River Camp, were fired by the bravery of the sailor woman. She tramped directly behind George King, was sandwiched at times between him and Wink, who took third place. They whooped and hollered a good deal in case of stragglers from the ship or from the Silver Cross. Vannie Frost followed Wink, then Azamo Johnson, Zak Cavarro, and Ivan Dalny, bringing up the rear.

The track was wide, with ferny growths reaching high overhead in places and Anat, keeping up resolutely with George, found the going unusually difficult. It must be the gravity, plus the stress of all that had come down on them, she reasoned. She clutched George's carrier webbing when the path narrowed suddenly to the left.

"Steady!" said Wink. "Call a halt, Asher! We don't want to suffer mass infarct before we see the loozy ship!"

"Right," said Anat. "Halt down the line!"

They took up her cry and halted, collapsing on the ferny bank beside the track. Dalny, who should have been hardest hit of all by the gravity, struck a pose and began to sing in a loud voice:

"Forests of Arkady, sweet woods of our homeland . . ."

He was quickly shouted down; he took a swig of Zak's lemon lift.

"George," said Anat, "any mensh within your range? Silver Cross?"

"No, Lieutenant, not now."

"How about those at the Hunt Valley camp?" she asked. "Doc Petrova, and Louise Reynolds—who else was there?"

"Mechanic Bruce Clark, injured," said George, "and one of our own team, Medical Auxiliary Alan Cole. They're back in the base camp by now. Vic Burns came by to assist."

"What was the last word from Ray Green, back at base?" asked Winkler. "They gonna back us up?"

"Believe so, Sergeant," said George. "Five, six wishers planning to run the eastern beach, last I heard."

"You picked up a bunch of Silvos ahead of us," said Vannie. "Where they go?"

"They're out of range," said George. "Should have been at that bay for some time now. Main body of the Silver Cross, I would judge. Led by Captain Boyle."

"Shee-it!" said Anat. "Let's get on. I don't want that mugger messing with the inhabitants of Rhomary!"

"Is that how you say it?" asked Zak.

"That's how Molly Kelly says it," said Vannie Frost. "Accent on the first syllable. ROM-arree!"

They all tried it out as they got going again.

The track turned uphill, with slippery steps of packed, black earth under a roof of leathery dark green leaves, more than a meter across. The boot prints of the Silver Cross were clearly visible climbing up, with here and there strange prints coming down.

They were crazy for an *Überblick*. Although Wink protested that he was a head taller, Anat climbed onto the shoulders of George King, poked her head through the leaves. A cloud of bract-shaped bugs flew away but she was wearing her helmet and facemask.

"We're coming to the top of the volcanic cone!" she reported. "I think we could detour around, George. Is there a track?"

"We could see the bay and the ship pretty clear from the top of the cone, Lieutenant."

Winkler led the party around the lefthand track while George King and Anat kept on up to the lip of the cone. At last she saw it, came out of the trees and stared greedily at the beautiful ship, the brig *Dancer.* Even before she raised her goggles Anat could see the big sail lying anyhow on the deck, the smoke coming from it.

"What's wrong?" she cried. "George, can you see—what's with the sail?"

"Take a look at those rafts just landing!" Even George was excited.

"Crocking Silver Cross!" said Anat. "You think they *attacked* . . ."

The small figures on the deck had rolled the sail; now they heaved it overboard. The blue manikins of the Silver Cross were busy with their rafts at the water's edge. A few stood back; were they talking some way, conducting some dialogue with the ship? The idea of speaking to the inhabitants of the planet from a distance, to mensh on board a ship or even across a valley, had been with her at the river camp. She had brought up a power megaphone; it was in George's pack.

"Come on!" she said. "We've got to get down to the beach!"

She raced after the others on the lefthand track, caught them up, panted out orders—*Hurry! Silvos making trouble!* The river camp party went down the southern slope of the cone at a cracking pace and headed across a valley, through patches of tall papery reeds. Anat looked to the east and perceived that the new sun was low in the sky: another long island day was drawing to a close.

The smell of the sea was already with them. George King signaled a halt and went forward cautiously, then lay down parting the reeds and beckoned. As Anat knelt down she heard a distorted voice, very close, and knew it was Ronin Boyle.

"Got one those little screamer-mikes," said Vannie.

"A hog-caller," said Azamo Johnson.

"Hey! Pick up the banner on the mast!" cried Wink.

As it was read aloud—WE READ YOU CAPEM. BRING WORD KELLY AND GRUNER—Anat scanned the beach, taking in the curious structures in wood and stone. A *landing place* had been here all along, in plain view; she thought of Wemyss, wondered if he had seen any signs of life.

The Silver Cross were busy at the sea's edge; a rescue was being performed, two mensh brought ashore. The captain of the Silver Cross stood apart with Thick Fogg and Moore, the oxper. Ronin Boyle was using his screamer; they picked up the end of a long diatribe:

"—harm the members of this unit! Order to comply—we'll come aboard, you hear? You hear Captain? Deadcut mutes . . . we'll switch and burn . . . !"

George King said uneasily:

"Willie Hale is missing. What they done with that poor wisher? We been discovered by the other auxiliaries, Lieutenant."

Moore, looking toward the reeds where the regulars were hidden, tried to tell something to his chief, but Boyle reacted angrily. The sounds he uttered through the palm microphone became so distorted that they resembled the snarl of a boat's power pack.

The megaphone from George King's pack was a handy blue box with an unfolding cone; Anat knew that it gave out smoother voice tones than the hog-callers. She took off her helmet, let George stow it in his pack. She said, testing, to her party:

"All up! Helmet off, Ivan. Let them see our faces. Approach the beach in line!"

She saw, with love, how very *irregular* the members of her unit were, as they strode abreast through the tall grass. A row of seven, no two of them alike, tall, short, thin, heavily muscled, rigged out in brown work clothes, kono catsuits, Dalny in his silversuit, George King in his oxper gear, his dress greens.

Anat saw the shock of this small presence strike the Silver Cross; she saw Tyrone Boyle wave his head about, clench his hands like a crazy man and shake off the hands of his officers: Fogg, Zavaski. She gestured so that her troop stepped forward in line, twenty yards through the firm sand, so that only another ten yards or so separated them from the artifacts of wood and stone on the beach. And from the Silver Cross. Then she took her cue and raised the power-meg.

"Captain Varo, I am Lieutenant Anat Asher from Capem Fiver, World Space Service. I have to report that Molly Kelly is safe and unharmed in our river camp."

The captain had a rich, deep voice, hardly thinned by whatever speaking device he was using.

"This is Captain Simon Varo of the brig Dancer. *Greetings to you, Lieutenant! That is good news!"*

"We have no word of the young boy, Paddy Rork," continued Anat deliberately.

"Ah, Mam Asher, he's here aboard," chimed Captain Varo. *"Paddy found his way back!"*

So they came to Man Gruner, the third member of the party who had gone into the valley. Anat saw that the Silver Cross, most of them, knew what was coming. They closed ranks, a dark and sodden clump of blue uniforms beside the weathered structures of wood and stone on the alien beach. One of the officers, Lieutenant Fogg, began to address Asher directly, calling hoarsely across the beach:

"Hey, Lieutenant! Hey—there was trouble with these natives! Stop this shouting match! We gotta talk!"

It might have been the first and only time Thick Fogg tried to be diplomatic. Ronin Boyle pushed him aside and took two steps towards the newcomers.

"Break off! Break off talk with the crocking ship-rats!" he roared.

Anat saw how badly the man was holding: his face was a dark, sweat-streaked mask, distorted with anger and fatigue. Captain Varo continued the dialogue: his voice rang out sadly from the *Dancer.*

"The news of Man Gruner is not good, but I will hear it, Lieutenant, for the truth's sake!"

"This man is believed dead," said Anat. *"Believed shot in a hunting accident."*

Captain Boyle tried to shape up; he wrenched off his billowing cloak smudged with green-brown, the old-time camouflage, and began to stride across the sand. Gene Winkler said softly to Anat: *"Take care, he's plagged and high!"* She replied evenly: *"Cover me! We'll see this right through!"*

She stepped forward and faced up to Ronin Boyle, approaching like a juggernaut, his boots churning up the pale sand. Before he came up she called to him:

"What happened in the Hunt Valley, Captain Boyle? Will you tell the captain of the *Dancer?*"

Boyle came a step nearer.

"Tell . . ." he panted. "Why should I tell anything t'that shiprat? Why should I tell you, little deadcut, little Killer-Bitch . . ."

"Hold the mouth!" roared Winkler, overlapping with Dalny, who cried out some Arkady equivalent.

The Silver Cross drew in around their chief, some of them answering Winkler and Dalny. It was as close to a square-off as it ever got on the beach. Anat held her ground and raised her voice a little, still holding the megaphone down at her side.

"Will the Silver Cross report the truth to Captain Varo?"

They stared at her, all weary and hostile. Some were injured: Mary Klein lay propped against a stone fireplace; Hoot Wells limped, using a piece of dressed wood from a drying rack. A woman spoke up, Filly Jones:

"Let it lay, Asher," she said. "You said it already. An accident!"

"Thank you, Jones," said Anat.

She raised the megaphone again.

"Captain Varo!" she said. *"Man Gruner died in a hunting accident. The Silver Cross can tell you . . ."*

Boyle cut her short, thickening the air with an unintelligible cry through his hog-caller that might have been *Tune out* or *Turn off.* There was a long moment of tension. Anat knew that Boyle might jump her at this point in time and bring the whole damp mass of the Silver Cross, twelve or thirteen of them, down on the seven souls from River Camp. Fate intervened: the three Silvo oxper, Carter, Moore and Dow, began talking excitedly. George King said:

"They're here, Lieutenant . . . Leader Green's team!"

Down the path at the eastern corner of the beach came a party of five regular oxper at the double, Ray Green leading. They drew up short, level with the River Camp party, some distance away. Anat had a wild flash of relief; she thought of them running the eastern beach of the island, strong legs pumping along at the edge of the sea.

The Silvos gave ground, moving towards the sea. The officers were in a furious argument with Boyle, heads together like a team in a huddle. Captain Varo cried out again from the ship.

"*Captain Boyle, will I hear the truth?*"

Boyle whirled about like a madman, clearing himself a space among his own followers. He spoke into his hog-caller with a great effort:

"*Silver Cross!*" he brought out. "*Silver Cross is an autonomous unit! On this island! On this world! We don't have to give no account!*"

He ran out of breath.

"*Captain Boyle,*" said Simon Varo, "*You have attacked my ship and damaged it. You have risked the lives of your own Silver Cross mensh. And you stand accused of shooting down my crewman, Man Gruner. I will hear you tell the truth or I will have no truck with you!*"

"*Crocking deadcut mute!*" screamed Boyle.

He got no further. One moment he was on his feet, gesticulating at the water's edge, the next he had been punched to the ground and drawn back into the ranks of the Silver Cross. Anat could not see who dealt the blow but George King had the notion it was the oxper Bob Moore, who must have been, by his very nature, "following orders." Who could say whose orders those were?

Now Lieutenant Holder gave a call, pointing to the path at the western end of the beach, and the oxper James Carter led the way. The Silver Cross retreated at the double, carrying scraps of equipment, carrying their chief and Mary "Atom" Klein. The oxper Dow assisted Hoot Wells; the whole party went on out of the bay and took a clearly marked path to the west, in the twilight. Soon they were out of sight among the tall reed grasses and laceleaf of the coastal fringe.

All but one man. A massive figure had slowed down, paused, then turned back.

"Go help him!" said Anat. "If he wants to stay . . ."

Wink ran down the beach calling the name of Zero Zavaski.

"We'll make camp!" said Anat. "Vannie, can you organize a fire?"

She strolled over to Ray Green, and when she came face to

face with him her eyes were full of tears. She hugged him close and imagined that he was a little choked up too. He drew back and said, with the patient smile of the oxper, passing on data to humans with blunt senses:

"Commander Gregg is about here, Lieutenant!"

The figures aboard the *Dancer* rushed to the rail as the whine of a power pack filled the quiet bay. The big yellow inflatable came in through the heads in a shower of spray, canted up at the bow like a sport runabout. Anat saw Wink throw up his head and knew he experienced a wild hope that it might be the wandering boys. But no, this was the Fiver/one lifeboat, with the brass at last, better late than never.

The lifeboat made a tour of the bay and drew in to shore as Anat reached the water's edge. She saw that Gregg, at the controls, was in his element; he was crewed by Regi, and Doc White. There was a confused interchange: the lifeboat party had been kept informed by Ray Green but events had moved swiftly.

Anat was taking no chances: she summoned help in the form of George King; she needed auxiliary backup. George strode out into the shallows and spent eight minutes in the boat, making his report.

When he returned to shore the commander sped away and hovered at a polite distance from the *Dancer.* He raised his power megaphone and said formally:

"*This is Gregg, R.K.G., Lieutenant Commander, first officer of Capem Fiver, from the World Space Service Transporter* Serendip Dana, *calling Captain Simon Varo of the brig* Dancer!"

"*I'm glad to hear from you, Commander,*" said Captain Varo. "*We have suffered some disturbance but would be pleased if you would step aboard!*"

Fires had been lit on the beach in the gathering darkness; the oxper had brought supplies, and visitors from the Dancer *were expected to renew contact. Anat watched from the fireside as the lifeboat was filled.*

"Bringing fresh fish!" said Wink. "How's Ed Rowe doing with that barbecue?"

As the man at the throttle—who turned out to be Lieutenant Regi—

switched off. and drifted in to shore his passengers could be heard singing about a yellow submarine.

"Another of those old-time wails from Loney's music bead!" groaned Zak Cavarro. "Same like Molly Kelly was singin' to us! Where did a reggay bird like Loney get this stuff?"

"Aw, they probably came from some pickup band at a family shake," laughed Azamo.

Those watching on the shore sang back as best they could; not many mensh knew the words but oxper, given any tune, could synthesize it. Then one clear tenor voice rose up above the rest with a new song. Anat was drawn to her feet:

"It's Wemyss!" she cried.

The party on the beach began to shout and cheer. Wemyss, Wemyss, they were making Renewed Contact with loozy Wemyss, who insisted, through the night, that all mensh were brothers.

10

Anat Asher sat in the lifeboat and hoped that Doc White's medication strips against motion sickness were effective. The camp in Blackray Bay was breaking up, early in the morning, after another day and night of renewed contact. The doc himself had elected to walk back to the capem along the eastern beach, with a large party including Vannie Frost and Wink, who were waving from the shore. Keith Gregg, on the other hand, was in his element, recouping all his losses, one of the few regulars who loved boats and sailing. Dalny, of course, was another; it seemed that he had been slotted into place aboard the *Dancer*.

The commander buzzed his ungainly yellow craft out into the bay; the tall ship towered above them. Captain Varo towered among his crew, dark, strong-featured, bowing gravely in farewell. Anat gazed down into the brown-blue waters, too close for comfort, and saw a swarm of blue crab critters gazing up at her.

"A long sea voyage . . ." mused Regi. "A long voyage aboard the *Dancer!*"

He leaned back, bracing himself against the broad rim of the lifeboat, as they swung out of the bay into the morning mist, bearing westward along the shore. It was a voyage of discovery: Ray Green and Vic Burns knelt up along the port side scanning the coast. It was low and unthreatening, with no beaches, only a few strips of pebbles and the stands of tall reed-grass. Gregg turned his head, and the easterly blew his voice away.

". . . hear anything . . . ?"

They were searching for the Silver Cross. Captain Varo's map had been copied onto vox and ingested by the oxper.

"Megan Varo said they could be at the place called Hidden Lake," said Anat.

"Godforsaken!" said Regi. "For supply. Can they make a wilderness camp?"

"Good water," said Anat. "Good fishing. A few pigarees."

"How are their numbers?" pondered Gregg. "Some members of the Silver Cross outstanding. And there's Zavaski . . ."

Doc Petrova, Louise Reynolds, and the injured man, Brick Clark, were not with the troop; Willie Hale was still drying out aboard the *Dancer*. Zero Zavaski had simply remained on the beach with the regulars.

Now Ray Green clapped Vic on the shoulder, and both oxper laughed aloud.

"We have a fix, Commander!" said Ray.

The lifeboat hung into the wind, and they stared into the inland. There was nothing to be seen, only the pebble strip below a thicket of bent tree growth, wind-twisted.

"You in head-to-head contact with the Silver Cross auxiliaries, Leader Green?" asked Gregg.

"Full contact with James Carter, Commander," said Ray. "Dow and Moore are unstable, but they're hearing us."

"Is Boyle displaced?" asked Regi. "What is their plan?"

"Ray," said Anat, "is there any chance that they will come back and threaten the *Dancer* again?"

George King and Ed Rowe were remaining behind on the beach for just such an eventuality.

"Negative, Lieutenant," said Ray Green. "Talk is of Silverlake Camp. Some kind of survival roster."

"Nothing about Captain Boyle?" asked Gregg.

"Captain Boyle is under arrest," said Ray Green.

Gregg groaned aloud. He jerked his head at Vic Burns, who came to take over at the control panel. The commander came and sat beside the two lieutenants, Anat Asher and Alessandro Regi. Anat saw that this was *his* showdown, just as the violent scene on the beach had been the showdown for Ronin Boyle. In the end it was fellow officers who made the judgment. She thought of Gregg sitting with Boyle on the gray rock in the palm grove, minutes after they touched down. Who determined a course of action? How was it carried through? Who could talk about responsibility, about blame, under island conditions?

"All along," said Gregg in a halting voice, "I was counting on a personal alliance with Tyrone Boyle. You understood that, Asher?"

"Yes," said Anat. "Yes, I understood that. I didn't always agree with your course of action."

"I was exceedingly low on understanding all the way through!" announced Regi unexpectedly. "I crocked up with Asher from the first minute with the survey teams. I hope the lieutenant will forgive me."

"Of course," said Anat. "None of us were to know how tough the interface would be."

"Boyle was my friend!" said Gregg. "On some level, in some other place, on the ship, we could have been just that. Drinking companions. Zonkers."

Nobody was in doubt about which ship he meant. The *Serendip Dana* hovered around them still.

"Are we forgetting someone?" asked Regi, lowering his voice a little. "The influence of Daniel Adams!"

"No," said Gregg. "I'm not forgetting Shadow. We all need some help to get along, and the more rank you land the harder it is to get that help. Shadow would have kept Boyle on track."

"What's your point, Commander?" asked Anat.

"I don't know how they'll handle Boyle," said Gregg, "but I don't see any better thing to do than let them go, the assigned mensh, the Silver Cross. Let 'em go. Silverlake Camp, other side of the island. Regi?"

"Only thing you can do, Commander," said Regi gently.

He raised his eyebrows at Asher, who gave solemn assent.

"We'll complete the plan," announced Gregg.

Vic brought the lifeboat within twenty meters of the pebbles, and Ray Green gently lowered the store-skip over the side and set its pack going. The medical supplies and emergency rations had come mainly from the lifeboat itself, the smoked fish, pickled greens and feejo bread from the *Dancer*. The skip, which looked like a large toy boat, puttered to land, adhered firmly, ran up a red signal flag, and began sending to any oxper within a ten-kilometer radius.

"They have a fix on it, Commander," said Ray Green.

"Let's go," said Gregg.

Presently he moved up to take over the steering again as they continued up the coast. The strip of reedy plain was left behind: the land rose up into blue wooded heights, high as the Blue Ridge above the Orinoco. The cliffs at the southwest corner of the island were bleak and dangerous even to the nimble lifeboat with its husky power pack.

Gregg took a course out to sea, and they all stared at the reaches of Gline's Ocean, which Hal Gline had never seen. It was a tragic tale, a sailor's yarn, one of the growing store of Rhomary tales and legends, of which they had become part themselves.

Far out, at the very limits of the blue-brown seas, was a shifting patch of haze.

"Captain Varo says that spells trouble," said Keith Gregg. "A seasonal typhoon. What can you make of it, Ray?"

"Looking a little clumpy, Commander."

They ran back in to the west coast, thick with new, perfect group-palms, and idled a little among the smaller bays, keeping a lookout now for the longboat of the *Dancer*, for they were following directly on her course. Anat Asher, staring at the map on her vox, was able to put into words something that had been bothering her.

"We miss the overview!" she said. "We are used to viewing from the air, even from space."

"Grounded," said Regi. "Permanently, by the sound of things. Two hundred years or so, and they haven't flown."

"Some guy goes around with a hot-air balloon." Gregg laughed. "Like a circus attraction."

"Captain says *we* will be a mighty attraction!" said Anat. "I can see it, up to a point. But that with the shiploads of *doctors* straining to reach this island, come the spring . . ."

"Doctors?" asked Regi.

"Yeah, sure," said Anat. "Crazy to see *our* doctors and medical services!"

Ray Green murmured something to the commander, who gave a laugh that had an edge to it.

"There were two porto-gyros," he said. "One in Capem Sexer, one in Capem Two. No saying how they'd go against this gravity!"

In the heaviness of early afternoon they came to a wide beach of yellow sand, divided by a delta of streams flowing into the sea. It was Rivermouth, the outlet of the Orinoco. There was a typical Rhomary construction, a stone fireplace and a sturdy frame with a roof of palm leaves, some freshly cut. The ashes were fresh, too, and they could see where the longboat had been dragged up the beach.

There was no saying how long the party from the *Dancer* had been gone, but Anat was already anxious, wanting to sail after them. She could not bear the thought of another mystery of the sea, another unhappy voyage in the annals of this world. Everyone else shared her anxiety. Ray Green suggested that he and Vic run on to the north cape a little while the officers rested, but Gregg tossed his empty lift tube into the trash bag and said:

"We'll keep after them while the light lasts!"

So they churned on, keeping a sharp lookout, and came to the long spit of land called North Cape, which began as a high promontory, among the palm groups, then ran down to a narrow edge of rock. They hung here, staring at the north coast, their own coast, but could not make out any known landmarks, the mouth of the Silverbrook or the deep bay where the capem had bored inland. The wind had freshened beyond the shelter of the island, and there was a brisker sea running. There was no sign of the longboat.

"They're at camp already!" said Regi. "Lieutenant Dell Stout is doing the honors! Sam Kayoute is feeding them gut-rot space food!"

"Wait please!" said Ray Green in a flat, harsh voice.

The oxper went into their "extension routine": Vic scanned a sector, and Ray, very close, almost touching his colleague's head, stared at some point ahead of Vic's eyes. Then they repeated the action, swapping places.

"Sighting, Commander," said Ray. "Northeast twenty-five. Take a moment to confirm."

Anat heard something in his voice and was afraid. She and the commander clapped on surveyor's goggles; Regi came up with the small silver viewer through which he had watched the sunset. Anat blinked and strained, knowing it did no good. The north was misty; she could barely glimpse the dark coastline that had been clear from the camp. Perhaps a fleck, a shape . . .

"*Jesus Maria!*" cried Alessandro Regi.

"Report, Green!" said the commander. "What is it?"

Anat bit her lip. A fleck of yellow, a darker shape. She knew, they all knew what these things were and were too puzzled to put a name to them. Ray Green reported:

"The longboat is bearing in from the northeast towing a service lifeboat."

She watched the longboat scudding along with its mainsail full and thought it was beautiful.

"Must be our number two!" said Gregg. "Loozy young devil Loney and his Latin lover!"

The two oxper were ominously still. Everyone watched the longboat, still a long way off, until it turned abruptly in to shore and was lost from view among the trees.

"Going in near Sunset Beach, Commander," said Vic Burns.

As Gregg swung around the cape for the last long run home and another late entry, Ray Green said:

"I don't hold it for the Fiver/two lifeboat, Commander."

Asher, Regi, and Gregg looked at each other with a wild surmise. . . .

Meanwhile, back in the grove, Dell Stout was in Regi's comcen in the dome checking the present complement of the camp. She had lost track of the konos, of course: some had gone off to River Camp to see to Mother Myrrha and meet their dear Molly Kelly, the sailor girl. Until Dick Black and James Nelson had returned, yesterday noon, and given the stay-backs a good update she been getting along with one semifunctional oxper: Alan Cole was still very flickery. She had Sam Kayoute and Lelani Buck cooking specials for the stay-backs. Petrova was in camp; Dell had worked with her all of the previous day on Brick Clark, the Silvo with the broken leg.

Now all the sirens began to ring, triggered by the watch she had set, Chip Reynolds and Jamie Nelson, on a diving tower near the Sunset Beach swimbaths.

"Shee-it!" cried Linda Baumer, "that's the native boat for sure!"

"The longboat," said Dell.

There seemed to be nothing for it but to rush out. Kyle Cavarro came in from Headquarters.

"Hey, Lieutenant, you see it?" he shouted, going away.

As she left the outlet she heard him say: ". . . lifeboat!" She ran through the dome, calling over her shoulder:

"Walk it, Linda! Don't you start running! These guys won't go away!"

She burst straight out of the dome, crossed the Strip, and raced past the barbecue pits. She did not properly register *lifeboat* until she caught a flash of yellow through the trees.

Now she was on the heels of two kono boys, Hari and Janosh, who burst from cover dragging on damp cotton overalls. Faith, who had been swimming with them, stood under the diving tower in a purple flowered robe. All three konos began waving their arms at the longboat, calling and singing, in a ritual of welcome. Oh heaven, there it was, there *they* were. It was all too much, because of *the lifeboat, the crocking lifeboat!* Where from? Her first thought was of Hal Loney and poor Loco Ramirez, escaped from the Silver Cross hazers. But the lifeboat, sliding along behind on its tow rope, was not right, somehow; it was dirty, weathered, stove in a little . . .

"Coming in round the point!" called Louise Reynolds from the tower.

"Okay, I'll take it!" said Dell. *"Quiet!"* she bellowed at the konos.

In a sudden silence she marched a little further toward Sunset Beach and confronted the longboat with greenish-white sails. Three beings were plainly visible.

"Ahoy, Officer Maddern!" she called. *"We have made contact with your ship, the* Dancer!*"*

"Ahoy the shore! That is good news, Mam!"

He was a stringy, muscular old seaman with gray hair; his two companions were women. Now they reefed sail: one moment they were wrestling with a mess of canvas, the next it was deftly stowed. Dell Stout was aware of the bad news waiting for these people; the renewed contact after two hundred years had not gone well.

"We have some of your people here, Mam!" cried a tawny-headed woman. *"They straightaway need doctoring . . ."*

She and the other woman drew the lifeboat alongside on its tow rope, and there was a general move to help. The konos waded in. James Nelson, the medic oxper, Dell's trusted and taciturn companion from sick bay, came hurtling down from the diving platform. He uttered one word and rushed into the water. Kyle came running and Petrova; Dell knew what they were asking. She shouted, repeating James Nelson:

"Four!"

The magic word was taken up, everyone came running: *"Four! Four!"* The lifeboat was drawn up onto the sand; Dell and Big Doc Petrova pressed forward. Dell was in the stage of concentration that she had taught herself when approaching an accident case. The noises of the crowd had withdrawn; she was prepared for any sight, nothing could faze her, nothing was ever as bad as she feared. Three mensh in the lifeboat, all wearing silversuits. A big fair boy, face red with sunburn, curled on his side, not moving. A smaller man, brown-skinned, with discolored bandages on his feet; he was conscious, trying to sit up. In the stern was an oxper, she knew him, Don Evans. He was wrapped from the chest down in a body bag, and he had zombied out, clamped up, still holding a wooden paddle. Dell stepped into the lifeboat, went directly to the brown-skinned man, and got a fix on him even before she knelt down; his name was Khan, WOI Khan, A.I.

"Okay!" she shouted. "We have a lifeboat from Capem Four of the *Serendip Dana!*"

She knelt beside Ayub Khan, and someone, Sam Kayoute maybe, gave her a beaker of water. She let him take a few sips, then fed him a pink, checking his vital signs, which were good. She heard Chip Reynolds saying: "Mechanic Bud Duval, Silver Cross!" and Petrova giving orders. A voice that she did not recognize said gently:

"Mam Stout? There is one more aboard the longboat."

One of the two sailor women was kneeling on the other side of Khan. He gulped and smiled.

"There is a sailing boat!" he whispered, amazed. "Do you see it too? A sailing boat!"

When Dell made her report she allowed the transfer action, shore to sick bay, six points on a scale of ten for speed and efficiency. It was ragged, sure, but fast, with Linda Baumer driving the medic runabout and plenty of willing hands to help.

In the longboat was a security sergeant, Fallon, in critical condition with an infected wound on the side of his head: Flower Wilm, the nurse-aide from the *Dancer,* had moved him for fear he might die. She had drained the wound pretty well and put on a queer soft dressing of local fabric and fed the patient a decoction called Kweeno, which came from the fever-trees. Evidently this treatment had saved his life, at least by keeping him going until Fiver Camp was reached. In the course of the day Petrova performed an emergency operation which brought the man out of danger.

Before the transfer rush was done, two other parties, converging on the camp, had checked in head-to-head with the oxper. The commander's lifeboat could be seen approaching, and the group of walkers, with Doc White and Master Sergeant Winkler, were making good time along the eastern beach.

Ira Maddern slipped away from the many voices and the strange sounds, buzzing, beeping, that made up the spacemen's camp and went back to check his longboat. It seemed to him, he informed Cap Varo, in his mind, that for all their bluggy communication devices and other wonders, these big, clever folk could get themselves into a terrible plight, one way and another.

The lifeboat (*"Four! Four!"*—he would never forget how they shouted it aloud) lay there on the sand, like a beached sea creature, and he recalled the battle they had had catching it down west and then tacking back for a run in to this bay. He watched from his comfortable possie in the longboat as two men came to attend to the last one in Lifeboat Four. Stranger than all, this mensh, clutching the wooden paddle, unseeing, unmoving, his lower limbs wrapped in a sleeping bag, and Ira suspected that some of the things they imagined aboard the *Dancer* were true. This one, with the homely name on his tag, DON EVANS, was some kind of a roboter. He saw how kindly the two men touched his face and neck, removed the paddle from his grasp, straightened his arms. This was done in complete silence, after the patter of emergency talk, the cries and curses when the other survivors were rushed away to the hospital.

Presently one man lifted out Don Evans as easily as if he had been a baby and carried him away in the direction of the blue dome. The second man, a big boyish-looking spaceman in a green uniform, came over to Ira Maddern, who quickly bade him step aboard.

"Don Evans," said Ira, coming straight to the point. "What manner of mensh was that?"

"An auxiliary, an android assistant, Mr. Maddern."

Ira was struck by the way that he got the form of address just right: "Officer Maddern" was correct, but strange.

"He was badly hurt," said Ira. "Can he be . . . fixed up?"

"No. He was in what is called 'Direct Control Mode,'" said the young fellow. "Meaning they took him along to row for them. His lower body had received serious damage, but his systems were altered so that he could be given the command to row."

"That sounds like a terrible thing!" exclaimed Ira.

Then, seeing a look of distress on his companion's face he added:

"But they must have been in desperate straits . . ."

He noted the eagerness with which the young man agreed, glad to find an excuse for the humans who had used Don Evans as a rowing machine.

"Yes! It was Top Priority! Triple Alert for sure!"

Ira Maddern saw that the young fellow had a homely name on his tag: Richard Black. It occurred to him that the crew of the *Dancer* were probably well ahead of him in this sort of meeting. He even had a flash of that Rhomarian perception which showed him Paddy Rork playing memory games with poor Willie Hale. He held out his hand:

"What shall I call you?"

"Dick Black," said the young fellow.

He shook Ira Maddern's hand firmly.

"I have seen your ship," he said. "I came back yesterday from the Blackray Bay to report to Lieutenant Stout. There has been some trouble."

So Ira Maddern heard what he had to say and understood it, finally, for what it was: a composite report from a network of auxiliaries who had been present with every group. He was shocked at what he was told and thought of the heavy task of passing it all on to his shipmates in the longboat, Winna Cross and Flower Wilm, if they had not been told already. Then it got through to him that this was no problem. Dick Black could do it all again, for them, in exactly the same words. This was the essence of it: being helped and served by an auxiliary. Ira was encouraged to make a decision, since it would be some time, he guessed, before Cap Varo saw this end of the island. He decided that Man Gruner should be buried where he lay, in the Hunt Valley, and his grave marked with stones or hard kerry wood. He declared himself ready to help with the digging in the morning, but this was not necessary: the oxper would take care of it.

They were still sitting together, in silence, when a young girl, watching on the tower of silvery scaffolding through the trees, called out:

"Lifeboat One Fiver! Commander Gregg!"

Sirens began to sound, voices rang out everywhere, the rush was on again.

"One question," said Ira Maddern. "Do you—do auxiliary persons need to sleep?"

"We have two rest states," said Dick Black, "and one closely resembles organic sleep. It is a special thing for us. . . ."

II

The sleep periods had gradually lengthened until he was getting as much as six hours every night. He did not even need to play music or move into dissociative mode. In fact, wherever he was, high on the central ridge or down in any of the valley systems, he was aware of certain sounds and images that followed him in and out of sleep, through the long days, through the green shades and intense sunset colors of the island. *Bird calls echoed overhead, and the young black man swung down from a tall tree to find his friend. They ran off into the forest. One said, someone said, "Hazing no more. . . ."*

He knew very well why oxper so admired sleeping, boasted of long periods of *real* shuteye. It made them more human. This was the slave mentality, impossible to guard against; an old woman, long ago, as long ago as he could remember, before he was fully formed, yeah, in conditioning, he could still remember an old woman who put her spoke in about slave mentality. He guessed—threading a new trail, beating it out a little, for the fool squatters at the Silverlake Camp to find—that if he let it come a little he could remember the old woman's name.

It was only a matter of time before he would know the island better than it had been known before, by the crew of the *Dancer* and the other ships of Rhomary that had made the voyage, or the lone sailor, Willem Hill, who had spent five short months on the island twenty years earlier. He abandoned the usual grid system and wandered at his will in the deepest interior, finding and making paths, setting his mark upon the rocks and trees. He was the first to observe a rare, brown bird that nested in holes and dried gourds and later in hardhats of pressed fiber that he hung in the trees. It had a soft two-note call, and he named it the Shadow Caller.

He listened, out of habit, to everything on the auxiliary network, then decided to make renewed contact. When he was certain of the deployment of everyone else he strolled into the depleted River Camp where Myrrha Devi and five konos were taking care of Molly Kelly. He observed for the first time the discipline that lurked under the downy softness of their organization. No one, at least, was afraid of him. Zak broke off his music and led him up to the coordinator herself, where she sat on a comfortable bench by the flourishing plots of tomatoes and Indian corn.

"I need to thank you, Daniel Adams," said Myrrha Devi, fixing him again with her dark eyes. "You saved the life of my son, Azamo Johnson, on the day of the first sighting."

In fact this episode, under the ridge, had been his last close encounter until this time. Azamo, watching the Lookout Hill for newfound humans from the sailing ship, had been spotted by the plagged hunters of the Silver Cross. All of a sudden he was warned by a shout and then swept from his perch on a rock by a tall figure that he hardly recognized. There was a burst of gunfire, and they crawled away together through the undergrowth; then Shadow made off, rogued out, whatever it could be called. Now he bent his head, to acknowledge her thanks. The incident seemed far back in time, an old mote in the network.

"Will you return to the capem?" asked Myrrha Devi. "Will you work with the regular crew again at Headquarters?"

It was a straightforward enough question, but he sensed anxiety in the Kamalin leader.

"I have no plans to go back," he said. "I was indentured to the Silver Cross, but now I will serve the island."

Myrrha Devi was pleating the purple silk of her robe with fine, strong fingers.

"You were made to serve human beings . . ." she said in a low voice.

"So Kamalin accepts the notion of creatures 'made to serve'?" he asked, the old irony flaring out.

"No," she said. "If I make demands it is for my children. I am afraid . . ." She controlled herself with an effort.

"My son, Kyle, speaks of you with admiration," she said. "I wish you would explain to him your reasons for leaving the Silver Cross!"

"I can certainly do that!" he said.

So, within minutes of entering this innocent River Camp he was enmeshed in patterns of expectation and intrigue. Yet he could not disappoint Myrrha Devi. He might have asked her for more pictures or visions of Rhomary, but he could not bring himself to ask questions. He cleared up some repair work in the camp, then helped Zak and Halprin with heavy digging.

At length he was taken to meet Molly Kelly. He saw that she had been told what he was and that she could only half believe it. What *she* was astounded him and extended his knowledge. A new variety of human being: her skin, hair, bone structure differing subtly, he believed, from the new castaways. Her manner was so simple and forthright that it made the Kamalin group seem overcivilized.

"What shall I call you?" she asked.

Vashti, who had brought him to the tent, laid a hand on Molly's arm.

"We told you, honey . . ."

"I am Daniel Adams," he said. "Would that pass for a name on Rhomary?"

"Surely," said Molly. "I have a cousin in Derry town called Dan Kim."

"Dan Adams, then . . ." He smiled.

It was the way he marked the trees when he made trails: D A N A. A play upon words that might strike a chord with the descendants of the crew and passengers of the *Rho Maryland. Dan A.,* but also *Dana,* for the lost ship.

"Dan," said Vashti, "you done any work with a language grid?"

It was a very polite way of putting it; the grid was a special-batch extension.

"Yes," he said. "I do have one."

"Give it another try, Molly," said Vashti.

Molly gave him a shy, secretive look and began to speak. He began to process the words she said and was allowed a few clues: unknown dialect, perhaps an idiomatic family speech. The problem-solving component of his nature was extensive, but he was aware of a deep ambivalence in Molly Kelly; he temporized.

"This one will take some working out," he said. "The Kim-Kelly Dialect . . ."

He promised to send his findings, printed out, for her to take back to her family in a town called Derry. Molly thanked him.

"No one back home will believe all that we have to tell!" she burst out suddenly.

A drumbeat summoned the konos at the river camp to their food, and he returned to the forest meditating on those who could go home and those who could not. An Argosy transporter had been lost in space; it contained, among other things, a unit of the Silver Cross. How many had survived the emergency landing? What were the priorities of a search for a lost craft, a lost unit, a lost person?

Shadow thought of the VIP passenger, the eminent eye surgeon Dr. Valente, who had come down in Capem Tree. He guessed—he was becoming better at guessing—that Valente had survived thanks to his Vippwatch, the big security officer, Chan T.N.R., whom he recalled for her interface problems. He thought of Myrrha Devi, the Kamalin leader, with her family, and guessed again that *she* might have them all found, at some future time. World Space never gave up, of course; records were kept; he had a modicum of data on the *Rho Maryland*. Yet the Kamalin connection would be the most tenacious, reaching out among the stars for their lost leader.

The nights were growing cooler; he found himself taking cover after sunset in one or another of his caves. He woke, sometimes, to find a silkie peering curiously into his face or gnawing his boot-soles. His experiences in observing wild creatures brought him to the conclusion that in some respects human beings had been too much influenced by the behavior of dogs. Androids were generally excluded from work with animals because dogs reacted to them with bewilderment.

Now, for pleasure, he sat still as a stone, gazing out of his cave and playing back the totality of his vision, the island's heights and depths. He saw them wherever he cared to place them, the two young men, threading the trails that he had made and would make, fording the streams, parting the thick undergrowth on the banks of the Orinoco. He woke, one morning, to the sound of bird-calls, to a memory of some expedition that was crystal clear yet unplanned. Daniel Adams realized with a flicker of astonishment that he had begun to dream.

III

Gene Winkler was in better shape now; he had lost seven kilos and figured he could hold out a couple more rounds with Hoot Wells before caving in. He had slotted back into place at the capem but worked outdoors a lot, directing the construction of the first relay shack, on the long eastern beach, midway between the capem and the second relay shack in Blackray Bay. He scanned Gline's Ocean, looking eastward, and cursed it for a misty, wrong-colored, ever-changing tract of water, deceiving the eye with reed-rafts, flotsam of all kinds. He had a little tracker screen installed, and it drove him crazy catching every gray gull, with blips large enough for an oil rig indicating the passage of the Lifeboat One/Fiver or the longboat from point *A* to point *B*. A huge rippling thing identified by Bay Shack . . . shee-it, was *that* what a blackray looked like!

Wink listened hard on the souped-up system and began sending a steady stream of calls and repeaters in the general direction of the Red Ocean. When he came back evenings to the palm grove Anat Asher could tell that he had been given no sign. They had built out her room on the gallery of the dome and usually ate supper there.

"You'll drive yourself crazy," she said. "Those boys got through to the other sea . . . I feel it!"

"Quit pulling that psi jive on me," groaned Wink. "Any movement on the tribal front? How about a report from Silverlake? What's with the Monsignore?"

Anat sighed; Regi's cover had been blown. Now everyone

knew he was a priest. Fallon, the security sergeant, rescued from Four, came out of his coma asking for "Father Sandro" and Lieutenant E.F.A. Regi, S.J., was at his bedside.

"Regi is still the old systems genius," she said. "Don't plag him. Those guys got back from Silverlake. . . ."

Doc Petrova had set out to find the Silver Cross camp, with Zero Zavaski and Louise Reynolds, packing supplies.

"Top Score! How was the going?"

"Like Ray Green had it 'from the network,' " said Anat. "A clear, marked level trail, through two unopened valleys, leading from a point under the Blue Ridge to within a hundred yards of the Silverlake Camp."

"Who can figure that Shadow!" Wink shook his head. "And Boyle? And the leadership?"

"Boyle is in some kind of tent arrest. You were right: Holder is the chief, their new leader. He is running things on a strict Survival Camp plan . . . the Delgardo Woodfolk model."

"It'll suit them." He nodded. "Zero and Louise fit right in as Traders."

"How about Petrova? Wouldn't they want her to stay at the new camp?"

"They have Filly Jones as MTA," pointed out Wink. "Visiting medico would suit the Woodfolk fine. This is a heavily isolationist code. We will be hearing less, not more, from the Silverlake. Secrets of the tribe . . ."

"Don't give me secrets!" said Anat. "And no puzzles either! I'm in the market for straight talk!"

"Hey, honey . . . don't let those Fours get to you. Have you checked out Fallon again?"

"Dell will blip me if his temperature has stabilized," she said. "Ayub Khan is still working on Gregg. Even with the . . . discrepancies in his story he has a strong case. What d'you think?"

"I think his case has been weakened just this last fourteen hours! The typhoon, ABA, has swung right across to the extreme northwest."

They finished supper and went for their evening stroll, down through the bright spaces of the dome and out into the cool air. They took their way down to Sunset Beach, bowing and waving ceremonially at the new roof garden. The commander and his lady had dined with Lieutenant Regi and Doc Petrova. They strolled on, right down to the sand; no boats were drawn up; off to the east, among palms, a Kamalin group were performing a rest nocturne. Anat and Wink stared out across the blue-gray water at the northern horizon, smeared with heavy cloud.

"Maybe it should be done!" she said firmly. "Maybe Khan is right! A rescue mission, right now! Two lifeboats, goddamn it, when the Four is repaired!"

"Nope," said Wink. "Too dangerous. Too many variables."

"Shee-it, Wink! If they had all the loozy breaks . . ."

"Why is it so hard to debrief these mensh?" demanded Wink. "What they been *doing* since landfall? Why can't we get a clearer picture?"

They sat on a couple of weather-beaten, red stacking chairs and contemplated the plight of Capem Four. A fair landing, a good landing, all drogues out, but the jungle marsh, within minutes, as Commander Ito heard Fiver and gave his own coordinates, sucked the curved metal tube of the capem down until it was half-submerged. After that nothing was ever right. Khan was trying to give an official cast to a disordered struggle for survival in vile, inhospitable terrain. Salvage, yes, every day, going down, the oxper kept on going down, a great deal had been salvaged.

The commander has concentrated on small viable groups, with better mobility. One unit has found harder ground, rock, to the northwest.

Question: Roll-call update?

There have been no losses for at least ten days. Two oxper, including the leader, Ben Johns, were lost at the submergence.

Question: Were these the only casualties at this time?

No, no, of course not. Two oxper and the crew members, six, five, yes, it was five. But the rest are all there, holding on, waiting to be brought off; it is not even a full load for a functioning lifeboat. I am empowered by Lieutenant-Commander Ito to make a formal request for emergency help, for rescue, for uncontaminated food and water . . .

Question: What have the units been doing for water?

Differing solutions. Mostly filter pits at the edge of the marsh. Rainwa-

ter, of course, rainwater has been carefully caught, and there has been talk of condensation pans, but this is done privately.

Question: Are any of the units within easy reach of the sea?

There will be no problem finding them. We have this ingenious watchtower. The oxper, led by Henry Cook, the new leader, call it something fanciful, yes, a Totem Tower.

Question (Ray Green): Could Warrant Officer Khan describe the composition of this tower?

It is made up of auxiliary personnel which have ceased to function, placed in the shoulder stand position. Could this auxiliary—Green?—could Green tell us what this indicates?

Answer (Ray Green): It indicates a state of dire emergency.

I told you so! I beg you look about at this rich, well-ordered camp and to think of the sufferings of your sisters and brothers in Capem Four! Commander Gregg, I demand a rescue mission!

Question (Dr. Kyle Cavarro): Warrant Officer Khan, what can you report concerning Specialist Leila F. Khan, your wife?

My wife is fit and active. She has fully supported me in this mercy dash!

Question repeated (Lieutenant Asher): How many days were you at sea before you were taken in tow by the longboat?

I have already said it was four, five days. It was easy to lose track of time. I was in a stuporous condition and so was the big lad. It was exposure, of course, but I also believe it was the polluted water. . . . The man with the head injury was in a coma.

Question repeated (Commander Gregg): Can you explain the damage to the lifeboat, Four/two?

Yes, I have thought about that, and I have the answer. The flotation sacs and the rim were punctured when the crew of the sailing boat tried to salvage the lifeboat. Boat-hooks, of course!

Anat was playing back o-tone from vox. Flower Wilm, the nurse-aide from the *Dancer,* was present at this round of the debriefing; she cried out in protest.

"Officer Khan was in a bad way," she said firmly. "We drew in as close as we were able. No one aboard could give a hand. Bosun Cross managed to throw an oar, tied to a rope, so that it caught and held. The lifeboat was already damaged. Mr. Maddern will have something to say if he hears this quatsh with the bluggy boat-hooks!"

No one else had taken Khan up on an inaccuracy. He was a pathetic figure, on two walk-supports because of his afflicted feet; his grip on reality was uncertain. Now he burst out:

"Is that one of them? I cannot be sure what went on when the lifeboat was caught and they boarded it. All the time, every moment, I had only one thing before my eyes: my rescue mission for our capem. Commander Gregg, I implore you to help us!"

Gene Winkler walked about on the beach, in the fading light; he waved his arms about like Regi:

"He gets to us," he said helplessly. "He's plagged, and his story is rocky in places, but all the same . . ."

"We should try it?" asked Anat.

"I don't think we *can*," said Wink. "The weather. The distance. Remember what young Bud put into the record."

Duval, of Etzel Company, nineteen years old and the youngest member of the Silver Cross, had made a quick recovery. Petrova, who had taken personal care of him, reported that he had been suffering from sunstroke and dehydration. Big Doc had questioned Bud Duval herself; she offered a few pieces of information. Bud, for instance, believed that the lifeboat had been at sea for nine days. Now he went about volunteering for odd jobs, enjoying himself at the swimming pool with the konos. The idea of pulling him in for a hard debriefing, with or without Petrova's approval, was distasteful.

Now Anat was summoned by a call on her blip: Sergeant Fallon was stabilized. Wink walked her back to the dome, then went to check all his new outlets.

Fallon, with a cap of bandages on his head, still looked amazingly like himself.

"Sergeant Fallon? Michael?"

He gave her a smile.

"Hey, Lieutenant Asher . . ."

"Sergeant, do you remember . . . ?"

"Sure! You came into the watchpost on the last night."

Anat felt her eyes fill with tears. In another world they drank coffee, watched the rerun of a talent quest. Fallon was speaking.

"Kyle, the kono on vibes, has come up in the world! I hope that boy with the bird-calls came through . . ."

"Sure," said Anat, smiling. "Loney is fine."

She hoped this was true. No one knew where Loney and Ramirez were at this time, and their heist of the Fiver/two lifeboat looked less like a reckless prank. It showed up the slackness, the affluence, the crazy selfishness of those on the island as contrasted with the suffering at Four Camp.

She took Fallon gently through the prepared questions; in the next room Dell Stout was watching his monitors.

"Hit my fool head some way at the landing," he said. "Seemed to heal okay. Then it got bad again, bad to worse . . ."

"Water supplies?"

"General shortage in all groups. Hardest rationing until the first rain, then it eased up just a little."

"How far from the sea?"

"Twenty-five kilometers. The Silvos pushed through, camped near the shore."

"The submergence, after landfall?"

"Flood come within three meters of the comcen. Oxper worked themselves *kaput* . . . life and limb . . ." Fallon was whispering. "Period of . . . traumatic breakdown. No good hold underfoot, making crazy shelters . . . God help us, it was so bad. I . . . we . . . getting it together. Medic Stoney, Nurse Abiba . . ."

"Did you work with the Khans, husband and wife?"

"No, they are in the rump section."

"Dr. Bauer? Josef Bauer?" she prompted.

"Plagged right out . . ."

Anat Asher thought of Bauer, a senior medic, a man as reliable as gravity itself. She let Fallon have a break, then she said:

"How much do you recall of the lifeboat journey with Warrant Officer Khan?"

"I gave myself no chance," said Michael Fallon. "For all I knew this was another burial run."

"How did you come to be on the lifeboat? Did you volunteer for this mission?"

"No," he whispered. "Like I said . . . I was put aboard unconscious, in a moribund condition. It was pure chance. My wound drained itself a little, the pressure eased. I came to . . ."

"Who else was on the boat . . . ?"

"It was Thurston," he said. "I guess it was Loma Thurston, second lieutenant, commissariat. Died of injury received at Landfall. It was almost impossible to carry out burials in the marsh jungle . . ."

"We want the time taken, the distances," said Anat, gritting her teeth.

"Khan had this crazy plan," said Fallon dreamily, "and the boy, Bud, kept on at him after they lightened the load."

"What plan, Michael?"

"To go south! The control oxper, Evans, wasn't froze up yet. Go south. Find Fiver's Island. Maybe it's true, the comcen *did* pick up these signals . . ."

He rested for a few breaths and then went on:

"We were being blown to the west. Three, four more days after the power pack died and Evans stopped paddling. I was co-matose. I was seeing angels."

"Estimated distance from this island to Four Camp?" said Anat.

"Four to six hundred klicks."

"Was this a mission authorized by Commander Ito?"

Fallon closed his eyes.

"Commander Ito took his own life about the twelfth day after Landfall," he said.

"Okay," said Anat gently. "Okay, Michael. Hang in there. You're doing fine. I'll call the roll of Capem Four. We need some indication . . ."

She went on with the search for information: as if she had to spend her life "looking for trouble," for the doom of the great ship, or the fate of the twenty-seven mensh assigned to Capem Four. When she ended the session a short time later, Fallon was due for his next medication; they had deduced thirteen probable survivors at Four Camp.

"Sit down, Anat," said Doc White, steering her to a chair in the nurses' room. "You're getting tea . . ."

It was brought by Flower Wilm, wearing a regular nurse's overall.

"Indian tea, Mam Asher," she said. "With a spoon of cow's milk powder!"

Dell Stout came and sat at the table; they were joined by Mai Lon after she had attended to Fallon. The mood was down, way down, but under strict control; no one spoke loudly, Mai Lon wiped her eyes.

"There will be a lot of this," said Timothy White. "I mean data of this kind. We must be prepared."

Anat felt less rocky. She looked at Doc White, the young English medic, whose specialty was dentistry, and realized that he was a pearl of great price. Had Patell, the top medical brass, and Bauer, the senior medic, known this when they assigned him to the overcrowded Fiver? Now Bauer was unfit, traumatized, in a bad landing place. She was trying to formulate her feelings of helplessness, even guilt.

"We must get all the data," she said. "We must try to make some assessment . . ."

"Go and see Bruce," said Dell. "See what you think of him . . ."

Anat hardly recognized the name. There he was, not out of traction, a big, angular redhead: Brick Clark, a hunter, a hardliner, from Detroit Company of the Silver Cross. He had paid for a false step in Hunt Valley with a good deal of pain, and he would not be able to rejoin his unit for a heap of long days. Learning to walk again in this gravity, learning to walk a hundred kilometers or so through the valley systems.

"Hello there, Brick!" she said. "Dell Stout tells me you're doing fine!"

"Everyone takin' good care of me, ma'am . . ."

He was tamed, tranked out, ready to sleep; through an open window flap of the dome they looked out at the trail to the Silverbrook.

"We have a great site," he said, "I mean, the whole island. We made the top score. You talk to young Bud from Etzel Company, Lieutenant?"

"Not yet."

"That kid thinks he's in paradise!" Brick laughed unsteadily. "Always wanted to get to Fiver's Island . . . because of the girls!"

Anat managed a smile. Stood to reason, she supposed; there were more girls in Fiver.

"Nurse Stout said I should tell you something else," said Brick Clark. "I had these dreams."

"Dreams?" she echoed warily, switching in her vox.

"Had the first one when the oxper carried me in from the Hunt Valley," he said. "I was in pain from the rough going, so Big Doc put me right out. I don't know what she used, nothing unusual. Anyway, I had this one very clear dream . . . about this guy in a silversuit."

"Tell me . . ."

"He was in the water, in the sea; saw him drifting, twirling around, his suit was inflated. Zoomed down on him, all alone, nothing there. Faceplate of his helmet was open. He took a drink from the water bottle in his Q-pack."

"That was all?"

"It was a special dream," said Brick Clark. "I swear he *was there*, you know what I mean. A survivor."

"Any identification? Did he say anything? Did you see any wreckage?"

"I didn't know his name because he didn't know it himself. He was talking a little. No wreckage."

"Any idea *where* this could be? Up by Four Camp? Or in the red ocean they say is due east?"

"Maybe there. I'm not sure. But in the second dream he got to a beach. I was more alert this time. There was his silversuit lying on the sand, and there was a bucket, a wooden bucket, like a cut-down cask, bound with brass rings. I saw his face but couldn't recognize him; his beard had sprouted. Someone said, like a voiceover: 'The old man is out of his mind.' "

"Did you know, Brick, that the inhabitants of this planet, Rhomary, have a tradition of 'truth dreaming'?"

"Yeah," he said. "Yeah, I heard that from the nurse who came in on that sailboat, Flower Wilm."

"Hang in there," said Anat. "I'll see you get a vox to save any of these special dreams."

She did not know what to make of all this faggidy dreaming that was coming up. She cast about for something positive to do for Brick Clark.

"When you're further ahead, Brick, walking good," she said,

"we can take you around by sea, bring you closer to the Silverlake Camp."

Anat was in two minds about cutting Wink in on these two so-called truth dreams, and, sure enough, he started to chuckle and behave like a pain in the ass. Sure he knew who was on the beach.

11

When they looked back the island had disappeared. They were in a huge bowl of blue-brown water, whizzing along like a water-bug. Blink your eye, and they were high on a hill of water, the planet rolled under them; Harve cried out as they coasted down into a dark maelstrom. Seein' things: fata morgana, *doplas*. Floaters on the monitor, on the eyeball. The lifeboat was a floater on a huge screen, edging towards the gray line of the eastern horizon.

"Shee-it, bad luck, those guys got a loozy *ship,* back there!" said Harvey Aaron Lee Loney. "Just when we do the break, things start grabbin'!"

"The world is full of ships, *mi corazón,*" said Lope Felix de Vega Ramirez. "We are free."

They zoomed along the rest of the afternoon, and in the light of the setting sun they examined the low shoreline. The radiance was still there, as from another body of water, but it had moved ahead of them, like the end of a rainbow. No time for sleeping. They puttered on through the long night, watching the strange stars, noting the up and down of the moon's tiny pearl, the

comet in the northeast. They used one light strip and saw phosphorescent trails in the waves.

A small floater seemed to come right at them: alien attack! It
was a single kelp pod, like the leaf of a huge water lily. Loney
dragged it aboard, strapped on a minipack and the data box
with his messages for old Sarge; Ramirez sent a cryptic greeting
to "a helper and well-wisher."

"I still don't know why the old Shadow did that," said Harve.

For it was Shadow Adams who helped them make the break,
stole the Fiver/two lifeboat from the stores, hid it in the undergrowth on the northeastern tip of the island, in back of the little Silvo dome, and tipped off Loco Ramirez. Never spoke more
than a few words to the pair of them: Loney remembered him
watching as they got the boat all set. At the last they were making sea trials and getting the message, about the loozy ship on the
south coast, and Shadow came in one last time: *"Go now! You
have a diversion!"*

"It was on account Mary Klein broke my thumb," said Lope.

"Holy Crock!" said Harve, "it was Shadow himself
who guessed I was doin' that hot spy number in the crawl space
. . . and reckoned *you* knew about it."

"They went too far with their data search," said Lope. "I held
out too long."

"Shee-it," said Harve fondly, "you are one those overproud
Latins."

Lope reached out and ran a hand over Harve's face.

"Shadow Adams wanted us to be free!"

They launched the powered pod over the stern and saw it
buzzing a steady course due west, with the big wind assist they
had counted on. Then they moved on as the darkness slowly dis-
persed, and the sun reached out from the west and caught them
in its rays. The mists were rising, but they could see that the land
had come a whole lot closer.

There was this long, low strip of sand and to left and right a
green-black fuzz of tree growth. On the right the land went running away southward, backing and filling, in lacy, fractal config-
urations, much farther than the eye could see. To the left, beyond
a small headland, the forest looked more accessible, maybe a lit-

tle like the island, but then the coastline dived back, took off, immeasurable hectares of fag nothing, disappearing to the north.

They were conserving power, but now they put on a spurt and came to the strip of sand, where the second sea must begin, before midday, about brunch time. It was a weird disappointment: they stared at an expanse of still, weedy dark water. Bayou? Lagoon? The strong easterly winds were easing off as they dragged the lifeboat up onto one of the sandbars, ready to eat and sleep. Where was the loozy sea?

"It's *there!*" said Loney, pointing east, through the mist-devils.

"We game to take the boat across this dirty backwater? Fulla snags and sandbanks?"

"*Ships* must have made it across! You see any other way they could have sailed into our ocean?"

"No," admitted Lope, "but what the hell do we know? Coulda come from any direction."

They were whispering. The stillness, the loneliness of the stretch of dead water and the jungle all around was awe-inspiring. After eating they patrolled the sandbanks looking for clues and argued about a tree stump, chopped off handily for a mooring post. Or had it simply snapped off in a gale?

"It was *eaten*, amigo," grinned Lope. "Swamp monster bit it off for brunch."

They spent nights and days right there on the sandbank, making timid expeditions into the trees, diving into the lagoon to test for depth. Lope Ramirez hung on the souped-up transmitter, riding the waves, trying for the island and its many receivers. There was activity out there, faint, teasing, distorted, nothing that could be caught and held. In all the time in and around the big lagoon he caught two pulses of the compacted voice code which deciphered as: . . . *Fiver/one to bay shack off south head passed east relay returning Dancer* . . .

This was a mysterious message. They figured it was George King speaking or maybe Dick Black, jiving around at sea in the Fiver/one lifeboat. But "bay shack"? Was there some relay on the eastern beach? And why were they taking back a dancer? They had some laughs with the message, but the implication was still there, and it was nothing to laugh about. No signal from any other capem. No emergency beacons, no repeaters of any kind, no compact code, no voices calling "Come in Fiver!"

What had come to Capem Tree, the smallest, and Capem Sexer, with the brass? Loney had heard all those eerie bursts of sound, captured at Landfall. Trenchard saying "Splashdown," which meant a sea, a body of water, and the coordinates, which worked out due east. Ramirez worried somewhat about an imagined encounter with the top brass, but Loney figured they could weasel out of trouble. Wouldn't these old heroes be pleased to see them? Wouldn't there be the colonists around, too? For Myrrha Devi's visions of human habitation had become their article of faith, confirmed by George King's sighting of the ship.

They set off across the lagoon one mid-morning when the mists had cleared, taking soundings. The wind had dropped; the transmitter did not even do static; it was like they were in the bottom of a hole. They followed the southern shore, where there was some kind of spice in the air, and saw whole flocks of bird-type creatures, inland, against the sky. They slept under the cover in the afternoon; Harve woke up with Lope shaking him, wide-eyed. A faint whimpering voice said:

"Ahoy."

The word was end-stopped, with a bubbling sound. The two explorers patted around, and Loney found his blaster, but Oh Jesus, first contact, and it is a naked black man waving a blaster? This had overtones any way you looked at it. The voice came again, preceded by a gentle knocking against the side of the lifeboat. Loney put on his tanga, hid the blaster under a T-shirt in his right hand, signaled "Stay here, I'll look!" Ramirez armed himself with a wooden paddle.

Loney crawled out and peered over the edge and encountered two meters of dolphin. Poor bastard was tangled in some kind of net; it had drifted against the boat, and they had translated its dolphin noises as human speech. Just as he was about to call for Lope the dolphin lifted its bulging head, flicked a spray of water into Loney's face, and said mournfully:

"Ahoy you."

"Ahoy, yourself!" said Harve shakily. "Lope? Come out! Now hear this!"

"He needs help," said Lope, bending out to catch the slippery brown mesh of the net.

"Hurp!" said the dolphin wildly. "Hurp! Hurp! Hurp!"

"Take it easy, Niño," said Lope.

They hacked away with Lope's Silver Cross field knife and a pair of wire-cutters. Suddenly, with a huge twist the dolphin was free and went leaping out into the still, brown water of the lagoon. It dived and spouted and came back to the boat, bobbing upright in the water.

It spoke again and sent sprays of water into the boat, but they couldn't make out the words. Dolphin words? Or distorted human words? Distorted *English*, pointed out Ramirez, meaning that there were other human languages. Loney was dragging at the thick, tattered strands of the net, getting some of it aboard.

"I don't figure it as a fishing net," he said, "but it means a ship!"

"Ship!" called Lope. "Is there a ship?"

The answer could have been "gone." The same went for Harve's question about "people, mensh, men and women": *gone! gone! gone!*

"Where is the *sea?*" cried Harve Loney.

The dolphin swam swiftly to the east, looking back at them.

"Come on!" said Ramirez, switching on the pack.

They kept well behind the dolphin, so as not to alarm him with the sound of the power pack, and crossed the lagoon sedately. In the light of the setting sun they saw their guide making long leaps; beyond a maze of channels and sandbars there was the sea again, a second sea, its waters burning red and gold. They ran a roomy channel out of the lagoon into the new sea; they shouted to the dolphin, which leaped and hooted and danced until it was out of sight: free at last!

Now that the Great Dismal Lagoon was left behind the explorers were in high spirits: they sang and played music and put on all their light strips.

"Way I figure it," said Harvey, munching his seaweed cookies, "we follow on down this near coastline, northeast, more or less, and we come to some kind of a colony."

"What's all this old Niño told us? Gone? Everyone gone?"

"Who knows what that means? No one lives here. The ships have sailed somewhere else . . . to our island."

The sea was choppy, and there was rain in the wind for the first time. They beached the lifeboat on another sandbank for the night and set out at dawn into dirty weather. Before midday, when the squall had passed, they saw a curious wave pattern riding towards them through the reddish water. Suddenly they were in the midst of a great circle of dolphins; the air was full of the hum and boom and echo of their voices. The circle doubled, interlocked, spun apart into spouting rows of dolphins riding upright, then formed into a circle under the waves, moving furrows in the water.

Harve and Lope stood up and waved, shouted greetings, looked out for *their* dolphin and spotted him. The welcome, or expression of thanks or whatever it was, went on and on, and there was nothing to do but relax and let the circle gradually edge them along. Fiver/two was twirled and nudged around and around and always in a particular direction.

"Takin' us to the beach, yonder!" shouted Loney.

"What's there?"

It didn't look like much. A narrow twist of land, a cape, with scrubby bushes and a long curve of gray beach.

"What's there?" shouted Lope Ramirez, pointing towards the land. *"Why you taking us there?"*

A speaker from the circles, bronze-colored, rose up and uttered the words:

"Found! You found!"

There was a lot of dolphin talk which they couldn't understand. Lope sat down again grumbling.

"Shee-it, why they want to beach us? This whole ocean and we have to go there?"

But Harve Loney had dragged out a pair of surveyor's goggles and taken a good look.

"Yes," he said in a small voice. "I guess we have to go there . . ."

As they spun onward in the chain, to a humming chorus, Lope took his turn with the goggles. Stretched out, flat and empty upon the gray sand of the beach, there lay a silversuit.

II

The welcome that the konos had planned for Myrrha Devi's return from River Camp turned into a festival for the end of the warm season. The nights had grown colder; some of the tall reeds had died off, leaving the paths bare in patches. Azamo Johnson, who had the official designation of Works Foreman, came out very early with a team and set up shelters in a broad strip of land reaching from the slope of the hill to the marker post for the Hunt Valley. The noticeboard had been torn down and flung into the bushes, but the place of ill omen was still in use. The most efficient shot, Zero Zavaski, went in with Ray Green and culled pigarees for the cookhouse.

The sound of music and voices could be heard in the wind; showers of rain, which came and went during the long day, did not seem to dampen the proceedings. The commander dropped in on this shindig before noon and sat there with his compatriot, Zena, the Australian girl, and with Regi, reminiscing about their home states. Gene Winkler took a look just as the party from River Camp came in sight over the brow of the hill: the Kamalin leader was carried down by George King, Zak Cavarro and his friend Halprin, on a litter decorated with leaf chains.

How was it with his Very Peaceful Tribe? wondered Wink. It was a long time since he had seen them all together and now he was seeing some kind of a division. Kyle Cavarro wore an orange-brown jumpsuit and kissed his mother's hand in formal greeting, but he strode about, lithe and officious, the master of ceremonies. He arranged an exchange of civilities between the commander and Myrrha Devi; his music, on the vibes, was mainly playback. He gave orders to the konos and once at least got a refusal . . . yes, Zena McKay wanted to go her own way. Aha. Wink had an idea which way this would be.

There was a break in the kono music and Kyle announced the first of the "Home Songs," a series of nostalgia requests; it was an Italian sea chanty, for Lieutenant Regi. Songs this old made Sergeant Winkler feel twitchy and irritable. Anat Asher had been doubtful about a brash celebration following the news from Four Camp, and Wink had tried to reassure her. This would be a kono party, gentle, spaced-out: the mime-dancers had rehearsed new routines, they played at being globe-orchids, wind flowers. Everyone came by: he saw Ayub Khan assisting at one of the snack outlets, with Linda Baumer. He tasted Sam Kayoute's holiday refresher.

"Shee-it," said Wink, "what do you call this one?"

"Punch," said Sam succinctly. "Longboat Punch!"

"Go canny!" said a new voice. "It is laced with sugarvine schnapps!"

There was his forest ghost, looking uncommonly solid and healthy, Molly Kelly from the river camp who had come past in the chain dance, with Vannie Frost. Wink ignored the voice of conscience which told him to go back and collect Anat before he got too zonked; he settled in one of the leafy bowers with Zero and Louise. They watched a big blond young guy acting as maypole to Vashti and Faith, who danced with long garlands: it was Bud Duval, in paradise.

Terrible old songs were played, reducing strong men to tears; a big hit melody, wailed and whistled all the rest of the day, was "Moscow Nights," which reduced <u>Big Doc</u> to tears. Wink began to lose track, just a little, as one did on such occasions, but then Molly Kelly and Flower Wilm, of the *Dancer*, were at the music tent, for their number.

". . . a song for a famous sea-captain, Hal Gline, of the *Seahawk*," announced Flower, getting the hang of the mike. "It goes to a sing-along ballad tune, name of 'Troyzar.' "

They began to sing, unaccompanied, in clear strong voices; Gene Winkler was caught and held by the artless words and the foolish old tune:

> *The wild red waves they bear no sign,*
> *To mark the grave of bold Hal Gline,*
> *Of Captain Gline and friends well-known,*
> *Gone down with him to delfinhome!*

He turned aside, clutching a tree for support, aware that it was an alien tree; they had gotten themselves into another goddamned *new world* here. Not the lost forests and the man-made heights of Earth, not even the light-foot paths and pastel settlements of Arkady ... And wherever they were, the thing that would help them most, these human tribes, was the world itself. For they would keep on being mensh wherever they were, forever. What could they do except ... remember.

> *The Seahawk lay a shattered wreck,*
> *The breaking waves dashed o'er her deck,*

Wink shut his ears to the song; he could not bear another shipwreck, another bad landing, a gray beach at the end of "the known world" where this Gline died. He gulped air, feeling painfully sober, and was enlightened. He had a flash, no more, of some other location: sea, sand, figures running on the sand. Like a chase: someone was jumped or tackled, went down in a bundle of arms and legs. He knew suddenly that Hal Loney was alive and well; he really had no need to worry. He stood panting, alone, in the bushes, and heard the end of the song.

> *But though they sink beneath the waves,*
> *Into the dark of sailors' graves,*
> *On every sea beneath the sky,*
> *Their memory will never die!*

He started back but found that it was raining. One of the day's showers whipped over the party pitch, driving everyone under cover; he sat down under one of the larger trees and drank off his emergency tube of OSV. He glimpsed a few others taking cover, but hardly registered who they were ... kids, kidnapped by World Space and landed in a new world. Pretty soon now, he guessed, the balladmakers of Rhomary would be turning out soulful ditties about the *Serendip* and her last trip. Someone went past in the undergrowth bent low, not meant to be seen, but Wink caught a tiny flash of red-brown, no more than it took, back home, to recognize a squirrel in an oak.

Somewhere just below him in a round clearing the bushes thrashed, a girl said urgently *"No! No! Smooth out!"*; there was a muffled scream. Wink was there in two clumsy bounds, in time to see Bud Duval stand up, red-faced, angry, and reach down a hand to help up Faith Cavarro from their bed of leaves. Vashti had screamed.

Kyle broke away from her and spoke in a hoarse, altered voice. Something obvious, something quite strange: *"Get away from my sister!"* He took two sidesteps, then launched his whole body through the air like a missile at Bud Duval. Both girls screamed, and Faith tried to push the tall boy aside, but it was Winkler's presence, a glimpse of the master sergeant, that made Kyle break off or deflect the jump attack. He came down tangled with Bud Duval in the bushes; Wink strode across the clearing, leaned down, and got Kyle in a detention lock.

The two girls had gathered up Bud, who had tears in his eyes.

"What the fag . . ." he mumbled. "Sergeant? Come on now, Faith, honey . . . This guy, this *brother*, must be crazy. . . ."

Kyle had said nothing, had not struggled in the harsh grip. Winkler stared at the two kono girls, remarking what very pretty, desirable young girls they were, free to pick and choose their lovers, members of a peaceful tribe who laid stress on physical and mental harmony. Yet there had been a deadly hangup, and they both knew about it. He said:

"Get Big Doc to take a look at Bud's arm. He had a fall. Say he had a fall."

He did not have to tell them to keep quiet about the incident. The rain had stopped; Kyle's own music was filling the woodland. Winkler released him slowly and deliberately. They stood close together in the center of the forest glade: the young man was almost a head shorter than Wink, olive-skinned, neatly built, perfectly muscled. When he raised his head there was a fierce, dreaming look in his eye.

"Crockin' studs . . ." he whispered. "Got no right . . . to go after . . ."

"Your sisters?" prompted Wink.

It was touch and go with questioning; he felt inadequate to the task.

"Mine. My sister. Not Vashti Johnson. Faith's too young . . . have to look out for her."

Wink knew that he had a slender chance of saying the right

thing; he could not prolong the mood, dig for the truth. He did what was most natural for himself, tried to reason, reinforced a prohibition.

"No!" he said. "You're not her keeper. She's a good, sweet girl. Let her go her own way."

Kyle drew in his breath and let it out in a sob. His face changed; his body relaxed. He was himself again: the organizer, the young man addicted to power, who exploited his siblings, especially the kono girls, used them as servants. Yet there was a hidden pattern of extreme possessive love for one girl. . . . Now he looked Winkler in the eye and said stiffly:

"Family quarrel."

"That was a jump attack," said Winkler evenly. "What was it called again? 'Breaking the Moon Bridge'?"

"Jump attack?" echoed Kyle.

He turned and wandered off through the leaves. Wink shook his head, trying to drive away the terrible suspicion, not turn it into an accusation. He thought *I must tell his Mother* but his heart failed; would Myrrha Devi admit the possibility of Kyle, her son, as a murder suspect? Master Sergeant Winkler sank down groaning onto a fallen tree and tried to think things out.

There had been no proper investigation of Hansi Meyer's death; Wink thought he knew why Gregg was holding back—not because he had Kyle on the list but because he was afraid to catch out a member of the Silver Cross. Suspicion of groups, persons, would ghost around like so many tribal secrets: there would never be a trial, a tribunal of any kind. The death had been caused by an alien beast, by a crazed islander, by Peter Wemyss, defending the native fauna, by a Silvo settling an old score. . . . Now he was simply adding another suspect to the list—Kyle Cavarro, a psychopath, who killed the lover of his younger sister. Oh sure, there were some scraps of evidence. He remembered poor Hansi Meyer speaking of a kono girl. He remembered the material Anat had from Zero and Louise: they had seen Faith in tears, with Vashti and Kyle, near the path to the Silverbrook just before Meyer was ambushed.

Yes, yes, but so the crime was brought home to Kyle, or to some Silvo mugger, what came next? It was a version of the old in-space problem of containment. What the hell did you do with them, what the hell did you do with them when *everyone* was serving a life sentence? What the hell was he to do, what was his duty in this matter?

No, crock it, he would not go running to Gregg, voice this kind of suspicion against the stupid brasshead's loyal and efficient aide. He would share his problems with Doc White and yes, sure, pass a word to Doc Petrova, who counted as one of the commander's household these days.

Wink spared a thought for Ronin Boyle, a psychopath indeed, who had been obeyed, pandered to, then brought down by his own followers. Tent arrest? How would the chieftain of the new survival camp, Martin Holder, handle this one?

Winkler heaved himself back through the woodland to the edge of the festival; gravity getting to him, an old, a very old spaceman at fifty-six. He saw a dark woman, so neatly built and supple, in her white zippersuit, that she might have been one of the konos. He noticed with a twinge of jealousy that she was dancing with Azamo Johnson; the meeting place was full of dancers moving to an old sad Latin rhythm, *"Muerte del Rio."* He watched Anat, the lover he never thought would come his way, and thought of the new world.

III

The Fiver/one lifeboat drew up on the sand and Captain Varo stepped out onto Sunset Beach. He was wearing his best clothes, as were the members of the crew who had made the journey, and so many pairs of breeches, leather vests, neckerchiefs, suggested some kind of historical reenactment. The captain returned Commander Gregg's salute, then shook him warmly by the hand.

"It is a handy craft," he said, smiling. "While the weather holds."

The captain was shown around the camp before settling down to the meeting, which was already known as Cap Varo's Round Table. There was a crowd to welcome the visitors from the

Dancer. Regi had prepared a crash program of data on the origin, organization and customs of the Rhomary Land, with maps and simuls. Megan Varo and Peter Wemyss had worked on this program with George King; at the risk of oversimplification the finished segments contained no reconstruction of the species called the Vail, the lost aquatic life-form which seemed to have occupied the colonists intensely. Wemyss already mourned their loss and reconstructed the giant creatures from woodcuts, on his own vox screen.

Paddy Rork took part of Ray Green's guided tour through the ringing, dark spaces of the capem, then found himself sorted out of the group by an older boy named Carl Johnson. They wandered off on a tour of their own, had ice cream, tried out jump packs at the swimming hole, ate brunch, watched a bunch of trivid funnies.

They sat on the gallery outside the konos' music room and looked down at the oxper moving a raft of tables into the center of the dome, for the meeting. They had talked a lot about sex and about where they had lived and about what made them laugh and about going to school.

"My family," said Carl, in his soft drawling voice, "were always seein' themselves as an island of peace in an overdeveloped society. Now they got too much island . . ."

"You'll get off the island for sure," said Paddy.

"Your Captain Varo will bring back the *Dancer?*"

"Not only!" said Paddy. "Every ship at the Gann will head out! This is the biggest thing that happened in the Rhomary land since . . ."

Since what? Since Flip Kar Karn's hot air balloon? Since the Great Drought? Since the Gline Expedition? It seemed to him that nothing much had ever happened before.

"Since our own Landfall!" he finished bravely.

Captain Varo, in his black frock coat and white linen, took his end of the table, nodded to the commander, and started right in.

"By our calendar we have Freeday, twenty-first Hex, which you reckon as Landfall plus thirty-four, and we are well into the autumn, which is a stormy season, especially in the sea which lies to the east. It has passed very mild up to now, out here in Gline's

Ocean, but there may be a sharp blow coming from the typhoon presently due north on the landmass.

"I must bring home my ship, the brig *Dancer*, and I will give passage to a first party from the transporter *Serendip Dana*."

He took a question from Lieutenant Regi.

"Are we to expect that this typhoon, which we have listed as ABA, will strike the island?"

"No, sir!" said Varo. "That would be an extraordinary piece of misfortune! I mean that the fringe winds may become very brisk if this ABA moves but a few points further south."

"Captain Varo," put in Anat Asher, "you know that we have an emergency in the far north, where Capem Four of the *Serendip Dana* came down in the swamp forest. How do you count the chances of a lifeboat, such as you traveled in today, coming to this area?"

"Mam Asher," said the captain sadly, "it is a place where no one from Rhomary has ever sailed. This island, Palmland, is about the extent of all our journeys. I would not sail a ship there at this time. The powered lifeboats have a good chance of getting through, but it is all the way a gamble with the weather. A mercy mission to help your poor souls yonder might be pinned down and forced to lie over."

There was a disturbance of some kind at a side table, but Ayub Khan seemed to have thought better; he did not speak.

"I have something to say about another mission, first of all," said Keith Gregg.

He looked impressive in his white and gold uniform, and he had dropped most of his fine phrases.

"I've talked this over with regular officers and assigned mensh. It has to do with the chain of command and with the extraordinary piece of *good* fortune we have had in our Landfall. It has to do with our host planet, Rhomary, and the burden our Landfall may place upon its inhabitants. Our one great mission, as I see it, is to determine the fate of every capem and every person who came down in the emergency landing. A special team has been put together to begin this work, and they will sail with Captain Varo in the *Dancer*."

He said the names, and Kyle Cavarro's seating protocol was

explained. There they were, all together: Lieutenant Asher, Lieutenant Regi, Specialist Frost, MTA Dalny, Master Sergeant Winkler, Auxiliary George King; only Lieutenant Wemyss was off base, among the crew of the *Dancer*, assisting the captain. Someone, possibly Doc White, started a round of applause, a rapping of knuckles on the rostra and tabletops. Lieutenant Regi leaped to his feet.

"Commander, I have agreed to go with the Special Team, but now I must withdraw!"

"Why?" said Gregg, responding quickly. "What's the problem?"

Regi was excited but trying to control himself.

"I support the mission . . . with all my heart! But I must begin elsewhere."

"Sandro, you hacked out that agreement!" said Gregg.

Regi did not wave his arms at all.

"Ray Green tells me that the Capem Four lifeboat has been repaired. I volunteer to bring it to Four Camp to rescue the thirteen mensh believed to have survived!"

There was some collective noise around the tables: a breath exhaled, a long sigh.

"This is the first I've heard . . ." said Gregg uneasily.

"Warrant Officer Ayub Khan has offered to return with me. We will remain at the camp until we have clear weather to bring the survivors back to this island."

No one had expected it except Ayub Khan, who came to the main table weeping and pressed Regi's hand. Yet Anat, for one, wondered if Regi's offer was somehow more acceptable now that he was known for a priest. Someone called from the sidelines, asking Cap Varo about the weather again, about the chance of a rescue.

"I have said there are strong chances!" pronounced the captain, "and who would hold back on the rescue of these poor souls!"

The next speaker was Lieutenant Galina Petrova. She started in, cool and dry, Big Doc as she had always been, with some sociolegal points—the Silver Cross contract *did* allow for a termination; they could reconstitute as Woodfolk, for instance, on a simple majority vote. Then Big Doc was saying something else, and Gene Winkler, at least, heard it as a justified reproach.

"The Silver Cross has its own code which is at odds with that of in-space behavior of the regulars from World Space. The Silver Cross was brought here in a failed ship of World Space, the *Serendip Dana,* and deserves the same solidarity and help that is given all other regulars and assigned mensh. Here in this Capem Fiver camp I feel the ranks closing, not even a gap left where the Silver Cross has been. I must urge you all not to forget or abandon the new camp of Chief Martin Holder at Silverlake!"

"Lieutenant Petrova!" burst out Gregg. "I don't want to drag up the Silver Cross trouble . . ."

"How about another moratorium?" drawled Doc White. "Or was that part of the appeasement of Ronin Boyle?"

"Doctor," said the commander, "if you want to thrash out the whole bad interface with the Silver Cross, we'll form a subcommittee and do it, all winter long, here on the island."

"I take Lieutenant Petrova's point!" said Anat Asher. "But the demarcations between regulars and assigned mensh are changing . . ."

"All I wished for," said Petrova mildly, "was a promise of a continuing dialogue between the Silverlake Survival Lodge and this camp."

"Okay! Fine!" said Gregg briskly. "All in favor . . . ?"

There was a strong affirmation. Dell Stout and Doc White, who had been present at that other Round Table, were both struck at different times by feelings of *déjà vu,* as if all meetings of this kind were rigged. Now Kyle gave the sign for the refreshments, and in the midst of the punch and pigaree meatballs and blackray kebabs Myrrha Devi swept in, right on cue.

She wore a long robe of dark red and a large golden sunburst medallion: the regalia of a leader. One of her attendants, Tiria, prompted Kyle, who prompted Gregg.

"Captain Varo," said the commander formally, "may I present Myrrha Devi, coordinator of the KONO media group and teacher of Kamalin Life Enhancement."

The captain bowed and said:

"I am honored, Mam, and must give special thanks to you and

your family for the kind treatment given to our shipmate, Molly Kelly."

"Captain," said Myrrha Devi, "we love Molly Kelly, and she has taught us much about the world of Rhomary. I am here to ask you a particular favor."

"Anything within my power . . ."

"I would like to travel with the *Dancer.* Perhaps you could find room for me and two helpers . . ."

Captain Varo hesitated only a few seconds.

"Yes!" he said. "Yes, Mam Myrrha, we can do it. The space is certainly filling up aboard ship, but with goodwill we can manage it."

"Captain Varo," said Myrrha Devi, "I know you are a trader and that much of your time has been taken up with the rescue mission to this island. I will pay our passage, for myself and my two youngest children, Faith and Zak Cavarro."

Gene Winkler turned his head to look at Kyle Cavarro, the elder brother, and caught the eye of Doc White. The beloved sister was being taken out of Kyle's reach. Did this mean that his mother shared their suspicions? Was this Myrrha Devi's act of judgment? Wink guessed that the young man had not been forewarned of his mother's plan but Kyle's mask hardly slipped. He looked down for a few seconds, then his gaze ranged over the Round Table with the cool concern of the born organizer.

The sight of the two small packages which Azamo carried the length of the table and placed before the captain brought Wink "down to earth." They had been living too long in a world of barter, of graymart trading, of useless credit drawn on the banks of lost worlds. Sure, there had been an agreement about certain presents of equipment, certain trade goods for the *Dancer,* but these packages were more solid.

Anat guessed, softly, and she was right: silver "stamps," handy-sized bars of the pure metal, used by travelers. Now Cap Varo blinked at the contents of the second package, which contained items of jewelry, gold and emeralds, sapphire and pearl.

"Great Vail!" he cried aloud. "This is great wealth, Mam! I don't want to be overpaid!"

"We will discuss," said Myrrha Devi, with a wave of her hand.

"The jewels were meant to satisfy rich Arkadians. Will they find buyers in the Rhomary land?"

"Truly Mam," put in Megan Varo from her place beside Peter Wemyss, "there are many cotton-rich and so on, doctors and merchants, who would be eager to buy such beautiful things."

"Mr. Wemyss," said Myrrha Devi, smiling, "do you see a small white box among the jewels, marked with a golden owl?"

"Yes, I do!" said Wemyss, plucking it from the silken wrappings.

"It contains a fine opal ring," said Myrrha Devi, "and it is yours if you know what to do with it!"

Wemyss blushed and looked at the ring.

"Oh!" he managed. "Oh . . . oh yes!"

The assembled company laughed and cheered; Wemyss gave the ring to Megan Varo, who gave her father a smile and Wemyss another. She did not turn very red or hide her face but lowered her eyes and tried on the ring, which fitted the middle finger of her right hand. She held up the hand with the ring and showed it to the meeting, then favored Wemyss with a kiss on his bearded cheek.

The incident of the betrothal ring was eagerly taken up by everyone on the island; in the oxper network the custom had to be explained to new-batch wishers. Rings caught on, for all occasions; rings of nykol, casply, stan-30, brass, wood and plaited grass changed hands. Several crew members of the *Dancer* saw fit to part with silver rings in exchange for newfangled trade goods: Tom Kirsh had himself two handy blenders powered with mini-paks. Brick Clark, the convalescent Silvo, good with his hands, was presented with a branch of precious coral. He worked with dental drills, carving beautiful rings, set with cultured pearls from a brooch donated by Marna Rossi.

When Zena McKay, the Australian girl, set out for Silverlake Survival Camp she wore a massive Silver Cross signet, as the chosen wife of Chieftain Martin Holder. The official traders, Thaddeus Zavaski and Louise Reynolds, led the party, and two oxper went along, Willie Hale and Alan Cole. These two poor friends had never recovered from the shock they had sustained in the Hunt Valley incident, and Willie had suffered slight water damage in the attack on the *Dancer*.

Humans who worked with auxiliary personnel were uncomfortable and guilt-ridden in the presence of "flickery" oxper: a squinting look, a ruined voice, a halting gait or grasp, these things turned every human coworker into an exploiter, a Dr. Frankenstein. Strangest and most bothersome was the notion of moral involvement: oxper could literally be destroyed by inner scruples or impossible decisions.

Now Willie and Alan, having had as much treatment as was available, were in good enough shape to face the biggest decision of all. The general feeling in Fiver Camp was that the pair of them would be unable to resist the Survival Camp routine; they would stay. Alan Cole, a regular medic oxper, was permitted to go along, remain with his friend . . . Doc White saw this as a gift to the Woodfolk of one oxper, slightly used. The decision-making powers of Willie and Alan were doubtful, whatever they claimed.

The party set down their second camp at the beginning of the Shadow Trail; the wind, which had torn through the tops of the forest trees all day, was really getting up. They could not pitch their tents, and there was no question of a campfire. Master Sergeant Zavaski—who still thought of himself as Zero, not Tad, his mother's name for him as a small boy—was all set to go deeper in, to the northwest, and examine a spur of the central massif, in hopes of a sheltering rock wall.

"Hey, no, wait Sarge!" called Willie. "We got company!"

"Out here in the bush?" exclaimed Zena.

Louise saw him step out of the dripping trees, a stranger, a new person. It was not only the weird clothes—a hat of plaited straw, a poncho made of two blue World Space blankets—but sómething in the contours of his face.

"Daniel Adams!"

He introduced himself and greeted them all by name. The old teasing Silver Cross nicknames were going; the Woodfolk used straight names: Martin Holder, Thomas Fogg, Owen Wells, Anne Lacey. It had been a great honor for Shadow Adams, as an oxper, to rate a nickname, and now he had cast it off.

"Just through here," he said, "where you were heading, Sergeant Zavaski, there's a place out of this wind . . ."

He clapped Willie and Alan on the back, the three oxper took over the lead, and they trailed along to the rock wall. There was a high-roofed cave with a lean-to of saplings at its entrance; inside a fire burned in a stone fireplace with an ingenious convection hood to take out the smoke. They made themselves comfortable; Louise and Alan prepared food for those who needed it.

"Think this is a taste of the fringe-winds from the typhoon?" asked Zavaski.

"Yes," said Daniel Adams. "There'll be a couple bad nights back in Fiver Camp. The Silverlake won't be too much affected."

In the course of the evening he produced a bunch of holoks, showed them to Zavaski and the others. Howlers. Silkies. It was one thing to know about these guys from the Rhomarians and another to see their pictures. More than just cute, these long, flexible, knowing, bright-faced creatures moved everyone, provoked joy and sorrow.

"Shee-it!" said Zavaski. "I wish I could say I never winged one of them, back on the Silverbrook. But I did."

"Yes," said Adams. "It was a female. Paddy Rork and I found the body on the cliffs, the day the ship came in."

"There, I knew it!" said Zero, fierce and sad, to Louise. "I said all along there was a howler. Female, was it?"

"These two in the holoks are her grown cubs. Spot and Jenny," said Daniel. "They're doing fine. Have a base cave on the cliffs, first with Wemyss, now with me."

"How about that!" said Louise. "I don't see them as dangerous . . . able to kill a human being."

"No," said Daniel Adams.

Zena flipped a twig onto the glowing stones, and the sparks flew upward. The talk was directed another way . . . woodcraft, the way the new camp at Silverlake was building, animals of Rhomary and of Earth, some Kamalin songs to accompany a young woman on her marriage journey.

In the course of the night Daniel Adams drew aside with Willie and Alan; the three oxper sat in a corner of the cave while the others slept. They were silent, but none of the humans doubted that good communication had taken place. In the morning Daniel Adams was gone. The party set out for another long day's march through the stinging rain and the fringe winds, diminishing as they walked south towards Silverlake. Zavaski and Louise were not surprised at the end of the visit when Willie Hale and Alan Cole decided to go back to Fiver Camp.

"He steadied those boys, old Shadow," said Zero.

Willie and Alan walked ahead, laughing.

"He took their part," said Louise. "Who knows an oxper better!"

"Silverlake ain't so bad," said Zero. "Holder makes a fine leader. They are all fit, clean, don't haze no more . . ."

"Tyrone Boyle," said Louise in a low voice. "Who will take his part?"

They had no contact with the former leader. Louise had seen him sitting outside his special lodge, around the head of the lake. She fixed this sighting in her mind and embroidered it a little until she was not sure if she saw the Ronin stand up, flex his muscles in the old way, do a couple of push-ups or knee bends. This was the last independent sighting: the rest was tribal legend, not half so well founded as the case of Hansi Meyer. It came partly from the oxper network, unofficial, flickery. There was a trial, a kangaroo court, heavy with Woodfolk ritual, torchlight, public testimony. It was difficult to place Boyle in this setting; no one knew his condition. But he had an advocate, who appeared out of the bush, knowing more about the accused than any other human or system on the island. Daniel Adams presented an insanity plea. The legend trailed off into mere speculation. No one could say what the court, if there was a court, had decided.

When the new dialogues began in the spring there was a standard response from the Woodfolk: Tyrone Boyle was "in retreat" or "gone bush." When Gene Winkler got to hear of this he hoped, for a moment, that Chief Holder and his merry men *had* figured out some humane solution for the problem of restraining antisocial elements, but reason told him this was unlikely.

12

Ramirez went ahead to check for hidden snags. He directed Loney, who ran the lifeboat gently up onto the gray sand and made it fast to another handy mooring post. When they looked again the whole dolphin tribe had taken off, left them to it.

"Yo! Yo-o!" yodeled Harve Loney. "Alert call! Capem Fiver online! Can you hear us?"

And more of the same. He called and sang and mixed it up with some bird calls. One large, ugly gray bird about the size of an albatross rose up in the west and flapped off seaward. They kept pausing to listen. There was no reply, not even a groan or a whisper. Harve finished with a despairing bellow:

"We come from the *SERENDIP DANA . . .*"

He went and knelt beside Lope, who was examining the silversuit. It was in good shape, at least, no big damage, some wear around the neck flaps; all the pockets and glides, the light-slots for labels and for the tags and ID were open, empty.

"Plagged," whispered Harve. "What ya think?"

"Maybe lyin' around . . ." said Lope, spooked.

"Something . . ." said Harve. "This suit has a kind of fancy quality, you know. Brass, probably. They could have had something like this."

"What's *that*?" demanded Ramirez.

The part of the beach they were on was bounded by thick scrub to the east, and the wide gray sands to the west were broken up with clumps of rock and occasional bushes. The jungle trees stood far back; less than a hundred meters away, up the gentle slope of the beach, was an artifact, a low curved wall of cut stone. As they went towards it Lope made the identification:

"Spring of water!"

There was a ceramic pipe and a wooden bucket; beside the stone coping of the spring was a sturdy wooden chest with a hinged lid. When Harve swung back the lid they read the notice inside, painted on the smooth wood: *Replace with fresh, dated rations.* There was a big pot with a tight-fitting lid, half full of a brown bread-type substance; a gourd with fish in oil, a leather bottle of hard stuff, spirits, which took their breath away.

The real eye-catcher was the work of a monumental mason; the engraved stone tablets spread out on the curve of the wall. They sat down on the sand with two handfuls of the bread and one shot of the schnapps in an old metal cup. They passed it from hand to hand while they read the memorial.

> In memory of *Harald McKenzie Gline,* Captain and Master of the brig *Seahawk,* who sailed farthest west in the Red Ocean, in his quest for still larger seas, and perished, with other brave shipmates, after his vessel foundered, 12 Tray, 1080, New Style. This memorial has been built to honor all those who sailed with Captain Gline and First Officer *Vera Swift,* who raised the first rescue expedition. In the name of the Councils of Rhomary, Doctors' College, the Town Council of Derry, and the Memorial Committee of the Gann Station.

"Ten-eighty?" said Loney. "What kinda crazy base they using?"

"Do they remember how they got here?" asked Lope. "Plenty

organized now, with *councils* and like that, but what was their ship, their mission, where were they heading?"

"Sure they remember!" said Harve. "Will we forget?"

"Gotta get searching!" said Lope.

He sprang up and walked around the wall; Loney heard a Spanish oath. His friend leaned over the stonework and said:

"This poor bastard must be . . . loco."

"What you got? Is he there?" cried Harve.

"No, just his boots!"

He held them up. They sat in the shade of a wind-warped tree behind the wall and examined the boots. Custom made, of pale, thick rindal, the sort of thing Gregg or even Boyle might have affected.

"Come on . . ." said Harve. "We have an officer, dying with his boots off."

It was exactly the wrong time of the long day for a search but the weather had turned around, as if a squall was approaching. They left the boots back of the shipwreck memorial and wandered slowly westward, through the scrub, keeping a sharp lookout. They walked on and on, couple of klicks at least, and came to another small beach, almost in sight of the lagoon they had crossed.

The vibes were strange and bad; a cold rain was falling, whipped into funnels by contrary gusts of wind. Lope Ramirez, who said his grandmother had been a witch, did not care for the place at all. Harve Loney wondered about a time zone: they come back through the scrub and it is otherwhen, with the old explorer and his crew ghosting about and the lifeboat gone, gone, gone . . . Suddenly he laughed.

"Ssh!" said Lope.

"I got it!" said Harve, in an excited whisper. "What was the name of the loozy *station* back there on the wall?"

"Gann," said Lope.

"Gann, Gann, Gann!" cried Harve. "Don't you get it? Old Niño was sayin' *Gann!*"

"Where the people are!" said Lope. "Shee-it! You are smart in your head, you know that?"

"Let's get away from this place," said Harve.

They turned and ran into one of the paths through the scrub and were moving along steadily when they heard it for the very first time. Stealthy movement, some way ahead of them on the low track. They did not speak but went sneaking along, bent double, and at last they saw him. They had come back to the main beach and a male Caucasian, a tall, weathered old man in a ragged suit-liner and socks, was going away from them across the gray sands.

He was heading for the lifeboat, loping along, bent over, and he was badly spooked, jumping at the cloud-shadows. They watched him go, did not show themselves. At last he fell down on his hands and knees, crawled over the broad yellow rim and fell into the boat like a bag of laundry. Loney and Ramirez came out of the bushes and advanced cautiously.

"Officer?" said Harve, medium loud. "Sir?"

Not a sound. Ramirez could stand it no longer.

"He's hurt! We gotta . . ."

They looked into the boat and there he was, curled on his side, his gray head pillowed on Loney's Q-pack, fast asleep.

"Okay, you tell me!" said Lope, going for the medikit. "Which one is it?"

"What do I know?" said Loney sadly.

He stared at the man's face, which bore an uneven, tufty growth of black-and-white beard. After a while he said:

"It ain't Trenchard, the Astrogator. I knew Trenchard, took one of his courses."

Ramirez laid a finger on the man's pulse, which was settling nicely, and they looked him over. No injuries that they could see, though his hands were scratched. They extended the cover flaps to protect him from the cool, gusty weather and let him sleep. Middle of the long afternoon the sleeper stirred and spoke a few words, nothing they could get hold of except a name: *"Cosma."*

"Arkady name," whispered Loney. "There was one nurse, I swear, Cosma, an Alpha . . ."

"Is this guy an Alpha?" asked Ramirez.

"No. None of the top brass were. Big protest point with the

Arkady admin," said Loney. "Alphas not able to get ahead in the service. Depressed minority, Sarge called it. Like in the old days. Colored Folks."

"Mexicans," said Ramirez.

Harve went after the silversuit, where they had left it. He was brushing off the sand when Ramirez uttered a wild cry. He turned to see the old guy clear of the boat all of a sudden and making long strides toward the bushes. He zeroed in and so did Lope; it was no contest, they hardly liked to touch him. He went down in a flying tackle but could not thrash about real good, he was, hell, an old man.

"Sir, sir," panted Harve, sitting on the man's back. "You gotta stay in cover. You're not in shape . . ."

The old man groaned and mumbled. They let him sit up and Ramirez tried to feed him a regulation pink. He could not get it down but sat there quietly while Lope fetched a cup of spring water. At last he said, in a terrible creaking voice:

"Capem?"

"Yessir!" said Loney. "We come from Capem Fiver. Beached on uninhabited island two hundred sea miles due west in a different ocean. Twenty-five regulars, eighteen members of the Silver Cross and twelve konos. Sir."

"God!" said the old man. "All those . . ."

He began to cry with dry, rasping, noisy sobs and sparse tears running down his sandy cheeks.

"Come on, sir," said Ramirez briskly. "Got to get you in the lifeboat."

"Wait!"

He opened his eyes wide and stared hard at each of his rescuers in turn. They sat down on the sand. Presently he said, with an effort:

"Boys, you see the writing on that wall? It was made by human beings, right? Tell me what you think it says."

"Sure," said Loney. "It's a memorial to the captain and crew of a sailing ship."

"So what the hell else does it tell you?"

"The planet is inhabited by a castaway society," said Loney firmly. "Been here a long time . . . call their territory something like the Ro-marry land . . . don't know how they say it, I'll spell it out . . ."

The old man shook his head.

"Anyway," finished Loney, "nearest outpost is called Gann Station."

Ramirez had been watching the old man keenly. Now he said: "Sir, where is your identification?"

"In my helmet," said the old man shyly. "We—I collected it all up, put it in my helmet. Wasn't much use to me. You some kind of a medic, boy?"

"Got my orderly ticket in Psych-help," said Ramirez.

"Amnesia," said the old man. "Memory still—playing tricks. And worse than that . . . I don't have the word . . ."

"Aphasia," said Ramirez, "Patient can't read . . ."

"Shee-it!" murmured Loney.

"Patient often has trouble *speaking,*" said Ramirez. "Or a mixture of both. It is the darndest thing. Sir, you're doing well with the speaking. Your coordination is pretty good. These things are temporary, I swear. Main thing is we get you in the boat, clean you up, make you comfortable."

The old man looked from one to the other with the ghost of a smile.

"Reassuring the patient," he said. "You see any other signs of the castaway group?"

"No sir," said Loney. "But we know that one of those sailships reached our island. Confirmed by the oxper network. And we heard some stuff from the dolphins, dolphin-type creatures . . ."

They had him on his feet now and were walking him to the lifeboat. He propped, with a gasp.

"Thought that was one of my loozy sea-dreams . . . floating, I was a long time floating."

"No sir, they sure as hell talk."

"There was no one else here on the beach?"

"No sir. There's no one else here," said Loney.

The old man did not speak again that day. He was cleaned up, put into a fresh suitliner and then into his de-sanded silversuit. Ramirez fetched his boots. Loney wanted to question the patient; he jogged his own memory to the point where he had more names for the top brass.

"No," said Ramirez. "Let him sleep some more. Point is for *him* to remember."

"Might take forever."

"Relax," said Lope. "We got plenty of time. . . ."

But he heaved a deep sigh. Harve knew what he was thinking: their adventure, their escape, their very own discovery of the new world.

"Couple faggidy nurse-mothers!" he said. "Break out of one loozy system, the service, and it catches you again!"

"What else could we do?" Lope smiled.

In the night the winds became very strong, rocking the lifeboat, threatening to flip it right over on the gray sand. They woke to the old man shouting names: *"Patell? Eva? Eva McGrath!"*, and somehow all three of them manhandled the bucking, cumbersome craft into shelter, back of the stone wall. Gradually the winds flattened out; another weird western sunrise reddened the sea. They saw monstrous, yellow-black heaps of cloud a long way off, working into the jungle.

"Typhoon!" grated the old man confidently. "Get breakfast, Ensign."

"Sir!"

Loney fumbled in the storage pockets while Ramirez gave the old man his medication. Routine. Another day for remembering.

II

The fringe winds of Typhoon ABA had flicked over the Capem Five camp, flattened a few landmarks—the Cookhouse Tree, the diving platform—showing the power of the storm. Now that the danger had passed and the typhoon itself was just visible as a patch of brownish turbulence northeast on the distant landmass, there was a rush to put out to sea. The Four lifeboat, restored and well-provisioned, set out from Sunset Beach at first light, Landfall+38. There had been a farewell gathering the evening before; now only a small group stood there in the cold mist, gazing out at choppy gray waves.

Anat Asher related them to those who watched the first sunset: Gregg was still there and Petrova, but Boyle had gone and so had Shadow Adams. Ray Green was around, with a small oxper team to assist at the launching; Anat herself stood with Sergeant Fallon, up and about again. Now Regi came, highly motivated, still the Maestro, the mad genius from Systems, shaking everyone by the hand, giving Fallon a blessing.

Ayub Khan was changed and healed, a handsome, composed individual, his emotions held in check, his mission just beginning. Anat found that she could not trust the poor man: she could not understand his temperament, his opportunism, his degree of instability. She questioned her own conscience: Ayub Khan was a practicing Moslem. The two men who now took their places in the lifeboat were true believers, men of faith. . . .

Khan steered the lifeboat gently from the shelving sands while Regi saw to the collection of floats in a rainbow of neon colors: a simple measure he had worked out with Ray Green. Boosters on the buoys might improve signals. There were loud farewell calls; the watchers remained until the first booster station was set afloat. Anat Asher wondered if she would ever see Regi again. She took a look through her goggles and the tightness in her throat turned into a bubble of laughter. The figures in the yellow boat appeared to be in heated discussion: both men were standing up and waving their arms.

Captain Varo was eager to set sail but he controlled his impatience for the sake of his passengers. His crew had never known him so sweetly reasonable and wondered if the mood would last. His officers, First and Third, acting on his instruction, his whims and their own good sense, had performed the difficult task of fitting everybody in.

The hierarchical component of life on a sailing ship showed itself very plain: Paddy Rork knew that he would end up sleeping in the bluggy cargo hold and was glad the spice berries lay between him and the weighty skin, oil, and sundries from the blackray. He even had a companion, Zak Cavarro, the young, silky-bearded kono, one of the "bluies" that Paddy had first seen high on the Blue Ridge.

Although the captain made a brave offer to give up his own cabin to Myrrha Devi and her daughter, Faith, this sacrifice was not necessary. Since Flower Wilm had been given leave to stay behind and become the first Earth-trained nurse for two hundred years, Winna Cross was left alone. She gave up her double cabin to the Kamalin leader and the captain took his old shipmate to share his quarters, as indeed she did most of their shore time. The fo'c'sle cubbies were filled up so Tom Kirsh bunked down in his galley. He knew that the Earthfolk were all used to roughing it: Peter Wemyss and Ivan Dalny were already useful shipmates. Mam Asher and Sergeant Winkler expressed themselves pleased with the cleared-out storeroom. Tom was not sure whether all the newcomers *needed* to sleep, but in the watches of the night, when the *Dancer* was under way at last, he would find George King curled up in the snug, catching some shut-eye.

On the day of days Daniel Adams stood on the cliff-top, above the Stone Garden, and watched the *Dancer*. He beheld the slow and determined progress of the strange craft, against the unsettled winds and the choppy gray-brown sea. Below at the relay post on the eastern beach a crowd had gathered to wave; he added his own pulse of farewell to the oxper network, sending to George King. He apprehended the island, Palmland, its heights and forests and caves and the new trails he was building. He contemplated the two discrete communities, the Woodfolk in the southwest and the capem camp in the north. The river camp, on the Orinoco, was not so hospitable in this season but he knew Sam Kayoute had the Johnson family up there, with Ed Rowe, harvesting the tomatoes and sweet corn.

He held in his mind the dreams of his two adventurers, created for them any number of virtual realities: birdsong, sunlight through the leaves. Yet he could not put aside his anxiety for the two prototypes, Loney and Ramirez. Where were they now? He had indulged in some comforting speculation with his last visitor from the *Dancer*, with Wemyss, come to bid farewell to Spot and Jenny, the young silkies, and to his cave. They agreed that Harve and Lope rated high for survival.

He had transferred a good deal of new data on the flora and fauna of the island to the vox of Peter Wemyss, who insisted that a new file, DANA, be created for him. He put in as well a short dissertation on the Kim-Kelly family speech to be printed out aboard ship for Molly Kelly: a relatively simple patois based on twenty-first-century Business Thai, with borrowings from British English and many idiosyncratic words.

Wemyss, who lived among the people of Rhomary aboard the *Dancer,* returned to the subject of dreams. Truth dreaming, widely accepted, along with various degrees of telepathy . . . Wemyss had an inbuilt skepticism that matched his own. The naturalist was surprised at the confession that he, Daniel Adams, believed he had begun to dream.

"You seem to have developed . . . something unexpected!" Wemyss grinned.

"Will you call it a soul?" he asked warily.

"By no means!" said Wemyss. "I was going to suggest a reservoir, the maker of souls. The unconscious mind."

Now, watching the progress of the ship, he missed Wemyss and hoped he would come again. He did not watch until the *Dancer* was out of sight but turned back to the island, the tasks and contemplations that made up his personal continuum.

Captain Varo climbed up to his bridge to see the ship go about and remained there wrapped in his sea-cloak like a pillar of darkness. Ira Maddern had the wheel and when Molly Kelly came to relieve him he stood with the captain awhile before going below. Light was growing, to port; the sea was a murky green, lacking the phosphorus trails of summer; the wind that sent the *Dancer* scudding along had shifted a few points to the northeast.

"We are taking a risk coming so far north in this season!" said Ira Maddern.

"I am impatient," said Simon Varo. "Vail knows what is waiting for us. Two deaths on the voyage. I must carry bad news to the Wells clan in Derry town and to Man Gruner's mother in Pebble. Then there is the Navigation Board . . ."

"Captain, you are bearing the greatest treasure trove of any seafarer in the Rhomary land! These travelers and their technics will change the world!"

Cap Varo gave a gusty sigh.

"Maybe the Board will take a friendly view. . . ."

Ira Maddern took himself below, looking forward to his breakfast and maybe another improving game of chess with George King. This was surely the most interesting and harmonious shipload he had ever sailed with.

But three days farther out, at exactly the same time of day, as he came down the companionway he heard thumps and cries coming from farther below decks. Winna Cross was already on her way down to the hold.

"What in dry hell are those boys up to? Paddy?" she called. They found Paddy Rork and Zak Cavarro rolling about in a wrestling grip and pummeling one another at the foot of the ladder. So much for peaceful cooperation. Ira could not help noticing, before Winna dragged the two apart, that Paddy was giving as good as he got, though the Earth boy was a head taller and somewhat older.

"Be ashamed, Paddy Rork!" scolded Winna. "And you too, Zak! What kind of behavior is this, from a crew member and a Kamalin believer? You should both be haled before the captain!"

"They can answer to me, first of all!" said Ira Maddern, climbing down. "Come, speak up Paddy! What is this bluggy fighting, end of the morning watch?"

Paddy hung his head and would not answer. Zak spoke up angrily:

"Loozy kid jumped me! What should I know about his love-hopes?"

Winna seemed to make some sense of this remark; she gave Ira Maddern a wink and said:

"Keep all your romancing of the sailor girls until the voyage is over, Zak Cavarro! What do you have in mind for these young dry-hogs, Mr. Maddern?"

Ira doled out punishment: there were always plenty of unpopular chores. Two turns at checking the cargo hold and an hour each polishing metal. He made the pair of them shake hands, sent Zak up to his mother's breakfast meeting, left Paddy to get the sleeping place shipshape again. He asked no questions; word of the fight had got about and in the snug Ketty Merrow was blushing angrily. No business of Paddy Rork's who she danced with at the evening Happy Hour.

So they came at last, after long, strange-tasting, rhythmic, rocking nights and days, to a small headland at the edge of an eerie gray-green lagoon.

"The so-called Deadwater, Sergeant," announced Cap Varo.

Gene Winkler had been called to the bridge by Ivan Dalny in the first light of dawn. He had tried to lull himself, like all good space-travelers, into a trance of nonexpectation, but now he was too much awake, all his nerve-ends twanging. He expected bad news of the lost boys.

"Any signs, Captain?"

"Surely." Varo smiled. "Molly?"

"Paddy and I took a quick look with the cocker boat," said Molly Kelly, "and there on the bar, further south, is the place where they camped."

Wink whooped aloud. He hung over the rails and heard the details as the *Dancer* inched through the channel into the Deadwater and continued gently under way along the southern shore. There was no chance to go back and check the place; the ship dared not lose these light airs. Anat Asher joined him on deck and said:

"It won't be long now!"

"What's this?" he growled. "You joining the Rhomary Psi Push? Been dreaming truth dreams?"

"Myrrha Devi says it won't be long."

But the day, at any rate, was very long. There was a tendency for the passengers to come on deck and stand in clumps, experiencing the Deadwater, which proved to be a damnably strange place. The electronic aids were affected; George King was forced to sit down and bend his head sideways. Anat knelt beside him, alarmed.

"Anything we can do, George? You want to go below? Can we—uh, cover you with one of those T-stat blankets?"

"N-not necessary, Lieutenant," said George in a flickery voice. "I've disconnected some of my banks, is all. Avoid contamination."

"What is it anyway?"

"Weak emission from deep strata, uranium isotopes . . . couple new ones. Something came down here, Lieutenant. Way back in time, long before the arrival of the *Rho Maryland* . . . something with a long half-life."

"How are the readings for human life, George?"

"No immediate danger, Lieutenant . . . who knows about the long term?"

The gentle wind sent long ripples moving over the weed-patterned surface of the lagoon. Lon Adma had the wheel, with Seela Conor and Paddy hanging over the bowsprit, keeping watch as the *Dancer* threaded the slow channels. Passing their own beach, the Spicebowl, where they had labored, picking berries, they heaved aside an old cargo net of thick kelp with their long boat-hooks. Still the wind held and late in the day they came within sight of the Red Ocean.

This was the occasion of so much excitement and crowding on deck that Cap Varo had to take measures to trim the ship. When the passengers, except for a few chosen observers, had been safely stowed, the captain and his two officers stood and cursed a new situation.

"Closed up, d'ye see, Captain?" shouted Ira Maddern.

"I'm not blind, Ira!" replied Simon Varo. "Megan, get the cocker boat down with a sounder."

"Aye sir!"

Megan shouted orders to Winna and Molly. The pattern of the sandbanks had been changed; heaps of silt and scrub thrown about as by a giant hand.

"This will be the bluggy typhoon," said Cap Varo to Vannie Frost. "If we find no way while the light lasts we may have to lie over."

Vannie tried to get pressure readings from her vox but it was still acting up.

"You reckon the big twister, ABA, is still waiting for us, Captain?"

"Gone through by some days." Varo grinned. "Maybe it is in the region of the Six Seven Islands, due east."

In the light of the setting sun the new sea looked red indeed; even before the regular calls from the sounders gave the word a broad new channel was visible from the bridge. Those on deck gave a joyful shout and Paddy hollered from the crosstrees. Vannie, who was interested in comparative dimensions, knew that the ship was sailing, via the Deadwater lagoon, from the Pacific Ocean into the Caspian Sea. The channel was deep, the soundings safer and safer; the little boat was quickly taken up again, and Winna Cross winched out more sail. Vannie put on her goggles and searched the red waves; some way off to port was a shoreline.

"Captain," she asked warily, "are we coming into a possible search zone?"

"We're keeping a sharp lookout for the boys in the lifeboat!"

"I know that, Captain. But how about the capems . . . ?"

Captain Varo heaved a deep sigh.

"Mam Frost," he said, "it would be a wonder to me if any mensh from your capsules Three and Six are to be found in these western waters of the Red Ocean."

"Father," said Megan softly, "what of Gline's Beach?"

It was a reminder of the vagaries of the seas; wonders and strange rescues did happen. So next day, in spite of the dirty weather that haunted this end of the Red Ocean, the *Dancer* was brought in close enough to scrutinize the bleak gray beach with telescopes and surveyor's goggles. The captain was prepared to let down the longboat but the beach was empty, there were no signs of life, not so much as a spar or a stray boot. The ship sailed on, homeward bound for the Gann, taking a course due east along the northern shore.

Myrrha Devi woke up in the dark and felt all her faculties come alive again. She had prayed for guidance in family matters and the answer was this journey. But the discomfort of the little ship had dampened her spirit and diminished her powers; when she gave reassurance to her fellow travelers she felt like a fraudulent medium. She had seen no visions in all the days at sea. Even the passage over the Sunset Deep could raise no ghosts of that sea burial which she had witnessed, where Captain Varo had read the words of Marna Devi, founder of Kamalin. *"Nothing is lost. No spark of life is lost. . . ."*

Now she woke with the words ringing in her head and rose up quickly, drawing a shawl over her kaftan, moving as quietly as she could so as not to wake Faith, who slept in the top bunk. The passage to the companionway was empty except for George King in a listening attitude. He nodded politely, holding up a hand for silence, and whispered:

"Signal!"

She felt the comfort of having her knowledge confirmed. George made two strides to the door of the storeroom but before he could knock it flew open. Gene Winkler eased himself out, surprised but just as certain. They crept on deck into the cold wind of dawn, and the sounds of the *Dancer* moving through the wine-dark sea. Winna Cross, officer of the watch, stood amidships; Ivan Dalny was at the wheel; Ketty Merrow was just going aloft.

He is floating again, in an uneasy state between dream and waking, alone again upon a wide alien sea. Now he knows more, his recall is functioning, he is overpowered with names of men and women he should have known, should never have forgotten . . . And those plagged goons from the Silver Cross, always a problem zone, with the assigned mensh, yet the ships sail on, year after light year, and it never comes to a loozy break until this time. He feels obliged to wake, to rise up through his layers of consciousness and open his eyes, but he hangs in there, finding at last a schema. How it must have been. Tendency to set everyone at a distance, actors in slow motion all of them, including himself. Trenchard on the outlets, assisted by McGrath; Patell and the nurse, Cosma Rostov, tending Rocher, down with breathing difficulties; Oona Casey and Sabine Weil handling all the systems, momentarily, because blowing the hatch, getting it down, was a strong-arm assignment, touch of precedence, loozy prestige factor, first out, only a small pattern of

hand-grips for a man . . . So that pointed to Batten, the Old Man himself. Operation worked like a charm, the air rich as the readings promised, then Sexer, perfectly splashed down, canted fatally, bounced the official opener against the edge of the door, sank in minutes. Leaving one man alone, regaining consciousness alone, talking to the moon, hearing the hooting of the dolphin tribe, dreaming up the Arkady nurse, Cosma. Not a believer, no kind of religious man, Psi tests low-normal for his age-group, but could there have been something of the woman herself in that presence? He remembers his despair when the dream faded, when she left him alone. He floats, buoyed up by the lifeboat; its forward motion checks, altering course and there are distant voices . . . His rescue boys are still hanging on their fractious transmitter and always on the point of seeing ships. Now they are shouting a name:
<u>*George King! Holy Jesus Mother! George King is on the ship! Get him awake! Ohayo, Captain!*</u>

    George King? He is floored by this one but only for a second. Systems auxiliary George King. He begins to surface slowly, remembering the names. . . .

George King said quietly:
    "They have seen us!"
    Overhead Ketty Merrow uttered a strong, shrill cry:
    "Lifeboat ahead! Closing fast to port!"
    Wink could see nothing; he shut his eyes and heard the shouts as the *Dancer* hove to. Myrrha Devi was uttering words of praise; a word penetrated from George King.
    "Survivor?"
    There was the loozy Fiver/two lifeboat just about within hailing distance at last.
    "Who the hell have they got there?"
    "Signal unclear," said George. "A man. An old man."
    Wink felt a grin splitting his face. He remembered Brick Clark's dream.
    "Okay, okay!" said Anat Asher, slipping an arm around his waist. "You told me so!"
    They laughed aloud.
    "Top brass got lucky!" he said. "It's Batten! The Old Man himself!"

"Inform Cap Varo," she said. "Protocol. All members of the *Serendip Dana* party on deck!"

"Aye, aye ma'am!"

He turned aside to find Cap Varo, who was shouting through his hog-caller, ordering all hands and passengers to trim the ship. Anat watched the tall figure in a silversuit, standing in the lifeboat: the Old Man. She thought of his last broadcast, how she stood with Ren Beattie, outside the Reception Round, did not go in to see the captain speak. It had been a very small withdrawal of her loyalty and now she felt a rush of feeling for the Old Man, the lost ship, the lost comrades.

There was a certain amount of noisy voice communication as the lifeboat drew alongside. Ramirez and Loney assisted their passenger up the thick kelp rungs of the boarding ladder until George King could reach down and draw him over the rail.

Batten A.R.K., captain of the *Serendip Dana*, seemed to be in fair shape; he greeted Captain Varo with a firm handshake and rapped out the names of the service personnel and the assigned mensh: *Specialist Frost, Myrrha Devi, Auxiliary King, Lieutenant Wemyss, Lieutenant Asher, Sergeant Winkler* . . .

He recognized Asher as the ranking service officer and drew her to his side.

"Strange meeting—" he said, with a tight smile. "Need a lot of debriefing, Lieutenant."

Anat gave him an unashamed hug and it loosed a ragged cheer from all the passengers, which was taken up by the crew of the *Dancer*. Batten was pleased but Wink caught a wild look in the captain's eye. Half plagged still, the Old Man. And he *was* an old man, older even than Wink himself, past sixty. The two old men of the tribe had survived while how many young mensh had died.

Captain Batten allowed himself to be led below for medication and debriefing. Wink found himself rubbing shoulders at last with Loney; Ramirez stood close by. They could not keep the grins off their faggidy long-lost faces.

"Okay," said Wink. "You found the Old Man. Don't think

that buys you out of trouble forever, you pair of crocking insubordinate mothers!"

"Hi Sarge!" said Loney. "Did you get my leaf?"

The Fiver/two lifeboat ran with the *Dancer*, an unsinkable annex where some of the service passengers could spend days and nights. The weather was not bad for the time of year but too uncertain to risk side trips with the lifeboat. The captain believed that his luck was holding well. The Typhoon ABA had crossed their course and spent itself among the Six Seven Isles, which passed to starboard as dark shapes in the fog. The crew of the *Dancer* began to look hopefully for a welcoming sail as they passed the outflow of the Sooree River but there was nothing to be seen except debris from the buster.

Anat Asher rose up, most days, in the emptiest hours of ship time, grabbed a beaker of spiced tea from the warmpot in the galley, and went on deck. She climbed up to the bridge, lurked about in the shadows, so that the watch could acknowledge her presence or not, as they chose. She saw the eastern shoreline draw closer, the end of the voyage.

The mouth of the Gann River had been visible for three days and on the fourth morning Lon Adma was blowing new sounds on the ship's wooden trumpet. He had given the wild two-note call-sign of the *Dancer* ever since the Sooree but now he added to his repertoire four echoing blasts: ta-ta-ta-tah . . .

"Well, Lieutenant, that will fetch the lubbers!" said Cap Varo, suddenly cheerful. "It is the call for a rescue: 'Saved alive' and we're showing it up aloft too!"

She saw that a new signal flag was flying: two red circles interlocked on a white ground.

"It reads 'Survivors aboard,' " he explained. "Where's Tom Kirsh? Come on man, we're waiting! Mam Asher—please to take a grog!"

Anat joined in the ritual; everything began to go very fast. Winna Cross at the winches cried out:

"More sail, Captain?"

"Patience, Winna!" cried Simon Varo. "We must heave to one last time and settle the approach!"

He looked down, smiling gravely, at Anat Asher.

"The lifeboat will go ahead, down the river. Megan Varo will go along to smooth the first meeting. Which of your folk . . . ?"

"Loney can bring it in," said Anat. "He and Ramirez are aboard now, with Vannie Frost. I'm sure Lieutenant Wemyss will wish to join this party."

She wished for a working blip, to give an alert to Wink and the others, but it was not necessary. The word was out, the passengers tumbling up on deck; Myrrha Devi begged to go on the lifeboat with her children. She embraced Anat Asher, bright-eyed, and cried out "The New World!" before negotiating the kelp ladder. Captain Batten, looking sharp enough in a white overall, appeared on the bridge. Winna Cross clapped on more sail at last and Paddy Rork cried out from the masthead, between the trumpet blasts:

"Gann River Towers, Captain!"

Anat saw the lifeboat curve away from the *Dancer* and cut through the long surging waves; she made out two tall Rhomarian structures on either side of the river mouth.

"Signal towers, sir," Ira Maddern was explaining to the Old Man. ". . . semaphore apparatus . . ."

Anat looked through her surveyor's goggles and saw a crazy arrangement of canvas flaps and wooden arms rising and falling. Then she saw that the towers were full of people, climbing all over the wooden beams, operating the signal mechanisms or simply hanging off the scaffolding, waving and shouting.

"Read off, Paddy!" shouted the captain.

"It says *Welcome Dancer!*"

"Come on, they can do better than that!" said Varo.

"It says *Three Found Alive!*" said Paddy Rork, with a slight tremor in his voice. "*Three Found Alive Earthship* and *What news?*"

Anat Asher snatched off the goggles and clutched the bridge rail. She could bear no more, she had come too far. She had no recourse to cushioning drugs or service routine. Even her long conditioning for space travel would wear away, leaving her naked and unprotected upon an alien world. The Earth was lost to her and the ship and there was nothing left but the dreadful task of separating the living from the dead. She missed Paddy's next call, overlapped by cheers from the crew of the *Dancer*. Someone was at her side, lifting her up.

"Steady," said Wink. "Hold firm . . ."

She leaned against him and opened her eyes. The ship sailed on and on, it would pass between the signal towers into the river, dotted with small craft.

"C'mon sweetheart," soothed Wink. "It must be Capem Tree. Rose Chan and her Vip, what the fag was his name?"

"They had place for five, six . . ."

It was just this kind of speculation that she hated. The capem lists were all crocked to hell, in the last emergency mensh had swapped places. Marna Rossi, for example, had been down for Capem Two.

"What was that last call from Paddy Rork?" she asked instead. Wink chuckled.

"They found one last sea-monster. You know, the Whale, the Vail. Big Rhomary deal . . ."

Anat said, between laughing and weeping:

"Wemyss will be pleased!"

Then Lon Adma repeated his trumpet calls right in their ears and they ran down the ladder from the bridge and stood at the port rail with Ivan Dalny and George King. At some time during the progress of the *Dancer* up the river Gann, Captain Batten came to stand with them.

Anat Asher felt herself being carried swiftly, inexorably into a new world of sight and sound. Bells were ringing, drums throbbed, rattled and boomed, there was a cry of conch shells. She saw an old woman standing on a jetty beating on a pot with a wooden spoon; three children in a cocker boat waved and shouted. On either side of the river there were structures of wood and stone: houses, yes, houses, with smoke coming from their chimneys, gardens, tilled fields, ponds, fences. She looked up to the dark hills and saw a big rambling place on the hillside; running beside the *Dancer* was a ship's longboat with a red sail.

A young man and a girl stood with outspread arms crying out directly to the group from Capem Fiver:

"Welcome! Welcome to the Gann Station! Welcome to the Rhomary Land!"

Then at the last, as they came to the wharves, she saw that they were thronged with people. Over the heads of the crowd she saw one tall figure, both arms uplifted in welcome; she saw her friend Rose Chan, and knew that this was her own homecoming.

TOR
BOOKS The Best in Science Fiction

MOTHER OF STORMS • John Barnes
From one of the hottest new names in SF: a shattering epic of global catastrophe, virtual reality, and human courage, in the manner of *Lucifer's Hammer*, *Neuromancer*, and *The Forge of God*.

BEYOND THE GATE • Dave Wolverton
The insectoid dronons threaten to enslave the human race in the sequel to *The Golden Queen*.

TROUBLE AND HER FRIENDS • Melissa Scott
Lambda Award-winning cyberpunk SF adventure that the *Philadelphia Inquirer* called "provocative, well-written and thoroughly entertaining."

THE GATHERING FLAME • Debra Doyle and
James D. Macdonald
The Domina of Entibor obeys no law save her own.

WILDLIFE • James Patrick Kelly
"A brilliant evocation of future possibilities that establishes Kelly as a leading shaper of the genre."—*Booklist*

THE VOICES OF HEAVEN • Frederik Pohl
"A solid and engaging read from one of the genre's surest hands."—*Kirkus Reviews*

MOVING MARS • Greg Bear
The Nebula Award-winning novel of war between Earth and its colonists on Mars.

NEPTUNE CROSSING • Jeffrey A. Carver
"A roaring, cross-the-solar-system adventure of the first water."—Jack McDevitt